ERAFEE

Book 2

The Untenable

David F. Farris

www.erafeen.com

Written by: David F. Farris
Cover illustrated by: Alessandro Brunelli

Sphaira Publishing, 2017

IBN-13 978-1548768461
IBN-10 1548768464

To everyone who has supported me:
Thank you.

Disclaimer:

If you haven't read the first book in the *Erafeen* series, *The Jestivan*, I highly advise you do so before continuing. It's free as an eBook, so go ahead and get a copy.

Enjoy.

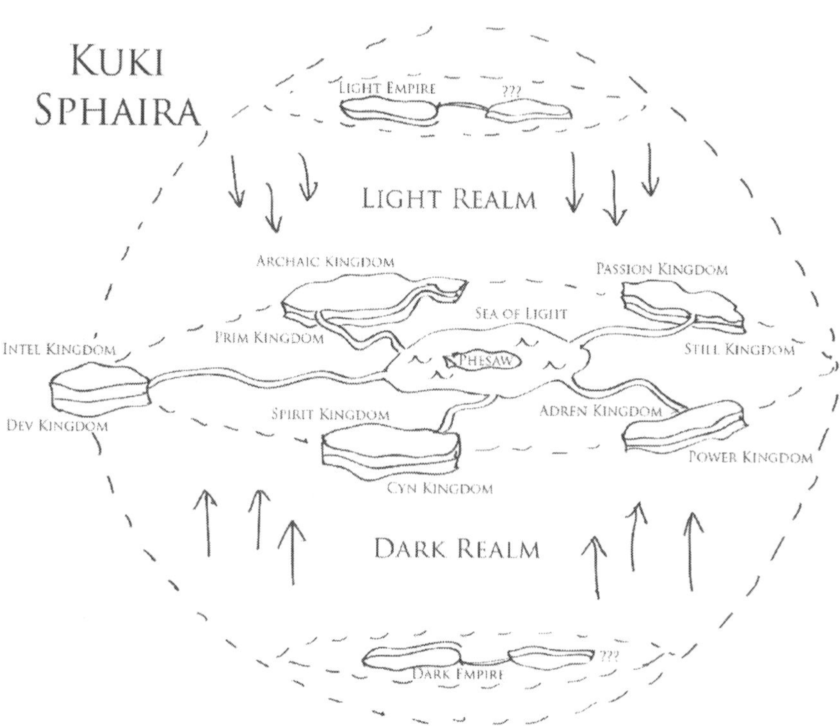

*This is a 3D module of Kuki Sphaira. A ball of air with floating islands and rivers. There are no landscapes or structures because its purpose is to better position the reader in the world in respect to other kingdoms and realms. Arrows represent flow of gravity. Dev, Cyn, Power, Still, and Prim Kingdoms (Dark Realm) hang on the underbellies of floating islands. Intel, Archaic, Spirit, Adren, and Passion Kingdoms (Light Realm) sit atop. More detailed maps of individual kingdoms ahead.

INTEL KINGDOM

(LIGHT KNOWLEDGE KINGDOM)

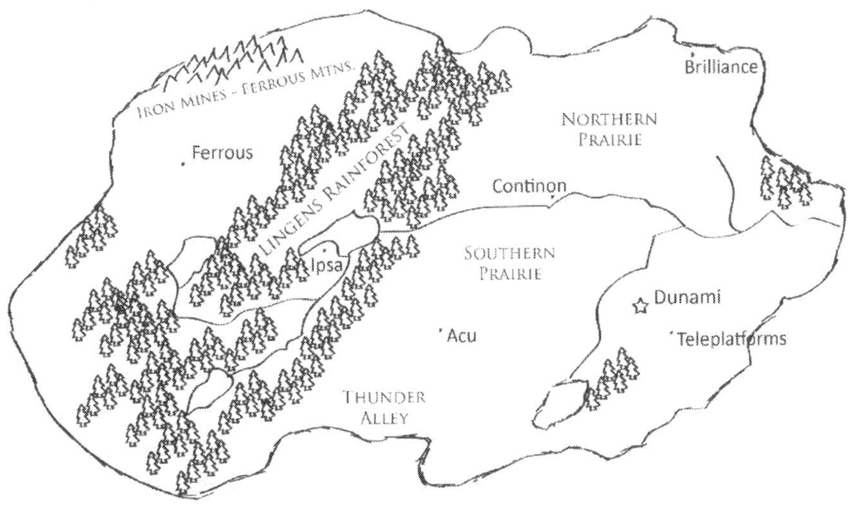

PHESAW

(CENTRAL SCHOOL OF THE LIGHT REALM)

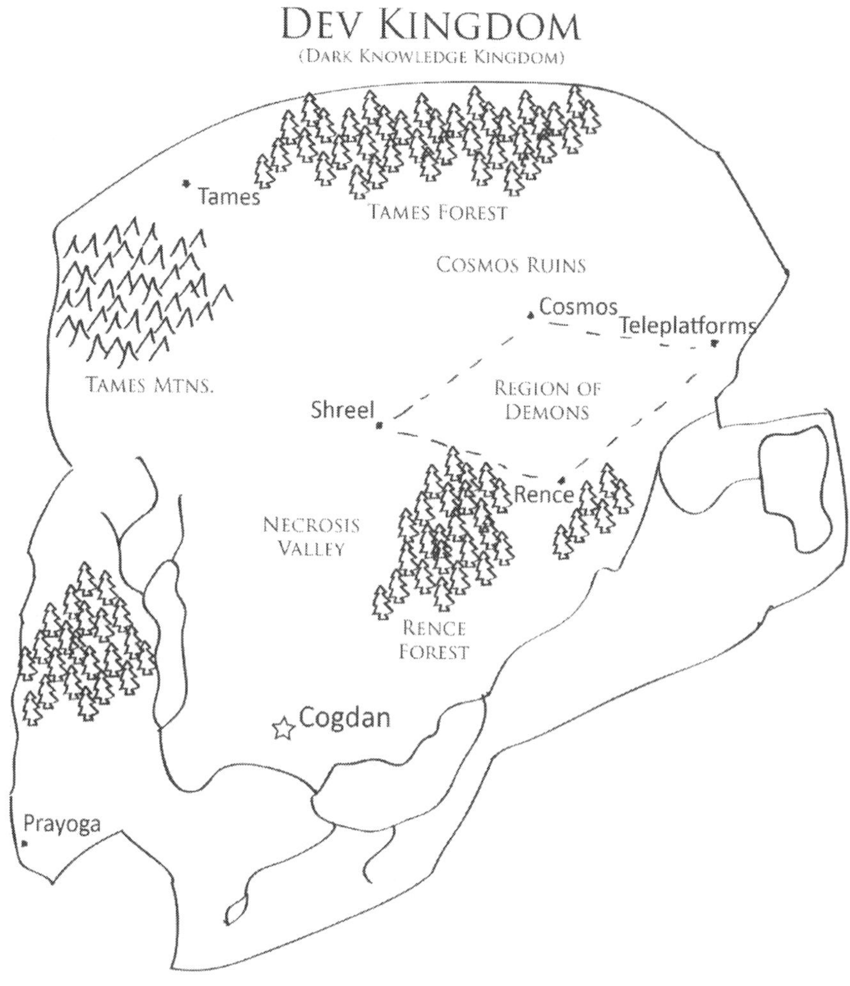
DEV KINGDOM
(DARK KNOWLEDGE KINGDOM)
Tames
TAMES FOREST
COSMOS RUINS
Cosmos
Teleplatforms
TAMES MTNS.
REGION OF
DEMONS
Shreel
Rence
NECROSIS
VALLEY
RENCE
FOREST
Cogdan
Prayoga

PASSION KINGDOM
(LIGHT EMOTION KINGDOM)

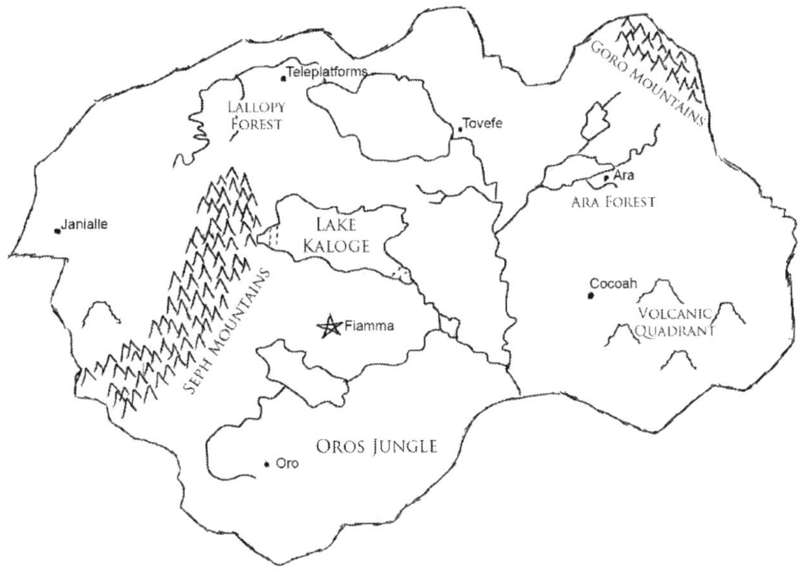

ARCHAIC KINGDOM
(LIGHT MORALITY KINGDOM)

STILL KINGDOM
(DARK EMOTION KINGDOM)

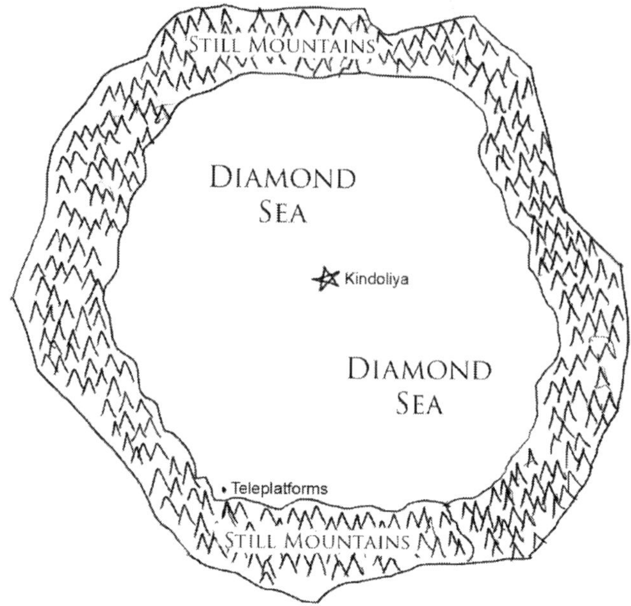

CYN KINGDOM (THE VOID)
(DARK SPIRIT KINGDOM)

Light Realm

Intel Kingdom (mind, electricity):
Bryson, Simon, Lilu, Director Jugtah, Princess Shelly, King Vitio, Grandarion, General Lucas, Major Lars

Passion Kingdom (heart, fire):
Olivia, Himitsu, Director Venustas, King Damian, Fane, Horos, Rosel, General Landon

Spirit Kingdom (soul, wind):
Jilly, Tashami, Director Neaneuma, Queen Apsa, Wert, General Minerva

Adren Kingdom (body, speed):
Toshik, Yama, Director Buredo, King Supido, Toth, General Sinno

Archaic Kingdom (mind, ancients):
Agnos, Rhyparia, Director Senex, Itta, Prince Sigmund, Ophala, Vliyan, Preevis, Mayor Trolk

Dark Realm

Dev Kingdom (mind, psychic):
Vistas, Flen, King Storshae, Illipsia, Tazama

Still Kingdom (heart, ice):
Apoleia, Queen Salia, Ropinia, Titus, Tria

Cyn Kingdom (soul, supernatural):
Chelekah

Power Kingdom (body, strength):
Vuilni, Bruut, Warden Feissam

Prim Kingdom:

Not all characters are listed.

1
Deception

Walking up the crude stone steps proved difficult in the darkness. Twice the man awkwardly twisted his ankle on a dead soldier's armor and cursed into the pitch black.

As he wended his way between the heaps of corpses toward the top of the spiraling staircase, he could see candlelight seeping down from above, and the end of the trail of bodies. He picked up his pace. Once at the top he turned to the right and headed down the torch-lit hall, his kingly robes of burgundy softly billowing behind him. He was in the dungeons of the palace, evident by the stone walls and floor.

He took another right down an adjacent hall and ascended a wide set of stone steps. The floor shifted into a blood red marble, signaling his arrival into the palace's main level.

A voice stopped him in his tracks. "Prince Storshae!"

The prince turned around to see a very young guard. Judging by his simple uniform and the complete absence of badges or medals adorning it, he was a new recruit.

"How are you, sir?" the man asked as he bowed to his prince.

Storshae gazed curiously at the novice, who looked back up with round eyes of awe. "Quite well," Storshae replied. "Based off your lack of etiquette, I'm assuming you're new here?"

"Yes, sir. I was recruited while you were away on your mission."

The prince studied him for a moment before nodding his head and turning back in his original direction. "Come. Let's take a walk."

The two men strode through the quiet lobby side by side. It was early into first-night—one A.M. at the latest—so the staff was mostly asleep.

"What has you awake at such an hour, sir?" the guard asked.

"Visiting family."

"Oh …" The guard looked away in shame, understanding what his prince meant. "I'm sorry, sir. My parents always tell me stories about how great of a king he was—your father, that is."

Storshae was silent as they walked out of the palace's front entrance and into the starlit courtyard. The young guard's face was knotted with unease as he looked around.

"Is it wise for you to leave the palace by yourself at this time, milord?"

Ignoring the question, Storshae asked one of his own. "What is your goal in life?"

"To become the Dev General, serving as your right-hand man and the fiercest fighter in your army." It was an immediate response, as if it was something he had made his mind up on a long time ago. "General Ossen was highly skilled and greatly revered, but I am up to the task of stepping in … which I will prove in time."

Storshae's face grew stern. "Hopefully your time spent climbing the ladder will dissuade you of such a fate."

The guard frowned at the peculiar remark, but he continued to keep pace with his prince. He became perplexed as they approached the palace's main gate. They had walked a considerable distance. And just as he made sense of where they were headed, the bells of the palace's towers began to clang behind them, reverberating like thunder across the night sky.

The rookie was confused. The windows that lined the castle walls illuminated as the people within were awoken by the ear-rattling bells.

"What's happening, sir?" The guard whirled around to see Storshae still strolling calmly through the gates. The prince made no effort to look back. The guard chased after him as holographic displays began lighting up the sky. An older gentleman occupied every one of them.

"Attention, citizens of Cogdan," the voice boomed across the city, somehow loud enough to be heard over the bells. "This is an emergency alert of the highest magnitude. Thirty-two soldiers are dead within the palace walls. Prince Storshae has been found incapacitated in the dungeons. There is an intruder among us. Lock down all exits from the capital. The culprit will not escape."

The young guard looked over at Storshae. "You're right here. What are they talking ab—" His sentence was cut short as a blade ripped across his throat. He collapsed to his knees … why was his life ending at the hands of the prince he had vowed to protect? As he clutched at his neck, trying to stop the blood spraying from his wound, he saw his killer turn around for a brief moment.

It wasn't the prince anymore. His face was tired and old, his eyes sunken in from a debilitating night. A fresh cut ran across the aging skin of his left cheek. His long white beard was stained with blood. But the oddest feature was his eyebrows—so hairy at the ends that they hung down the sides of his face.

"Please forgive me, young one."

2
Gravity

One month later … April

Bryson was lying in bed with an open book plopped on his face. With all the ruckus in the house, he had given up on reading. He should have been used to it by now, though.

Clack! Bang! Boom! Clang!

He rolled his eyes before pushing himself out of bed and heading down the hall. He turned and gazed into the kitchen with a frown. Forks, spoons, knives, and plates soared across the room and smashed into pieces against the wall. Cabinets stood open at varying angles and drawers were yanked out to different lengths. A woman was on her knees, her top half swallowed up by the bottom cabinet that she rummaged through while flinging pots and pans over her shoulder.

"Keep this up, and I'm not going to summon you down as much as I do," Bryson said.

The kitchen finally fell silent, and the woman backed out of the cabinet. Her face was a flustered red, and her normally straight blond hair was a mess of matted lumps.

"I can't eat with these utensils," she whined. "I ran out of Jilly's chopsticks."

"Well, if you didn't eat like a whale, this wouldn't be a problem. You go through food like it's air."

Thusia bounced lightly onto her feet, paying the insult no mind. "Let's visit the Spirit Kingdom and get some chopsticks!"

"No."

"Why not?"

"I have a life," Bryson said. "I have school. I'm not taking a day-length journey for the sake of some chopsticks."

Thusia's eyes narrowed and her lips pursed. She had an amazing ability to switch moods, tones, and expressions in an instant. "You have an unhealthy obsession with that book."

"That has nothing to do with it," Bryson lied. "Besides, I haven't read that thing in days."

Thusia released a hearty laugh and clutched her stomach. "Please, stop! You're killing me."

Bryson simply stared at his Branian as she gasped for air. Thusia shoved him to the side and sprinted past. He chased her down the hall as she threw blasts of wind over her shoulder with an evil grin.

By the time Bryson reached his room, Thusia was already seated on his bed with a book in her hands. "Is that why I found this open on your bed?" she asked. Once again, her tone had shifted. Ten seconds before, she had been roughhousing through the house like they were siblings. Now she was giving motherly words of advice. "You keep reading it over and over again, looking for answers that don't exist. Stop beating yourself up, Bryson."

Thusia dropped the book onto the covers. "I'll see you later," she said with a whimsical wave, then disappeared into the light.

Bryson walked to his bed and looked down at his obsession. It had gone through a lot of wear and tear lately. The cover's edges were tattered. Pages lay uneven from being folded in as bookmarks. And a stain from spilled orange juice blemished the title: *Ataway Kawi: The Third of Five.*

*   *   *

A day later, Bryson stood in a part of Phesaw's campus he had never ventured into before—an open field of grass that stretched for a few miles behind Phesaw Park, far away from the school's main building. It was so far out he could see the small mountains of the Rolling Oaks looming over the High Sever—a sky-scraping wall that separated prohibited land from the campus.

His fellow Jestivan stood scattered throughout the field, equally as confused. They had been training intensely for nearly a month, but the directors had warned them that a day would come that would outstrip all the others. Today was that day.

But only one director stood with them, and he was the unlikeliest of all. The Jestivan had to tilt their heads down to see his face, for he was no taller than three feet. In fact, the grass reached his mid-thigh. His gray hair was wiry and extruded in all directions, and his beard was equally as messy. His tiny glasses sat askew on his nose. This was Archaic Director Senex, adorned in his usual sandy brown director's robes.

"I was expecting someone like Director Buredo," Himitsu mumbled. "Senex couldn't reach me if we stacked two of him together."

"Good morning, Jestivan," Director Senex said. "What if I was to inform you that one of your peers is capable of flattening a neighborhood … maybe a town? What would you say to that?"

"I'd say, 'aw shucks, Director Senex, that's so flattering,'" Himitsu retorted.

The other Jestivan laughed, but Archaic Director didn't find it to be funny. "This is no laughing matter, Zana Himitsu. Each of you is capable of exceptional feats. Some in different ways than others. Everyone knows that Agnos can out-think even the greatest scholars of Phesaw. And we all know about Yama's unparalleled speed, making her invisible to even a trained eye." Senex paused for a moment. "But what about sheer power? Brute force?"

"Olivia," Tashami answered. "Her punches and kicks can crack stone."

"Indeed, that is physical power. But I'm talking a different kind of power—a much scarier kind ... *clout.*"

The Jestivan frowned as they tried to read between the lines of the vague lecture. Bryson couldn't help but be a little annoyed by the Archaic Director's method of teaching. It was the exact sort of thing that Intelians hated about Archains.

"Prepare yourselves," Senex warned. "Stand tall, brace your joints, and gather air into your lungs."

These were odd commands, but the Jestivan did as instructed. The director nodded gently and the air grew heavier. The Jestivan looked around in confusion. Some slowly lifted their arms in front of themselves to experience the extra effort needed to do such a simple task. Others simply watched the grass beneath them flatten against the ground.

Even though the difference was subtle, Lilu began to panic. She started panting then collapsed on all fours. Trauma from the restaurant collapse, Bryson thought.

"Stop it, Rhyparia!" he shouted.

Normal gravity returned, and the Jestivan stood quietly as Lilu sobbed. Bryson ran over and knelt beside her. "Are you okay?" he asked as he pushed her green bangs her face.

"I'm fine." Lilu quickly stood back up, and Bryson heard her mumble something like, "How embarrassing."

"Lita Lilu, you must clear your mental hurdle," Director Senex said. "That was a fraction of what we'll be training with in the next two months. Rhyparia will learn self-control, and the rest of you will develop speed and strength. You'll be lighter on your feet after prolonged exposure to increased gravity. Your muscles will grow stronger, but you'll feel like you're carrying half the weight."

Senex studied the faces around him. "I know what a lot of you are thinking. I'm not going to be the one who answers questions about Rhyparia. If she feels comfortable, she'll answer them ... but not here. Do that on your own time."

Rhyparia lowered her bandana over her eyes and stuck the point of her umbrella in the ground.

"Please return to your classes," the Archaic Director said. "Have an ethical day."

The Jestivan split into smaller groups as they headed back toward the main campus. Toshik walked in solitude, as he often did whenever Jilly was preoccupied with Yama. Jilly was happily thrashing Yama's sword around. Tashami and Agnos walked with Lilu, who was as far from Rhyparia as she could get. Ever since Lilu had learned of Rhyparia's ability, she avoided her at all costs—unless it was forced like today.

Bryson, Olivia, and Himitsu walked with Rhyparia, who stared at the ground with her lone visible eye. The three of them had known of her ability for a while now. Bryson and Himitsu had witnessed the destruction she caused at the crater's rim during their battle at Necrosis Valley. Olivia had apparently known it ever since the restaurant collapse during the Generals' Battle five months ago.

But none of them had ever brought it up. She had killed many innocent people, but it truly was an accident—not that that made it okay. But if the royal heads and directors were giving her another chance, they weren't going to argue. Rhyparia was one of the kindest Jestivan, up there with Jilly, Olivia, and Tashami.

Lilu's friction with Rhyparia had put Bryson in a difficult spot. He had surprised himself by leaning closer to Rhyparia through all this, even despite Lilu's distaste.

He understood that Lilu was hurt and scared. But Rhyparia was hurting more. The guilt that lay on her shoulders had to be backbreaking. The lost lives of innocents, the safety of her friends, Archaic Director Senex's fate—and her own—outweighed Lilu's broken ribs.

"What classes do you guys have next?" Himitsu asked, breaking the silence.

"Women's history," Olivia blankly replied.

"Music," Bryson said.

Himitsu glanced at Rhyparia, and after realizing she wasn't going to answer, he said, "Too boring for my taste."

"Haven't practiced any piano for months," Bryson said, "so it's a relief to get back to it. What about you?"

"World of Assassins." Himitsu didn't bother hiding the excitement in his voice.

Meow Meow finally made himself heard: "Learning how assassin blood can affect other kingdom's energies differently than your Passion Energy, eh?"

"Yep. There are some truly unique abilities out there … makes my black flames look silly. Don't even get me started on Spirit Assassins." Himitsu paused. "Did you know that Thusia has assassin blood?"

Bryson frowned. "What? How? What's unique about her ability?"

The ink-haired Jestivan gave him an evil sneer. "That's all I'm saying."

For the rest of their walk, Bryson thought back to when Thusia had displayed her wind abilities, but nothing stood out to him as unique.

As they were saying their goodbyes outside Phesaw's main building, they heard people screaming. Bryson was gone, accelerating to his max speed percentage almost instantly. As he curled around the outside of the school's Emotion Wing, he saw a large crowd of students and staff massed at the bottom of Telejunction's towering hill. Two women ran up the side of it: Directors Neaneuma and Venustas.

A man was collapsed in the lush green grass, and Bryson recognized him immediately. The last time he had seen him was in a tavern in the town of Rence, disguised as a man he wasn't.

As Bryson fought through the crowd, they split apart to let him pass. Olivia and Himitsu were only a little ways behind him. He knelt next to the fallen man alongside Venustas and Neaneuma.

"Grand Director Poicus, wake up," Bryson pleaded.

The old man's breathing was fragile and shallow. Blood seeped from fresh stab wounds, and other parts of his robe were stiff with dried blood.

Poicus gazed up at the boy. "Shut down … Telejunction."

"Why?" Passion Director Venustas asked.

"Dev Assassins … three of them."

Neaneuma and Venustas's eyes widened, and Venustas quickly charged up the hill, her blazing red robes flaring in the breeze.

"They're already here," said Himitsu, who stood a few yards down the slope. "I can feel them."

"No, no, no, no," Neaneuma mumbled to herself.

Bryson was befuddled. How did they get in without anyone seeing? And where were they now? And what did Himitsu mean by "feeling" them?

Olivia brushed past Bryson and picked up the Grand Director. She turned and headed down the hill with Poicus cradled in her arms. "I'm taking him to the nurse's building," she said.

Bryson sat in a stunned quiet as he watched the growing crowd step aside to make an open lane for Olivia.

3
Olethros, Rim

A small city of wooden buildings and dirt roads sat at the foot of the Light Realm's tallest mountain range. The few paved paths ran through the wealthier spots, which were hard to come by in Rim—an afterthought in the Archaic Kingdom.

At five stories tall, one building sat higher than the rest near Rim's center. It was constructed as a perfect cube. Brown drapes typically hung from the many flag poles lining the building's exterior. But ever since the invasion, gleaming yellow flags fluttered instead.

The citizens of Rim despised the yellow. It was the color of their rivals—the Intel Kingdom. The banners that hung on the walls of the first floor were always in danger of being burned or ripped down as onlookers cheered in the streets. They didn't care how many times they were arrested by the Intel soldiers who patrolled the city, nor did they feel responsible for the actions of King Itta. The capital, Phelos, was on the opposite end of the Archaic Kingdom and never showed them much love in the first place.

A man gazed out a fifth-floor window, observing the streets below. He too was adorned in yellow, though in civilian clothes unlike the armored guards. "We don't hurt them at all," he sighed, "yet they act as if we're spilling their blood across the streets."

A second man, this one in brown robes with graying hair encircling a bald spot, also occupied the room. "With all due respect, Major Lars, you may not be attacking them physically, but you are attacking their pride. Maybe you should get rid of the flags before someone accidently lights the entire city on fire."

Lars collapsed on a sofa. "I still let you run things. Literally, the only things that have changed are the soldiers who patrol the city and the colors displayed throughout. I don't care about the history of the Archaic and Intel Kingdoms, or the Mind War. I have no resentment for your people."

Mayor Trolk's lips pursed. "I understand that, and I approve of how you're handling things. It will just take my citizens a little more time. Remember, it could be worse. There are violent riots in the capital. Adren soldiers have died at the hands of Archaic civilians."

Lars leaned back in the cushion. "You're right."

He only had a brief moment to relax before the building began to rattle. He leapt off the couch, eyes wide and arms out to keep his balance while the tremors roared. They lasted for nearly a minute before abruptly coming to a stop.

Trolk chuckled. "You've been here for months and you're still not used to it."

Lars groaned. "I hate those mountains. They disturb my sleep too."

The mayor rose from his chair and walked toward the window in order to get a good look at the behemoths of the Light Realm—the Archaic Mountains. "People have volunteered for the past 1,500 years to find out why the earthquakes and avalanches occur so frequently. Some travel from other kingdoms … a few from the Dark Realm. But none ever make it back."

Lars cocked an eyebrow. "Sounds like the Void—notorious for crazy, inexplicable legends. Ghosts and whatnot. It's probably just nature doing its duty. The mountains must be eroding quicker than most."

"If you say so," the mayor replied. The low murmurs of the city streets below seeped through the walls as the men soaked in their thoughts. "You know what? I think it's time you visit Olethros."

Lars gazed curiously at Trolk. "Why the sudden change of heart? I've been asking since I got here."

"Maybe the citizens of Rim will gain a bit of respect for you. They'll look at it as you wanting to connect to them in a more genuine way." Trolk turned and headed for the door. "Let's go."

Soldiers in gold escorted the two most powerful figures in Rim out of the central building while pedestrians and people traveling by coach turned and tipped their caps with a nod. Those gestures of respect weren't directed at Major Lars, and he knew this. And almost as a way of making sure he that he did, a fist-sized rock slammed into his ribcage.

Laughs erupted across the paved street, and a young boy darted away as his brown hair bobbed between the masses. A pair of red-faced Intel soldiers went to chase him down, but they were instantly halted by Lars yelling at them to stop.

"Get back here and don't lose your wits over something so petty," he snapped.

Lars and Trolk stepped into a draped carriage that was waiting in front of the building. The ride went smoothly at first, then it became bumpy and uneven, signaling their arrival into the poorer sectors of Rim. After half an hour, they finally came to a stop.

Mayor Trolk exited the carriage, asking Lars to wait for a moment. He had to make sure everything outside was safe and explain Lars's presence to the Archaic soldiers. Olethros was the only part of the city where Lars allowed Archaic soldiers to be stationed—mostly because Trolk had warned that its inhabitants would attack any unfamiliar faces, especially those of their rival kingdom.

Trolk stuck his head through the curtain. "Come on."

As Lars stepped outside, a wave of pity swept over him. Homes had been smashed to rubble, and crows cawed as they circled the skies and sat perched on broken bits of wood. Directly behind this expanse of ruin was the daunting presence of the Archaic Mountains. Olethros sat right at their feet.

They approached a short barbwire fence where soldiers in brown stood outside. Lars could feel their eyes burning holes into him.

The Intel major's heart broke further as they crossed the border. Skeletons of all different types lay contorted in the wreckage—dogs, cats, horses, and humans. The animals that were alive gnawed on the bones of the dead.

It was quiet, for neither Lars nor Trolk wanted to talk, and the two Archaic soldiers escorting them had no reason to. Lars understood the despair, but where was the danger that he so often heard about? A pile of rubble to his right rustled, and a couple pots tumbled down its side. As he whirled around, a head popped out—a laughing child with a face in need of a wash.

"You're still it, Sebas!" the boy shouted. "I'm the best hider!"

Another kid ran up the pile from the opposite side. "I hate you!" he screamed. Then he spotted Lars and Trolk, and his face shifted into fear before he bolted off the other way.

Lars recognized him as the boy who threw the rock earlier. Again, he ignored him and continued walking. In fact it made him even happier that he had let him go. If that kid lived here, there was reason for his anger.

Here and there a tiny shack rose above the ruins. It was free to live in Olethros, Trolk explained, so it was the only option for families with no income. By the looks of things, Lars began to think that maybe the city should pay the people for living in such a landfill.

Then Trolk said something that really caught him off-guard: "Some families simply choose to live here."

"Insanity," Lars remarked. "Is there a rough population size?"

"Three hundred, give or take."

After wandering for close to an hour, they walked toward a particularly small shack. This one didn't even have a roof—unless blankets and patched cloth counted as such. The same two brunette boys from the pile of rubble were play-fighting with planks of wood right outside the front curtain. When the boys saw who was approaching, they dropped their weapons and ran inside. Lars smirked. They were cute.

A man and woman walked out of the shack. The man was tall, skinny, and feeble. The woman was short and rather round for someone who presumably didn't get much food.

"This is a family that lives here by choice," Trolk whispered. "It's sad. They have a lot of children."

"Welcome, Mayor," the father said. Trolk gave him a half-hearted wave and a strained smile. Then the man noticed Lars's golden robes. "An Intel official?" he asked.

Lars gave a slight nod.

"We visited your kingdom last year!" the woman said. "The Generals' Battle was a travesty."

Lars scowled, irritated by the couple for some reason he could not place.

"Is that so?" The major's tone hinted at disbelief.

"Yes, sir. We were invited by Grand Director Poicus himself."

"And how do you have a connection to a man of such stature?"

"We're the parents of a Jestivan," the woman said proudly.

There was a prolonged pause accompanied only by the crows soaring above. The setting sun behind the mountains cast the group in an eerie shade.

"Which one?" Lars asked.

"Lita Rhyparia."

"I see. Talent can come from anywhere, I suppose … even desolation."

The mother's eyes narrowed. "Your theory on the cause of this desolation, Mr. Lars?"

"An avalanche. I don't think that's a theory, however … more of a documented fact."

The woman smirked. "Yes, of course … an *avalanche*."

The mayor hurriedly pushed Lars away. "That's enough of them. Good day, Mr. and Mrs. NuForce."

Lars begrudgingly obeyed the dismissal, but he knew that he would have to return here again. Death, disease, and poverty weren't the only factors plaguing this sector; Olethros was rotting in deceit.

4
Toono Arrives

An unimposing man with dirty-blond hair calmly stood on a teleplatform with no roof, no outer cage to shut people in, and only a few eroded stone poles positioned throughout for people to hold onto. A bandage was wrapped around the top of his head, directly above his eyes. A taller woman and younger girl whose onyx hair fell to the stone floor stood beside him.

It was quiet—that unique silence only found in the Void. The incoherent whispers of the dead and distant roars of the linsani shrouded the thin air around them. There were no guards here, or anyone at all. A building sat off to the side, but it had likely been abandoned for decades. The Cyn Kingdom didn't have to worry about intruders because no one in their right mind would voluntarily set foot in this place.

Toono closed his eyes, relieved to be departing. He put his hand on Illipsia's head and rustled her hair. It was impressive to see a girl so young withstand the Void's melancholic aura with her sanity intact.

"Go ahead," Toono whispered. "Get us out of here."

The young girl flicked her finger in the air, and a lever in the distance turned halfway. The howl that released from the platform made it clear that it didn't get much use. The noise would carry for miles across the Void's thin, still air.

The stone teleplatform gradually picked up speed, and the surroundings became a twisting blur of navy blue and gray before changing into a blinding blue. It was second-night in the Dark Realm, but the mid-afternoon sun would be high in the sky where they were arriving.

Toono's hand was hidden in his cloak, prepared for any possible threat. The entirety of the Light Realm's elites knew the ability of the man who once stood guard in Relic Alley, so his ancient would be a dead giveaway.

The platform slowed. It was still a stone floor, but better manicured. The Seph Mountains sat on the Passion Kingdom's horizon, rising above the thick forests. A vast blue lake stretched for leagues to their left. And a single trail extended directly ahead. Toono couldn't help but feel relief at the touch of the gentle breeze.

Three men in tight-fitted red combat gear approached from a terminal. The capes tied around their necks flowed behind them. They looked like suits more fitting for Adren soldiers.

"If things go south, stay calm and simply execute," Toono mumbled. "Remember, I'll be in Lallopy Forest."

"Who goes there, and why are you arriving from the Cyn Kingdom?" asked one of the men as they stopped at a safe distance.

"My name is …" Toono paused with a placid gaze. Maybe it was the lingering effects of the Void, but his patience had withered while he suffered in that kingdom. The young man sighed as he gripped his ancient, deciding to not bother with a charade.

He withdrew his staff with a violent swing, making contact with one soldier's jaw as he did so. The man fell to the ground. His two colleagues alertly skipped back several steps. And as they planted their back foot, they thrust their hands forward, sending trails of flames toward Toono.

Toono flicked his ancient in front of his mouth and quickly exhaled. A bubble began to form, but before it closed, he turned the wand perpendicular to the ground and swept it to the right. The bubble took the shape of a long pipe before finally closing at the end of Toono's motion, forming an inflated force field.

The two waves of flames hit the wall and rebounded in different directions as Toono leapt on top of the bubble and created two more. He bounced high into the air, using his force field as a spring, and at the apex of his jump, flung each bubble at the Passion guards. The speeding blobs cut through their defensive fire and blasted both men into the ground.

By the time Toono landed, more soldiers had exited the terminal. Toono sidestepped every attack, countering the same way he took down the first three. Occasionally he'd dodge a punch or kick by someone who was able to get close enough before throwing a combination strike of his own. For a man who had once hated killing, Toono conducted the massacre with a grim efficiency. The Void had apparently done its work, and maybe a little too well.

Bodies littered the grass. A teleplatform stopped spinning as people arrived from a separate kingdom. Kadlest, Toono, and Illipsia quickly threw their hoods over their heads, not looking in the newcomers' direction. If these civilians had any proper wits, they'd simply walk away and not make a scene.

Toono waited, eyeing the group from the shadows of his hood. There were two young girls and presumably their father. The girls opened their mouths to scream, but the man cupped his hands over their mouths and squeezed them tight against his body. Walking carefully through the mess, he kept his eyes forward, not even entertaining a glance at the trio.

Toono looked back at Kadlest and gave her a nod. She smiled and stepped onto a different teleplatform with Illipsia by her side. He walked over to the control room and flipped the proper switch. Within moments, his companions were gone.

Toono gazed at the battered, bloody bodies and scorched patches of land, wondering how he would clean this mess up.

5
Revisited Bonds

A month had passed since Poicus's arrival. Students and staff milled through campus as if nothing was unordinary, but they all knew the truth. There were three highly trained assassins somewhere on the island, waiting for the perfect moment for a calculated attack.

For this reason, no one was allowed east of Phesaw Park or Wealth's Crossroads onto the vast prairie leading to the High Sever. This meant no more group training sessions with Archaic Director Senex and Rhyparia's ancient, since that was the only safe location.

One would think that finding the assassins would be easy with an entire campus on high alert. There was no way they could have gotten past the High Sever to hide in the Rolling Oaks, and the main campus was far too busy to hide in. But then it made more sense when Poicus sat the Jestivan down for a meeting inside the central auditorium, where their induction ceremony had been held nearly a year before.

The Grand Director stood weakly near the lip of the central stage. Looking into his eyes was impossible since they were always half closed now. He was already an old man, and his stint in the Dev Kingdom seemed to have added years. Fending off Dev soldiers to get into King Rehn's grave, fighting with Prince Storshae, and then the long journey back to the teleplatforms while being pursued by assassins was telling of how great this man was.

"To my Jestivan." Poicus paused, and may have tried to smile. His voice was weak. "Thank you for your support while I was recovering. You all visited me frequently—even Toshik."

Poicus meant it as a joke, but it had to stab at Toshik. Bryson glanced behind him, where the tall swordsman sat. His face reflected shame, and Bryson, for a brief moment, felt badly for the stuck-up jerk.

"Some of you gave me helpful updates on the condition of the campus, some gave me promising news about your progress here at school, and others … well, one of you made sure to bring me candy every day and tell me the elaborate stories of your amazing adventures through lollipop forests and taffy seas. If only I could dream as vividly."

The Jestivan laughed softly. Only Jilly's imagination could be so bizarre.

"I'm here to provide you information, much like our meeting before the Generals' Battle. It's time I tell you the ability of a Dev Assassin. They can cloak themselves, becoming invisible to anyone's eye."

"Why weren't we informed of that sooner?" Yama asked. She glared at Himitsu. "You're supposed to help your teammates. That means give us important information such as this."

Himitsu opened his mouth, but Poicus spoke first: "I told him not to inform any of you. Tell me, Lita Yama, what was the use of you knowing such a thing? That there are killers around, but you can't see, hear, or even smell them? That would only foster paranoia, and that isn't a constructive mindset when making decisions."

"I can touch them, though, can't I?" she fired back. Agnos shook his head at her impertinence.

Poicus studied the young woman for a moment. "Yes, you can touch them. Good luck, however, ripping your sword randomly through every inch of space on Phesaw's island—including beyond the High Sever. If they can cloak themselves, there's no stopping them from gaining access to the Rolling Oaks for safe hiding."

Yama glared, but her indignation had been deflated.

"You're probably wondering why the school isn't in a fit of chaos right now," Grand Director continued. "Surely these assassins would be hiding in the nooks and crannies of our halls and dungeons, silently killing anyone who walks past. Fortunately they can't do that for a few reasons."

Most lecturers would have been pacing by now, but the only movement was an occasional wave of the director's arm—perhaps all the energy he had to muster.

"An assassin's greatest weakness is another assassin. They can sense each other, and that would make them silent killers no more. Luckily we have Himitsu, and he's been sleeping in this auditorium ever since the Dev Assassins infiltrated our campus. Since this building is most deserted in the night hours, that would be the most obvious time to penetrate its walls. Himitsu prevents this, for he would be awoken by a disturbance around him … and nobody wants to face a Passion Assassin in the night. The darkness is their specialty.

"This leaves the day hours, but even then it's unlikely that they'd try anything—not without a well thought-out plan at least. Directors Venustas, Senex, Neaneuma, and Buredo are patrolling each school wing. And now that I'm somewhat in better shape, I can lend a helping hand."

Bryson eyed him suspiciously. Was this that what he called "better shape"?

"We also have reinforcements arriving from other kingdoms. Nothing drastic," he added, noticing the uncomfortable gazes of the Jestivan. "A few skilled—and *law-abiding*—men and women whose specialty is hunting down elusive criminals. They are hunters of varying types that work for the royal families.

"Then there is the fact that a Dev Assassin's cloaking ability is temporary. They can only stay hidden for a limited time—a couple minutes' span at most. And with what I've learned recently, there is another reason for my optimism.

"So, Jestivan, trust me when I say that we'll be okay. It was a mistake for the assassins to pursue me into the Light Realm, and even they know it. And remember, summer vacation is only a month away, after all."

Poicus smiled at a few of the faces in the seats. "But from what I've learned, it won't be much of a vacation for some of you. I'd call the Void the opposite of one. With that said, you're all dismissed."

The ten Jestivan slowly rose from their seats. Some stretched the lead out of their backs while others yawned. It seemed an odd reaction to such alarming news. Perhaps Poicus's attempt to calm them was successful. He did make it sound like he had everything covered. Besides, what could three people do in a campus filled with the Jestivan, directors, and mysterious hunters?

As Bryson began walking up the never-ending staircase to the arena's outer walls, someone called for him from behind: "Zana Bryson."

He turned to see Poicus looking up at him. "Please stop by my office in an hour."

*   *   *

Bryson brushed his bangs from his eyes before pushing open the Grand Director's door. He was nervous, but not because of a meeting with Poicus. He was scared to be in this office and unsure of how he'd respond to his most recent memory of the place.

And sure enough, as he stepped into the room and looked at the elderly man seated at the desk, he could only see Debo sitting there—his tall, lanky frame hunched over a copy of *Ataway Kawi: The Third of Five* while his ear piercings shimmered in the sunlight of the window behind him. Bryson stopped as he stared blankly at his painful memory. He nearly turned around and walked right back out.

"Have a seat, Bryson," Poicus instructed. The pity on his face was pronounced. "I'm sorry about Debo."

Bryson stared for a moment before responding. "You can call him by his real name."

"You're right," Poicus said. "There was a certain book missing from my shelves, so I inferred that you had gotten to it already."

"I had someone grab it for me."

Poicus nodded. "I can sense your discomfort, so I'll make this quick. I doubt Himitsu would have told me about this if it weren't for recent circumstances unfolding, but I know of your Branian."

Bryson gritted his teeth. Trying to explain how he had gotten a Branian would only remind him of his complete lack of knowledge about his mother and the hidden secrets of his father. After losing Debo, the last thing Bryson wanted were reminders of his orphanhood.

"She can help our school, Bryson. We need as many assassins as possible in order to apprehend the intruders."

Bryson's face relaxed. "Well that's not my decision," he said. "It's hers."

A light formed next to the young boy and morphed into a woman's shape. Poicus's heavy eyes somehow spread in awe as the slender frame became visible. Thusia wore a white and shamrock green frock with a matching green bow attached to its belt. Her heels were also the same color, and she had a white ribbon in her hair. Her merry cheeks rose into her eyes after realizing who was seated in front of her.

"Grand Director Poicus!" She floated over the desk and hugged the old man.

"Thusia," he stammered, turning a deep red. "I can't believe I'm seeing you again."

"Miss me?"

"The entire school has missed you."

Thusia walked back to Bryson's side of the desk. "I'm sure Jilly has filled my role well," she said.

"Two different kinds of crazy," the director said with a wink.

She glanced down at Bryson and hugged him. "Hi, buddy!"

Bryson couldn't describe the euphoric feeling she gave him. He felt warm and safe when she was around—he thought it must have been close to what having a mom felt like. Debo had always made Bryson feel safe and loved, but warmth didn't come with it.

Poicus watched Thusia and Bryson with an inquisitive twinkle in his eyes. "Thusia, I must request your assistance."

"Sir, yes sir!" she replied as she snapped to attention.

Poicus laughed, then coughed weakly a few times. "Bryson's going to stay on campus until the school year ends—maybe through the summer too. Can you stay down here, with the Light Empire's permission, of course?"

"Sure, but for what?"

"Bryson hasn't told you, I guess."

Thusia sternly glared at the top of Bryson's head, who was purposely avoiding her gaze. "No, he hasn't."

"There are a few Dev Assassins somewhere on the island."

She smacked the back of Bryson's head.

"Hey!" he shouted while rubbing his skull.

"I'll help," Thusia said. "I'm guessing you need me to sense them, give Himitsu a hand."

Poicus nodded. "And we'll have a couple more reinforcements arriving in the coming weeks. You'll need to stay hidden while roaming the campus. An oversized cloak will do. No one can see your face. If word gets out that a dead Thusia has been spotted, the royal heads will be jumping down my throat."

Her lips formed a rigid line. "Understood."

* * *

Yama leaned against the clerk's counter, watching her blond-headed friend run amuck throughout the aisles of Tabby's Gift Shop. Customers also stared with incredulous smiles as the Jestivan's most energetic member dunked herself headfirst into barrels of chocolates and climbed the tallest shelves in order to reach the most overpriced goods.

Jilly shot down one aisle, then turned right back around with a look of sheer horror as she realized she was in the fresh vegetables section—or what she deemed "death." As she tore through another barrel—this one filled with stuffed animals—the elderly storeowner weakly smiled as her prized merchandise was tossed across the floor. Yama placed a pile of coins on the counter as a way of saying thank you for putting up with Jilly's rowdy behavior. It was the same routine every visit.

"I found it!" Jilly shouted as she resurfaced from the pit of fur. She held a white stuffed horse above her head. "Bobuel, the pony!"

Knowing damn well it wasn't a pony, Yama gave her friend a thumbs-up anyway. "Good job." She flipped another coin toward Tabby and followed Jilly out the door.

They exited onto the sunny cobblestone streets of Wealth's Crossroads and headed toward Lilac Suites. Jilly made galloping noises with her mouth as her new toy bobbed up and down in her hands. Then she'd tilt the horse onto its hind legs and make a loud neighing sound—though it sounded more like a sheep to Yama, who burst into a fit of laughter.

Jilly instinctively guffawed along with her for no reason at all. She had no clue that Yama was laughing at her—not that she'd care. Jilly simply loved to laugh as much as possible, and that always pried Yama out of her harsh mood.

While the two of them walked through the patch of grass that divided the front walkway of Lilac Suites and the main roundabout of Wealth's Crossroads, Yama caught someone out of place in her peripheral vision. She snapped her head to a woman she had only seen once in her life, roughly a decade before. The woman ducked around the building and out of sight.

Rage flooded Yama's face as she abandoned Jilly, who looked around with a baffled expression. The violet-haired swordswoman was already in pursuit as she bent around the building's corner. She pinned the woman against the brick wall, her left hand grasped around her neck and her sword pointed toward the bottom of her chin. "What do you think you're doing here?"

The woman gave a crafty grin. "I should ask you the same. With Toono being 23, that would mean you're 21 … We may have only exchanged a few words so many years ago, but I pegged you for a girl who would be well on her way to pursuing her own ambitions by now."

"My ambition is to be better than everyone else," Yama coldly stated as she pressed the tip of her blade into Kadlest's chin. A trail of blood ran down the polished steel. "Phesaw grants me the most worthwhile avenue at this point, with individual training by Adren Director Buredo."

Kadlest was breathing carefully, but the cold metal penetrating her skin didn't stop her banter. "You look more like a prepubescent girl with that frivolous friend of yours rather than a woman with an agenda."

Yama choke-slammed her against the bricks. "I will kill you."

Kadlest winced. "But you won't. You're too curious about Toono."

"I don't care about him. He made his decision."

"That he did," Kadlest said with a victorious smile. But it quickly turned to scorn as she added, "However, he wants you by his side again."

Yama hesitated. "No. Absolutely not. Besides, if he desires something of me, tell him not to send a messenger—since that seems to be what you've been demoted to. He can confront me directly."

"As impudent as always," Kadlest calmly replied.

"Remember that it's only because of him that your head isn't skewered on my blade right now." Yama shoved the older woman to the side. "Get out of my sight."

Yama returned to the front of the suites, looking for Jilly. It was evident that without the Spirit Jestivan, she had no balance. There was only one other time in her life that someone had such an effect, and that was when Toono was her Charge.

6
Home

Toshik dragged himself toward the gate of gold that surrounded his house. His father had requested that he come home for the weekend, which was a nuisance for two reasons. One, the travel time from Phesaw was more than half a day. Two, he knew why his presence was needed.

As the two guards nodded at the tall swordsman and opened the gate, Toshik gave a deep sigh as he took a moment to stare at the yard. Trees were scarce, but vibrant green grass blanketed the entire ground. A luxurious building made of woven bamboo—a plant native to the Adren Kingdom—stretched atop a gentle hill.

There were several different wings with a house of such size, each serving different purposes. Some were one-story tall; others multiple floors high. Toshik couldn't count on one hand the amount of times people had mistaken his home to be a vacation resort.

He walked up the sloping stone path, giving a friendly wave to a servant who was tending to a rock pond in the distance. He thought back to his days as a child, splashing and swimming with not a care in the world as his mother sat on the rocks and teasingly kicked water into his face.

He entered the house and headed toward the business quarters. It was quite a walk through different hallways, exchanging nods and friendly hellos with dozens of his father's employees. Finally he came to a massive door on the back wall of a room full of cubicles.

When Toshik slid open the door, his heart rate picked up as he saw the man accompanying his father. He had been prepared for this, but evidently that didn't matter.

"Hey, Toshik." The greeting came from his dad, who was leaning back in the chair behind his desk. The single large sheet of glass behind him spanned the entire wall, looking out at the home's hundred-acre backyard.

"Hello, sir," Toshik replied. He then turned to the other man. "Hello, Spirit Major."

Instead of responding, the man fixed Toshik with a rigid glare.

"Have a seat, bud," his father said.

Toshik obeyed the request, careful to not show his anger.

"How was the journey home?" his father asked.

"About as one would expect—long and boring."

"How are you and Jilly?"

"Perfectly fine, sir." Toshik's answer reeked with bitterness.

"Major Wert has told me differently."

Toshik's father was leaning back in his chair as if he was happily digesting a large meal. Interrogations were simple for him. He shot off questions like he was striking up a conversation—after decades of being a successful entrepreneur, he engaged in business as if it were pleasure, and the line between his associates and his family had been utterly erased.

Toshik purposely avoided the major's eyes. "I don't know what would make him think such a thing, father."

"I was at the Generals' Battle," the major said. "And where do you think I found my daughter?"

Toshik glanced at Wert from the corner of his eyes but didn't answer.

"I found her in the lap of another woman, playing and mingling," he spat, nearly enraged. "Meanwhile you were inebriated in a bar."

"Who is this woman, Toshik?" his father asked.

"Yama … another Adrenian, sir."

"And you're letting her win over Jilly's heart?"

Toshik paused.

"Answer the question, boy!" Major Wert yelled.

"Jilly's making that choice," Toshik said.

"Scare the Adrenian girl away. Threaten her into leaving Jilly alone," his father suggested.

"She's faster than me, and more talented a fighter, sir. She isn't scared of me at all."

That managed to break his father's cool demeanor. He stood and leaned forward, hands on his desk.

"You better make something happen, son. Major Wert is about to be promoted to an elite position, as am I. My talents as a swordsmith have made me the wealthiest, most powerful businessman in the Adren Kingdom. I have connections throughout both of Kuki Sphaira's realms. If—*when*—the son and daughter of these two powers come together in matrimony, there will be no limit to our bloodline … the Brench-Lamays. We will be looked at as equals to that of the kings and queens of all ten kingdoms. It's possible we could even hold sway over such powers. Do you understand the weight of what you're trying to accomplish?"

Toshik studied his father's eyes. "Yes, sir."

"You protect Jilly at all costs. Do not let her spirit overpower her rational thought, which we know is bound to happen if you're not around. I heard about your adventure into the Dev Kingdom. I'm proud you were able to keep her safe. Now all I need is for you to pry this Yama girl's fingers off of her."

"Yes, sir."

"Good. Thanks for stopping by, son." His father sat back down as if nothing happened. "You can stay the weekend if you want. I need to talk to Wert, if you don't mind."

Toshik rose from his chair. As he was about to exit, he was stopped by a remark from Major Wert.

"How about you protect Jilly better than you did your mother and sister."

Toshik paused but didn't look back. His mouth creased downward as his eyes dulled. A puking sensation sat in his throat, making his response sound weak and morose:

"Yes, sir."

* * *

The teleplatform slowly came to a halt as Olivia arrived in the Passion Kingdom. She and a few students and staff from Phesaw stepped off and regained their bearings. Several soldiers approached to search them. Ever since the slaughter of fourteen soldiers a couple weeks back, security had been heightened. Even General Landon had been stationed here for the first week.

Olivia lazily lifted and extended her arms as one of the soldiers patted her ribs and triceps. She went through this every day, so it had become routine. She took this time to study the scorched field around them. There was still roughly forty men and women stationed at the terminal, but the search parties seemed to have dwindled lately. It was likely they had given up. If they hadn't found the culprit by now, he was long gone.

The soldier granted Olivia permission to proceed into the kingdom. She strolled down the lone center trail with Meow Meow's snores as the only sound to interrupt the quiet. With her mind so blank, the cat's dreams of fish overpowered her senses.

She dipped into the forest to her right after rounding a bend in the trail, out of sight of the terminal. Lallopy Forest was vast and thick, and a notorious hideout for outcasts and criminals. Five days before, one of the search teams returned from the forest with one of their own hobbling on a broken leg. The guilty man had accompanied them in chains.

Wake up, Meow Meow.

The kitten hat's eyes jarred open. He was an extra pair of eyes and ears—and a much more useful nose. Olivia followed the same path she always took. She counted trees before turning in different directions and she looked for purposely broken branches that marked danger zones such as traps, criminals, or predatory wildlife.

Meow Meow's nose twitched. *Someone is following us.*

Unfazed, Olivia continued walking while making sure not to look back. A twig snapped behind her. She ignored it.

Pick up the pace, Meow Meow warned.

She gained speed and began to weave between trees in effort to throw off her pursuer's sense of direction. But that wouldn't matter if this person was a veteran of the forest like she was.

Olivia hopped onto a sturdy branch and leapt, grabbing a higher branch with both hands. She swung forward and landed in the crotch of a nearby tree. She ran from branch to branch with the expectation that she had shaken her pursuer.

Meow Meow's nose wiggled again. *They're still on our elevation. Get home immediately. You're not outmaneuvering this person.*

Olivia accelerated as she ran through the canopy. She knew exactly where she was. She planted her left foot on a thick branch and surged forward through the leaves, then hit the ground with a forward roll and immediately sprang back to her feet.

A wall of dirt jutted up from the ground in front of her, where the crust of the land was broken into two different elevations. It was only a little bit taller than Olivia, but it stretched for miles to the sides. A massive boulder sat against the wall where she stood. She slowly pushed it out of the way. Even for her, it took a lot of strength. A hole was revealed, and she walked inside before sliding the boulder back into its original position.

She was in the front hall of her home. It was pitch black, but she could easily walk through the passage after so many years. Turning right down a different pathway, she could see candlelight seeping through the cracks of a door. Her mother was in that room, but this would be a terrible time to greet her, for she could hear her mother's heavy breathing and the occasional thud of a fist against wooden furniture. She was having a breakdown—nothing out of the ordinary.

Olivia calmly turned the other direction, heading toward her room as her mother's outbursts grew distant. The only light in her bedroom came from a patch in the ceiling, where branches, sticks, and other foliage were interlaced to act as a skylight and a ventilation system.

She sprawled across the bed and fell asleep.

*   *   *

Olivia and Meow Meow awoke a few hours later to the sound of heavy rustling above them. She sat up and gazed at the speckled patch of moonlight. A shadow shifted in the light. Someone had found the natural vent in the floor of the forest above—most likely the person who had chased her earlier that day.

The foliage above snapped as a person fell into her room and landed cleanly in a squat. Olivia placidly stared at her guest while Meow Meow growled softly. The man stood tall, allowing his face to be illuminated by the moonlight above. A bandage encircled the top of his head.

"Hello, Olivia."

He knew her name, yet she had never seen him before. "Hello," she replied.

"I'm here to talk to your mother."

"She's not fit for company at the moment."

"I see," the man said. "Can you inform her of my arrival?"

Olivia paused. *I don't know about this*, Meow Meow said to her.

Ignoring the kitten's uncertainty, Olivia asked, "What is the message you want me to give her? I'll inform her and then come back and retrieve you if she permits."

"A friend is here to plead for her partnership."

Olivia got out of bed. "And your name?" she asked while stepping into her boots.

"Toono."

She glanced at him with empty eyes, and he stared back at the scars on her face from the whips of the Dev soldiers.

*   *   *

The orange hue spreading over Phesaw Park and its many cherry blossoms signaled dusk's arrival. Nine of the Jestivan occupied the only location that was clear of the trees—a rectangular patch of grass that sat near the park's heart. Olivia always had to be home before dark, but the rest were eager to put in some extra work. Eight Jestivan sparred in pairs while Agnos sat against a tree off to the side, watching without much interest.

He wasn't the only spectator. A wall of students bordered the practice field. Unlike Agnos, they were enthralled by what they were witnessing. Older students sat in the front rows of the crowd along with the youngest students who could get away with standing. Behind these first few rows, others were hopefully craning their necks toward the action.

A cloaked figure sat next to Agnos—Thusia, who was sensing for any possible assassins.

The Jestivan switched partners every three minutes. It didn't require a break in the fighting. Toshik bolted away from Bryson, and Tashami quickly took the swordsman's place with a lunging knee already prepared. Sidestepping to the right, Bryson palmed downward onto his partner's knee and immediately rebounded the back of his hand into Tashami's face—a routine one-two combination.

The snowy-haired Jestivan wasn't rattled. He was used to Bryson's speed by now. All of the Jestivan were familiar with each other's strengths, weakness, and styles.

A gust of wind smacked Bryson from behind, knocking him toward Tashami and into his fist. Bryson needed to pay better attention to his opponent's hand motions—especially with Intel, Passion, and Spirit residents. They told a lot about an attack. Only the best of the best could manipulate their energies without the use of their hands, such as a select few of the royal heads and their kin. The Jestivan simply weren't quite there yet.

Their limbs moved in a blur of hand-to-hand combat. A burst of wind would whizz past Bryson's ear, and he would return the favor with an electric-coated punch. Many blows were dealt, but landing one was rare. And although the fighting was serious and heated, no one was mentally or emotionally affected by any of it. They had grown used to beating up on one another; they only wanted to improve.

The most important benefit was for the slower Jestivan to grow accustomed to the faster movements from the likes of Yama, Toshik, and Bryson. Though the others couldn't move at the same speed, they could still learn to visually read the speed and react with an appropriate block or evasive maneuver. And though they weren't at an Adrenian's speed percentage, they were becoming faster themselves.

Bryson noticed this. He felt lighter on his feet, but he also saw it in the others. Tashami was proof of it. He didn't fight like this a mere couple months ago, which was credit to Rhyparia's ancient. It made them feel feather-light in normal gravity.

As the sun disappeared behind the trees, the spectating students clapped three times in unison. The Jestivan had instructed them to do so, as a signal to stop the fighting. Bryson and Tashami briefly grabbed each other's hand with a smile.

"Good job, Tashami," Bryson said.

"I'll never get used to that speed and electric combination," Tashami said through heavy breaths. "At least with Yama and Toshik, it's just speed."

"Thanks, man. Glad to see you're not holding back as much as you used to. Break out of that shell a little. Especially since you'll be entering the Void soon."

The ivory-haired Jestivan ran a hand through his hair. "Will do."

As Tashami walked away, Bryson looked for Lilu. Most of the Jestivan had already been swallowed by swarms of students, but she sat in the grass by herself. He took a seat next to the royal girl, whose green hair had a radiant yellow chrysanthemum pinned in it. She looked ahead at nothing in particular, obviously lost in thought.

"You're getting faster," Bryson said.

It took a second for Lilu to turn her head toward him. She was astonishingly alluring—even with beads of sweat running down her face. "We all are," she pointed out.

"Not Agnos."

Lilu smirked. "He doesn't count."

Bryson glanced behind him. Agnos was gone, but Thusia remained seated at the edge of the training field. He knew she was watching them from beneath her hood, for she constantly teased him about Lilu.

"I'm proud of you," Bryson said.

"Excuse me?"

"How you've grown accustomed to the gravity training. You're tough."

"If that surprises you, you don't know me."

There was the hostility again. Bryson ignored it. "Rhyparia really wants to sit down and talk to you sometime."

Lilu flopped back in the grass with an exasperated sigh. "What does a murderer want with me?"

"Do you even realize the death toll your bloodline has racked up over the centuries?" Bryson snapped.

A hand struck Bryson in the face hard, snapping his head to the side. He rubbed his jaw, not bothering to turn back, as he knew that she had already gotten up and stormed out of the park and toward Lilac Suites.

Bryson pushed himself off the ground and headed toward Thusia. She had rolled up the sleeve of her cloak and was giving him a very pronounced thumbs-down sign—as if he needed to be informed that he completely butchered that conversation.

A young boy sprinted out of the crowd as his red hair whipped behind him. He jumped into Bryson's chest with a thud.

"Hey, Simon," Bryson said with a laugh.

"Bryson! That was so fun to watch! You're the coolest Jestivan!" Simon exclaimed.

"I sense a bit of bias."

"What's that mean?"

Bryson smiled. "Never mind. What have you been up to?"

"Archery. Been practicing with the bow Debo got me during the Generals' Battle."

"I think you might train more than any of the Jestivan do."

Simon frowned. "Not really. You remember what it was like to be at school at my age. So many classes, so many rules. The grownups are always watching us."

"Ah, yes. I hated that."

"I made a new friend!"

"Who?" Bryson asked, wide-eyed.

"She's over there," Simon said, pointing behind him.

"*She?* Ooh, a girlfriend." Bryson scanned the crowd and saw a girl staring intently back at him. "The one with the black hair and big eyes?"

"Yep!" Simon replied as he waved her over.

The girl broke away from the pack, and as she came closer, Bryson realized that her hair was much longer than he'd thought. It would have trailed along the ground if she didn't have a ball of it wrapped around her wrist.

Bryson beamed. "Hey!"

"Hello," she mumbled.

"I'm Bryson."

"LeAnce?" she asked, her gaze turning from one of wonder to a sharp focus.

"Indeed! What's your name?"

"I'm Illipsia." Her eyes veered toward the ground. "It's an honor to meet you."

7
Pilot of Spy and Sky

The staff and students gathered at the foot of Telejunction's massive hill, much as they had on the day when Grand Director Poicus arrived in a bloody mess. This time, however, there were smiles everywhere. Bryson, Rhyparia, Himitsu, Toshik, Jilly, Olivia, Grand Director Poicus, Director Senex, and Director Venustas stood in front of the crowd, looking up at the hill's crest.

Tashami, Agnos, Lilu, and Yama were walking up the hill, ready for their journey into the Void. They were flanked by a hunched Director Neaneuma and lean Director Buredo, who would accompany them into the Dark Realm. Bryson couldn't help but think of how nice it would have been to have such help in the Dev Kingdom a few months back.

As the Jestivan reached the top of the hill, cheers erupted from the crowd. Bryson looked to his right and smiled. Jilly did a decent job at holding back her tears, though her lips were trembling. She wouldn't see Yama until summer vacation ended.

Bryson glanced back up the slope at Lilu. This was the second time that they were parting on bad terms. Not that it was his fault.

The crowd continued to roar as the recipients waved down the hill. There were shouts of encouragement and good luck. Bryson studied Director Neaneuma's weary face. She was the most important piece to their group, for she would be the one to spiritually drive the Jestivan through the Cyn Kingdom's deflating atmosphere.

Lilu, Tashami, Agnos, and Yama prepared with the Spirit Director every day for the past few months. Their mission: tracking down the Unbreakable.

The cheers died down as the Jestivan and directors disappeared into the gated portion of Telejunction—the area designated for cross-realm platforms. It was finally hitting Bryson. With his fellow Jestivan's mission underway, it meant tomorrow would be the last day of the school year. And what a year it had been. In a little more than twenty-four hours, Phesaw's campus would be deserted of roughly eighty percent of its normal population as students and teachers made their way home.

Bryson turned and scanned the dispersing crowd, expecting to see Thusia in her usual oversized cloak of sky blue. She was supposed to be waiting for him, but she wasn't in sight.

"She's running toward the library," Himitsu whispered in Bryson's ear. "Very quickly, too."

Bryson bolted immediately. The farther away from Bryson that Thusia traveled, the weaker she'd become. The only reason a Branian could even leave the Light Empire was because of the person they were attached to.

Bryson knocked into lingering packs of students, then sped toward Phesaw's brick library—the Warpfinate. He hated the place. It felt like a cold, abandoned cave, even during hotter months. His face soured as he pushed open the towering heavy doors.

The lobby was dreary—and strangely empty. The librarian's desk was unoccupied, so Bryson walked right past it. Bookcases rose hundreds of feet into the gloom as he entered a maze of words on paper. Bryson wrinkled his nose. Unlike Lilu and Agnos, who both spent a lot of time in the Warpfinate, he absolutely hated books.

The quiet was too resolute, even for a library. There was no turning of pages or rolling of book carts to fill the hollow void. Bryson chalked it up to it being the end of the year. For fear of fires, candles weren't allowed in the library, so the only light came from the occasional Intelight perched on a bookshelf. But even they were dim.

After minutes of walking in a straight line, Bryson finally reached the end of one aisle before turning left down another. He wished he had grabbed one of the maps from behind the librarian's desk. Usually there were guides who helped students through the city of books, but they had vanished too.

Footsteps broke the silence. They were hurried, heavy and grew louder with each step, and Bryson's heart rate increased with them. This couldn't have been Thusia, for she was naturally stealthy.

A few Intelights were spaced evenly in front of him, and with how close the footsteps were, he should have seen the person they belonged to. Then he was violently knocked into the towering shelves beside him as the footsteps passed. His stomach dropped—a Dev Assassin.

A hand on his shoulder made him jump. He turned to see Thusia's cerulean eyes and thick golden eyelashes glowing in the shadows. "Get the Grand Director. Tell him there's an emergency in the Bricks." Her eyes grew stern. "Do not follow me."

Thusia skipped away with a purposeful and fluid movement. Though it was unorthodox, it was her own style of travel, and she could cover several yards in one stride.

Bryson didn't follow her, but he didn't go straight to Poicus either. He sprinted in the direction that Thusia had come from. He continued running until he saw a light shining through the gaps between shelves. He also caught whiff of a putrid smell. He punched through some of the books and crawled between the shelves as a shortcut.

He turned a final corner and stopped in an open area. A patch of grass lay before him, enclosed by a shin-high wall of bricks. A smaller circle of bricks stood in the center of the grass. A lively fire was ablaze within the circle. This was normal. The Bricks was the only place where a fire was allowed, and it was monitored by a librarian at all times—but not now.

The fire was unruly, and Bryson's lips flattened when he saw what was feeding it. A steel beam ran from one bookshelf to another, across the expanse of the grass. Tied to the beam and hanging upside-down directly above the fire were three people roasting in the cackling flames. None of them struggled or screamed, for death had already come.

* * *

"We're going to have to shut down the school for the summer," Poicus said as he slowly paced behind his office desk, leaning on his cane. His naked agitation seemed very unbefitting of a Grand Director. "Nobody can stay here. It's too dangerous. No, no, no. They hit us at the perfect time."

The office was more crowded than Bryson could recall. Thusia was sitting with her legs crossed on one of the display tables off to the side. Himitsu was leaning against one of the bookshelves. Directors Senex and Venustas stood on either side of the Grand Director's desk.

"There was too much commotion," Thusia reasoned. "I could barely sense him, so Himitsu probably couldn't sense him at all."

Himitsu faintly shook his head.

Poicus walked to his desk and read over a piece of parchment that Bryson had recovered from the Bricks: "This is only the beginning. It could also be the end if Praetor Poicus hands himself over."

Poicus rubbed his eyes. A bird landed on the windowsill behind him. "Part of me feels like I should give myself up. I'm not having the lives of students and staff in danger because of me," the old man said.

"No!" Thusia shouted.

"I would agree with her," Senex said. "That would hurt Phesaw in a way that could not be fixed. You are far too important. This place stays safe simply because of your presence."

"Obviously that is not the case," Poicus replied.

"If anything," Himitsu said, "what that Dev Assassin did speaks to Director Senex's words. They did that out of fear. From what Thusia said, they're trapped in the Rolling Oaks, and they can't get to Telejunction while there are four assassins guarding it … not to mention Thusia and me patrolling the campus."

"I would have chased him farther," Thusia mumbled. "But I was too far away from Bryson by the time I reached the High Sever."

"Director Debo was already a big enough blow," Venustas said. "He was more talented than any of us. We cannot lose you too."

"Then they'll have to be disposed of, and promptly. But I cannot fight," Poicus said as he glared at his cane with disgust. "Forget fighting, I can barely walk."

"Send us after them," Bryson said. "They killed three. We'll kill three." His voice was cold.

Poicus studied Bryson. "Your rage is potent, but do not let malice overcome you. I will not entertain such an idea from a person with that mindset. You must look at it as a necessary duty in order to prevent the deaths of more innocents—not as revenge. Do not dig the same grave as your father."

"What did revenge have to do with my father's death?" Bryson retorted.

"The man I knew your father to be died long before his heart ceased."

Bryson closed his eyes at the sudden jolt of pain. Thusia's eyes lowered as her head tilted toward the ground.

"We can't let them camp out in the Oaks," Venustas said, steering the conversation back on course.

"Of course," Poicus agreed as he gingerly took a seat, resting his cane against the desk. "I've already planned for the moment when we go after them. The directors need to stay on the main campus. With Buredo and Neaneuma gone, and no Intel Director, we're already down in leadership. And Senex must stay here to continue molding Rhyparia. Olivia won't be at Phesaw over the summer—and I wouldn't send her regardless.

"So we'll send two groups beyond the High Sever—each group containing one experienced assassin-blood. I'll inform Jilly and Toshik that they will be joining Himitsu and one of the assassins who guards the cross-realm platforms."

Himitsu frowned. "I'm assassin-blooded. Why do we need another in the group?"

"I said 'experienced,' Zana Himitsu."

The look on the young Jestivan's face made it obvious he took it as an insult, but he didn't argue.

Poicus ran his fingers through his snowy beard and looked at Bryson next. "The choice for you is clear. You'll have Thusia." The Grand Director gazed at the Branian. "You'll keep his head clear."

"Yes, sir," Thusia replied.

Director Senex's eyes widened. "You said that the Dev servant you brought into the Dark Realm lost her life. That means all we have is Tally. Communication will be vital to this mission. Without that link, how will everyone keep informed?"

The bird that had perched in the open window flew into the office and onto the desk. Its wings sporadically twitched as it hopped from one spot to another. "This little starling," Poicus said.

Himitsu pushed himself off the bookcase and slowly approached the bird. He leaned over and brushed a few falling strands of black hair from in front of his eyes as he stared into the bird's eyes.

"Are you serious?" he mumbled.

The door to the office opened and an older woman took a step in. Her skin was a dark tan, and her straight jet-black hair was cut short. Her outfit consisted of strange articles of clothing that Bryson had really seen before, all of it different shades of brown. But what stood out most was her staff. Long and pure white until it reached the top, where it formed a perfect circle engraved with elegant designs. Hanging from the staff's loop were ten beautiful feathers, each with their own pattern.

The bird that had been scuffling around the desk flew across the room and perched itself on the staff's loop. The woman gave its beak a peck. Himitsu walked over and embraced the woman in his arms.

"Hello, son," the woman said, her voice muffled by Himitsu's chest.

"I missed you," Himitsu replied.

"I've missed you, too. I'm sorry. There has been so much happening with your father and me."

"How is he?"

The woman shook her head. "We'll talk about it later."

"Everyone, I'd like you to meet Ophala," Poicus said.

Ophala gave an awkward wave around the room. She gave Thusia a courteous nod and simply said, "Thusia."

"Ophala," Thusia replied.

The Archaic Director nodded. "I see. Well, as expected, you've planned accordingly, Praetor. One of my favorite students."

Ophala gave a weak smile. "Flattering, Director Senex. And you don't look a day over twenty."

"We were lucky. King Itta would never have lent us such an important piece of his military." Poicus was speaking more to everyone else than he was to Ophala. "With him no longer in power and the other four light kingdoms in control, she was more accessible.

"Ophala is the leader of the Archaic Kingdom's branch of spies. The official title of such a position is a 'Spy Pilot,' and the title is oddly fitting for her—given the nature of her ancient. Throughout the Light Realm she has earned the name of Ophala, the Pilot of Spy and Sky."

Himitsu wore the evilest grin, as if he was the one receiving all the glory. Ophala, meanwhile, had scrunched up her face like she was painfully uncomfortable. "I feel like I'm winning an award. Thusia is the one who was a Jestivan. Let's boast about her."

Thusia playfully stuck out her tongue, and Poicus's eyes twinkled. "Old friendly rivalries never die, I suppose." He stood up. "With that said, Ophala can catch everyone up to speed later today or tomorrow. She will inform you of the mission's details and how it will be orchestrated. This means each of you will get a taste of a *professionally* prepared and tactically executed battle plan from the mind of a very experienced specialist. She is your pilot, figuratively and literally."

The little starling perched in her staff flapped its wings and released a flurry of whistles.

*   *   *

The moon sat high above Lilac Suites and the rest of Wealth's Crossroads. A massive chandelier cast a golden light throughout every floor of the magnificent suites. Besides the group gathered in the lobby, the building had completely emptied for summer vacation.

Bryson was seated at a table with Jilly and Thusia, which led to plenty of laughs. Just one of them could make an entire garden bloom in the midst of winter. Himitsu was busy at another table, undoubtedly discussing all sorts of things with his mother. There was a lot for the two of them to catch up on.

Toshik sat alone on the second floor with his legs between the rails and dangling off the edge. His arms were also through the rails and folded against each other while his face was pressed into the wooden bars as he solemnly stared down at Jilly.

A chime sung as the front door to Lilac Suites opened. Everyone turned to look at the guest. His face was covered in age spots and wrinkles, and his hair was a thinning chestnut brown. His eyes were narrow, as if old age had caused an extra fold of skin to droop over his eyelids.

This couldn't be the man they were waiting for—the assassin who Director Poicus had assigned to lead Himitsu, Jilly, and Toshik. Bryson couldn't help but think how lucky he was to have Thusia.

"Good evening, Fane," Ophala said with a gleaming smile as she stood up.

"Good to see you, Ophala," Fane replied as he shook her hand. His voice was deep and sturdy—incongruously so for a man of his age. And his stride was that of a young prince. He carried himself with confidence, with his chin up and chest out.

Ophala walked behind the bar and started opening cabinets. She grabbed a mug and dunked it into a barrel, then faced the others with a wide smile.

"What's a meeting without ale?" She took a sip from her mug and let out a sigh of satisfaction. "Any takers?"

Himitsu rowdily pounded his fist on the table three times. "That's my boy," Ophala said.

"Might as well," Fane thrummed in his deep voice. "I assume it'll be a while before I get a taste again."

The rest of them declined. Bryson was too young, Jilly and Thusia didn't drink, and Toshik surprisingly wasn't interested.

Ophala chugged the contents of her mug, then slammed it on the bar. "You're aware of the myths of the Rolling Oaks—the beasts, the unstable environment in certain spots. Those stories are enough to keep most out. But roughly a millennium ago, a foolish band of students acquired a taste to explore the unexplored. When they never returned, Grand Director

Charaton commenced the most daunting project ever pursued in Phesaw: the construction of the High Sever. It took sixty years and many, many loans from the Light Realm's kingdoms before it reached completion.

"Now the High Sever is patrolled around the clock with archers lining the windows, soldiers from all five kingdoms at the top, and trained beasts locked away in the bottom floor of the wall. So how is it that three Dev Assassins can cross it without being noticed? Surely, even if they can cloak themselves, the fact that they can only do so for a couple minutes of time would make it impossible. Crossing that wall would take a lot more time than that."

"The lake," Bryson said.

Ophala smiled. Bryson never represented his kingdom too well in regard to book smarts, but when it came to anything strategic in nature, his mind shined.

"During this mission, I will have many tasks," Ophala continued, "and keeping an eye on the lake will be one of them. Bryson, with Lita Thusia by your side, two people will suffice. She is fully capable of hunting down and eliminating an assassin. Not only was she a Jestivan, but now she's a Bozani too? How can she lose?" She laughed at her joke and threw back another gulp of ale.

Thusia stuck out her tongue. "The gap between us has widened even further than it was."

Ophala held her mug in the air as if she was giving a toast. "To the rival I never had a chance at surpassing." She scanned the scattered faces of Fane's group. "You four will have the numbers, but you can't stay too close to each other. Himitsu must stay in range of Fane, but spread out far enough to expand the reach of your abilities to sense the assassins. Jilly can travel with Himitsu while Toshik goes with Fane."

"No," Toshik called down from the second floor. "Jilly stays near me."

"No can do, and I will not waver," Ophala said. "You're welcome to discuss your concerns with Grand Director Poicus, but I must inform you that he and I worked on this plan together. Each pair absolutely must contain one assassin. Otherwise mistakes will be made and lives will be in danger."

Toshik looked to be thinking on it. "At least let Jilly go with Fane. I'll go with Himitsu."

"Do you trust Fane more than your friend?" Ophala asked. "You don't even know the man."

"Himitsu is simply a teammate, not a friend. And yes, I do trust Fane more."

"Interesting," Ophala said. She looked at Himitsu and Fane. "Are you okay with this?"

The two of them nodded. "Fine. Jilly will stick to Fane, and Toshik to Himitsu. And while the six of you venture into the rolling hills of forest, I'll be stationed at the top of the High Sever."

Ophala walked from behind the bar and grabbed her staff that was leaning against a table. Tapping came from a windowpane in the front of the building as a starling pecked away at the glass. Himitsu walked over and opened it, and the bird darted across the room and perched itself on Ophala's staff.

"You'll find travel sacks filled with supplies in your rooms. We head out in two days' time."

8
Rolling Oaks

Bryson awoke at four A.M., before the sun had shown itself. He got out of bed and stretched before heading to the washroom, where he examined his "T2"-shaped scar on his chest and lazily prepared for the day ahead. Then he flopped back onto his bed and withdrew the contents of his traveling bag, quadruple checking that he had everything he needed: plenty of dried jerky, some apples, a hatchet, flint, ink, quills, parchment, small blades, and a spare cloak that would serve as shelter from the elements.

One item did not belong, however—a tattered book with Debo's real name on the cover. Thusia, who was regaining her stamina and energy in the Light Empire, would have surely disapproved of this, but Bryson didn't care. He had gone home the day before to grab it. He hadn't been in the house in a little more than a month, so it was a painful visit.

Bryson threw the bag over his shoulder and pulled his hood over his head as he exited his room. He squinted as the chandelier's Intelights assaulted his groggy vision. Did they ever turn that thing off?

"Bryson!"

He gazed over the fourth floor's rail, down into the lobby below. Jilly looked up at him with wide eyes and a smile as blinding as the chandelier. As he reached the lobby, she ran toward him before abruptly stopping on her tippy toes. "Are you ready for another adventure?" she asked.

"I am," he said with a weak smirk. Everyone was already in the lobby and fully prepared. He must have lost time while staring at his book.

Bryson and Himitsu walked together as the group crossed the prairie under the moonlight. The two friends wanted to talk a bit before they parted.

"Toshik, eh?" Bryson teased.

Himitsu groaned. "Kill me now."

"He's gotten better, and it'll be good for the two of you."

"I could light him on fire in his sleep," Himitsu said, seeming to ponder the idea.

"You could become a duo."

Himitsu laughed. "Funny."

The High Sever clawed deeper into the sky the closer they got. Bryson wondered what it would be like to have to stand at the top of the wall every day. His eyes fell to the woman walking at the front of the pack with her staff in hand, for she would call that place home for the next few weeks.

"I thought both of your parents were Passion Assassins," Bryson said.

"I don't know why. I don't recall ever telling anyone about them."

"True. You're quite secretive about them."

"I have to be. My parents hold dangerous positions and rely on being hidden. My dad is a Passion Assassin. He's currently imprisoned by King Damian, along with pretty much every other assassin of the kingdom. He taught me everything I needed to know about hiding where you cannot be seen."

"And what exactly is Ophala?" Bryson asked, fascinated to finally be hearing about Himitsu's parents after all these years.

"My mom is from the Archaic Kingdom. Her staff—the Cheiraskinia—is her ancient. She isn't assassin-blooded, but she grew up learning a similar art—that of being a spy. Both assassins and spies require lengthy tactical planning and meticulous execution of their plans, and oftentimes they'll work hand-in-hand. The spy scouts while the assassin hunts."

"So basically what we'll be doing in the Oaks," Bryson said. "Ophala will be scouting from the High Sever, relaying information to and from the assassin of each pair: Thusia, Fane, and you."

Himitsu nodded. "My dad taught me how to hide in the shadows. My mom taught me how to hide in plain sight." He smiled. "They would always bicker when I was young about which tactic was superior. But they made sure I learned how to perfect both arts."

"Hiding in plain sight would be more difficult," Bryson responded after thinking about it for a moment.

"Let me ask you this then: if you're walking down a market street flooded with merchants, carts, pedestrians, and carriages, and you're about to stroll past a dark and abandoned alley … what are you going to be most wary of?"

Bryson knew what Himitsu was getting at, but he gave him the wrong answer he was looking for: "The dark alley."

"Meanwhile there are hundreds of strangers surrounding you, and that's where your real threat is. They could be right behind you in plain sight. So it's not that simple. People tend to be extra cautious in the dark, making it that much harder for an assassin to lurk. And they tend to flock toward the crowds when they're scared, automatically thinking they'll be safe around so many people."

The group reached the bottom of the High Sever, where a giant iron gate was closed shut. A bobbing torch approached from the other side. When the soldier realized that it was Ophala, the gate slowly rose from the ground.

"My mom and dad used to be a scary pair," Himitsu murmured. "They caught many notorious criminals."

Bryson looked at him. "Used to be?"

Himitsu's face was expressionless—eerily similar to Olivia's. "Crap happens."

A cacophony of beastly noises roared from both sides as they passed through the gate. Howls, roars, vicious barks, and some sounds not capable of description penetrated the stone walls. The guard was dismissed, and a torch-carrying Ophala led them through the rather narrow hall, with the dirt of the land as their floor.

They occasionally passed a ladder that would climb the wall until stopping at open passages that likely led to other sections of the structure. When they reached a second iron gate, Ophala turned around. Her black hair blended with the shadowy backdrop of the Rolling Oaks just beyond the gate.

"This is where we part," she announced. "Bryson, get Thusia."

A bright light manifested as Fane grumbled with interest. Even Ophala looked intrigued. Bryson was used to the euphoric feeling that accompanied the summoning of a Branian, so it was easy for him to forget what it had been like the first time it happened—that sensation of a feather-light conscious and pure freedom.

"It's about time," Thusia said through a pearly smile. "Let's hunt down some assassins." She made fake fighting noises with her mouth as she punched the air in ridiculous sparring stances.

Jilly, of course, joined in. "Bad guys suck!" she yelled.

"Remember," Ophala said after patiently waiting for the charade to cease. "Thusia and Bryson, head northeast. Himitsu and Toshik, head east. Fane and Jilly, head southeast. I'll be at the top of the Sever, but my presence will be felt at all times around each pair. We went over the finer details the past day and a half. Any questions?"

Jilly's hand shot into the air.

"Yes, Lita Jilly?"

"I brought cupcakes. Is that okay?"

Ophala smirked. "Did you bring enough for everyone?"

* * *

Bryson strolled between the trees as if he were taking a walk in Phesaw Park after a day of classes. The early morning sun shined through healthy green leaves. He had only been here for an hour, but he couldn't help but feel relaxed. What had happened to all the strange creatures that were supposed to be out here?

Thusia's blond hair swayed gently in front of Bryson. She was moving with a sense of purpose and direction as Bryson simply wandered.

When Bryson infiltrated the Dev Kingdom, he had leads and objectives. The server boy at the transit told him that he'd have to travel to Rence. The oblivious soldiers at the inn in Rence inadvertently informed him of Storshae's travels through Necrosis Valley. There was always a location or direction to head toward.

This was different. For Bryson, it was like finding a bead of glass on the beach. But that's what Thusia was for. While she did the tracking, Bryson's mind wandered to Lilu and friends in the Void, King Vitio and Princess Shelly, Rhyparia's control training, how Olivia was spending her summer, and … Bryson glanced up at Thusia.

"Thusia."

"Bryson," she replied as she stepped cautiously through a tangle of thorny vines.

"How come you never told me you're a Spirit Assassin?"

"I assumed you would know," she said. "You're an intelligent kid—or at least you're supposed to be."

"Well, I didn't. What's your ability?"

Thusia made a disappointed sucking noise with her teeth. "You need to be more observant. It's not like I try to hide it."

Bryson was quiet for a moment. She was right—inattention was a weak spot of his. It reminded him of trying to read the hand motions of his fellow Jestivan during sparring sessions, and how he would almost always predict attacks incorrectly.

"I'll tell you what," Thusia said while climbing over a fallen tree. "You have a week. If you can't guess what my ability is by then, you have to kiss Lilu." Bryson's face turned red. "But if you do guess it, I'll tell you a story about your father and me."

Bryson stumbled over a tree root. He hated hearing about his dad, but that was from ignorant mouths or exaggerated fairy tales. If there was anyone who knew about the real Mendac, it would be the woman he once was in love with.

"You're on."

*   *   *

"What's it like always being a prick?"

Himitsu's question broke Toshik out of his trance. "I guess it's a byproduct of being so hauntingly handsome," the swordsman replied.

Himitsu laughed. This section of the forest was much thicker than Thusia and Bryson's. "I refuse to believe you're that idiotically shallow."

"Maybe you should. Depth isn't a specialty of mine."

"Your lust of women that only lasts for a night's span before you move on to the next … your complete obsession with keeping Jilly out of harm's way … your disgust of males … and your superiority complex. All of those things relate. Something sculpted you to be like that—probably tragic."

"Another word and I'll dig your eyes out."

Himitsu's face remained placid as he turned and stared at Toshik, who had lost his habitual cool. "I remember your reaction to the story of Thusia's sacrifice when we first became Jestivan. Your eyes screamed of anger. Your tone, disgust. It wasn't Mendac that made you mad, was it?"

Tears flooded Toshik's eyes, but Himitsu continued. "Were you mad at yourself? Did the story remind you of your own? Is that why you are who you are?"

Toshik's rage boiled over. He grabbed the handle of his sword and pushed off his right foot. In an instant, he had unsheathed his weapon and slashed at an angle downward. He made contact, but not with his intended target. Himitsu had dodged the predictable attack and was now standing off to the side. After all, he had provoked it.

Two trees that were in the path of Toshik's sword slowly fell into others before crashing into the ground below. They had been cut cleanly through. Toshik stared blankly in front of him, heaving from anger.

"Vulnerability … that's a start," Himitsu said. "We're going to be out here for a while. When you're ready, let's talk man to man. I know there's some depth under your shell."

9
Apoleia

Olivia sat in her dingy room with dirt walls on all four sides and a dirt floor below her feet. She sat in crude wooden chair directly across from Toono, a breeze curling in from the hole he smashed through her ventilation system in the roof.

"Don't you worry," he said. "I'll take care of Storshae when I see him again. I gave him specific instructions to treat you well." He continued to stare at her scars. "I hate the fact that I must work with him. But since he's King Rehn's son, I have no choice. We have a common interest."

Meow Meow's furry brow rose. Olivia plainly gazed back. "Why do you treat me differently?"

"Hurting you is unnecessary and, more importantly, against my character."

"But you kill people."

Silence bathed the room as Toono tapped his fingers on the chair's arm. "Illipsia and Kadlest should be here soon. Yesterday was the last day of the school year, correct?"

"It was."

"Maybe I should go to the forest's edge and wait," he said.

A curtain slid open, and a woman in her late-thirties stepped through with a maniacal smile big enough to break her cheekbones. "Dress warm, dress warm!" she exclaimed as she threw a wool coat into Toono's lap. "Where we're off to won't be kind. You don't want to lose any toes, do you?"

She had no ability to hold a steady volume, shouting certain words and mumbling others. Her long hair was violet, her eyes a bright blue—perhaps made even brighter by the contrast of the dark bags around her eyes and her thick-rimmed glasses. Several rows of vivid scars ran across her neck. Olivia was used to them. Occasionally one would heal only to be replaced the very next day by another. She could always hear her mom's screams whenever she'd cut herself. There were many scars on her forearms too.

Toono smiled. "You're excited, Apoleia."

Apoleia walked behind Toono's chair and ran her fingers across his shoulders, all while wearing the same crazy grin. Her eyes lit up. "That I am," she whispered into his ear. She then looked up at Olivia. "How's my baby feeling?"

"Well."

"Look at my baby!" Apoleia yelled. "Unflappable! A *real* woman!"

Toono nodded. "One of the truest statements I've ever heard."

FWAP! Apoleia's open hand made contact with Toono's jaw. He kept his head tilted as he looked to be processing the blow. Apoleia crouched in front of him and grabbed his chin. Her eyes were now filled with menace, and her smile had turned sinister. "If I ever see my baby in this condition again, I'll tear your limbs off and feed them to Meow Meow."

Apoleia meant every word of it. The kitten hat made a face of disbelief, as if he would ever find such a thing appetizing.

"I deserved that," Toono said.

Apoleia ruffled his hair. "Good boy."

Footsteps rustled through the brush above. Apoleia's eyes slowly scanned up toward the vent. "Our guests have arrived," she whispered. "Drop on in!" she bellowed toward the roof.

A tiny girl fell through the vent first, followed by a sturdy brunette woman. "What a cutie!" Apoleia squeaked as she squeezed the girl's cheeks. "You must be Illipsia."

"Hi, Ms. Lavender," the girl replied.

Apoleia stood and stared at Kadlest—for the first time without a smile. "Kadlest."

"Apoleia."

Apoleia turned and abruptly left the room.

"She's still a nutcase," Kadlest said to Toono.

Olivia obliterated the arm of her chair with an effortless squeeze. Her face remained passive as she said, "Don't ever call my mother that."

Kadlest looked at Olivia, who she hadn't realized was in the room before. Her eyes ran over the scars on her face and the kitten atop her head. "I see. My apologies, Olivia. I am Kadlest. It's nice to finally meet you." Olivia simply stared emptily back. "Well then," Kadlest said to Toono. "Yama's a no-go."

"I'm not surprised," he replied. He stood and hugged Kadlest and then Illipsia. "It was a stretch, after all. But perhaps I can help her change her mind. We'll have to save that for another time, however."

A scream reverberated into the room, but Toono simply waved his hand when Kadlest looked at him.

"And you, Illipsia? How'd you do?" Toono asked.

"I made a friend!" she replied. "And he'll be of great use."

Apoleia walked back into the room with a fresh cut across her neck. Blood slowly trailed down from it. Her eyelashes were matted against her face from tears, but she wore a toothy smile. "Shall we leave?"

The five of them exited the cave and headed toward the dirt road at the edge of the forest, where they split into two groups. Illipsia and Kadlest headed south toward the capital, while Apoleia, Toono, and Olivia went north toward the teleplatforms.

As the three of them approached the teleplatforms, they received curious glares from soldiers in red. It was the beginning of summer, so their giant wool coats and raised hoods was a red flag.

One of the soldiers stepped in front of them. His face was badly sunburnt, and he looked miserable. "Where are you all off to?" he asked.

"We need to use the teleplatform that will take us to the Still Kingdom." Toono replied, careful to keep his face hidden.

"What's your purpose?"

"We have business to attend to," Apoleia said. "Please don't make this difficult."

"I'm sorry, mam, but with recent occurrences, access between realms is prohibited."

Apoleia snickered, raising the hair on Olivia's skin. It was the one sound that could affect her in such a way.

Her mother raised a gloved hand, extended her index finger, and gave it a slight flick upward. A jagged pillar of ice shot up from the ground underneath the soldier's feet, skewering him. His shout of pain lasted a brief moment and almost immediately trailed away as he died. Blood tumbled down the ice.

Apoleia giggled. "He's like a flag at high mast. What a *chilling* welcome to the Passion Kingdom he will serve as." She clapped as if to admire her handiwork.

They stepped onto the appropriate platform. Onlookers gazed from the terminal's windows, and soldiers stood in fear in front of the building. The man who controlled the teleplatforms wisely flipped the lever, initiating the platform to spin.

"You see, baby," Apoleia whispered into Olivia's ear. "Men are inferior. Dispose of the foolish. Instill fear in the cowards. Control the puppets."

* * *

Grand Director Poicus was seated at his desk, twirling the end of one of his eyebrows. His injuries were still noticeable, and he was beginning to wonder if he'd ever be the same again. "Alright, Tally," he sighed. "Connect us."

A young man stood in the center of the office. Tally was once one of Phesaw's two Dev servants, but after his mother's death while accompanying Poicus in the Dev Kingdom a few months back, he was now the only one.

A holographic display appeared above the desk. The first face to emerge was a dark-skinned man with a chiseled jaw—Adren King Supido.

"Good afternoon, Grand Director," Supido said.

"Hello," Poicus replied. "It's been a while."

The display cut to different faces as each person gave their own greeting: King Vitio's blockish face, then Spirit Queen Apsa's delicate features and Passion King Damian's chubby cheeks before ending with Sinno, the Adren Kingdom's general. He had been taken out first during the Generals' Battle with a combination attack from the other combatants. His skin was the color of sand after being soaked in high tide.

"How is my little brother?" Supido asked.

"I wouldn't know," Poicus replied. "Director Buredo left to the Cyn Kingdom about a week back, but I have no worries about him."

Queen Apsa's face appeared next. "Why did he enter the Void?"

"To serve as a proctor along with Director Neaneuma for the Jestivan who went with them."

"You sent Jestivan into the Void too?" Apsa asked.

"He sure did," King Vitio grumbled. "My daughter being one of them."

Poicus smirked. "Don't get me started, Vitio. Besides, they're in perfectly good hands. And this is what I called this meeting for anyway. Everyone needs to be caught up to speed—including me. With all that's been happening at Phesaw, I haven't a clue as to what's occurring across Kuki Sphaira. But this can change now that summer is upon us."

"Very well then," Supido said. "We'll go one at a time—starting with you, Praetor."

"A few things of note," Poicus began. "I'm sure you can tell by simply looking at me that I've seen better days. Within the past six months, I've infiltrated the Dev Kingdom, searched for Storshae only to find out that he had been in the Archaic Kingdom the whole time, sniffed out former Dev King Rehn's grave, fended off the current Dev King Storshae, ran for my life as I tried outmaneuvering Dev Assassins, and then ended up back here … along with the three assassins who followed me.

"They've been hiding somewhere in the Rolling Oaks. One of them managed to sneak into the main campus and kill a staff member and two students before then escaping. Spy Pilot Ophala is hunting for them with

Assassin Fane and four Jestivan: Bryson, Jilly, Toshik, and Himitsu. They departed a couple days ago.

"Meanwhile Lilu, Yama, Agnos, Tashami, and Directors Neaneuma and Buredo are five days into their journey through the Cyn Kingdom to find the Unbreakable in hopes of landing leads on Toono, who we all know is a supposed key player in Storshae's desire to bring back his father."

In the stunned silence that ensued, Poicus took the opportunity to say one more thing: "I will not answer specific questions about the missions. What I told you will have to suffice. But I will provide with you any intelligence they might gather when they return."

"What about Rhyparia and Olivia?" Vitio asked.

"Rhyparia is spending the summer in the grasslands of the Archaic Kingdom along with Director Senex, where she will train rigorously until she has a full grasp of her ability. As for Olivia, I'd imagine she's home for the summer with family. I wasn't going to send her on any missions—not with all she's been through recently."

"I completely agree," Apsa said.

"And would any of you have news of interest for me?" Poicus asked. "How's the Archaic Kingdom holding up?"

The broadcast cut to Adren General Sinno, who looked in dire need of sleep. "The majority of the kingdom seems to be functioning adequately. But the capital has been aflame with violent riots. We've lost twenty-two Adrenian soldiers in the past several months. Itta is locked away with maximum security, and the prince is being monitored at all times."

Poicus sighed. "Make sure you steer that boy down the correct path before it's too late."

"We're definitely working on that," King Supido affirmed.

"Excellent," Poicus replied. "What about you, Damian?"

A round face appeared on the screen. His smile curved sharply as he began to make hand motions. The Grand Director was fluent in sign language, so understanding it was second nature:

Ever since Vitio shared intelligence with us about the possibility of Toono having murdered the Prim Kingdom's prince, we have been slowly releasing our assassins from confinement. I've used Marcus—the Dev servant who extracts truths—on each assassin before letting them free, just to ease any qualms I might have. I cannot simply go off Vitio's word alone, regardless of how much I trust him.

Poicus nodded. "I assumed so, since Fane was brave enough to show his face to me. Otherwise he would have stayed in hiding."

King Damian's face twisted with alarm as he looked off-screen, and his transmission disappeared.

"What was that about?" asked Poicus.

"Ever since the Generals' Battle, the Light Realm has seen constant strife," King Vitio said.

Supido closed his eyes and nodded. "This Toono needs to be taken care of."

General Sinno frowned. "How much can one person really do, milord? You seem to be more worried about this random man than Storshae and his entire kingdom."

"General Sinno," Poicus said, "Toono has robbed a museum of one of the most cherished ancients in history. He has infiltrated a palace and killed a prince and general, and then escaped. He has weathered the Cyn Kingdom's atmosphere and Linsani roars for three months without completely losing his sanity, all while managing to effortlessly kill one of the Diatia. I would wager that he is responsible for the carnage at the Passion Kingdom's teleplatforms. Damian needs to be careful—and to protect his children at all costs. Toono is more of a threat than any army because he can travel inconspicuously."

Vitio sighed. "Toono has only attacked the Dark Realm kingdoms up to this point. It's possible that he has stopped with the murders. He could have had a grudge against the Prim Prince and the Diatia from the Void."

"Highly doubtful," Poicus said. "There is an objective—" He stared at his desk as realization dawned upon him.

"What is wrong, Praetor?" Vitio asked.

The director's eyes rapidly darted around. "I know why Toono attacked the guards at the Passion Kingdom's teleplatforms. Storshae had gone after Olivia because of Toono's desire for her—according to Vitio's account of what he heard in the carriage. Olivia was the key. Toono is looking for her!"

"Where did Damian go?" Apsa asked. "He needs to find her. Do we know where she lives exactly?"

Poicus shook his head. "She has always been quiet about her home life."

"None of us can do anything about it," Supido said. "With soldiers from each of our kingdoms occupying the Archaic Kingdom, our forces are already spread too thin. And to be honest, Praetor, you appear too fragile to hunt her down."

The director dismissively waved his hand. "I may be weak, and Director Senex may be busy with Rhyparia, but there is still one director here capable of searching for her. I appreciate the meeting, royals. I must go. Good day."

The broadcast cut out. "Shall I bring Director Venustas, sir?" Tally asked.

Poicus stared blankly at his desk as he thrummed his fingers against the wood. "Yes, Tally. Tell her it's urgent."

10
Diamond Sea

Passion King Damian shot out of his chair and gestured for his aide to repeat himself.

"There's been another incident at the teleplatforms," the aide signed. "An officer has been murdered. He was slain by ice."

Damian scowled. "We have more than a dozen soldiers up there," he signed. "How did that happen?"

A new presence slipped into the king's chambers. He was a stiff looking man with red hair and a red officer's uniform to match. "Embarrassingly, they were all frightened," he signed. "The control-man allowed them passage into the Still Kingdom after witnessing a woman effortlessly kill the guard with the flick of a finger. All they know is that there were three of them. And based off the ice ability, I'd say they were residents of the Still Kingdom trying to return home."

Damian's face flushed a burning red. "I want you to head out and fetch those soldiers within the hour!" he signed, his fingers a blur. "Bring a unit of twenty to replace them—and pick formidable men and women this time! People who can get the job done!"

Damian closed his eyes. "Bring the cowards back to the palace," he signaled, his hands moving more slowly now. "What a disgrace. To watch a comrade be killed, and not fight for him … there are no words to describe it!"

"Will do, milord," the officer responded with the kingdom's salute.

Damian sat back down, heaving as the chair groaned beneath him. "Bring the fallen soldier back to the capital. We will give him a proper state service. And we shall shame the selfish soldiers who watched him die."

* * *

Toono, Apoleia, and Olivia arrived in the Still Kingdom during the latter half of first-day—approximately ten A.M., two hours until nightfall.

Surrounding them was a never-ending canvas of varying shades of blue and white. The ground around them was the faded blue of an ice-capped body of water. It stretched endlessly in almost every direction—except for the menacing, ice-covered mountain range directly behind them. The string of mountains also stretched to each horizon, branching to the sides and curling around the ice-capped sea and connecting again hundreds of leagues in the distance—far out of eyesight—forming a mammoth circle.

Toono hopelessly gazed across the ice. All that could be seen was the perfectly flat skyline.

"Over there," Apoleia pointed.

Toono squinted. Finally he saw it—just a tiny a speck. If he held his hand out in front of his eyes and were to pinch his destination between his thumb and index finger, no insect could crawl through the space. But that speck was everything, for it was the capital of the Still Kingdom—the lone city in the entire kingdom. It sat at the center of the Diamond Sea, which was named for how it gleamed when looked at from high up in the Still Mountains. The Diamond Sea had always been frozen, and it was impermeable to any manmade device.

Apoleia laughed. "Toono, you should probably remove your grasp from the support beam."

Toono was so immersed in the beauty of the environment that he had forgotten he was still standing on the ice-covered teleplatform. He tried prying his fingers from the beam, but they were glued tight. He took a deep breath before ripping his hand away with a wince. He held up his hand and watched the blood begin to seep through the torn skin.

Apoleia laughed and banged on her knee. "Why are men so stubborn and stupid?" Then her tone flipped to something nastier: "Now put on the gloves like I suggested!"

Toono didn't argue. He had been stupid. They stepped off the platform and began their walk to the capital.

"So there really is nothing from here to Kindoliya," Toono asked as he struggled to put on his gloves.

"Nope," Apoleia absently replied before her mouth quirked into a teasing smile. "Just the storms."

Toono turned to Apoleia with narrowed eyes. "You mentioned nothing of storms."

She shrugged. "Slipped my mind." She glanced down at Olivia. "Baby, do you remember me bringing you here when you were a child?"

"I do," Olivia said. Meow Meow frowned.

"This is where I turned you into a strong woman … and at the age of five!" Apoleia roared.

Toono gazed at Olivia. He had never met a more peculiar individual—well, there was her mother of course, but they were on opposite ends of the spectrum. Apoleia's past turmoil had driven her to instill fortitude in Olivia.

The sun slipped behind the icy horizon. It was noon, and second-night had begun. Toono's breaths were now a pearly white against the blackened sky. His lips and nose had gone numb. "Dammit," he cursed.

Apoleia stopped and turned. "Does the poor widdle baby need a rest?"

Toono unslung his gear and dropped it to the ice. "Yes. Yes, I do."

* * *

A few days passed with nothing to guide their journey but a speck that had grown into a blob. There were no trees, wildlife, or landmarks, just an infinite expanse of flat ice. Even the daunting mountains behind them had shrunk considerably. Slowly, they were making progress.

Toono and Olivia never talked. With Olivia, that was normal. Toono simply wasn't able to speak. The only section of skin exposed to the harsh cold was that around his eyes. He had wrapped layers of cloth around his mouth, nose, and ears under his giant wool hood. Apoleia's constant humming of the same tune would have annoyed Toono if he weren't so distracted by the temperatures.

All of their gear was on Olivia's back, who had proven she could do a better job at carrying it than Toono. Though she always had her strength, she had also proven to be more skillful at maneuvering on the ice. Apoleia laughed hysterically when Toono asked Olivia for the favor.

The day progressed slowly, just like the others. The only difference was the mass of gray clouds forming above them. Toono looked up at the ominous ceiling, the first departure from the clear skies since their arrival in the Still Kingdom. A strike of lightning appeared to the east, and a clap of thunder sounded a few seconds later.

"A storm," Apoleia said.

"What kind of storm are we talking about?" Toono asked.

"One that requires shelter."

Looking around, Toono decided to point out the obvious. "That doesn't seem doable."

A chunk of ice exploded a few miles to the east. The resulting mist of white dust gently floated back down to the surface. Something had collided with the ice-capped sea.

"If you were wise," Apoleia said as she continued leading the pack, "you would have your ancient at the ready."

It happened twice more, eruptions of ice cutting through the air. Then they became more frequent—and closer. The ice under their feet quaked with each collision.

Toono's eyes widened. It was hail, but the hailstones were blocks of ice the size of cannonballs plunging down from the sky. Some looked more like boulders. And as the storm bore down on them, the tremors became constant beneath their feet. Everything in Toono's vision vibrated as holes were blasted into the ice on every side of him. Water shot from the ground like geysers, spraying his hood and instantly freezing in a stubble of droplets. His body was shaking just as violently as the ice.

Apoleia had removed her hood, and her wet violet hair fell sloppily down her back. Her mascara streaked down her face from the wetness of the sea. While Toono felt like he'd enter cardiac arrest at any moment from the cold, Apoleia was embracing it. He couldn't hear her over nature's destruction, but her face was contorted with maniacal laughter. This was her home, and she was thriving in this environment.

Toono had never experienced war. He was part of a generation of children who had grown up without it. This must have been what it was like. The claps of thunder were the cracks of cannons from across the trenches, and the glacial missiles raining around them were bombs and shrapnel. Olivia was casually sidestepping the frozen projectiles, completely unfazed.

A block of ice almost pancaked Toono, and he finally withdrew his ancient from beneath his coat. He turned it upside down, the single bottom hole placed in front of his mouth. He blew into it and created a bubble that enclosed the three of them. It was flat on the bottom, parallel with the sea's surface, but the top was domed. The sounds of crashing ice were replaced by heavy thuds as the hail struck the bubble. The tremors didn't stop, but at least he was safe.

Apoleia frowned. "You were supposed to take cover, not trap me in here too."

Toono was breathing heavily. "I apologize. There wasn't much time to think."

"Panicking. That's unbefitting of you," Apoleia replied as she waved her hand and sculpted a chair of ice to sit on.

"Yes. But if there's anything that can affect me in such a way, it's nature."

For once, the woman appeared calm—it almost looked like boredom. A small hole in the ice exposed the water below. Apoleia stared at it for a second, then said, "Olivia baby, hand me the net."

Olivia plopped their gear onto the ice and sifted through it. She withdrew a net, four wooden poles, and some brown twine. She quickly assembled the separate pieces into one, tying the poles together and placing the net at the top, and handed it to her mother.

"Thank you, baby." Apoleia stood back up. The pole was taller than her. Toono had questioned why they were bringing such a small food supply before departing the Passion Kingdom. And his worries had only intensified once he realized how desolate the Diamond Sea was. But now he understood.

The woman thrust the net into the water. "Come to die, fishy fishies," she cackled. After a few minutes, six fish with pure white scales were feebly flopping against the ice.

It took an hour for the hailstorm to recede. Once it was over, the sky was painted a pitch-black, and Toono had released the bubble. He and Olivia were huddled next to a small fire while Apoleia slept off to the side. Olivia absentmindedly fed Meow Meow some fish guts as she gave Toono a gaze of stone.

"What is it about nature that frightens you?"

Toono looked up from the dying fire. He wasn't used to hearing her say more than two words. "The unpredictability."

Silence followed as the two of them studied each other. Toono decided to elaborate. "When I was little, all I wanted to do was learn about our world—about Kuki Sphaira. I read a lot. Actually, I read all the time. That's all there really was to do in an orphanage. I would sneak into the offices of the teachers and read books meant for people more than twice my age. Eventually they took notice and welcomed it. They started giving me books.

"I'll never forget my eighth birthday present—a relic. A pair of glasses. One of my favorite teachers at the orphanage passed them down to me. Those glasses allowed me access into a completely different realm of reading material."

Toono paused. "Sorry, I'm rambling. Basically when I was little, I spent a lot of years preparing to go against nature in its scariest form just to find a book—*the* book. All those years of research brought to light the weight of what I was trying to achieve in life, and the nearly insurmountable dangers that came with such aspirations."

"Do you mean what you're trying to achieve now," Olivia asked, "with all these killings and the rebirth of Dev King Rehn?"

"No," Toono murmured. "The mission you speak of is different. I passed my earlier aspirations on to someone else, hoping that person could learn the origins of our world and that blue circle in the Dark Realm's sky."

"Agnos," Olivia said.

Toono smiled. "My best friend."

* * *

A towering wall of ice circled the Still Kingdom's capital. Kindoliya was filled with bustling streets and buildings decked in snow—some were constructed completely of ice. The crowds made a gentle hum at the top of the city's barrier, where soldiers dressed in powder blue coats were stationed. From their vantage point, only the highest tips of the Still Mountains were visible across the vast expanse of the Diamond Sea.

"How's that wife doing, Leo?" Titus asked as he casually leaned against the wall's stone rail.

"Ha!" Leo coughed a cloud of white steam. "This may pay well, but with the weeklong shifts, that woman has all the time in the world to explore every shaft of ice in this city—if you know what I mean."

Titus chuckled. "I do. But at least you're getting paid to stand up here and do nothing." He gazed across the frozen sea. He frowned. "Hand me your spyglass."

"You're seeing things," Leo replied as he handed it over. "There's never anything out there."

Titus extended the golden device and looked through the eyepiece. Three people were standing in the middle of the sea. Each of them was bundled in a heavy wool coat. His mouth dropped. "We need to send word to the palace," he said.

Titus handed Leo the spyglass. Carved into the ice in front of the group was a message:

Bring us to the Queen.

11
Rehn, the Oracle

A flickering candle floated through the hall, the ivory white hair of the man holding it bobbing behind it in the darkness. Tashami reached a door where an orange hue seeped through the crevices. He pushed it open, wincing as it creaked.

Inside, another young man sat at a desk illuminated by a brass rack of candles. A book was open under his chin as he turned and gazed at Tashami. "Your efforts to stay silent are futile. You should know this by now," Agnos mouthed.

Tashami slowly closed the door. Agnos shook his head with a smirk and looked back at the book he was reading. "You'll be waking Directors Buredo and Neaneuma if you keep your antics up. We're supposed to be sleeping."

Tashami shrugged and carefully crawled under the covers of his bed. "This is annoying," he whispered.

Agnos responded by exaggeratingly widening his eyes and placing his finger against his mouth. "Whispering is too loud," he mouthed. "Just move your lips."

"Sorry. What are you doing?"

"Looking through these letters from the Unbreakable."

"Still?" Tashami asked. "What for?"

Agnos turned over a page. "I'm making sure Spachny is the correct town. We're assuming he hasn't been moving around. I'm scanning the letters for any mentions of other locations."

"So thorough."

"In a kingdom like this, one wants to keep their adventures to a minimum … and far away from the Linsani."

Tashami stared at the ceiling, the occasional flip of a page breaking the silence. "You and Yama aren't unbearable together with the directors around," he said.

"The directors are irrelevant to that," Agnos said. "At the moment we share a common goal. We both believe we'll find answers about Toono here."

"I don't know why you're so eager. From what you've explained to me, he seems to have turned down a bad path."

"I do not refute that. But that doesn't imply that he didn't mean a lot to me at a certain point of my life. And as much as it pains me to say this, he means a lot to Yama too."

Tashami closed his eyes and sighed. "I don't care about Toono. I just want to find my father."

The quiet returned. Agnos closed the folder of parchments and stared at the name scribbled on the cover: *The Unbreakable.*

"I know, Tashami. And we will," he said before blowing out the candles and heading to bed.

* * *

The following morning brought forth another dreary sky as a gray sea blanketed the Cyn Kingdom from above. Lilu stepped out of the roadside inn and took a deep breath of the thin, cold air. It was the only building they had seen for a couple weeks, and following a few days' rest, it was time to depart.

Across the dirt path was a forest of scattered trees—all dead and gray, coordinating perfectly with the atmosphere that hugged their branches. The ground was littered with fallen sticks and crumpled leaves. They were in the thick of the Almawt Woods.

Six horses were tied to trees, and Lilu crossed the dirt path and began preparing her ride. She tossed a saddle over its back and strapped it securely into place. As she stroked its mane, she was careful to not touch the raw sore on the side of the horse's neck.

From inside the inn's walls Lilu could hear the playful banter between Tashami and Agnos and the murmurs of Directors Buredo and Neaneuma. No one native to the Cyn Kingdom spoke Sphairian, so her teammates seemed unconcerned that they would be heard.

Yama stepped out of the building in a tight suit of white and silver.

"Morning," Lilu said.

"Morning."

Yama approached her horse, which was stark white and had only bones as legs.

"How'd you sleep?" Lilu asked.

"Could've been better," Yama sighed as she threw her wool saddlebags over her horse.

Lilu nodded and studied the horses, each of which had their own grotesque blemishes. "I know what you mean."

Yama leapt onto the saddle. "This has been a frustratingly slow journey. To think we still have at least two more weeks of travel before we reach Spachny. I seek answers here, but how long will it take to find them? And beyond that, it feels like the life is being sucked out of me."

"More like blown out of you," corrected Lilu, going silent as the roars of the Linsani reached her ears from the other side of the kingdom. "Just imagine if we didn't have Director Neaneuma here to ease that feeling. Her spirit is overpowering."

The topic of spirit was a sour one for Yama, and her amber eyes slightly fell.

"You miss her," Lilu said.

"I do."

"Who is it that you miss more? The one who abandoned you, who you now find yourself chasing answers to? Or the one who's waiting for you back at Phesaw, hoping you don't abandon her?"

"They are two separate circumstances," Yama said after a long silence. "Yes, I have feelings for Jilly. But I am an Adrenian, and the protection of a Charge is one of our most important duties. The bond I had with Toono was different than love or friendship. It was family. The only hint of family I've ever had."

"Should I take that as your answer?"

Yama glared at Lilu. "All I seek is information about Toono's shift in attitude and goals. To answer your ridiculous question, I don't know who I miss more. But I know who I care more about returning to, and it's not Toono."

Lilu studied Yama for a second. It wasn't a very convincing answer. Lilu turned back toward the inn and responded with a simple "Understood."

The rest of the group eventually gathered and prepared their horses before departing east again. The morning hours of first-day dwindled away and the afternoon hours of second-night passed. By the time they were in the evening hours of second-day, a couple of the Jestivan were ready to pass out and topple off their saddles.

Spirit Director Neaneuma recognized this. It was too quiet in the Void, and the constant trotting of hooves had become painfully repetitive in her ears. She looked toward the sky in search of an interesting topic to bring up. A strange blue circle caught her eye as the clouds briefly unmasked it.

"You know of the moons," Neaneuma said, just loud enough to be heard above the hooves. "You know of the stars. You know of the sun."

Lilu and Agnos snapped out of their half-asleep trances. Agnos ducked, narrowly dodging a low-hanging branch aimed at his face.

"When you say 'our sky,' do you mean the Light Realm's?" Lilu asked. "The sky we see above us now is not the one we see back home. The Light and Dark Realm face opposite directions, since one hangs beneath the other."

"Yes, Lita Lilu. Besides what I named, what else can you see in the sky of the Light Realm?"

"The crusted underbellies of two other islands. The larger one being the Light Empire. The smaller one … an unknown. But the Dark Realm has that too. They have the Dark Empire and an unknown island."

Neaneuma nodded. "Strange how our world works—the symmetry, that is."

"There is one glaring difference however," Agnos said.

The Spirit Director chuckled. "Of course, Zana Agnos. I feel foolish for asking, but do you know what they call that blue mystery sitting in the sky?"

"Earth."

"That's right, but it was nameless until some thirty years ago … Well, let me rephrase. It had many names. The Dark Realm is full of folklore about that blue marble."

"Dev King Rehn was the one who gave it the title of Earth," Agnos added.

Yama was curiously gazing at Earth as it slipped in and out of the clouds. She had never seen it in the Light Realm, or heard about it either.

"I used to read about it when I was younger," Agnos said. "And I still try to learn more, but information is difficult to obtain. It'd be nice being able to pick the brain of Dev King Rehn."

The trotting hooves took over once again. Agnos blankly stared at his horse's mane, lost in thought. He just realized why Toono would want Rehn to be reborn. Toono and Agnos had spent years of their childhood with their heads buried in books, but they could never find the *one.* And their only lead to that book was a dead end that contained too many dangerous variables.

Toono must have given up on that hunt and pursued an alternative method that would provide the same answers. His desire to rebirth King Rehn was to learn from him. The Dev King was called *Rehn the Oracle* for a reason. He could see things that others couldn't. It's why he was so dangerous to the Light Realm.

Agnos gazed back up at Earth. *So you're still hunting the same answers, Toono. You're just altering your strategy and avenue of attack. You look for a dead man. I look for an ancient book from 1,500 years ago, which is why you gave me these glasses.*

You took an immoral path. Me, the opposite. Which will succeed?

*   *   *

Kadlest stepped out of a tiny building compacted between two much grander ones and unfolded a map.

"Take a look at the brochure for me," she said, handing it to Illipsia.

As Kadlest studied the map of the Passion Kingdom's capital, Fiamma, Illipsia scanned through the brochure until she found a section about the palace.

"There's an organized tour of the palace grounds every evening between four and five P.M." Illipsia said. "It only covers the gardens, courtyard, and such … nothing inside the actual palace though."

"That's a start. How much?"

"Sixty pintos per person."

Kadlest folded her map and nodded for Illipsia to follow her down the street. "That inn is already eating up most of our money. And we'll have to take that tour every day in order to properly study the grounds and its weaknesses. Looks like we'll need to coax some money out of people."

"How will we do that?" Illipsia asked.

Kadlest grinned. "Well the fact that you're already adorable is a start. We'll just have to smother you in some dirt and dress you in rags. Then we'll stick you on the curb and watch the coins of pity pile up. Who can deny a starving mother and daughter?"

Illipsia frowned. "We look nothing alike."

Kadlest pushed away a street vendor and took Illipsia's hand. "All they'll see are two dirt-smothered females. Remember, there are plenty of tools we can use against men. And that includes their misplaced pity for us."

Illipsia looked up at the men who walked past. She didn't despise them, nor did she think they were cruel. They were just people like her. Weren't they?

12
Assassins, Spies, and Beasts

A large tent was pitched among the trees, with separate rooms for Bryson and Thusia. A fire was ablaze in Bryson's room, just big enough to cast shapes on the fabric, but not big enough to set the tent's roof ablaze. They didn't have to worry about the brightness—Thusia would sense it if someone approached. Bryson was reading the biography about Debo—or Ataway Debonicus Kawi, that is.

The curtain folded back and Thusia stepped in. She stared at Bryson, whose hood concealed his face. He didn't bother to look up.

"It's been a week," she said.

Bryson turned a page. "So."

She forced a motherly smile as she approached the fire and sat across from the boy. "Did you learn what my ability is yet?"

"Yes."

"Then why haven't you told me?"

Thusia watched as the boy continued to stare down at his book. He finally broke the silence: "I wasn't sure if I actually wanted to hear a story about my dad."

Her smile vanished. She stood up and took away the book, then sat down with her arm around him. He leaned his head on her shoulder, his eyes red from previous tears.

Thusia sighed. "We met right after our introduction into the Jestivan. I was seventeen. He was only fourteen. He was young, but something about him sparked my interest. He had already lost all of his baby fat, and his jawline was as sharp as a man's. His nose was narrow and his eyes …" Thusia paused, searching for a way to describe them. "They were cold. A beady blue. A young, naive soul doesn't have eyes like that. But there was a hint of something else that would surface whenever he would look at me—kindness.

"And there were other factors that made you forget his age. His mind was unparalleled and his personality was that of a weathered father. Undoubtedly he was an old soul—the complete opposite of what I was. But that's usually how it works.

"Mendac found interest in me. That much was clear. It had a lot to do with his background, for he had never met someone like me before. All he knew were swollen minds—not swollen souls. That was his first year at Phesaw, so nobody knew who he was. He was still living in the city of Brilliance when he received his invitation into the Jestivan."

This was news to Bryson. He would have assumed that he attended Phesaw his entire childhood like most kids. Living in Brilliance explained a lot about who his father was. That city was the foundry of the Intel Kingdom's unparalleled technological might.

"We quickly learned Mendac's role in our little group of 'elites.' He could talk you in circles. You know how Agnos is. Picture that, but tenfold—which wasn't always a good thing. But it wasn't just that. He was a master of energy weaving. Ugh, he could power an entire auditorium of Intelights by himself—at fourteen! But I guess that was to be expected. He was raised by a weaver in a city of the best weavers in Kuki Sphaira after all.

"Mendac quickly became the leader, and I became the blanket that kept his heart enveloped in warmth. I was the reason why people could ignore the monster that lurked so conspicuously within him.

"It was either the first or second month of the Jestivan's existence. The five of us Jestivan were hanging out at Tango's Peak—that's what the hill where Telejunction sits was called. I was being my typical silly self. Saikatto, the Adren Jestivan, wasn't up for my antics. I think he was having a bad day.

"Well he snapped and raised his voice at me, and I'll never forget how fast Mendac had Saikatto pinned to the ground. His hand had a death grip around his neck as he sat on top of him, viciously assaulting him. If you were to look at only his face and the blur of raining fists, you'd think he was reading a book. It was frightening.

"I pushed Mendac off in my own fit of fury. I didn't care if he was defending me. There was nothing to defend against. It was the first time I showed such rage in my life. Try picturing Jilly mad. That's how strange it was.

"Mendac basically exiled himself from our group for a few months after that. He did it out of shame, not for his actions against Saikatto, but for the pain it caused me. Some good came out of it though. During the time he spent alone, he enrolled in philosophy."

Bryson fought back a gag.

"As you know, philosophy is mostly taken by Archaic students. He was the lone Intelian in that classroom, but he was driven to learn more about morality, ethics, and human interaction. This was when Mendac's legacy really began. An Intelian taking a philosophy class and mingling with Archains? You'd think he'd be the target for ridicule. But that wasn't the case. His intelligence broadened into different areas. He gained wisdom, and as a result he gained respect from his peers and elders. Eventually we allowed him back into the Jestivan with faith that he had grown as a human. Even Saikatto forgave him."

Thusia fell silent, and Bryson assumed that she had finished. "*Did* he grow?" he asked.

Thusia tossed a handful of dirt on the dying fire. "Story for another time. You were probably right earlier. You don't want to hear stories about your dad—believe me. Good night, Bryson."

*   *   *

Bryson's fitful sleep was plagued by constant dreams of his father. The image of a man's face being repeatedly hammered into the ground was unnerving. What was worse was the rage that Bryson experienced, as if he was his father.

Productive sleep arrived a few hours into the night, but with it came a dream even more haunting. Bryson was sitting in a classroom next to Agnos. Archaic Director Senex stood on a stool at the front. A single word was written on the board behind him. It wasn't in Sphairian—the primary language of almost all ten kingdoms. Bryson glanced over at Agnos, who was silently moving his mouth. His shaggy black bangs flirted with the circular frames of his ancient—his glasses.

Bryson leaned over and tapped his friend on the shoulder. No response.

He waved his hand in front of Agnos's eyes. Not even a flinch. Agnos simply continued to inaudibly mouth nothing.

"Hey," Bryson said. "Hey." Still nothing. He looked at Senex, who was gravely nodding his head like a metronome. It was like Bryson was stuck in a two-second loop.

But as the dream progressed, the depths of the room became shrouded in black. A woman's screams came from the shadows. And that too would repeat itself … all while Agnos mouthed unknown words and Senex nodded at him.

*   *   *

It was still dark when Bryson awoke early the next morning. He blinked to rid the sleep from his eyes, then heard what that had awoken him—a hooting sound. He looked to his right and nearly jumped off the ground as two gigantic yellow eyes with round black pupils glared at him from across the pile of ash.

It was an owl. Only its eyes were visible, but they were telling enough. Bryson stared back at the owl, wondering how it ended up inside the tent. He had heard hooting throughout the night—maybe it smelled the dried meat in the travel bags.

It hooted again, cocking its head to the side like it was waiting for something. Bryson went to reach for a bag and grab some jerky for it, but Thusia waltzed in and shook her head with a laugh. "Bryson, Bryson, Bryson."

She knelt down in front of the bird and pet it as she retrieved something from its beak. It immediately flew out of the tent. Thusia took a seat and unfolded the parchment.

"Owls too, eh?" Bryson asked.

"There are several types of birds she can control," Thusia said as she read through the letter.

She crumpled the note in her hand. "Good news. Fane disposed of his target and they're joining up with Himitsu and Toshik."

Bryson was pleased but not fully satisfied. "Now it's our turn. One avenged; two to go."

Thusia looked at Bryson with sad eyes. It took him a moment but then he flushed, ashamed of the note of joy in voice.

* * *

"This is practically a mountain," Bryson groaned. "We've been out here a week, and nothing."

Thusia froze in her tracks. "Are you bored?" she asked. "Then I have good news for you. He's near."

Bryson straightened up immediately, his motivation returning out of thin air. He scanned the perimeter, though their target could be anywhere within a few hundred yards. Suddenly Bryson's heart was beating louder than he could think. He was confronting a person skilled in the art of stealth killing—someone who made a living out of it.

Thusia was an assassin too—and a Branian, but even that didn't ease Bryson's mind. She waved, and a starling flew over to her. "How close are your bats?" she whispered. The tiny black bird pecked Thusia's shoulder three times. "All right, send them. Bryson, stay by my side."

Together they walked to the summit of the hill and stood at its grassy crest. Dark green waves of trees rolled in every direction.

Something screeched in the dense forest behind them, and the cries grew louder by the second. A wall of wings erupted from the trees. The bats seemed to move with no sense of direction, dipping and diving as they pleased.

"Thank you, Ophala," Thusia muttered.

The bats converged into one super cell and swarmed an empty spot in the field, forming an irregular shape of flapping wings. Then Bryson realized what was happening. The shape was that of a person. Though Thusia could sense the assassin's presence, the bats could pinpoint him with their echolocation.

Bryson bolted toward the black swarm. The bats scattered as he threw a punch. He stumbled forward as he missed his target, but he felt the enemy evade. He planted and pivoted his foot, digging up a chunk of grass, and threw a hook kick to his right that swept harmlessly through the air.

Meanwhile the bats flew in two separate packs, following the invisible assassin and occasionally diving down to point out a location. Bryson continued his pursuit, only throwing an attack when one of Ophala's helpers located the enemy. But nothing hit, and bats began to fall from the sky, their bodies crushed or wings torn.

Thusia was practicing a bit more patience with her approach, wisely observing from the side. She knew to not attack without studying the battleground first—especially when the opponent had already been waiting. She knew that Bryson understood this too. But his anger and taste for vengeance had gotten the better of his mind.

She caught a glint in the bottom of her vision. Something hidden in the grass reflected the sunlight. She knelt down and picked up a gleaming steel dagger, then scanned the ground around them. Sure enough there were dozens of tiny blades in the grass—the assassin was telekinetically launching them at the bats.

A glimpse of metal flashed to Thusia's right and she conjured a blast of wind in its direction, knocking the dagger out of its intended path toward

Bryson. She did the same with another projectile to her left. Meanwhile more bats plummeted to the ground. There were simply too many knives for Thusia to defend the bats while protecting Bryson and herself.

She continued to slap the daggers out of the air with sudden strikes of wind as Bryson hopelessly tried to land a blow on the enemy. Then he finally managed to land a punch, and the assassin appeared as he did.

He was young—maybe a few years older than Bryson. His hair was an almond color and cut very short. Bryson struck him in the face twice more, taking a giant stride forward each time. The assassin didn't fight back. Blood flung from his face, spraying across the grass and coating Bryson's fists. With a vicious uppercut, Bryson sent the young man's jaw toward the air and his body fell limp into the grass. But as Bryson went for a finishing blow, a sudden wall of black impeded his assault.

He stared at the roiling wall of wings that obstructed his path. In their screeches Bryson could almost hear Ophala screaming at him. He slumped in the grass and stared into nothingness. He felt rage for being stopped, and guilt for not stopping himself. He raised his open hands and stared at the blood. He thought he might cry, but then he frowned. Why was Ophala trying to save the assassin—a man who killed three innocent people, then displayed them like trophies?

As Thusia continued to observe from a distance, Bryson's hands clenched into fists. He burst through the wall of bats and threw a punch with electricity pulsing down his arm. He abruptly stopped his fist, for it was the slender body of Thusia who stood in front of him. They held each other's gaze for a few seconds as she shielded the enemy. There was shame in her eyes. She bent down and locked the man's ankles and wrists in chains.

"What are you doing?" Bryson barked.

"Being human."

"By protecting someone who embodies everything inhumane? He killed innocent people!"

"Rhyparia's killed innocent people," Thusia snapped. "Grand Director Poicus has killed innocent people." She stood their captive up. "Let me ask you something. Do you want to kill this guy for revenge or to make a statement?" She didn't give him a chance to answer. "Listen, I believe in an eye for an eye in some cases, but this isn't one of them. You want revenge—to make this guy feel what those innocent people felt." She shook her head. "It cures nothing."

Bryson's eyes had dulled.

"I wasn't the one who killed those people," the assassin said. "I stayed back, for I wanted no part of it, nor did I support it." His voice was weak. "However, I am young and have no say. All I wanted was to avenge my father—one of the many soldiers your Grand Director slew in Cogdan. When Prince Storshae asked us who wanted to pursue him, I was first to volunteer. But this … I did not foresee all of this."

As the assassin hung his head, Thusia glared at Bryson before turning away and guiding her prisoner into the forest. The grass was littered with fallen winged soldiers, and Bryson was at the center. As he glanced at each carcass, he realized how much of a monster he was. Hopefully Agnos would return from the Void soon, for he was the one who could help him.

* * *

Two lanky young men strolled into a clearing in the woods, where moonlight splashed across the forest floor in segmented spaces. They didn't walk next to each other, but Toshik no longer dragged behind as he did at the beginning of their journey. Conversation was at a minimum, but the occasional small talk was an improvement over the stiff silence.

"What do you say—call it a night?" Himitsu asked.

Toshik nodded and began setting up the tent while Himitsu gazed at the moon. An owl landed and gripped his shoulder with its talons.

He laughed and tilted his head. Owls weren't exactly small birds. "Hi, Mom."

It hooted softly.

"I hope the other teams are okay," Himitsu said as if the owl could reply. "I'm not too worried about Thusia and Bryson, but I don't know that Fane guy. But I guess you trust him. You were great friends if I remember correctly. You and Dad were always going out with him and his wife." Himitsu closed his eyes. "Sleep has been coming easier the past few nights.

My nerves aren't on edge. The fact that you're all around me is calming … I love you."

The owl nuzzled its head against Himitsu's cheek.

"It's ready."

Himitsu turned to see Toshik poking his head out of the tent.

"All right, man."

As Himitsu began walking toward the tent, a chorus of owl calls rang out from the trees surrounding them. Toshik scurried outside and placed his back against Himitsu's. They spun slowly with their eyes glued intently on the shadowy wall of the thick trees encircling them.

"Is he here?" Toshik whispered with his sword drawn in front of him.

"No, I would have sensed him," Himitsu replied.

Four sets of slanted green eyes appeared in the darkness. They glowed as they reflected the moonlight, low to the ground and sinister.

"Conjure your flames and hide us," Toshik said.

"If I do that and the assassin is somewhere in a treetop watching us, my ability will be exposed."

Toshik grit his teeth. "Looks like we're doing this the old-fashioned way then."

The four creatures stepped out of the forest and into the open pit. Their gray fur gleamed with a blue hue. Everything about their faces resembled a wild dog, but their backs were covered with white quills that stood menacingly erect.

"They're spunka," Toshik said as the beasts slowly advanced. "Agile and light on their feet. Those spines on their backs are as lethal as the sword in my hand."

"How do you know all this?"

"They're native to the Adren Kingdom."

Himitsu deliberated using his Passion Energy after all. Those spines were at least two feet in length. The thought of fending off these spunka with just his raw physical talent unnerved him. He was subpar in hand-to-hand combat even with his flames.

Toshik seemed to have known what Himitsu was thinking. "Take this." He handed Himitsu a longblade from his waistband. "Fight your two off for as long as you can manage. I'll dispose of mine within thirty seconds. And watch their tails. There are smaller spines hidden within the fur."

Himitsu stared at the blade in his hand. In the midst of his self-doubt, a blast of wind almost knocked him over. Toshik had engaged two of the spunka.

Himitsu stared as his two spunka lowered their black snouts to the ground, arching their backs so their array of shimmering spikes were fully exposed. Their long furry tails aggressively lashed back and forth.

They leapt at Himitsu at the same time. One targeted his ankle with an open mouth of yellow fangs, and the other leapt and swung its tail at Himitsu's face. He clumsily yanked his foot out of harm's way and ducked as the tail whipped past.

There was a wet gargling howl as Toshik slew one of the spunka. Knowing that help was arriving quickly, Himitsu worked up a bit of confidence. The next tail that was swung at his stomach just narrowly missed being hacked off by his longblade. He skipped backward several feet and then sidestepped left as a spunka snapped its jaw shut with a vicious growl. He parried with a downward slash, metal clanging against metal as he made contact with the spunka's spines. They weren't as fast as Toshik, Yama, or Bryson, but their quickness wasn't to be overlooked and they were crafty.

Himitsu screamed as a shearing pain dashed up his leg. He shook his leg but the spunka's powerful jaw continued to tear through the muscles and ligaments of his ankle. The other spunka leapt at Himitsu's face with a mucus-smothered howl. He leaned on his good leg and used the animal's momentum to toss it to the side. Screaming in pain, he hacked into the neck of the spunka chewing through his flesh and bone. It didn't cut cleanly through, but the clamp around his ankle softened. He drove down his blade twice more, and blood rose through the gray fur.

As Himitsu freed his leg, the other spunka pounced on his back and tackled him into the patchy grass. With his face in the dirt, he felt the heat of its breath against the back of his neck and its claws digging into his skin.

A gust of wind smacked him in the face as he heard a sickly yelp above him. Himitsu twisted onto his back to see a headless spunka collapsed at

Toshik's feet. Toshik flicked the blood from his sword before sheathing it at his hip. His gaze held on Himitsu's mangled ankle for a moment.

"Stay here," Toshik commanded before heading toward the tent. He returned with a thick branch, bandage, cotton balls, and a bottle of fleepshire—a numbing agent derived from a plant in the Spirit Kingdom. Himitsu couldn't remember the name of it. Thusia had packed it for everyone, calling it the pride of her kingdom. But she called everything that—including chopsticks.

Toshik sat next to Himitsu. He put the cotton against the opening of the bottle and turned it over.

"You won't be walking properly for a long while," he said as he dabbed the liquid on Himitsu's wound.

Himitsu grunted as the fleepshire burned at first touch. It took a few seconds to actually numb the area.

Toshik began wrapping Himitsu's ankle. "You did well, though. There you go." Toshik sat back and admired his handiwork. "When was the last time you used a sword?"

Himitsu thought for a second. "I think when I was twelve, during my fourth year at Phesaw."

Toshik laughed. "I can tell."

Himitsu smirked. He looked at the dead spunka lying next to them. "Do you have an interest in animals? You seemed to know a lot about this one."

"Only the odd ones. My knowledge of spunka comes from my family business. Their spines are a popular material for swords. People spend a pretty coin for them."

"You should make use of these guys then," Himitsu suggested.

"Useless. These are babies."

"Are you kidding me? What do the parents look like? Wait, does that mean they're close by?"

Chuckling, Toshik waved off the worries. "The mom abandons her litter at birth, then proceeds to kill the father. The offspring raise themselves as a pack of siblings for the first few years of their lives before splitting apart."

"That's twisted," Himitsu replied.

Toshik stared at the headless creature, clearly lost in memories. "You don't want to see a momma spunka. Not only do her spikes reach four feet in length, she can stand on her hind legs. And if she were to do that, she'd be taller than you or me."

Himitsu shuddered.

"As a child, my parents would never let me hunt the adults," Toshik continued. "But they would let me practice by killing the babies. 'Practice' is a terrible word for it though. I recall almost losing a limb a few times."

Toshik fell silent again. Himitsu didn't want to ruin the moment by saying anything stupid, but he did anyway: "Sounds like a family business. What does your mother do?"

"She was the Head Huntress." Toshik got up and arched his back. "Barring any other surprises, I'm going to rest. Hopefully I'll dream of some rain to bathe in. I stink."

Himitsu smiled. "At least you packed a comb."

Toshik grinned back, but his eyes were sad. He laid the branch next to Himitsu. "To help you walk," he said before heading toward the tent. "Night."

Himitsu stayed seated for a while. Toshik's use of the word "was" didn't slip past him. He wanted to know what had happened to Toshik's mother, but patience was important. Pushing the Adrenian would only make him revert to his old self.

While gazing at the stars, he felt it—another presence. His skin prickled. The Dev Assassin had just entered Himitsu's range. He gingerly rose to his feet, using the makeshift walking stick as support. He almost fell as his ankle gave way. The fleepshire was definitely working, and he couldn't feel anything below his shin.

Bats screeched from within the forest to his right as he wobbled toward the tent. He glanced in that direction and saw a shard of metal gleaming in the blue moonlight. Himitsu ducked under the missile and collapsed as his worthless ankle buckled underneath him. He raised his hand and formed a wall of black flames to hide behind. More missiles plunged through the fire as he rolled away.

"Dammit!" Toshik shouted as he stumbled out of the tent. "What now?"

"Be careful!" Himitsu hissed. "He's telekinetically throwing daggers from the trees."

"You hide me while I pursue him."

"Just follow my flames."

* * *

Toshik followed behind the advancing wall of flame with his hand readied on his sword handle, slowing down his pace to match the fire. He noticed several other black walls randomly sprout from the ground. Himitsu was forcing the assassin to attack multiple targets.

Toshik broke into the forest and weaved between the trees. He followed the calls of Ophala's winged scouts, which had grown distant. The assassin was escaping. Toshik picked up his pace, skipping over thick roots and turning corners by planting his foot against the base of a tree.

Eventually he saw his target. She had long blazing red hair that swayed behind her as she ran. Toshik unsheathed his sword and blocked a flying blade, redirecting its path into a tree trunk with a thud. He was much faster than her, and soon he was raising his blade for the killing blow. Then he felt something jerk him into the air. A giant net had closed around him. He could hear the bats grow distant as the assassin chose to keep running rather than try to finish him off. He sliced through the rope with his sword, and as he fell he saw a nest of knives waiting beneath him. A trap within a trap.

He thrust his sword into the tree that he was plummeting next to. His descent barely slowed as the blade cut down the middle of the trunk, and the friction sent shockwaves of pain through his hands. He grunted before finally coming to a stop, dangling above the knives, which now lay harmlessly flat on the ground. The assassin must have gotten too far away to control them anymore.

Toshik pressed his foot against the tree and ripped his sword free. After dropping to the ground he stood with his hands on his knees, listening for Ophala's winged helpers. He couldn't hear them over his panting. He ran for a couple of minutes before stopping once more. Dead quiet—no wildlife, no rustling of leaves in the wind. He leaned against a tree in exhaustion, realizing that he had lost her.

Footsteps rustled from some fifty paces ahead. He stood tall with his sword drawn in front of him. It was far too dark to see anything.

"I can hear you, woman," Toshik said.

"Woman?" a gruff voice fired back.

Toshik's head tilted slightly as the person approached, then he relaxed as he made out the man's chestnut hair and the loose skin on his neck. Fane had the Dev Assassin thrown over his shoulder. Her clothes smelled and looked burned.

"Where's Jilly?" Toshik snapped.

"Boo!" Jilly shouted as she jumped out from behind Fane.

Toshik yelped as he stumbled backward. Fane smiled as the girl howled in a fit of laughter.

"I finally got you!" she gasped, gulping for breath and wiping tears from her eyes. "It took eleven years, but it was worth it!"

Toshik stared at her dirty face and messy blond hair. After more than a week of living in the wild, her smile and spirit were as childlike and infectious as ever. He grabbed Jilly and embraced her. She went quiet. As her head burrowed into his chest, he thought about the last time he showed any kind of meaningful affection to a woman. He thought of his mother, Jun.

He squeezed Jilly tighter. This hug was long overdue.

13
Kindoliya

The steel gate clattered shut. Olivia watched the guards walk off in their powder blue uniforms and take their positions at the base of the stairwell at the end of the hall. They had stripped her of her wool coat and dressed her in dirty clothing. The cold stone floor stung her bare feet.

She walked to the wall and placed a hand on it. The same chill crept through. A mattress stood in the corner. There was a hand pump in the floor for water … and a bucket to serve as a toilet. Meow Meow groaned on her behalf.

Olivia grabbed the mattress and allowed it to fall onto the floor. It landed with a thud, implying that it was probably as frozen as the stone. And as she sat on it, she realized it was truth.

I think I'm getting too comfortable with this being-a-prisoner thing, Meow Meow thought.

It won't be long, Olivia replied. *Give it a day or so. Mom needs time to speak to the queen.*

Where do you think Toono is?

In a deeper cell.

Meow Meow chuckled. *He probably thought Apoleia would help us dance right in.*

I doubt that, Olivia said. *He is intelligent and understands how royal families work. They investigate everything before they act. They would be stupid not to. Consider who's been killed in the past year: the Prim Prince, Cyn Diatia, Archaic General Inias, Dev General Ossen, and Debo. But Toono has kept a low profile, so none of those kingdoms even know of his existence, let alone suspect him of the crimes.*

Their minds went quiet for a moment.

I just like to underestimate his brain, Meow Meow thought. *Makes me feel better about myself.*

Then when he proves you wrong, it just makes you feel ten times worse.

Meow Meow sighed. *Let me have my flawed logic.*

Olivia got up and walked to the pump. She cupped one hand under the nozzle and pushed the lever with the other. Nothing came out but a high-pitched squeal of rust. She pumped it three more times with no success before returning to her mattress to stare at the stone ceiling and drift off.

*   *   *

Olivia awoke to the sound of heavy footsteps. She had no idea how much time had passed while she slept. It could have been an hour—maybe an entire night. She sat up and rubbed the sleep from her eyes, awaiting the approaching visitors. The first figure she saw was her mother's, flanked by two Stillian guards.

"I'm sorry it took so long, baby," Apoleia said with a frown.

"What time is it?"

"It's nearly ten A.M." her mother replied as a guard unlocked the gate.

Olivia winced as she stood up. The mattress hadn't been kind to her back.

Apoleia rushed in and gave her daughter a hug. "Toono will take a bit longer. The queen isn't too fond of him so far."

"Can I visit him?" Olivia asked, looking at the three fresh cuts running across her mother's neck.

Apoleia studied her daughter. "Maybe." She slipped on her hood, concealing her face. "Let's go."

Olivia followed her mother out of the dungeons and through the winding stairs and halls of the palace. Instead of gold, the décor held true to the frigid temperatures: varying shades of light blue, gray, and silver. Ice sculptures were commonplace throughout the many chambers. The most impressive, however, was a grand masterpiece that sat at the center of a circular room.

"The Icebound Confluence," Apoleia said. "The heart of Kindoliya Palace, serving as the hub of all six wings."

Royal staff and people of assumingly high stature were bustling about, somehow not colliding into one another as they sifted through parchment in their hands. Doors swung open and closed in all directions.

Olivia looked up to see the sun. The circular wall soared upward for many stories, but there was no ceiling at the top. Throngs of people packed the spiraling staircases that curved along the wall.

Olivia, Apoleia, and their two escorts pushed through the crowd to the ice statue at the center of the room. Grand in size and fine in detail, the structure took on the shape of a layered cake with four tiers, stretching nearly forty feet into the air. Circling the bottom of the cylinder sat fifteen humanistic figures of ice, all assuming their own pose.

Olivia studied each one with a blank stare. One stood tall with its hands on its hips and chest out. Another sat on the cylinder's edge, its feet resting on the room's marbled floor. It was casually leaning back, staring at the sky without a care in the world. A pair of figures sat close together with their arms swung around each other's shoulders as if they were best friends.

On the second level of the sculpture were five figures, and there were three more people on the third layer. A singular ice figure stood at the top, shining in the sunlight.

"The Statue of Gefal," Apoleia said, leaning in close to Olivia's ear. "Built by Still Queen Lilia in the early 300s. It represents the hierarchical structure of the Dark Empire's Gefal. The fifteen at the bottom are the Bewahr, the protectors of the royal-blood firstborns."

So there are fourteen more beings like Fonos … I thought there were only four, Olivia thought.

A bit unsettling, Meow Meow replied.

"Surely not all of the Gefal are from the pre-300s," Olivia remarked.

"Of course not," Apoleia said as she guided Olivia around the sculpture. "This lady here, for example … Still Queen Francine. You can tell this by the gigantic gavel strapped to her back. Her reign was in the 700s. The Stillian royal head updates the Statue of Gefal every century or so. She was added in 934."

Olivia stared at the figure at the very top. "What about the other three tiers?"

Apoleia paused. "Not much is known about them or their roles."

"What about the poses? Why are they all different?"

"They distinguish their personalities."

"But how would anyone know—"

Apoleia laughed. "Slow down, baby. They're just educated guesses."

Apoleia led Olivia to one of the six doors. Unlike the others, nobody walked in or out of this one. The door's icy surface was engraved with grooves and ridges that formed some sort of maze. Apoleia placed her right thumb, index, and middle finger at the beginning of three trails. She then did the same with her left thumb and pinky on two other grooves. Her ice began to weave through five different paths. For the most part she followed the maze, but she would occasionally ignore the boundaries and go off in her own direction. The five trails of ice converged at a snowflake carved into the door, and Apoleia's ice filled it out.

"You have three seconds to step in," Apoleia warned.

The door melted, and they stepped through before it reformed. The guards didn't follow them.

Olivia observed their new surroundings. It almost felt like they had stepped into a different world. The floor was a purple marble, and gold accented some of the wooden fixtures located throughout the grand foyer. This looked like a proper palace.

"This is the family wing," Apoleia said as she removed her hood.

Olivia was more preoccupied with what she just witnessed. "Was that *weaving?*"

After a second of what looked to be confusion, Apoleia snapped her finger. "Oh, you mean the door?"

Olivia gave a slight nod.

"Yes," Apoleia said with a stern undertone that implied she should drop the subject.

They walked across the empty foyer and through an archway into a hall. "Is this where we're staying?" Olivia asked.

Apoleia let out a single laugh that echoed through the hollow space. "Never." She said it with a familiar maniacal grin. "Never, never, never, never, NEVER."

She's a bit loud for the residential quarters, Meow Meow thought.

"We're here for one reason and one reason only," Apoleia said as they started up a flight of stairs.

They continued their journey through the maze of halls and stairs before finally reaching a dead end with a single painting that hung on the wall—a vast landscape of a mountain range blanketed in ice. Apoleia grabbed the side of its frame and pulled, revealing a small door. It opened to a modest space with a narrow bed and a nightstand. Sections of the wall seemed burned, and others had sloppy plasterwork sealing off holes.

Olivia started to enter, but her mom grabbed her bicep with a crushing squeeze. "Do not go in. Simply look."

There wasn't much to look at, so Olivia looked up at her mother instead. Tears were running down Apoleia's cheeks, and her lips trembled slightly. She rarely allowed her daughter to witness her break down, but Olivia saw that there was no way Apoleia could hold it back. *This* room … *that* bed … they were demons in her mom's dreams.

Olivia's expression was still that of stone, but something itched at her heart as a woman's scream pierced through her skull. Meow Meow noticed the disturbance and shook his head.

Control it.

*   *   *

It had been seven days since Olivia was released from the dungeons. She now stayed in an inn a couple miles away from the castle. She walked through the crowded morning streets of ice toward Frostbite, her favorite eating spot. Like almost every building in Kindoliya, it was made of its own unique kaleidoscope of ice. Flashes of purple, blue, and green would reflect off its surface from the sun's rays and streak across the street in the most hypnotizing and beautiful way. It almost seemed celestial.

Olivia walked in and approached the counter. The head clerk smiled and wished her a good morning.

"Hello, Danip," Olivia replied with an absent blink.

"Are you going to finally switch it up today?"

Olivia slightly shook her head, and Danip laughed. "You owe me fifty unsas, Throdj!" she shouted over her shoulder into the kitchen.

A young man cracked open a fruit with a mallet. He looked back and swore: "Frost of Francine."

Danip giggled. "Forgive him. He doesn't know any better. One signature cup coming your way. I'll make it myself so you can have the best of the best."

Olivia stepped to the side to allow other customers to make their orders. She didn't care who made her drink, but in Kindoliya the women were believed to be supreme at everything and anything, and she thought it best to play along.

Olivia loved the intricate and unique craft that went into such a simple concept like fixing a drink. First Danip grabbed a white glass mug from a rack hanging below the cabinets and put it in an oven. While it heated, she heaved open a gigantic ice door in the kitchen. What was inside was a mystery, but it had to be unbearably cold because Danip's teeth would chatter as she stepped out with a block of ice in her hand. To make a Stillian's body react to cold in such a way was not an easy feat.

Next Danip approached a different counter, set the block of ice on a steel board, and shaved the ice with lightning quick speed and precision. Powdered frost accumulated on the cutting board, then she returned to the oven and retrieved the scolding hot mug with a cooking mitten.

She sat that down and grabbed a mixing bowl, tossing a few slabs of caramel and a slice of butter into it. She whisked the mixture for close to a minute, then scooped the powdered ice into the mug, followed by the caramel-butter concoction. Next she arranged frosted strawberries and blueberries around the mug's lip in an alternating pattern of blue and red. Then she took four pinches of salt and sprinkled it all around the drink.

Meow Meow salivated as Danip approached the counter with a smile. She placed the drink down, just out of Olivia's reach. Olivia stared at the mug for a moment, then glanced at the clerk. "You forgot something."

Danip's lip curled up further. "Did I, now?"

"The straw." It was only the most important part of the drink. It made up seventy percent of the item's price, for the ever-ice it was made out of was a commodity foreign not only to Kindoliya, but all of Kuki Sphaira. It came from the highest peaks of the Still Mountains.

Danip leaned in close. "You don't get anything until you say it."

Olivia paused.

"Summit Buh-buh-buh-burrreeze," she recited, an already ridiculous brand name sounding even sillier in Olivia's monotone. It was supposed to mimic a shiver. Meow Meow instantly went into mass hysteria with tears forming in his eyes. Olivia's open hand slapped his face, cutting off the maniacal laughter.

Danip laughed too, then reached under the counter and grabbed a thick ice straw coated in sugar and salt. Placing it in the mug, she asked, "See you later?"

Olivia nodded and walked away. She found an open table near one of the front windows. As every morning, the shop was packed with all different kinds of people: laborers, professionals, a few royal employees, teenagers who used it as a hangout spot before school, and the occasional father with a small child. A tiny bell chimed constantly as guests came and went through the door.

Olivia took a sip of her drink. Her eyes closed from the satisfying combination of warm and cold, sweet and salty, and cream and solid. And then the chilled bite of a strawberry to accompany it was enough to make her forget her worries for a brief second.

I can't get over how out of place those things look, Meow Meow thought.

Olivia looked out the window. He was right. Among the pretty shapes and lights of the ice buildings and the fluffy white snow blanketing the ground were brutish animals sluggishly tramping down the streets. They were huge—twice as tall and long as a full-grown stallion. Unlike a horse, their heads were flat against their shoulders, with their nose jutting out only slightly. Three menacing long horns protected their face; one that hooked upward from under the chin and two that curled inward from behind both ears. A massive curtain of fur from their torsos splashed to the ground below, hiding their legs—assuming they had legs. Their coats varied throughout different shades of white, gray, and black.

Apparently the Still Kingdom was too cold for horses, so the only means of getting around outside of one's own two feet were these boulders of fur. Their purpose seemed to be public transportation—hence, the name "tram ram"—offering rides to paying customers who didn't want to hassle with the crowds walking or skating on the ice below. Ah, skating, one of Olivia's guilty pleasures.

If an Intelian like Bryson is allowed to play a piano, you're allowed to ice skate, Meow Meow thought.

I miss Bry.

Meow Meow chuckled. *I hate that I do too.*

Someone took a seat across from her. Olivia turned to see a face she hadn't seen in a week. A fresh white bandage had replaced the torn and browning fabric around his head. A part of her felt relief.

"Hello, Toono," she said before taking a bite of her ever-ice straw.

"That's how you greet me after a week?"

She ignored the question. "That's a big coat."

"It's freezing. Nowhere—and I mean absolutely *nowhere*—is warm. Even these buildings are basically gigantic freezers." Toono blew into his hands.

Well that's just dumb, Meow Meow thought. *What's that gonna do with gloves on?*

"Do you know I almost lost a finger in the dungeons?" Toono asked. "Apoleia almost allowed it to happen too." His voice was shaking slightly.

Olivia took another sip of her drink. "The palace's residential wing has a sauna."

"That would be helpful if I wasn't banned from entering the palace, let alone the residential wing."

"I'm not allowed in neither. Only when accompanied by my mother. Won't that make this mission more difficult?"

"We'll just have to be more creative," Toono said. "Are you staying at the inn across the street?"

Olivia nodded.

"And your mother?"

"A guest building within palace grounds."

"Let's hope she can keep her head on straight—well, as straight as she can manage. If she can avoid succumbing to her own rage, we'll be fine. But I doubt that'll be easy. I understand the painful memories that the palace holds."

Olivia was worried too. She usually had all the faith in the world in her mother, but this was different.

When Olivia was done with her drink, they left Frostbite and strolled down the street. It was well into morning, so the crowds had dissipated. Toono was shielding his face from the cold as snow lightly fell from above.

"You're in for a rough month," Meow Meow said.

"And I thought the Void was bad."

Heads turned as they walked past. Foreigners were nonexistent in Kindoliya, and with the way Toono was suffering in the freezing temperatures, he might as well had held a sign saying "I'm not from here."

"What did my mother tell you?" Olivia asked.

"'Revenge is a dish best served cold.'"

"No. 'Play the part.'"

"It's hard to play the part when my body's naturally reacting with blue lips and chattering teeth," Toono said. "I can't stop that from happening. I don't have Still Energy."

"Your lips aren't blue," Olivia said. "And clench your jaw."

"And scratch my ear," Meow Meow added with a smirk.

Good one, Olivia thought. The kitten hat snickered.

They spent the rest of the day together. With Apoleia's arduous business in the palace—a task that could last several weeks—the pair knew they'd be seeing a lot of each other. They ate lunch back at Frostbite. Olivia had to pay for Toono since he didn't own any Stillian coin. Unlike the kingdoms of the Light Realm, each of the dark kingdoms used their own form of currency—outside of the Power Kingdom, which had adapted the Light Realm's currency a few decades back.

After lunch, Olivia showed Toono one of Kindoliya's many ice rinks. She rented a pair of skates and got on the ice, which Toono apparently found either impressive or amusing based off the smile on his face. He refused to join in, watching from behind the wall instead. The day was capped off by another visit to Frostbite for dinner.

A couple hours before midnight, the exhausted duo sat in Toono's room. It was bare, with a few books stacked on the nightstand and his bubble wand leaning against the wardrobe. The room was constructed of wood, but there were still icicles hanging from the top of the window frame.

"Is there an official name for your ancient?" Olivia asked.

Toono glanced at his staff. "Every ancient has a name. Most Archains refrain from using them however. They say that mentioning your ancient by name will create an unhealthy dependence on it—so much so that when it's not within your grasp, your life erodes at an unnatural pace." He stared at it a moment longer before saying, "Orbaculum."

"If you say its name so casually, that means you either don't believe in it or you just don't care."

"I don't believe in the reasoning, but that doesn't mean there's no such thing as dependence. Think of ancients as an addictive substance—like the tobacco in a pipe. Except the victim of addiction isn't the person, but the person's energy."

Toono closed his eyes. "Thankfully I have stronger control of my energy than most, and speaking an ancient's name doesn't matter. People will go a lifetime without mentioning the name of their ancient, yet every time they lose physical contact with it, their natural death draws nearer. It's why the average lifespan of an Archain is shorter than in most other kingdoms. But some people can switch out ancients without a care in the world, and it wouldn't affect them in the slightest."

"Fascinating," Meow Meow said.

Toono was quick to break the short silence that ensued. "I'm reminded of the Prim Kingdom."

Olivia—who had a book about Kindoliya in her hands—blankly gazed at Toono and asked, "How so?"

"The situation. The aura."

"It eats at you."

"It does," he muttered. "I was scared in Prim. The whole time leading up to that murder of the prince was a nightmare." He stared at the floor. "It went against everything I had been. I didn't want to do it, but I had to." He drifted off in thought for a moment. "But in a way, the return of this feeling is good."

"And how is that?"

"When I departed the Void, I impulsively took the lives of about a dozen Passion guards who were stationed at their teleplatforms. I did it because I didn't want to bother forming an elaborate lie … what a cold and heartless reason. I had attributed it to the lingering effects of the Cyn Kingdom's atmosphere, but I wasn't quite sure. It frightened me. At least I'm still capable of guilt. I don't want to be here; I don't want to kill anyone. I simply need to."

After a brief moment of silence, Olivia said, "My mother loves to kill."

Toono's face wrinkled with a look of pity. "She doesn't love it. She feels she needs it. It's how she copes."

"I know," Olivia said. "Her persona makes it hard to remember though. That grin or laughter every time she takes a man's life."

"Her persona is what should make it easy to remember. There are so many extremes to her personality, and they shift in the blink of an eye. And that's because what once was whole has been shattered into millions of tiny pieces. There is no fluidity. She only knows how to express herself with maniacal anger or glee, but neither is the truth. Both are facades masking the miserable truth of her sorrow."

Olivia stared at Toono's blue eyes. He was a person unlike any other she had met in her life, and just as convoluted as her or her mother. Nobody was capable of understanding the two of them, but he was proving to be an anomaly … and nothing like a person one would expect to partner with a man like Storshae.

Meow Meow was impressed. *I'm a miserable being, and even I might like this guy.*

14
The Unbreakable

The mutilated horses gathered at an arching wired sign that served as the entrance to the town of Spachny. The four Jestivan and two Energy Directors studied the shacks that lined the road. The brooding sky drowned the dirt streets with a dense gray fog.

The three-week journey was over. Lilu's eyes had collected shadows, and the roots of her green hair were gray. Yama and Agnos showed the same symptoms, but Tashami and Director Neaneuma seemed unperturbed—a credit to their Spirit Energy. As for Director Buredo, he was beginning to show some strain, but not nearly as much.

Agnos was slumped against the raw neck of his horse, barely aware of his surroundings. His breathing was weak and shallow, and the only thing keeping him from passing out were the sounds of life reaching his ears. Spachny actually had a population, though the streets were hardly crowded.

"What's your plan, Zana Agnos?"

Agnos slowly lifted his head to see Adren Director Buredo earnestly gazing back at him. How was he handling this so well?

"Our destination is anywhere that's busy," Agnos mumbled.

"I hear people from every side," Yama said. "It's hard to sense their direction in this thin air."

"This way," Tashami instructed. He led his horse into an alley between two buildings.

Director Buredo seemed pleased, but held his counsel. He and Neaneuma had been silent for most of the journey, just as they had told the Jestivan they would be prior to their departure of Phesaw. They would force the young minds to make critical decisions on their own.

Agnos didn't object. He knew his mind, along with Lilu's, were perfectly capable of this task. And as much as he despised Yama, he was confident in her ability to perform in the event of an attack.

Tashami's guidance was correct. The alleyway led to a market square, if one could call it that. There were a total of four stalls and a couple dozen people mingling in the fog. They dismounted and tied their horses to a wooden beam before approaching one of the stalls to find it constructed with rotting wood. But that wasn't the worst of it. The meat on display was gray and spotted with fungus. Lilu's nose immediately turned up at the sight.

"Good grief," she groaned.

The merchant, who had been dealing with another customer, snapped his head around, undoubtedly from the sound of foreign tongue. "Zil ty ful?" he spat. Agnos's ancient translated it to "Who are you?"

Agnos was irritated. Lilu knew not to speak in front of a Cynnish. He turned to the man with an austere glare. "Lallo, fangali conmusuls." *Simply interested consumers.* He had been practicing speaking the language since Tashami showed him the Unbreakable's letters a year ago.

The man's angry gray eyes lingered for a moment longer before refocusing on his previous conversation.

Agnos glared at Lilu, whose face was red with either embarrassment or anger. He decided that the meat stall was off limits now, so he headed toward the middle of the market where a small cluster of people were gathered. They were all scruffy, seasoned men with white hair speckling their beards.

"Vanto, gandolas," Agnos said. *Hello, gentlemen.*

They split apart and stared at the sickly stranger. They were all taller than him, lanky like Toshik and Himitsu. "Vanto," one man said.

"I'm sorry to bother you, but I'm visiting from Gangladesh and am unfamiliar with the area. Do you know where I can find this man?" Agnos pulled a book from his cloak and pointed at the name: The Unbreakable.

A chorus of laughter tore through the thin air. *"More like the Broken,"* one man said. *"I've never seen a more deranged man. Well I suppose I've never seen him at all, but you can definitely hear him. Listen … do you hear that sound in the distance? It only barely reaches the ear."*

Agnos listened closely, trying to weed through the roars of the Lansani and the many conversations clouding his hearing. Then he heard it … a faint howl of despair.

"Thank you," Agnos said. He walked through the fog and returned to his group. He nodded in the direction for them to follow. Spachny, along with the other towns in the Cyn Kingdom, was ruled by no system but anarchy, and thieves were common. The exception was the capital, Batilearsh.

The wailing brought them into the outskirts of the town. The fog wasn't as thick, and the already humble houses were replaced by shanties crudely crammed together. Dirt roads waned into patchy dead grass, and the voices were fewer in number. In the silence the howling was more vivid and ghastly, sending chills down Agnos's spine.

They stopped in front of the lone house—as opposed to the shacks scattered about. It was two stories high, and both wide and deep. The grass in front rose to the waist, and there was no clearing for a path that led to the door. Director Buredo volunteered to keep watch out front while the others fought their way through the weeds. The two moons of second-night sat at an angle in the sky, casting an abnormal tangle of shadows on the ground.

Agnos knocked on the door, questioning whether it could be heard over the wailing within. It felt as if his eardrums might split. He banged his fist against the wood three more times, and the howls came to an abrupt halt. Now he wished it would resume, for the silence was even more overwhelming. Only the whispers leaking out of Spachny were audible, and the shallow, anxious breathing of the young Jestivan around him.

A loud thud from within the house made them jump. It was followed by a dragging noise. A couple seconds passed, then another thud. Then more dragging against the floor. This repeated until the source seemed to be directly on the other side of the door. Long moments passed, and the door remained unopened. They waited in a hush. Even Director Neaneuma's breaths were unsteady.

Agnos decided to knock again.

The door creaked open, and a frenzy of whispers were unloosed as if escaping from a punctured balloon. Everything inside Agnos felt like it was deflating—hope, promise, faith, will … spirit. Thoughts of suicide drowned his mind. For the first time in his life, he felt completely insignificant to this world—which happened to be his biggest fear.

Agnos fell onto all fours with his eyes fixed on the stone steps, but visions of blood spattering against a wooden floor flashed through his mind. Children's laughter and screams rang out among the whispers. Tiny invisible hands grabbed at his shoulders, and he wanted nothing more than to claw out his own throat.

"Stop it … Stop it!" Agnos shouted. "*Kill me!*"

A blast of cool wind blew over him, and the whispers ceased, as did the despair. He regained his awareness and saw the wrinkled face of Director Neaneuma as she knelt next to him. That was her wind, for such a thing didn't exist within the Void.

"Are you okay?" she asked.

Agnos exhaled and ran his hand through his black bangs. "I am now, Director. Thank you."

"That is the true power of Cynergy, Zana Agnos. A type of life beyond death … one that is full of misery and absent of body." She gazed through the door with a look of uncertainty. "But even that was beyond what I would have ever imagined running into this far from Batilearsh."

Agnos looked behind him to see that Lilu and Yama were recovering from the same experience. He drew himself to his full height and entered the house. The only light came from the moons glowing through cracks in the boarded windows. He began to wonder why he had volunteered to lead this expedition. The empty quiet was enough to drive him insane—silence shouldn't have existed in the Void.

He walked into another room, where a tattered sofa and armchair squatted in the darkness. Children's laughter echoed through the room while footsteps jumped about the abandoned room. A glass mug fell off an end table and crashed to the floor. More laughter, then a chorus of hushes.

"That was my dad's favorite mug, you squealers!" a whisper hissed from no tangible source.

"Your dad may be the Unbreakable, but his mug isn't!" Giggles erupted, but then footsteps from the doorway caused them to stop.

"That was funny, Panelle," came a deep and gentle voice. Agnos felt something walk through his body in the direction of the shattered glass. "A fantastic joke."

"What's a joke?" a child whispered back.

"It's something that makes you laugh, a great tool to ignite your soul. Jokes make people feel better."

"Do people tell jokes in the Light Realm, Mr. Patter?"

Mr. Patter, Agnos thought. *That's the Unbreakable, Tashami's father.*

"All the time, but not all are so nice. Jokes that harm someone's feelings are bad."

A knock came from the front door, causing Agnos to jump. "Guess what, children," said the deep voice of the invisible Mr. Patter. "You get a new foster brother today."

There was a burst of cheers followed by a stampede of tiny footsteps that went directly through Agnos and the others before immediately quieting as they left the room.

Agnos continued through the house. *Panelle.* He would ask Tashami about him later—assuming he made it out of this nightmare with his sanity.

Each new room contained its own scenario of whispers, but nothing that seemed of importance like the first. They returned to the main foyer and climbed a set of stairs. Upon reaching the second floor, they heard a loud snap followed by a thud. Once again, it seemed to come from no particular source.

Then the howls and groans resumed. Agnos covered his ears as he pressed on. He glanced down a hallway and saw light flickering through the crevices of a door. He motioned for Yama to take the lead, for this was her role. She strode forward, eager to assert herself in this haunting place.

Yama drew her sword, and the metal scraping against her sheath pierced the air like nails on slate. Agnos felt his hands tremble as she placed her hand on the door. Instantly the moaning stopped and the light disappeared.

They all held their breath. Then there was a thud on the other side of the door, followed by the sound of something dragging across the floor. It was the same sound that Agnos heard when they were outside the house.

"*Fools*," someone hissed in Cynnish.

"We seek the Unbreakable," Agnos replied in Sphairian.

The voice recited what seemed to be a poem:

A kingdom of graves,
The Gravedom, the Void,
Whichever you call it,
All gets destroyed.
Dead and rotten,
Broken and forgotten,
I let that boy in,
With hair like cotton;
Reminiscent of a son,
A clone or replica,
How I despise that boy,
The one they call Chelekah.

Yama stood at the forefront with her sword drawn while Agnos looked down the hall to their sides.

Tashami stepped forward. "Dad."

More silence.

"It's me, Tashami."

"That cannot be my son," the raspy voice replied. "He knows not to come to the Void. I remember making that clear long ago."

Tashami gently pressed his hand against the door. "I was only three. Please, let me in."

"No."

"Thank you for the letters," Tashami said. "There was a sense of comfort in knowing you were alive."

A pause.

"What letters?"

Agnos cocked an eyebrow at his friend. Tashami gestured for the book of letters, and Agnos handed it over.

"I have them right here," Tashami said.

"I sent no letters."

Tashami looked flabbergasted as he stared back at Agnos. Agnos decided to take over once again, walking up to the door. "Did you meet a man named Toono?"

"How would you know this?" he replied. "Did he tell you about his visit?"

"No," Agnos said. "You did."

All was quiet for a few seconds. "You've been tricked … lured," the Unbreakable said.

"By whom?"

Agnos snapped his head around as something cold grabbed his shoulder and giggled. No one was there but his comrades.

"My eldest son, Joni. You must leave now. Cynergy is not something to take lightly. These children, they will kill you … *Broken and rotten, dead and forgotten.*"

Playful giggles erupted once again, this time throughout the entirety of the house. The footsteps of little girls and boys pattered all over the wooden floors. Then the wailing started again:

With a knock on the door,
One swore, one more,
With a snap and a thud,
Six hung, six swung,
With a death and a roar,
One war, one war,
With a slice and a drip,
Dear Joni, R.I.P.

The haunting laughter morphed into screams as ghostly figures materialized in the halls. Agnos turned to see six children standing on the banister with rope around their necks. Most of them seemed to be at peace. One cried in horror. The banister snapped from under their feet, resulting in an immediate death as the rope arrested their falls.

"Get out!" Director Neaneuma yelled over the ruckus, conjuring gusts of wind in every direction to silence the children, each gust replaced moments later by more laughter or screams.

Agnos had a different agenda. He burst through the door of the Unbreakable's room. The window was open, so moonlight splashed over most of the expanse. His eyes frantically darted every which way until landing on a mass of shadows in the back corner.

"I need to know where Toono went!" he shouted.

A voice crept out of the darkness: "I liked that young man." It was a wonder how he made himself heard over the chaos outside the room. "He came asking about Batilearsh. I told him I knew what he was after because I hear the whispers of the dead from all over the kingdom. I knew he kills, but with a purpose. And I could see it in his eyes … a thirst. A dry kind of thirst, if that makes any sense."

"Where did he go?" Agnos repeated.

The man chuckled. "He sought someone who harbored great power. His target was a royal, but gaining access to Batilearsh is near impossible for even someone with Cynergy. So I gave him an alternative in the town of Nuadam, one that would benefit not only him, but me too …"

"*Who?*" Agnos shouted louder than he ever had in his life, his question thundering across the Cyn Kingdom's atmosphere like the first rumble presaging a summer storm.

The shadowy mass slowly lifted into a hunched stance and stepped into the moonlight. Now Agnos understood the source of the dragging sound. One of the Unbreakable's legs was stripped of skin and muscle from the knee down. His bones dragged across the splintered floor. And the skin that he did have hugged the rest of his skeleton. His hollowed out face nearly sent Agnos into shock.

"The boy who knocked on my door that day. The boy who took everything I had worked for at this foster home. The boy who convinced all of my foster children to take their own lives after I worked so hard for years to make them realize they were not victims to their Cynergy, that there was more to life than the death that concluded it. The boy who *ruined my mission in this kingdom!*" His tone turned venomous. "But most importantly, the boy who made my son Joni slice open his own throat, forcing me to send my only other son back to the Light Realm, as far away as possible from this nightmare!"

The children's screams intensified, as did the Unbreakable's moans as he wallowed back into the shadows of his corner. Agnos turned to leave and saw a distraught Tashami standing in the doorway. Tears were shining in his eyes. Agnos grabbed him and pulled him into the hallway. They darted down the stairs, passing the hanging children.

A ghostly figure obstructed the path to the front door. It was a young boy with white hair, about ten years old. He walked toward Agnos and Tashami with his hands clutched around his throat. Blood seeped between his fingers and poured down his hands and chest. This was Joni—or someone's Cynergy giving Joni shape. Agnos wasn't completely sure how Cynergy worked—nobody did.

A blast of wind wiped the figure clear. It had come from Tashami, who now led the charge out of the house. Agnos followed and leapt into the front yard, stumbling in the weeds. Buredo, Neaneuma, Yama, and Lilu were fending off Spachny townspeople. It was obvious they were holding back, and Agnos was surprised to see Yama's sword sheathed at her hip.

As Agnos and Tashami ran toward the crowd, Director Buredo and the others broke off toward the countryside. Their heavy footsteps and breathing splintered the air. They only stopped when Agnos finally collapsed.

The three-week journey through the Void's atmosphere had already depleted his energy. Tonight was the breaking point. He leaned on his elbows and hacked up chunks of snot. The images and screams of the children wouldn't escape his mind.

Tashami sat on the edge of the dirt trail, sobbing hysterically. Yama stood with her hands on her knees, her panting loud and rapid. Lilu had a silent look of terror on her face. They had left their horses in Spachny.

"I think it's time we head back home," Director Buredo said after the Jestivan had calmed down somewhat.

Agnos pushed himself to his feet. "North."

"Excuse me?" Buredo asked.

"We need to head north to Nuadam, Director."

"Look at your comrades. Do you appear to be in any condition to travel another couple days north? And we're getting too close to the Linsaniun Mounds."

Agnos studied his teammates, landing on Yama last. Despite the strands of gray in her violet hair and circles of exhaustion around her eyes, she stood tall and strong. "With Yama around, we have nothing to worry about. She is a warrior. Besides, you said we will make the decisions."

"What's the purpose?" Director Neaneuma asked.

"Mr. Patter told me that Toono killed Chelekah, who I now know was the Diatia, in Nuadam."

"What does that matter?" Yama asked. "Chelekah is dead and Toono is long gone."

"Well think about it," Lilu said. She was sitting next to Tashami with her arm wrapped around his shoulder. "The dead can communicate with the living here because of their Cynergy. We learned so much about what happened in that house a decade ago because of those children."

Yama's eyes narrowed. "What are you getting at?"

"Chelekah could talk to us if we find him. Toono might have said something in private—or what he thought was private—around Chelekah's carcass."

Agnos was distracted as someone giggled behind him. He slowly turned around but nobody was there. A piece of parchment lay on the ground. Agnos picked it up and read it:

Thank you for letting me see my son again. I never wanted him to come back to this kingdom, but I'll admit that seeing his face sparked something within me. I want to help you in any way I can, but all I can give you are shreds of information that I've collected from the whispers that have happened to travel through these parts.

Toono possesses five white gems that he claims to have stolen from the Archaic Museum, and I believe they are one part of bringing a dangerous man back to life. He must kill one person per kingdom while in possession of the gems. They must be powerful individuals … individuals with strong energies and rare talent, likely royals or elite citizens. The Prim Prince was the first. The Cyn Diatia was second. Now he has eight more kingdoms to visit—five Light and three Dark.

I wish I had more to share, but I have received no news from the town of Nuadam. It's not like I can hold a conversation with the dead—nobody can. What I hear is by chance. And even I, someone who has developed a strong ear for this sort of thing over the years, cannot hear everything. Good luck.

Agnos sighed—some of it exhaustion, and some relief. Up to this moment, all he knew was that Toono had stolen a "dangerous relic" according to Archaic King Itta.

Now Agnos knew that Toono had acquired Anathallo, an ancient piece fabled to have the ability to revive a life. He must have learned how to make it work; no ancient texts provided a clue. Agnos stared at the ground—something just didn't add up. What did Olivia have to do with this? Why'd he send Storshae after her?

He sighed and handed the letter to Yama. "Our mission here is done. Let's head back to Phesaw."

15
A New Regime

Bryson lay in the lush manicured grass in one of Dunami Palace's courtyards. He stared at the overcast sky, happy to be back in his home kingdom and away from Phesaw and Rolling Oaks. Tashami, Agnos, Lilu, and Yama were still in the Cyn Kingdom with Directors Buredo and Neaneuma. Rhyparia was training in the Archaic Kingdom with Director Senex. Olivia was spending summer at home like she did every year. Toshik and Jilly had also headed home after returning from the Oaks. And Himitsu had left with Ophala and Fane to go greet his father, who had been released from the confinements of Passion King Damian. A younger Bryson might have loved the peace and quiet currently bathing Phesaw's campus, but the past year had given him an appreciation for company.

A thud and a rip snapped him from his trance. He lazily looked down to see an arrow stuck in the ground. It had torn a hole through his jacket.

"All right, that's it," Bryson said, yanking the arrow from the sod. "No more until the princess gets here."

An excited red-headed boy looked at Bryson with wide eyes. "What's she like?" Simon asked as he lowered his bow.

Bryson smirked. "Like five Meow Meows combined."

"Meow Meow is nice to me though."

"True," Bryson said. "Well, she's a princess. You get what you expect." He heard armor clattering in the distance. "Right on cue."

Shelly walked out of the hall with four steel-clad guards flanking her. She wore a modest dress of aqua, as she had no interest in training. She was simply here to teach. The guards set up targets in their instructed positions before retreating to each corner of the yard.

Bryson gazed at Shelly with amusement. "Are they really necessary?"

"One can never be too careful, Mr. LeAnce," she mockingly replied. "You might finally succumb to my irresistible beauty and steal me away." She pressed the back of her white-gloved hand against her forehead as she tilted her head toward the sky.

Bryson laughed, reminded of when Lilu reenacted his mishap of descending the stairs at the ceremony for their induction into the Jestivan.

"This is Simon, the archery prodigy I told you about," Bryson said.

Shelly studied the little boy. Simon bowed exactly how Bryson had showed him to. "Hello, milady."

Shelly pointed at a wooden pallet in the distance that was carved to look like an adult human. "Hit it," she said.

Simon smiled and loaded his bow with an arrow, pulled back, and released in one fluid motion. He did it so quickly that when Bryson looked at the target, an arrow was already pinned in the figure's head, between where the eyes would be.

"You're well on your way to becoming a champion archer in our army," Shelly said.

"I'm going to be a zana of the Jestivan."

"I'll happily pass on the torch," Bryson said as Shelly rolled her eyes.

"What's so special about the Jestivan, Simon?" the princess asked.

"They're talented and brave!"

A flash of white blinded Bryson as a crack of thunder shook the air. Bryson's hair stood up as the electricity pulsed around his skin. He blinked a few times to rid the daze from his eyes. Simon lay in shock on his back. A patch of grass had been scorched to black ash.

"Can the Jestivan do that?" Shelly asked. Then she turned to smile at Bryson. "If you're not too startled, let's get started."

"Still can only muster up on one bolt, eh?" Bryson teased.

"Do you want to find out?"

"What's first?"

"Hold out your hand and curl your index finger."

Bryson obeyed.

"Good. Now create sparks."

He did … tiny ones.

"You're not controlling that. Weave it into a shape or pattern."

Bryson focused hard on his energy. He could feel it subtly pulsing through his body, and if he paid careful attention, he could feel the zigzag pattern it traveled in. He tapped into it at his fingertips and pushed it out of his body and into nature. The sparks began to spiral upward, but fizzled out just as quickly.

"It really is astounding how behind you are with your energy. You didn't take any beginning courses when you were younger at Phesaw?"

"Debo always made my schedules, and he made sure they never involved any classes involving energy or weaving. 'Focus on your body,'" Bryson quoted.

Shelly sighed. "Look, I get it. You excel at elite levels in speed, technique, and strength. But with all those natural physical skills, you would be unstoppable with some electricity to back it up. Do you know why I told you to curl your index finger?"

"To—"

"To teach you that weaving eventually becomes as natural as bending a joint or flexing a muscle." Shelly turned to Simon, who had peppered the target with several more arrows. "Torchtop, what's the first rule of weaving?"

"Crawl first, milady."

"Right!" Shelly said, looking back at Bryson. "Start simple, then build. I can't teach you much because it's something you must learn to control on your own … and it's more of Lilu's specialty. Once you learn to do that, it will become second nature—like bending your knee. Then you can start learning the hand and finger manipulation of weaving." The princess frowned. "When you register for classes this year, I suggest you finally take a weaving class."

Weaving was an obscure concept to Bryson. Shelly always spoke of it, but she never really broke it down to something he could understand. He forced some Intel Energy out of his body, managing to ignite another spark from his fingertips.

"Bryson!"

The blockish King Vitio was strolling toward them. He wore a sky-blue tunic embroidered in a gold that matched his beard and hair.

"Vitio, hey," Bryson said, extending his hand, which Vitio batted out of the way in favor of a hug.

"It has been so long, my boy! How have you been? How were the Oaks?"

Bryson smiled. "Mission accomplished. How about you?"

"Fantastic. There is so much happ—" He paused as he looked down.

"This is Simon," Bryson said.

"Are you an archer?"

Simon nodded.

"He's very good, Father," Shelly said.

Vitio looked at the target in the distance. "And you managed to do that from here?"

Another silent nod.

"I must see this with my own eyes!"

The rest of the afternoon was spent training and socializing in the courtyard. Vitio even summoned one of his top-ranked archers to teach Simon a few things. Bryson's frustrations mounted with each failed attempt to weave his energy. He felt like Shelly had left out a lot of key information. Maybe Lilu could help—if she would ever forgive him.

After Bryson showed Simon where he'd be staying for the night, he took a late-night stroll with the king through the palace's third-floor chambers. He hadn't seen the king since his return from the Dev Kingdom in March, so there was a lot of catching up to do, though he was careful not to mention Thusia.

"And how's Vistas holding up?" Bryson asked.

Vitio's face grew stern. "I sense he's still a little more rattled than normal, but he's okay."

"I need to visit him one of these days … maybe get here early, before weaving lessons with Shelly."

"I may have heard a rumor about who will be stepping in as the new Intel Director this fall," Vitio said. "And if it's true, Shelly's lessons will prove useless. I know she's my daughter, but this person is one of the best three weavers in the kingdom."

"Who is it?"

Vitio shook his head. "Not a chance. Praetor would have my head if I let it slip."

"And how about the Archaic Kingdom … how is it holding up with Itta in prison?"

"Outside of a few riots, things are running smoother than we could have hoped for. Itta will be executed within the next ten to fourteen months. King Damian will have Itta interrogated once this business with the assassins is concluded."

"By Marcus? The truth extractor from the Dev Kingdom?" Bryson asked.

Vitio frowned. "Lilu tells you more than she should. But yes, that's correct. We just have to figure out the right questions to ask. As for the state of their kingdom, Adren General Sinno is in charge of things in the capital. You've probably noticed the absence of Major Lars—he's been stationed in Rim."

"Good choice," Bryson said. "I like him."

"We're assigning five people—one native of each light kingdom—to positions of power over the Archaic Kingdom. They'll make all the decisions, but more importantly, groom the Archaic Prince into a proper king. I believe three of them are parents to some of the Jestivan."

"Do you know who?"

Vitio patted Bryson on the back with his gigantic hand. "I'm not Lilu. I'll give you hints though. One's rich, one's strong, one's sneaky."

"Fair enough." They finally reached the door to his room in the guest corridor. Bryson tried again to give the king a handshake, and was once again enwrapped in a hug that nearly squeezed the lungs out of his body.

Bryson understood that the king missed his friend, and he was the closest substitute to fill that void. Though he had always hated being compared to his father, he had grown to appreciate Vitio's affection. There was a euphoria in the king that warmed his laugh and reddened his cheeks.

* * *

Six people stood in the council room. Enormous windows were draped with cascading curtains of brown and gold. The walls were paneled with lustrous maple, carved with scenes of famous events throughout the Archaic Kingdom's history. A grand chandelier with dozens of candles loomed over the center table that seated five—two chairs on either side and one at the foot. There was no chair at the head of the table. Instead an elderly man stood there with parchment in his hand. In front of each chair were a stack of papers and a bottle of ink with a quill.

The old man read from the parchment. "Today—the twenty-fifth of July, 1499—the five chosen individuals, as selected by the royal heads of the Passion, Adren, Intel, and Spirit Kingdoms, convene for the first time. With due diligence and, above all else, a moral ethos, they serve as stewards of the Archaic Kingdom and its prince."

The man looked up from the parchment. "With that said, please step up to the table and state your name and the position you will hold."

A plump man stepped forward. He was old and balding, and a set of glasses that were entirely too small for his head sat on the tip of his nose. "Grandarion Senten, Intelian representative, Chief Arbitrator, leader of the judicial system."

Next was a lady of great height. Her brown hair was pulled back in a tight bun. "Rosel Sania, Passionian representative, Chief Senator, leader of the political system."

A tall pinkish man stepped forward. A sword was sheathed to the hip of his business suit. "Toth Brench, Adrenian representative, Chief Merchant, leader of the economic system."

"Wert Lamay, Spiritian representative, Chief Officer, leader of the military."

"Ophala Vevlu, Archain representative, Spy Pilot, leader of the stealth unit."

They all took a seat. The older man at the head of the table rolled up his parchment and gazed at the faces once more. "Welcome to the Amendment Order."

16
Feast

A room occupied Olivia's vision—*the* room, the one hidden behind the painting of the Still Mountains at the dead end of that ominous hall. But it wasn't as she remembered it from her brief visit with her mother. The walls weren't damaged. Olivia had a feeling that she knew what was about to happen.

Sure enough, she heard a woman's shouting from within the room. There was no source of it. "*Stop it! I will have your head!*"

There was a crash, and a hole appeared in the wall out of nowhere, splintering in every direction. "*I will kill you!*"

There were sounds of a struggle as more dents were molded into the drywall. A woman's heavy, ragged breathing along with desperate grunts. Then the bed was knocked a few feet to the side. The menacing bellows transitioned into cries of panic … agony … despair.

"This isn't how it should happen!" the woman sobbed. "*We can't do this.*"

Olivia was jerked awake by someone's hand shaking her shoulder. "Olivia, wake up!"

She opened her eyes to the sound of Toono shouting over Meow Meow's hissing. His blue eyes were wide with shock as he stared at her.

She reached up to pet Meow Meow in effort to calm him.

"Are you okay?" Toono asked.

"Yes."

That was a lie. Olivia had always experienced the shouting and crying during her dreams. In fact, that was what molded the mask over her emotions at a young age. Her mother had used it as a tool to teach her. But there had never been a visual to accompany it.

"Do you need anything?"

Olivia rolled over on her side with her face to the wall. She repeated her mother's words in her head: *Vulnerability makes you weak*. After a long minute she felt the mattress rise. The door creaked open and clicked shut. She rolled back over and pressed her face into the pillow.

Meow Meow hissed, and Olivia balled up her fist and sent it through the bedframe.

* * *

The next morning passed slowly, filled with anticipation of finally putting plans into motion. It had been nearly two months since Olivia was dragged into the city of Kindoliya by Still soldiers, which had given plenty of time to overthink their schemes. Plans had been debated, altered, or completely replaced.

Today's meeting was different. There were no debates or brainstorming sessions. Instead Olivia and Toono reviewed their final plan of action, quizzing each other to make sure they knew what they were to be doing at what times, where they should be, and the titles of any important people they were sure to run into.

They sat at opposite ends of a table in Toono's room as sunlight leaked through the powder blue curtains. Detailed blueprints of the palace lay in front of them. Apoleia had smuggled them out. The blueprints covered the entire surface area of the table and draped over the sides.

Olivia pressed her finger to a diagram. "That is where it happens," she said. "That is your goal."

Toono snorted. "You mean the room circled ten times over?"

"Yes."

He chuckled, letting out a puff of steam. "I'll miss this place," he said.

"You have to escape this place to miss it," Meow Meow said. "Don't get ahead of yourself."

"You're right," Toono said. "Let's go over this one more time."

"Who are you looking for outside the palace that will help you get in?" Olivia asked.

"A man named Titus Finilguster; high-ranking guard of Kindoliya's wall."

"How many people did my mother persuade into helping us from within palace walls?"

"One."

"Name and position?"

"Tria Shau …" Toono shook his head. "The head chef, which still sounds silly."

"Describe her," Olivia instructed.

"Short, round lady with thinning gray hair. Looks like an evil old hag—and apparently she is one. But she's trustworthy, according to Apoleia."

Olivia nodded. "What's the first rule?"

"Silence."

"Second rule."

"Follow instructions."

"Third."

"Don't question the instructions." Toono smirked. "You're such a tyrant."

Olivia rose from her chair and started rolling up the blueprints. "I must head to the palace. My mother is waiting. She told me there are a lot of preparations for a lady before a banquet—dressing up, accessorizing, etcetera."

"I'm sure you'll look stunning," Toono said with an amused look.

"No mistakes," she said flatly.

* * *

Olivia sat in silence while her mother tugged at the ends of her hair with a brush. Her mother's lavish guest room was trimmed in wood, but everything else was made of crystal or diamond in the texture of ice.

A large family portrait hung above the bed. The men stood on the right half and the women on the left. Some had brown hair, others violet. X's had been carved into their eyes, and lines across their necks. Only two people had escaped the vandalism—a man and a woman. Undoubtedly, this was her mother's doing.

Olivia's head snapped back as the brush caught a knot. "I'm sorry, baby," Apoleia said.

Unfazed, Olivia glanced at a leafy green dress hanging from the bedpost. "That's not going to match my hair," she said.

Her mother let out a gigantic laugh. "What color would you like then, baby?"

"Yellow."

Bad idea, Meow Meow thought.

It went silent. Olivia knew her mother was scowling behind her, so she corrected her error: "Black."

Apoleia's voice quivered as she replied, "Anything for my little girl."

Close one, the kitten sighed.

Apoleia guided Olivia out of her seat and turned her around to face the mirror. She hardly recognized herself. Dark red lipstick, copious amounts of blush, purple eye shadow, and a thick layer of eyeliner distorted her into the exact opposite kind of woman she tried to be her entire life. Her hair had been tucked behind her ears in order to place her trailing diamond earrings in the forefront.

"I look weird," Olivia remarked. In her head, she said to Meow Meow, *You ruin the look.*

How dare you, the kitten replied.

Her mother's faced stretched with a grotesque smile. "You must present yourself well. All eyes won't necessarily be on you, but the ones that matter will."

Olivia turned her head side to side. "I approve."

Apoleia pecked her daughter's head, then turned and headed toward the closet. "After all, it is the princess's thirtieth birthday! We must celebrate properly!" she shrieked.

She's covering her scars, Meow Meow observed.

Olivia had noticed that too. *There's a first for everything, I suppose.*

Apoleia stumbled out of the closet with a dashing black dress in hand. "Eloquent, yet sexy."

"I'm sixteen."

Apoleia laughed. "Do you think that matters to these men?" she whispered into Olivia's ear. She held the dress in front of Olivia. It was the perfect size. "Besides you'll be seventeen in nearly two weeks, and *that* is what we should be celebrating tonight. I have my own preparations, baby," she said sweetly. "I'll see you later."

Apoleia rested her hand on the doorknob. "Tonight Kindoliya is vulnerable, blinded by the celebration of life. However, they fail to realize that with life comes death …" She licked her finger. "Let's remind them."

* * *

Olivia stood in the Icebound Confluence, staring at the Statue of Gefal once again. She thought back to her time as a captive of Dev Prince Storshae and wondered which figure symbolized Fonos, or whether he even was a part of the sculpture. Maybe Fonos had yet to become a Bewahr when this statue was last updated. Wait … she ran through the figures once more to make sure her eyes weren't deceiving her … they're all women?

Her mother, who had been discussing something with a passerby, broke free and pulled Olivia away.

"Let's go, let's go!" Apoleia exclaimed. "Off to Glacial Hall!"

Olivia followed her mother through a door and down a hall that ramped upward before opening into a grand lobby. The blue walls were paneled with long blocks of crystal. As Olivia took a step inside, something crunched beneath her feet. She looked down and saw a floor of ice shards sparkling back up at her. She gently kicked up a few crystallized fragments. It was like the sand on a beach—not that she had ever been to one. Something possessed her to look up. A ceiling of icicles glittered above.

A few people were mingling in the space, but the real party was occurring past the open doors on the far side of the room. Olivia noticed a few heads turn and stare at her as she walked past.

"It's good to be fashionably late," Apoleia whispered in her ear.

Olivia wasn't prepared for what she walked into. She stuck out like a sore thumb, as she wore the lone black dress among the canvas of blues, whites, silvers, and purples. Did her mother want her to stick out? Was that why she had suggested green at first?

The Glacial Hall was immense and opulent. At least ten crystal chandeliers hung on chains that stretched endlessly to the cavernous ceiling. The crystal floor was textured to look like massive snowflakes. A stringed orchestra played softly as royals and other expensive-looking people chatted.

Olivia felt the glares as she hesitantly made her way through the crowd. A draft from the dress's slit prickled her upper thigh.

A teenage boy stepped in front of her, his hair an inky black and suit a mousy gray. "Hello, ma'am," he said with a smile. He took her hand and gave it a gentle kiss. He had a crystal ring on each finger.

Olivia was caught off-guard. Men didn't just grab women's hands in the Still Kingdom—unless they wanted to be greeted with a knee to the groin in return. Perhaps this stranger knew that Olivia wasn't from here.

"Hello …" She paused. "Junio, son of General Garlo, correct?"

"That's what they call me," he said with a bow. "And what do they call you?"

"Sona."

Junio crooked his elbow. "Shall we, Sona?"

Olivia hooked her arm in his and followed him to the dance floor. Couples glided across the floor, weaving through the traffic in synchronized harmony. Junio put his arm around Olivia's waist and his other hand in hers, then stepped left with the music.

It was effortless for Olivia—the counts, the motions, the patterns. Her mother had taught her to be a fighter, but there were other lessons as well, such as the etiquette and art of being a lady. Certain aspects of being a woman were necessary evils. This was just the first time that Olivia had acted like this in the public eye. If any of the Jestivan had witnessed this, they'd have thought they had a stroke.

Junio smiled. "You're good."

"Thank you."

"So who are you?" he asked. "You're somehow related to the royal family, perhaps? But I don't recall seeing you around the palace." He paused. "A pretty face like yours would surely engrave itself into my memory."

Meow Meow gagged.

"Second cousin of the queen's sister," Olivia recited.

"Do you share the last name? *Sona Still.* That would be a pretty one."

Olivia shook her head.

"No matter. I'll accept any last name as long as it's yours."

Save me, Olivia pleaded.

About time, Meow Meow replied. *I've been licking myself all day for a moment like this.*

The kitten flung himself into a fit of hacking and wheezing. Junio backed away with a look of disgust as Meow Meow coughed up a massive clot of soggy hair. Olivia casually cupped her hands in front of her and caught the slobbery ball. With a look of sheer horror, Junio turned and marched off the floor.

Terrible idea, Olivia thought. *I'm supposed to be a lady.*

What else am I supposed to do? I'm a cat … I think.

Hiss. You just hiss. She gazed around. *Everybody is staring.*

A death grip took hold of her arm and dragged her through the crowd and out of Glacial Hall. Apoleia didn't speak until they had passed through the lobby and into a study room.

"I'm sorry, mother," Olivia said.

"This is the one time I ask you to paint yourself as a lady," Apoleia panted. "The *one* time!" Fire burned in her eyes.

Olivia stayed quiet, knowing that words would only make it worse.

"All that time I spent teaching you how to act as a royal, telling you there would be a time you'd eventually put it into play! *Well this is that time!*"

Olivia watched as her mother went into one of her more hysterical fits. She head-butted a wooden bookcase with enough force to send cracks through the surface, holding her head against it with a deranged menace as her teeth bore down on each other. Then she slapped her hand against her face and screamed before kicking an end table's legs in half.

"Where's a blade?" Apoleia muttered, her eyes darting frantically in every direction. "*I need a blade!*"

This isn't a response to you, Olivia, Meow Meow said. *She's nervous—scared that this plan won't succeed. And she can't handle the fact that this all relies on Toono, and she must sit back and wait … and it's possible she's being triggered by memories.*

Olivia gripped a pair of scissors that had been resting on the table when they walked in. She had preemptively snatched them up and was now hiding them behind her back. But this was Apoleia Lavender; there was no stopping her. The damaged woman sat in the corner of the room with tears splashing down her cheeks, ripping at the skin on her wrists with her manicured violet talons.

Olivia approached her mother.

"*Get out!*" Apoleia shrieked.

Olivia hesitated, then turned and left the room. Was she a bad daughter for leaving so easily while her mother was in pain? Her mom wouldn't think so, but Olivia did.

She took a breath once back in the lobby, the murmurs from Glacial Hall leaking through the doorway. She didn't want to go back in that place, but she had to. Her job was to keep an eye out for … *There he is.*

A man marched through the lobby and into Glacial Hall with long and purposeful strides. He wore a blue cloak embroidered in silver with a giant snowflake on its back—the insignia of a Still soldier. Behind him, being carelessly dragged across the floor through the shards of ice was another man cloaked in an identical soldier's uniform.

Relief wafted over Olivia. This news would please her mother. Their partners had made it inside, and it was time to initiate Apoleia's part of the plan.

* * *

Midnight had struck, and the sun was setting as first-night began. Toono stood at the edge of a dark alleyway between two buildings of ice, carefully eyeing the entrances to the palace grounds. There were three main points of entry for the guests who stood in orderly lines, preparing to be searched by the soldiers stationed at the gates. Toono counted thirty of them, which was a good thing.

The Still General must have counted on strength in numbers, but he didn't account for the possibility that there might be a traitor in the royal family's midst. And the more soldiers there were, the easier it was for one of them to split away unnoticed.

That was what Toono had been waiting for—to see someone slip from the crowd. But this was taking too much time. The cold had started eating at him about thirty minutes ago. He looked up at the snow-capped palace of ice. Olivia and Apoleia were in there, trying to pretend to have a good time while they anxiously awaited his arrival.

He heard a thud behind him. He snapped his head around to see an unconscious soldier sprawled face-first in the snow. The soldier standing next to him gave Toono a hard-eyed stare.

"Are you Toono?" he asked.

Toono nodded. "Titus?"

The man nodded as he knelt next to his comatose comrade and removed his cloak. "Here," Titus said, handing it to Toono. "Your ancient is in the location Apoleia discussed with you."

Toono threw the cloak over his shoulders, noticing how weightless it felt. He had been hoping for something a little warmer. The crystal snowflake on the back was impossible to re-create, as it was made from special crystals only accessible under the ice of the Diamond Sea.

Toono took a mug of ale that he had gotten from a pub earlier and rubbed a fair amount on the cloth. He pulled the hood above his head. It didn't seem adequate enough for concealment. Though the hood's hem looped to a triangular point that fell between his eyes, most of his face was still exposed.

Titus stared at Toono. "You're forgetting a piece." He reached into his collar and pulled up a mask that covered his mouth and nose.

"Ah, okay," Toono said, doing the same. "That makes a little more sense."

"You've been here for nearly two months and didn't know about our headgear? Apoleia told me you were intelligent."

"Forgive me," Toono said through a shiver. "The cold has frozen my brain."

"Marini here—" Titus gestured toward the body on the ground— "is your height and has blue eyes too. Therefore the only thing you should have to worry about is not speaking. Do not say a single word. They will notice the difference in tone."

"Understood. And thank you, Titus."

The soldier gazed out the alley. "I'm doing this for Apoleia." He looked back with unforgiving eyes. "Don't mess this up. Let's go."

They exited the alley. Titus strutted like the soldier he was, and Toono stumbled and weaved behind him like a drunken buffoon. As they approached the other soldiers, some stared at Toono with incredulous looks.

"Oi! Is Marini drunk again?" one of the men shouted. "Of all the days!"

Titus snatched Toono's wrist with a snarl, pulling him to his side. "I told General Garlo that this disgrace wasn't suited for such a duty," he growled. "Caught him puking his bowels out at the rink."

There was some scattered laughter. "Marini, you have a problem," one guard said.

Toono groaned, his head down as he slumped in Titus's grasp.

"Gonna take him to the general right now," Titus said. "It's time this delinquent gets what he deserves."

"You're supposed to be stationed here," a soldier replied. "General Garlo won't want to be bothered over something so petty. He is an esteemed member of the festivities."

"Really, Buln?" Titus snapped. "You know the general values the discipline of his men over a frilly banquet. And if you think otherwise, then stop me."

Buln stared at Titus for an uncomfortably long moment, then something made him turn around and refocus on the guests.

Titus dragged Toono through the gates and into the grounds. As laughter and gleeful conversation danced through the air, Toono could only think of how different his world was at that moment. He occasionally lifted his head to better orientate himself within the palace. But for the most part he kept his head low, trusting Titus to guide him to where he needed to be. It took a while, but the sound of instruments and a sea of murmurs finally reached his ears.

He looked up and saw Glacial Hall directly ahead. Glancing left, he saw Olivia, which was a bit confusing, seeing that she was supposed to be involved in the festivities. She turned around and slipped into a hallway.

Titus let go of Toono's wrist and slammed him against the wall that divided the lobby and the hall. "Stay here while I go get the general, you drunken fool," Titus growled, loud enough to be heard by any dawdling guests.

Toono slid down the wall, landing with a crunch in the ice-strewn floor. He knew wealthy eyes were staring at him right now, internally debating whether they should be disgusted by such a disgraceful sight or apprehensive of a skilled soldier in an inebriated state of mind. He slowly tilted his head toward the hallway that Olivia had entered. Apoleia walked out a moment later. She appeared flustered, her face sloppily cleaned up of tears. Cloths were wrapped around her wrists, but a smile was plastered on her face as she entered Glacial Hall with Olivia on her heels.

Toono twirled his fingers in his pocket out of habit, but there was no clattering of gems. They had been taken from him by General Garlo two months ago, along with Orbaculum.

"Where is the idiot?" a deep voice snarled.

A pair of buckled white boots stopped in front of Toono. A moment later he was kicked in the face.

"What's wrong with you, boy?" the man asked.

Toono crumpled sideways and grabbed his nose. He groaned and mumbled incoherent nonsense as he smeared the blood across his face and eyes.

"Escort Marini to my office, Titus," Garlo instructed.

The journey was long, for Garlo's office was on the opposite end of the palace. They had to return to the Icebound Confluence, then had to pass through a door that led to the military control wing. The long hallway was nearly empty, and most of the candles on the walls were unlit.

Garlo had been silent the entire time—likely from the anger consuming him. Titus said nothing as well, probably out of deference to his senior officer. The only sounds were their footsteps and Toono's sporadic groans.

Toono was guided through a door and placed firmly in a chair. In the brief moment he had to scan through the room, he saw a map of Kindoliya spread across a massive table and a four-poster bed at the far end … but no ancient. He stared down at his knees as he heard Garlo take a seat across the desk with an exasperated sigh. A minute passed with nothing said, and Toono assumed the general was staring at him in disgust, choosing his words carefully before speaking.

"Ashamed to show your face? Embarrassed?"

Toono didn't answer.

"But that's likely my wishful thinking. You're simply too intoxicated to even lift your head."

No answer.

"The princess turns thirty today," Garlo continued. "Our queen is stepping down to allow her daughter to take over that role. It's a day of celebration of our queen's past and princess's future accomplishments. At this very moment, Princess Ropinia is addressing a packed Glacial Hall with her mother by her side, ready to have the Crystal Crown placed on her head." He paused for a deep breath. "And because of you, I'm missing it. This momentous day, and you couldn't care less."

"Tainted day," Toono mumbled.

"What was that?"

"*Tainted* day," he repeated with conviction.

"Well …" Garlo stood up and walked around the desk. His massive fist collided with Toono's jaw, knocking him out of the chair as his hood fell down his back.

Toono lay still on the floor and looked up at the general. Garlo was a built man. His beard was full and a snowy white, connecting with his sideburns and framing his face in a perfect square. His eyes were black and surrounded by tight wrinkles, his nose a tad crooked.

Garlo stared at Toono for a good moment, probably trying to read between the blood and bruises that littered his face. Then realization dawned. "You're that guy from the Diamond Sea," he said, his face turning red. "Your name was—"

Toono cut him off. "You don't know my name," he said with a placid gaze as he pushed himself to his feet. He grabbed a book from the desk and swung it into Garlo's head. The general stumbled sideways a few steps. But he quickly retaliated with a tight jab at Toono's face. Toono casually bent sideways, grabbed Garlo's head, and slammed it into the wooden desk.

The general let out an angry roar and threw a flurry of icicles from his hands. Toono dipped and sidestepped between them. He then dove to the side into a roll to avoid a pillar of ice that shot up from the ground. Mid-roll he saw a staff lying on a long table on the side of the room. It had three holes at the top and a single hole at the bottom—his ancient.

Toono lunged at Garlo, and as the general tried to block the attack up high, Toono ducked low and thrust a sidekick upward into Garlo's sternum. Toono spun on his plant foot and hooked the general's neck with the back of his knee, then slammed him down onto a crystal table, shattering it into pieces.

Toono retrieved Orbaculum as the Still General gagged and wheezed. Flipping the ancient upside down, Toono blew into the bottom hole, creating a domed bubble and trapping Garlo within.

"I am a being of the mind," Toono said. "I rely on information. From books or word of mouth—the source does not matter. When you isolate yourself like Kindoliya has, you put yourself at a disadvantage. You have a frozen, barren sea. That's great. You have a wall that touches the clouds. Fantastic."

Toono walked over to the desk and looked down at the map sprawled across its surface. "You plan where all your guards and soldiers will be stationed and how they rotate week to week, but what good is that if you have nothing to defend against? Your military is a bunch of children playing war against imaginary enemies. And if you did have something to defend against, how would you know?"

Toono looked back at the general, who was slowly regaining his breath. "You wouldn't, and I am proof of this. You thought I was simply a friend of Apoleia's, so you let me go with a little slap on the wrist in the form of taking my weapon away from me. But there's the rub, eh? To think that

Apoleia is a friend of this city. Not only are you blind to the wider world—you can't even smell what's right under your nose.

"But I suppose it's not really your fault. This is what you were born into, which is why I'll allow you to live. Others won't be so fortunate." He returned to the side table and grabbed his five white gems—the Anathallo.

* * *

Olivia sat at a large circular table with her mother inside Glacial Hall. They were the only two who were seated. The rest were either dancing or socializing. The mother and daughter sat in an uncomfortable silence that was thick enough to smother the festivities surrounding them.

The orchestra finally came to a stop, and three dull thuds of a gavel quieted the crowd. Hurried footsteps and the scraping of chair legs replaced the din of conversation as the guests took their seats. Once order was restored, an older woman with a crystal crown stood up from behind the table at the head of the room. Her smile was unpleasant and awkward, as if she had never performed the expression before.

"Today, the eighth of August, 1499, is a momentous one. For 42 years I've led Kindoliya as the Still Queen, and in that time we celebrated our seventh consecutive century of peace. We have prospered in harmony and we stand as rigid as the glacial walls surrounding this city."

The queen glanced down at a younger woman who sat next to her. Olivia thought she looked embarrassed. "These years have been prosperous and peaceful, but time cannot be fought, nor should it. I have grown old, but my daughter has grown into a resilient young woman—the kind our kingdom has always been known for. Today we celebrate transition."

The queen removed her crown and placed it on her daughter's violet hair. "No longer a princess. I give to you Still Queen Ropinia."

What followed was interesting. The men clapped enthusiastically as they rose to their feet. But the women—every single one of them—stayed seated.

"I-I-I'm not sure what to say," Ropinia stammered. "I've known this day was coming for years. However, words still fail me." Her smile became an unreadable line. She scanned the faces of the hall. Her eyes may have lingered in the direction of Olivia and Apoleia's table, forcing Olivia to look at her mother, who wore a demon's smile.

"I've been told I should be excited, but what I feel is unease." The new queen glanced at the former. "My mother calls it anxiety—an emotion very unbefitting of a Stillian … especially a royal. Anyway, there isn't much to say. I promise to maintain this streak of peace, and above all else, I will lead the Still Kingdom with a Stillian woman's mindset …"

Olivia grabbed the ice gavel next to her plate and waited for the cue.

"*No hesitation,*" Ropinia said.

"*No hesitation,*" the women of the hall recited as they rapped their gavel three times in unison.

It was a Stillian tradition that Apoleia had taught to Olivia when she was young. In the Still Kingdom, the core value of any woman was her assertiveness. They were the decision-makers, and lightning quick ones at that. The gavel represented their authority to judge, while the ice symbolized the stability of their unwavering convictions.

Still Queen Ropinia sat down, and murmurs filled the hall again.

That was incredibly boring, Meow Meow thought.

I found Ropinia's discomfort intriguing, Olivia replied. *She regrets a lot.*

She has a murky conscious, but no power to cleanse it.

Male servants weaved through the maze of tables with large serving trays propped on their shoulders. A waiter served Olivia a plate of raw medallions of fish garnished with black and orange caviar.

Olivia's plate was nearly empty when Apoleia excused herself from the table. The others ignored her, having already learned that she wasn't much of a talker.

Olivia kept a keen eye on the head table where the big names dined. There were two empty seats. One belonged to General Garlo, who was being dealt with by Toono. The other was at Salia's side—the woman who just abdicated as queen. Her husband was supposed to occupy that chair. Salia whispered into Ropinia's ear and stood up. Olivia quickly left the hall before Salia could.

Apoleia stood patiently in the lobby, an uncharacteristic calm settled upon her face. She glanced at Olivia through her thick ivory-rimmed glasses with a gentle smile. Her tranquility unnerved Olivia.

"A chapter ends tonight," Apoleia said.

Flanked by two soldiers in blue cloaks, Salia Still strode into the lobby, her lavish purple dress trailing across the powdered ice. She stopped abruptly and looked from side to side.

"Are you going to see him?" Apoleia asked.

Salia hesitated, then said, "To bring him some food, yes. I suppose you would like to visit?"

That strange comforting smile appeared on Apoleia's face again. "I would."

"Very well then," Salia said.

"Can Olivia come?"

"No. Be happy she's here for this."

"Ple—"

"No, Apoleia." And with that firm denial, Salia continued walking without looking back.

"That's fine," Apoleia said to Olivia. "We made alternate plans. You know who to go talk to, baby?"

"Yes."

Apoleia smiled and gave Olivia a kiss on the forehead, then turned around and followed after Salia.

Olivia reentered Glacial Hall and glided toward the head table. With every step more heads turned in wonder as she approached the royal elites with such indifference—or maybe it was Meow Meow that had them baffled. A group of cloaked soldiers stepped in her way at the last row of tables.

"Let her through," a woman commanded.

The men parted, and Olivia stared at who gave the order. The woman wore a crystal crown in her violet hair. Confused eyes followed the young girl as she stopped in front of their queen.

Olivia bowed. "Hello, Queen Ropinia."

Ropinia beamed. For the first time a genuine smile graced her face. "You're beautiful—just like a younger her."

* * *

Toono stepped past Titus and into a section of kitchen, where line cooks were busily reducing sauces and paring fish. He melted in the overwhelming and satisfying heat that nourished his body.

A heavyset lady with thin gray hair encircling her head was already waiting for him. Head Chef Tria Shau made a hurried motion toward the bottom of a large serving cart. Toono crouched and slid in, placing his ancient next to him. He leaned back, mentally preparing himself for what came next.

Tria rapped the cart twice—her signal that Salia and Apoleia were on their way. A third tap would have meant that Olivia was accompanying them. The light from the candles in the kitchen allowed him to make out distorted figures through the tablecloth.

Soon the cart's wheels began to roll. Toono smacked his head as they hit a bump exiting the kitchen. As he rubbed his skull, the chef said, "We'll be meeting Lady Salia and Lady Apoleia in the Icebound Confluence."

"And how long will that take?" Toono replied from underneath the cart.

"This area of the palace is not easily traversable by anything with wheels, so it'll take a few minutes longer."

"We're sure she won't check under this thing?"

"She never has, so I doubt she'll start now. She has always trusted me. Lady Salia believes she is the only one who knows what she's hidden. Meanwhile Titus and I have had to live with knowing the truth."

The cart rolled along the floor for a few minutes.

"We never thought she'd come back," Tria muttered. "I admire the fact that she did."

Toono sighed and gripped the gems in his pocket. Eventually he heard a door open and a blast of even colder air pierced his skin like daggers. They had reached the open-aired Icebound Confluence.

"Good evening, Lady Salia," Tria said.

"It feels strange not being addressed as Queen anymore."

"A welcome strange, milady?" Tria asked.

"Give it a few more hours to settle in."

Toono realized he was unnecessarily holding his breath. He tucked his chin into his chest and breathed into his cloak. He didn't want the steam to expose him.

"Hello, Tria." Toono recognized Apoleia's shaky voice.

"Good evening, Apoleia."

"Don't use that name!" Salia hissed.

"My mistake, milady."

That lit a fire under Toono's skin. The nerve of that wretched woman to strip Apoleia of her name. The cart pushed off again.

"How is the husband doing?" Tria asked. "I see he still has his appetite."

"He hasn't left his bed in four days," Salia said. "Won't even get in his wheelchair and explore the halls." There was a chill to her voice that could have made any Stillian tremble.

Eventually a loud noise jarred Toono from his anxious thoughts. The cart rattled as a body fell against it. Apoleia and Salia grunted and breathed heavily as they wrestled. They had arrived at the painting in the hall that Olivia had repeatedly circled on their map.

"What are you doing?" Salia panted. Toono peeked out the tablecloth.

"Look at this painting!" Apoleia screamed as she slammed the woman's face into the artwork. "How many times has he silently rolled past here, struggling with the memories of his loss?"

"Loss of what?" Salia replied. "A woman with no strength?"

Apoleia swung open the painting, grabbed Salia by the throat, and thrust her through the wooden trapdoor. "No strength!" she screamed, but it ended with a weak quiver. "Look at you."

Salia lay on her back, eyes glued to Apoleia as she spewed venom: "In a kingdom of 'strong' women, it took a *man* to fight for me on that day! He sacrificed his body and voice!"

"To do what, exactly?" Salia asked. "To lose to the man who embarrassed you."

Apoleia's voice softened. "*Embarrassed* … that's the word you choose?"

Salia sighed. "You've lost your mind. This is clear." She nodded at Apoleia's bandaged wrists. "I suppose you're covering those for a reason."

Apoleia unraveled the cloths on her wrists and let them fall to the floor. Her fresh cuts bled the moment the pressure was relieved. She brought one wrist to her mouth as she stepped forward. She stood over the former Still Queen and spat a mouthful of blood into her face.

Salia scowled—her face had been impassive until then. "You don't even know who you're mad at."

"Many people," Apoleia whispered, leaning in close with a smile of bloodstained teeth. "My dignity was stripped from me. My place in this world was taken too. That was your fault, for you shunned me. By doing nothing, you did everything."

"Then kill me, and take away my place in this world."

"Gladly," said a deeper voice. Toono was leaning against the doorjamb with his hands folded.

Apoleia stepped to the side, and Salia's focus shifted to Toono. Her eyes narrowed.

"Go to him," Toono said. "It's been a long time since he's had a meal with you."

Apoleia took a few steps toward the exit, then turned and kicked Salia in the jaw before rushing out the door.

He stared at Salia for a while before stepping closer. "You will make this easy?" he asked.

"I have lived long enough."

"Longer than you deserve."

"And what do you have to gain from this?" she asked.

"You're another rung on the ladder to my goal."

"Just like a man to fight for such reasons," Salia sneered.

Toono drew his blade. "Coming from you, such an accusation holds no weight."

*   *   *

Olivia was sitting in Lady Salia's chair as Queen Ropinia held a pleasant conversation with her.

"Where is your mother? I saw her earlier." Ropinia paused, then looked to her left. "Matter of fact, where's General Garlo?"

Olivia changed the subject as she emptily stared into the distance. "I want to warn you."

The queen slowly stopped chewing her food. "Of what?"

Cries of horror and panic echoed through the room as the music came to an abrupt halt. A hooded man in a blue soldier's cloak stood at the doorway with a strange staff strapped to his back. In front of him, bloody and limp, lay the former Stillian Queen.

17
Summer's End

The classroom hollowed around Bryson as its depths were enveloped in suffocating shadows and distant screams. Steam puffed from his mouth as he took rattled breaths. He looked to his right to see Agnos seated at a desk with his attention toward the front of the room, where Senex stood on a stool in the lone patch of light. The diminutive Archaic Director was pointing at foreign characters on the chalkboard. His mouth was moving, but no sound came out. The same went for Agnos.

Bryson tried to stand but some inexplicable force kept him glued to his seat. He wanted to wake up but was trapped in this horrible dream. He glanced back at Agnos and was shocked to see his fellow Jestivan staring dead at him. That was a first. Agnos's lips continued to move as he stared at Bryson.

Then Bryson realized that Agnos was looking through him. He turned to his left to see a new face. He was shaved bald, his dark bronze scalp shining as if it had been polished. A tune was being hummed from the darkest reaches of the classroom. He strained to make it out, and then a piercing scream jerked him into the real world …

Bryson stared at the ceiling of his Lilac Suites' dorm room. The moonlight through the window splashed his room in a bluish hue. He wasn't panicked or scared, but he was covered in a dripping cold sweat. He couldn't do this anymore. He needed answers, and he knew exactly who to go to.

*   *   *

The following morning the Lilac Suites were bustling with staff as they prepared for the start of the new school year, which was two days away. Bryson sat at the piano next to the indoor waterfall that crashed into a pond. He eyed the keys, mentally playing his favorite song in his head: "Phases of S." He thought of how Debo would laugh when he saw Bryson obsessing over the same song as always.

Bryson heard familiar voices and looked up from the keys. Agnos, Tashami, and Lilu were walking down the final flight of stairs and into the lobby. They had mostly recovered since returning from the Void. Lilu had dyed the gray out of her hair, but faint wrinkles still lined her face. The other two showed the same wear on their faces, and Agnos's hair was streaked with gray. Tashami's hair—already a natural white—remained unchanged.

The trio walked across the lobby toward the door. "Wait, guys!" Bryson called as he jogged after them.

"Don't call me that," Lilu snapped.

"Hello, Lilu," Bryson replied in a snarky tone. They were still on bad terms, but Bryson found himself caring less and less. He was no less petty than her—as much as he hated to admit it.

"Morning, Bryson," Tashami said. "We're heading to Dinny's for breakfast. Wanna come?"

The bell above the front door chimed as Lilu stormed out.

"Thanks," Bryson said, "but I actually wanted to speak with Agnos for a minute."

"I'll catch up," Agnos said. "Order me an omelet."

Bryson and Agnos found a table farthest away from the other students. "How are you?" Agnos asked as he sat across from Bryson.

"Better, now that this boring summer is almost over."

Agnos smirked. "Isn't today your birth—"

"Stop," Bryson interrupted. Agnos looked hurt. "Sorry. I usually spend today with Olivia."

"Well that's understandable," Agnos replied. He looked down at Bryson's hands. "What is it you need help with?"

Bryson followed Agnos's gaze and saw that his hands were balled into fists. "Interpreting a reoccurring dream. I'm assuming you've read a book about dreams before."

Agnos chuckled. "I've read about almost everything. Describe the dream."

"You're in it."

"And what am I doing?"

"We're in a classroom, and you're sitting at a desk next to me, facing the front of the room and mouthing something."

Agnos put his hand to his face and looked out the window toward Wealth's Crossroads. "What else is happening?"

Bryson explained every facet of the dream he could remember—Archaic Director Senex, the foreign characters on the chalkboard, and the shadows and screams. As he did, he felt as if he was leaving something out.

"And when did you start having this dream?" Agnos asked.

Bryson leaned forward. "After Thusia told me a story about my dad," he said in a low voice. "How he attended a philosophy class."

"Okay, that makes more sense," Agnos said. "You're probably experiencing an event that Mendac lived through, but altered in a way that places people you know into the setting … but that's simply speculation. I'm going to require more information."

"But I gave you a lot."

"You gave me key points," Agnos said, matter of fact. "I'm going to need finer details. This is what you're going to do for me. From now on, every time you find yourself in that dream, you will ignore mine and Director Senex's presence. Focus on the characters on the chalkboard instead. I need you to memorize them."

"That's a tall task," Bryson said with a glum look.

"I understand that. But they're more than likely the most important aspect of the dream. Concentrate on a few of them at a time, and write them down as soon as you wake up. When you're done, I'll interpret them with my relic."

"At least it's a plan," Bryson said.

"And one more thing. Observe the details of the classroom. See if anything stands out—maybe I can figure out which room it is."

"Thank you, Agnos."

Agnos smiled and stood up. "Olivia always speaks highly of you, so I'm looking forward to this arrangement. Have an ethical day."

*　　*　　*

Rhyparia stared into the wrinkled eyes of Archaic Director Senex. It was weird to see him from this angle, as she was used to staring down at the top of his balding head.

Senex smirked. "Can you put me down?"

The director was swallowed up in the grass, which was taller than him. Rhyparia giggled as a path formed in the grass until Senex's head popped into view.

"Very funny, Lita Rhyparia," he said from his stepstool. "This has been a successful two months. You should be proud of yourself. You've learned more about weaving than I had intended to teach you."

"Thank you for everything, Director," Rhyparia said.

He gave a slight nod. "My pleasure. I know you're a good person and I want to make sure the world can see that." He sniffed the air and smiled. "My wife is cooking up something fantastic. Let's head back to the cabin. We'll pack tonight and depart to Phesaw in the morning."

The meadow swallowed Senex once again as he jumped off his stool. Rhyparia watched him walk in the opposite direction until he stopped and called back: "Lita Rhyparia, let's go. You don't keep a renowned chef waiting. Cold food is upsetting to—"

Rhyparia jumped and soared into the air, high above the gentle hills of prairie grass. A gradient of greens rolled east like the waves of the sea as the winds blew through the field. Archaic Director Senex was certainly down there somewhere, looking up at Rhyparia in amusement as she soared above him.

Forests, towns, and farms sat in the distance. As she climbed higher, she could even spot the Archaic Mountains, which looked more like anthills from her vantage point. She could see the desert surrounding the vast prairie. She released the most euphoric laugh of her life as a flock of birds ascended from the field below and joined her in flight. There were moments when she felt like she had wings instead of the umbrella that she held in her hand. The only thing stopping her was herself, and she was thrilled with the control she hadn't possessed until this summer.

She glanced below her and saw the cabin. With an abrupt halt to her flight, she dropped into a free-fall. Panic briefly overwhelmed her, but she quickly gained control of her descent. She landed on the roof with her legs dangling off the side. She watched as Director Senex carved a path through the prairie grass, hurrying home for dinner. She couldn't wait to see everyone at Phesaw again.

*　　*　　*

Dust kicked into the air as Intel Major Lars strolled through the streets of one of the poorer sectors of Rim. Homes and shops were sewn together on both sides of the narrow road to form two long walls of wooden buildings. People were dressed in cheap clothes, and many of them were barefooted. As he turned a corner, he saw a long line of people leading to a pipe that jutted from the ground. Each of them carried a bucket or two in hopes of getting water before the day's rations depleted. That pipe was the lone source of clean water—or what Lars hoped to be clean—in this sector. Only a few blocks around the mayor's building enjoyed the luxury of plumbing.

Lars was dressed in a stained green cloak, having shed his military attire for this incognito mission. He stepped through a door with a sign above it that simply read BAR. Few businesses in Rim were even legally registered. These were straightforward and simple people with not much in their pockets.

The barroom was mostly empty. A pair of seasoned men sat at a table, their conversation too low to be heard. A man in alarmingly short shorts stood off to the side of the bar with a pipe in his hand, his shirt unbuttoned to his navel, revealing the bronze glow of his chest. This seemed like an odd time of day to seek business of pleasure. The barkeep, an elderly man with pure white hair, was dusting off counters.

"Good morning!" he shouted with a smile.

Lars nodded and headed to a table in the corner, far away from everyone else. As he waited there was a commotion in the street. He glanced out the window across the room and saw two adolescent boys throwing wild punches. He was happy to see a pair of Intel soldiers step in and carefully separate them. One of the boys spat at the feet of a soldier. Lars closed his eyes with a sigh.

The door opened, and a man and woman walked in. The man was feeble and skinny. The woman, short and round.

"Mr. and Mrs. NuForce," Lars said as he gestured for them to take a seat. "How are you?"

"I'm not sure," the woman replied.

Mr. NuForce seemed fidgety. "What about you?" Lars asked.

"Nervous."

"There is no reason to worry," Lars said. "Itta is no longer the Archaic King. You're free to speak without the fear of losing your life."

Mr. NuForce straightened up and took a deep breath. "What is it you want to know, exactly?"

Lars reached into his cloak and withdrew a piece of parchment, a quill, and a bottle of ink. As he slid the materials across the table, he said, "I need you to write down the truth about what flattened the sector of Olethros."

Mrs. NuForce looked from the parchment to Lars with a frown. "Not what. *Who.*"

* * *

The capital of Fiamma was a beautifully manicured city in the northwestern corner of the Passion Kingdom. Its buildings were each individual works of art and pleasantly spaced to allow in sunlight at all times of the day. Abstract in shape, they rose in fans at different angles and in multicolored curves, with parks and gardens at their feet. At the center of the city lay Jarfait Meadow—one of the twelve must-see landmarks of the Light Realm, known for its imaginative and harmonious landscaping, and the intricate structures of limestone overlooking its perimeter. The tallest structure in Fiamma stood at its center: an enormous cylindrical pillar of stone that held the Great Flame—an eternal inferno that nearly dwarfed the edifice it sat upon. Even during the night hours, the fire cast a soft, flickering light on the capital.

Toono stared in awe at the blazing fire as he walked through the nighttime park. As always, a bandage encircled the top of his head, but he wore a top hat, vest, and pants all made of silk. A full brown beard and mustache had replaced his typical clean-shaven look, and a pair of wire spectacles sat high on his nose. Then there was the gigantic suitcase he lugged by his side, filled with a few books and Orbaculum. It was more like a costume than a disguise.

He threw the case on a bench and plopped down next to it. A few minutes later, two guests joined him.

He smiled. "Kadlest, Illipsia … I've missed you."

Kadlest laughed. "Who are you? Since when did the boy become a man?"

Toono shook his head. "I'm 24, Kadlest."

"Happy late birthday," Illipsia murmured.

"Thank you." He had celebrated his birthday with Olivia at the Frostbite in Kindoliya. He smirked, recalling Olivia smashing her slice of ice cream cake into Meow Meow's furry face after he'd tried to lick it.

"I assume everything was a success?" Kadlest asked as she took a seat next to Toono.

"Mission accomplished," he replied. "A little rough at the teleplatforms, but Apoleia made quick work of the few soldiers who were brave enough to fight her."

"I see you don't have it with you. Did you let her keep it?"

Toono closed his eyes. "The Still Kingdom was the first half of my agreement with Apoleia. I'll get it when we initiate phase two. But first I must attend to business here. How has the scouting gone?"

"Very well," Kadlest said. "The Light Realm kingdoms have been on high alert the past few months, so security has been impressive—especially here in the capital. But Illipsia and I have managed to spot weaknesses. We can show you them in the upcoming days, then devise a plan of attack."

"Illipsia will show me nothing," Toono said as he glanced down at the young girl, who was absentmindedly picking grass. "She returns to Phesaw for the start of the new school year. I want you to escort her to the teleplatforms tomorrow morning. Then you can return to Fiamma, and the two of us will proceed with our business here."

"I get to see Simon?" Illipsia asked.

"Yes, and you will use him to keep tabs on the Jestivan. Then when winter comes, you will return to the Passion Kingdom with what you've learned."

Kadlest titled her head. "Why not just have Olivia do this for you?"

Toono waved off the idea. "I can't."

"Oh. She doesn't know that there are two parts to the agreement. Quite deceitful, Toono."

"Don't remind me." He rose from the bench and groaned as he stretched. "I will need to contact Storshae tonight, so find us somewhere private."

"That's the one thing I didn't miss while you were away. I despise that man."

"I hate him too." Toono picked up his case, and Kadlest and Illipsia flanked him as he started down the path. "But he's important. His connections with King Itta and the Amendment Order Chiefs are vital avenues of information."

The trio walked in silence for the rest of the way. The summer heat was smoldering, even with the sun well into its sleep. The Great Flame attributed to that. With three sacrifices down, Toono was now focused on the fourth. He looked toward a castle that loomed above the rest of the city. Toono had three options: Passion King Damian or one of his two sons. But could he actually find his way through those walls?

18
First Exam

Bryson stood in his room in Lilac Suites, staring out the window toward Telejunction and the massive hill it sat upon. Thousands upon thousands of students swarmed down the hill as they returned from their vacations. Bryson caught himself smiling. Olivia was somewhere in that mass of people. It had been a long three months since he had seen his best friend.

But it wasn't just that. The team would finally be together again. Rhyparia would be returning today with Archaic Director Senex. Then there were Jilly, Toshik, and Himitsu.

Bryson grabbed his jacket off the back of his chair and left the room. His trip to the school's main building was relaxing and unobstructed, for most of the traffic was coming from the other side of the building. Even with the sun bearing down on him, he felt cold, yet he refrained from throwing his hood over his head. He had broken that habit for the most part. He was surrounded by great friends who lifted him up, and he had little desire to hide himself from the world.

As Bryson joined the tangled throng of students filing through the main doors of Phesaw, he received pats on the back and enthusiastic greetings. He smiled and returned the love to as many people as he could.

Bryson thought back to how different it had been when he returned to school on the first day of last year. Back then he had been ignored, or ridiculed for being Mendac LeAnce's failure of a child.

He decided to find a seat in the auditorium for the opening ceremony. Instead of secluding himself at the top of the stands, he sat near the front. Whispers of admiration surrounded him until the Intelights cut out. The center stage shined bright under the lone window in the ceiling.

Then it hit him. How could he have forgotten? As the directors took their places, Bryson stared at the empty podium, picturing the short rustled brown hair and gold ear piercings. Debo had always been able to pinpoint Bryson out of the crowd and give him a warming smile. Bryson threw his hood over his head and stared into nothing as Poicus addressed the audience.

"Phesaw is down a family member. His stay here was short—roughly nine years. But in that time he left such lasting impressions on anyone who attended school or worked here. Debo was a sarcastic, quick-tongued comedian who could assert his authority at the flip of a coin. The other Energy Directors even claim that he was the most skilled of their ranks."

Bryson snorted. Of course Debo was the most skilled. He was a Pogu, the second tier of the Bozani's hierarchy, right above a Branian such as Thusia.

"No one would be able to replace Debo in our hearts, but we were extremely lucky to find someone whose talents are worthy of an Intel Director. Without further ado I welcome one of Kuki Sphaira's top weavers, Nyemas Jugtah."

The students applauded as the floor opened up and a new presence appeared. He was a pudgy man with olive skin and thinning black and gray hair. He was of average height, and he wore a pair of gaudy gold glasses.

Poicus moved on to the steep increase in security. Telejunction was to be heavily monitored at all times by no less than twenty skilled soldiers from each of the five light kingdoms. He made sure to assure the students of their safety. At the end of the hour-long ceremony Poicus finally discussed news worth sitting up for.

"A year ago we instituted the second coming of the Jestivan. The directors decided to form this elite group for several reasons, but one was more important than the rest. Older minds are stuck in their ways, but the youth can still be molded. In the Dark Realm, the central school of Ipsas formed an elite group of students—much like the Jestivan—called the Diatia. The Jestivan and Diatia weren't created to counter each other, like a cynical mind would think. They were intended to complement each other."

A flurry of whispered conversations swept through the auditorium like steam escaping from a kettle. This was the first the students had heard of the Diatia. Bryson had learned of them from Agnos, who said that Toono killed a Diatia named Chelekah. But he had always assumed that they were their enemies.

"This was going to be a historic year for Phesaw," Poicus continued. "Alas, with the recent turmoil across the Dark Realm, our plans had to be cut back significantly. Instead of hosting all ten Diatia, we will welcome two. They hail from the Power Kingdom."

The murmurs grew into a hum. The Grand Director paused and waited for the noise to dwindle. "I'll allow you all to leave after this final note, for I fear your mouths won't be able to rest upon hearing it: Phesaw will hold an elimination tournament during the second semester. The combatants will be the ten Jestivan and two visiting Diatia, featuring one-on-one battles of raw skill."

But instead of erupting, the students were shocked into silence. Poicus's smile grew wider. "It will be a fun year. Good day."

Bryson waited for the others to filter out of the auditorium as he sat lost in thought about the glory this new opportunity might bring.

Most of the students would be heading to their first class, but Bryson hadn't made his schedule yet. Princess Shelly had convinced him to take a couple classes on weaving, but beyond that his plans were vague.

As Bryson headed out the towering front doors, someone said his name. He turned to see the new Intel Director seated on a bench near one of the windows that stretched from the floor to the ceiling, his ridiculous golden glasses reflecting the sun. Backtracking through the flowing crowds of students, Bryson approached the director and stopped a comfortable distance away.

"Hello, Director …" Bryson trailed off.

The man's thin lips were rigid and his eyes were cold. For being an older man, his skin seemed strangely smooth, and Bryson suspected that he didn't even need to shave.

"I'm going to need you to remember my name," the director said. His nasally annunciation was precise, as if his tongue wrapped around each letter. "You look just like him," he added.

"So I've heard, sir," Bryson replied.

The director retrieved a sheet of parchment from his cloak and handed it to Bryson. "I took the liberty of enrolling you in a weaving class before it filled up. It's basic level, nothing major. I won't be teaching it or anything."

"Directors don't teach students regardless, sir," Bryson pointed out.

The Intel Director's lips twitched. "I do things differently. If I'm not going to be experimenting in Brilliance, then I'll spend my time teaching at Phesaw. I prefer to train the mind in some way. I've noticed that the Energy Directors seem more like administrators, which I will not be."

"What will you teach?"

"Permanence."

Bryson thought for something to say. "Never heard of it," he finally admitted.

"I'm introducing the subject to Phesaw. Permanence is all around you—you just don't notice it. It's a major focus of research in Brilliance."

"I see," Bryson replied.

"When you prove you're ready for such a class, I'll make room for you. In the meantime, do try to remember my name."

As Bryson watched the man walk away, someone tapped his shoulder. "It's Director Jugtah," Simon said.

Bryson smiled. "Thanks, buddy." He rustled the boy's hair. "Speaking of names—" he nodded to the girl with her hair wrapped around her wrists—"what was yours again?"

"Illipsia," she said.

"That's right! Good to see you again. Your hair is so long."

"I've never cut it," she replied. "People tend to step on it."

"What classes are you off to?" Bryson asked.

"Agricultural science," Simon groaned. "Father makes me take it every year."

"Same," Illipsia said.

Bryson laughed. "Well have fun with that. I have to go register for—" He paused as he glanced down at the parchment that the director had given him. He hadn't registered Bryson for just one class; he had made his entire schedule.

"I'll see you later guys," he said, giving one last rustle of Simon's red hair. He headed to first period, which was in the depths of the school's Knowledge Wing. Debo had always made his schedule, and though he wasn't angry with the new director—Jugtah—he did feel a bit snubbed. He had been looking forward to choosing his classes on his own. At least Jugtah had thoughtfully included a music class.

Anxiety crept up the back of Bryson's neck as he approached his classroom. He was seventeen years old and a Jestivan, yet he was about to walk into a novice-level course with almost no experience in the subject. Children's faces turned to him as he stopped in the doorway.

"Ah, Zana Bryson, you're in the right class," the teacher said. "Take a seat." Her voice had the bright and cheerful lilt that adults used when they spoke to toddlers.

Kill me now. Bryson chose a desk in the back of the classroom, and chairs groaned as the other students twisted in their seats to stare at him.

"Welcome to Introduction to Weaving: The History. I am Professor Warwig. A little about me ..."

Bryson zoned out while the professor droned on about her personal background. Instead of Intelights, candles on the walls fought back the windowless gloom. Most of the class was spent introducing the students. One by one, they would stand up and give a little spiel about their hobbies and whatnot.

"All right students. We'll finish the first day of class off with something brief. Remember to take notes. I hope you came prepared."

Bryson snapped out of his trance and focused on the chalkboard as Professor Warwig drew a long wavy line.

"Does anyone know what this is?" she asked.

"Spirit Energy," a girl said.

The professor smiled. "Exactly! Gentle, organic, and fluid." She drew a second line beneath the previous one. This time the line was straight and thick. "I don't expect you to know this one, but I'll be impressed if someone does. How about it?"

Bryson didn't have a clue. Shelly had only touched on Spirit, Intel, and Adrenergy.

"We'll come back to this one," Warwig said after a prolonged silence. She drew another straight line, slashing across the board with the chalk.

"That's Adrenergy," a boy said.

"Great job!" Warwig beamed. "Quick, offensive, unwavering." She pointed at the unnamed line. "This is Still Energy. I didn't expect you to know it because it's a Dark Realm kingdom's energy. I just wanted to see if I'd have any outliers in the class this year."

Bryson closed his eyes. He wasn't even good enough to stand out from a group of twelve-year-olds. Well, that in itself made him an outlier.

"But we're here to learn about a specific energy, obviously," Warwig said while drawing a zigzagging line with harsh angles. "Intel Energy is one of the most rewarding energies for weaving. The most talented professional weavers of Brilliance aren't even sure of its limits. This year we will learn the history of weaving. We'll cover the entire Known History timeline and—"

The bell rang and the students leapt from their seats.

"Have a good day, everyone! The real learning starts on Wednesday!"

Bryson slung his bag over his shoulder and headed toward the door.

"Zana Bryson."

"Yes, Professor?"

She waited for the room to completely empty out before she spoke. "You seem displeased."

He stared at her for a moment, trying to phrase his next words without coming off as a jerk. "So we're not going to actually learn anything about the process of weaving in this class?"

"I'm afraid not."

"I just expected to …"

"Learn something useful?" Professor Warwig finished his sentence for him. "Director Jugtah constructed your schedule the way he did for a reason. If you have a problem with it, talk to him about it."

"Where is he?" Bryson asked.

She seemed taken aback. "He's on the third floor of the wing's B-sector."

"Thanks, Professor."

Bryson bolted out of the room. When he reached the Intel Director's classroom, students from first period were still lingering at Jugtah's desk. Bryson leaned against the wall and waited. His next class wasn't for another couple hours, so he had time to spare.

An unexpected face walked out of the room. It was Lilu, and she had a tulip pinned to her green bangs. She stopped and eyed him with surprise.

"You're in his class?" Bryson asked, trying to mask the bitterness in his voice.

"Yes. You sound shocked." She glanced at the schedule in his hand. "Introduction to Weaving … cute." Then she strutted down the hall with that annoyingly smug posture of hers.

When the room finally emptied, Bryson walked in. "Director Jugtah."

The director briefly glanced up before refocusing on a stack of parchment in front of him. "The great LeAnce has remembered my name," he teased.

"How is the history of weaving supposed to teach me the technical aspects of it?"

The Intel Director continued marking papers with red ink. "It doesn't."

Bryson stared at the olive-skinned man, waiting for an elaboration. "Then what's the point?" he asked when he realized he wasn't going to get one.

Jugtah dipped his quill in the inkbottle and stared at Bryson through his gold-rimmed glasses. "Because we don't cut corners. I don't care if you're a Jestivan or the son of Mendac LeAnce. The curriculum requires all students to take Introduction to Weaving as a prerequisite for any other weaving classes. If you aren't fond of this reality, by all means withdraw from the class."

"I'm—"

"However," Jugtah cut him off, "you should probably take a proper look at your schedule first, which you should have done before you confronted me in the first place."

Bryson looked down at the parchment. "The Science of Weaving."

"It's the only weaving class a student is allowed to take concurrently with the introduction," Director Jugtah said as he put quill to paper again. "You'll learn how different inventions tick, such as Intelights."

"I'm sorry, sir," said Bryson, red-faced.

The day progressed routinely. Bryson had lunch in the Knowledge Wing's dining hall before attending The Craft of Maneuver Tactics. He actually liked the class. It focused on preparing and executing tactical procedures to successfully obtain a goal in anything such as war scenarios, assassination attempts, thefts, or daring escapes of highly secure locations.

Some were sillier. In today's lesson, the professor had each student make their way from one end of Phesaw to the other without being spotted by classmates, who were each stationed at different locations throughout the school. Bryson loved every bit of it and saw it as an opportunity to learn some procedures he could use one day with his fellow Jestivan.

With Introduction to Weaving and The Craft of Tactics on Monday, Wednesday, and Friday, and The Science of Weaving and Master Musicians on Tuesday and Thursday, Bryson was content with the lineup—and a little bit embarrassed that he had complained to Director Jugtah.

He exited the school and headed toward the pink canopies of Phesaw Park. While the other students went to find their third and final class of the day, the Jestivan had training sessions with their specific Energy Director. But today they were to meet in the park's clearing as a group.

Bryson's heart raced when the trees parted to reveal a familiar kitten hat atop flowing violet hair. He sprinted at Olivia at his top speed percentage—a potentially reckless decision—and squeezed her half to death. She didn't smile, but that was Olivia.

"Hello, Bry."

"I'm so happy to see you!" He gazed at Meow Meow, who was pretending to be distracted by a butterfly. "And that includes this little guy!" Bryson said as he rustled the kitten's fur.

Meow Meow frowned. "Welp, the timespan of me being content with your existence lasted a good ten seconds."

Bryson laughed. "You're safe," he said to Olivia. "Grand Director Poicus said there were reports that Toono was pursuing you. He even sent Director Venustas. When she came back without you, I thought the worst."

Olivia stared blankly for a few seconds. "I spent my summer like any other: helping my mother."

Sensing her reticence on the subject, Bryson looked around to see who else was there. All the Jestivan were mingling in a huddled mess, talking over each other as they caught up.

Rhyparia was the first to hug him when he walked over. Compared to everyone else, it had been the longest since he had last seen her.

"How are you, Bryson?" she asked.

"Beyond elated now that everyone is together again. How'd your training go?"

She beamed. "I can't wait to show you what I can do now."

Rhyparia still wore her burgundy bandana, and the same sandy brown bangs swept over one of her green eyes. But the shakiness in her voice had been replaced by a happy self-confidence.

"Guess what," Rhyparia asked.

"What?"

"Lilu said hi to me." Shocked, Bryson glanced at Lilu, who was talking to Himitsu and Toshik. "She seemed a bit uncomfortable, but I could tell she was really trying."

Bryson felt conflicted. On one hand, he was happy that his message had gotten through to Lilu. But instead of accepting that she was wrong, she took it out on him. It was kind of childish, but he was happy for Rhyparia.

Himitsu caught Bryson's eye and stepped away from Lilu and Toshik. "Hey, buddy," he said as he reached in for a quick hug.

"You have fun in the Archaic Kingdom?" Bryson asked.

"It was amazing actually. Spent the past couple months in Phelos, which was a nice recovery from the Oaks."

"I've never heard anyone describe Phelos as nice."

"It depends where you stay," Rhyparia said. "Most Archaic Kingdom cities are like that: the epicenters are unfathomably wealthy while the rest crumbles to pieces."

"Yeah I didn't venture too far from the palace," Himitsu agreed. He leaned in and lowered his voice: "Toshik and Jilly were inseparable, and not in that insufferable way where Toshik goes on about her being his Charge … I think they're dating."

Bryson laughed.

"You lie," Rhyparia said.

"Believe what you want," Himitsu said with a sly smile.

"Are you guys excited to make new friends?" Jilly asked as she ran over.

"Hey, Jilly," Bryson said. "What new friends?"

"The Diarrhea."

Himitsu and Bryson folded over with laughter. Even Rhyparia laughed.

"The Diatia, Jilly," Bryson said.

"Yeah, that." She giggled and covered her mouth. "Do you think they'll be nice?"

"I think so," Bryson said. "The directors wouldn't have invited them if they were a threat. Is that Yama's sword?"

"Mm-hmm. She let me borrow it. Called me a great warrior."

"I don't recall saying any of that." Yama had crept up behind Jilly. "Nor do I recall lending you my sword. Hand it over."

Jilly unbuckled the sword from her waist and returned it to Yama. "You know I can beat you now?"

Yama looked amused. "Where did this newfound foolery spawn from?"

"Toshik taught me how to fight in Phelos," Jilly bragged.

Yama frowned. "What happened to the whole 'I'll protect you until the day I die' spiel?"

"He just believes in me now."

Yama's eyes narrowed, and Bryson understood why. Toshik was up to something.

Yama went to leave, but instead she raised her sword and thrust it into a blocking motion as the sound of metal against metal pierced the air. She twirled and slashed her blade downward with another sharp clash.

Bryson was one of the few who could see what was happening—and even he only made out a blur. Toshik was next to draw his sword and fend off an attack. Bryson followed the streak of silver that was attacking the two Adrenians. Was that Director Buredo?

Soon other distractions appeared. The Jestivans' feet slid through the grass as they were tugged in the same direction. Bryson spun to see a menacing twister of gray clouds contorting the surrounding atmosphere. What in the world was happening?

Bryson and the rest of the Jestivan ran away from the towering tornado as it lashed out wind and rain. Then several blasts of fire surged toward Himitsu and Olivia. Himitsu threw a trail of black flames back in the direction of the mystery assailants. Olivia, who was well ahead of the pack, picked up more speed as her calves and thighs bulged with each planted foot.

A crack of lightning struck ground directly in front of Bryson, and he stumbled backward. Then another bolt materialized to his right, followed by a clap of thunder that shook the organs in his chest. This was even more terrifying than the Generals' Battle.

Bryson sprinted as best as he could while the winds tried to rip his feet from the ground. Yama and Toshik were fighting as a pair, as were Olivia and Himitsu. Tashami and Jilly simply ran.

Then there was Agnos. He stood still with knees locked and torso low to brace himself against the twister's suction. Then he was ripped from the field, his body flailing as the gales from the twister's torque swallowed him whole.

A shout of anguish escaped Bryson. As he turned back to give chase, someone grabbed his wrist.

"He'll be fine!" Lilu shouted over the thunder and wind. "Rhyparia's got him!"

Bryson hesitated, then followed Lilu to the clearing's edge, where the weather was normal. The Jestivan gasped and heaved. Some slumped against trees. Some stood with their hands on their knees. Others simply lay on their backs in the grass. Rhyparia and Agnos were still missing.

"You said to trust her," Bryson panted.

"Look up," Lilu said.

Rhyparia was fluttering down from above with her umbrella in one hand and Agnos under her other arm.

She smiled as her feet finally reached ground. "That was fun."

Nobody replied. Even Jilly was speechless. It took someone else's voice to break the silence: "A year ago most of you wouldn't have survived that."

Grand Director Poicus twirled the tails of his eyebrows. "That was your first exam of the year." He grinned. "You passed."

19
Peg Course

Several buildings surrounded the roundabout of Wealth's Crossroads. There were Lilac Suites, the lavish dorm building that sat at the head of everything; Tabby's Gift Shop, Jilly's favorite building in the whole wide world; Dinny Diner, a popular hangout, especially at breakfast; Talonbrew, a bar for the older students and staff; and the Golden Gobbler, the fanciest restaurant in Phesaw. Reservations had to be made at least two weeks in advance—unless you were a Jestivan, who had a table reserved for them at all times. Most of them refrained from using it, disapproving of the favoritism.

On the third Friday night of the school year, two beautiful young women sat at a small table nestled between many others. Their conversation was drowned out by the enthusiastic couples nearby, the scraping of silverware and occasional laughter.

The girl with violet hair and amber eyes wore a sleeveless gray dress. Her lipstick was a deep red. She took a bite out of her steak and stared at her dinner partner, whose face was contorted with disgust. "Something wrong?" she asked mid-chew.

"That's so nasty!" her companion shrieked. "The blood is dripping on the plate!"

Yama smirked as she ran a slice of bread across the red juice. She slurped it slowly and winked. "Mmm …"

"I hate youuuuuu," Jilly whined, followed by gagging noises.

"Not all of us can get by on chicken tenders," Yama said with a wry smile.

Jilly picked one up and wiggled it between her fingers. "I prefer something gummy." She tossed the chicken into her mouth. "And sugary too!" Her mouth dropped open—a mash of chicken and breading visible on her tongue—as she was distracted by a slice of chocolate cake being carried by a waiter.

Yama's face went still as she took a moment to compose herself. "What is this, Jilly?"

"What is what?" Jilly asked, her head swiveling as she visually followed the chocolate cake.

"Are we enjoying each other's company or is this a date? We never seemed to clarify what we were doing last year."

Jilly fell silent, something only Yama was capable of making her do. "We're friends, Yama."

"Friends don't kiss."

Jilly blushed. "I was confused … I think. There were a lot of things we did that felt wrong."

"That's your father's influence."

"No." Jilly answered quickly. Then she looked down at her last chicken tender. "I don't know what's right," she mumbled. "I just know that I don't want to feel like a bad person."

"You're not a bad person," Yama assured her.

Jilly smiled. "Thanks!"

"So what about Toshik? I heard you spent a lot of time with him over the summer."

"I like Toshik."

"You like me. What's the difference?"

"My father likes Toshik."

Yama's face went white. The two girls gazed at each other—Yama, ready to set the building on fire; Jilly, ready to douse that fire with tears. With a death grip on the handle of her steak knife, Yama swung it through her glass of wine, cleanly slicing it in half. "Think for yourself," she said, kicking back her chair and storming out of the restaurant.

* * *

The cobblestone streets of Wealth's Crossroads bathed in the many Intelights bordering its path. Windows glowed gold as people celebrated their Friday night. Bryson strolled alongside someone he hadn't been on good terms with for a while—Lilu Intel.

They were only walking together because of Intel Director Jugtah, who had pronounced their spat selfish and unbecoming of the Jestivan. But that wouldn't have been reason enough for Bryson. Jugtah had pointed out that even if Bryson had to progress through classes at the same rate as any other student, nothing was stopping him from learning on his own. The director suggested Lilu as a tutor, and Bryson had begrudgingly followed his superior's advice.

"So what have you learned so far?" Lilu asked.

"I know how an Intelight works now. Not that I've made one, though."

"Let's hear it."

Bryson did his best recital of his Science of Weaving textbook: "To create an effective Intelight, you must first be able to harness nature's Intel Energy. Then you must—"

"And do you know how to do that?" Lilu cut him off. "If you don't, the rest of what you were about to say doesn't matter. Using your body's Intel Energy is one thing—tapping into nature's is a whole different story."

"No," Bryson replied, annoyed. "I told you Jugtah won't let me take an actual weaving class. I'm just reading kids' textbooks."

"Well that's what I'm here for."

"No offense," Bryson said, "but Shelly has been helping me with this for a long time now, and I've progressed well."

Lilu stopped and laughed. "My sister? Yes, I've seen the two of you parading around the palace's courtyards. I suppose shooting some sparks from your finger is a respectable product of half a year's training?"

"It's not exactly—"

"Let me explain something to you," Lilu snapped. "Shelly is all about power—or *clout*, as weavers call it. Think Yama and Toshik. Think Jilly. Think Rhyparia—although she's changed lately. They exert their energies with sheer force. Sure, Shelly can do a bit of weaving, but nothing intricate."

Bryson shook his head. "How is that possible? She's connecting her Intel Energy with nature's. I thought that was the basis of weaving."

"Let's keep this between me and you because this is the only time you'll hear me give my sister a compliment. When she summons a strike of lightning it's almost all her, not nature."

"Is that even possible?"

Lilu nodded. "Yes, but that's why she can only muster up one bolt. An extremely talented weaver—coupled with having some clout to back it up, mind you—can create an entire storm of lightning."

"Then how do I weave?"

Lilu smirked. "We'll start in the library tomorrow."

"I can't do that. I'm spending my weekends at home with Thusia while I do speed training on the pegs."

"You're busy lately. According to Rhyparia, the two of you have combination speed-gravity sessions every weeknight by the High Sever. And Agnos told me about your mysterious visits to the library every other night. And you're training at home on the weekends too?"

"I can squeeze you in," Bryson said.

"'Squeeze you in'? So it has come to this." She paused and stared deeply at Bryson. There was that purposefully overdramatic acting he had come to know her for—like she was mocking him. "Where did we go wrong, Mr. LeAnce?"

"You sound like your sister."

"Maybe you want me to be my sister." She turned back toward Wealth's Crossroads, her golden dress fluttering loosely around her knees. "I guess we'll get started when you have time. Good night."

*   *   *

Bryson awoke the following morning from dreams a bit different than the normal doom and gloom. He recalled Princess Shelly appearing in a few, and he thought of what Lilu had said.

Thusia's massive snoring carried through Debo's house. Bryson stumbled out of bed and down the hall. Thusia had one arm dangling off the couch in the living room and a leg tossed over the back. Her mouth hung open as a drool spot swelled on the pillow underneath.

He smiled, left to the front room, and sat down at the piano. He placed his fingers in resting position and began tapping a single key: *Seclusion*, the first phase. It then slowly progressed into a more complex tune—*Sorrow*. Then his fingers began skating across the keys at a pace only the most talented musicians could achieve. This was *Spite*, the final and most aggressive stage of his favorite song, "Phases of S."

This was only the sixth or seventh time Bryson had been able to play the piano in the past year, yet his fingers were as precise and nimble as ever. He was a natural, or at least that's what Debo always told him. Playing the piano—especially this song—was engrained in his muscle memory. His fingers instinctively struck each key as his mind drifted into other thoughts. He finished the song and stared down the hallway, where there used to be an everlasting orb of light that shielded a closet door.

He returned to the living room and noticed Thusia sitting up on the couch and staring at him. "Nice bed hair," he said.

"Do you know who wrote that song?" she asked.

"No one does," he replied as he walked into the kitchen and retrieved a carton of milk from the ice pantry. Thusia sat silently as he started a fire in a charcoal grate and held the frozen milk above it. "Why?" he asked.

"I don't think it's a coincidence that you know it so well."

"Do you know who wrote it?"

Thusia got up and stretched. "No," she yawned.

His eyes narrowed. "Why are you lying to me?"

She walked across the living room to a painting on the wall. It was a portrait of Debo and a nine-year-old Bryson, who was playfully tugging at one of Debo's ear piercings. Debo's face was contorted with laughter and pain.

"Because that's what he wanted," Thusia said. She turned from the painting and followed him into the kitchen. "There are certain things he wanted to keep secret in order to protect you. And I respect that man, so I will follow his lead."

Bryson groaned. "Somehow still managing to lie to me from the grave."

"*Protecting* you from his grave," Thusia corrected, slapping the milk out of Bryson's hand and into the fire.

"What was that for?" he whined.

"You don't drink milk before physical activity in the hot sun, idiot," she said. She grabbed a cup and held it under the faucet. "I'd like to make it through the morning without watching you vomit out your insides."

She handed Bryson the glass. He grabbed it and frowned. "I like milk."

"And I like chopsticks," she replied, "yet you don't hear me whining when I'm forced to use a fork."

He laughed. "I beg to differ."

They walked out the back door and began to stretch in silence while listening to the birds. Bryson was glad for Thusia's company, but he didn't understand why she participated in his training. She treated it as a joke more than anything else—not that he was complaining. She kept it fun, and gave him a chance to witness her abilities as a Spirit Assassin.

Bryson stepped up to the peg course—a training method very familiar to people of the Adren Kingdom, for it was an advanced speed, agility, and balance exercise. Thirty wooden stilts stretched in front of him at varying heights. He recalled all the times he watched in awe as Debo would run this course with ease.

Debo never let Bryson participate, claiming he wasn't ready. Naturally this annoyed Bryson since Adrenian children would start using peg courses at age ten. But Debo would counter by saying that was a mistake. They weren't good enough yet, and it could actually stunt their progress.

But Bryson was seventeen now and faster than most Adrenians at his age. In fact Yama was the only student he knew who could best his speed. He was even able to match Toshik's pace. And balance was something he excelled at, which was the most important aspect of this exercise.

He stepped onto the lowest peg using with the ball of one foot and his toes. That was the most effective method for running the course. It allowed for quicker twitch movements, but more important, it instilled healthy habits for combat. Moving on one's heels was a sure sign of a sloppy fighter.

As he prepared to push off, he watched as Thusia hopped from the ground and floated onto one of the highest pegs—some thirty feet in the air. For someone with the ability to float like a feather in the wind, these pegs were pointless. She stuck her tongue at him from high above.

Smiling, Bryson bolted toward a stilt. His foot made contact with the peg and he shot in a different direction, careful to weave around the taller pegs as he rapidly climbed his way to the top. He had never seen a monkey, but this was probably what it felt like to swing through the Passion Kingdom's jungles.

He upped his concentration as he reached one of the more difficult areas of the course. This section required him to hop up an inclining spiral of pegs. Over the course of the constant turn, his body tilted until it was nearly parallel to the ground. After three weekends of peg training, he had yet to pass this part. His heartbeat raced as he neared the top. Then his ankle rolled and he tumbled sideways, his face smacking against wood. He grabbed a stilt to slow his plummet, but that was likely a mistake. Now the pain was in his hand as it blistered and burned from the friction. He fell to the ground with a thud.

"That was nastier than the others," Thusia called down as she danced from peg to peg.

Bryson wanted to curse at her. His ankle, face, and hand were in immense pain. He stood up, wincing as he arched his back.

"Maybe we should wrap it up early today," she suggested.

"Debo always said to train under circumstances that hinder you, not cater to you. I'd say that pain is a hindrance I must get over."

"Using Debo's words against me!"

Bryson trained for the rest of the morning and into the early afternoon. He kept falling at the same point, but he was getting better at falling without hurting himself. Finally he did the unthinkable—he made it past the spiral and into the highest layer where Thusia was perched. He immediately fell off, but progress had been made. Instead of congratulating him, Thusia yelled at him like an irate mother when he tried to start again. His ankle had swollen to twice its normal size.

Bryson limped into the house and came back out with a carton of frozen milk. He sat down on a bench and pressed the carton to his foot. Then Thusia walked over and smacked his ankle.

"Thusia, why!"

"You deserve it," she said as she sat down. "It will hurt worse tomorrow. You won't be leaving the bed for the rest of the weekend."

"But I—"

"Ah-ah-ah, no buts."

They were silent for a few minutes except for Bryson's quiet hisses of pain as he readjusted the milk carton.

"What are you pushing yourself so hard for?" Thusia asked.

"There are threats everywhere. Toono is out there. Storshae is still alive. And I'm sure there are others. I don't even know how to weave, and it's embarrassing. I'm behind, which is completely unacceptable for someone who's supposed to be a captain of the Jestivan."

"Trust me, you can hold your own, and you're a highly capable fighter."

"Well I want to be better. The only reason I'm even alive is because Debo rescued me. And I still needed help from you … and Rhyparia, Toshik, Himitsu, and Jilly."

"You're supposed to need their help," she said. "They're your teammates. You don't need to fight every battle by yourself."

Bryson let out a deep breath. "I know that, but I'm doing this for myself. Something's coming, and I want to be ready for it. The Jestivan didn't just spring up for no reason."

Thusia closed her eyes. "Well, I'm here with you every step of the way. Remember that."

"I know."

20
A Bleak Realization

Intel Major Lars marched through Rim's central building. His jawline was even more pronounced than usual as he clenched his teeth. A man wearing a brown suit chased after him.

"You must believe that I didn't know!" the man pleaded.

"That makes it worse, Trolk!" Lars bellowed. "You're the mayor, so you should have known!"

"An avalanche made sense though!"

The two men turned a corner and sped up a flight of stairs. "No it doesn't! Nearly 1,500 years pass by without an avalanche powerful enough to reach Rim! Why would that change so drastically, so suddenly?"

Lars burst through the door of his office. A slender man with black hair was sitting on the leather sofa, flirting with one of the secretaries. "Flen!"

The Dev servant slowly turned to look at the fuming face of Lars. "Fine, we'll take our business elsewhere," he said.

"No. You're staying." The major turned to the young woman and pointed at the open door. "Out."

As the woman exited the room, Flen collapsed into the sofa. "What is it?"

"I need to speak with King Vitio. Now."

Flen stared at Lars, then closed his eyes. "As you wish." When he reopened his eyes, one had turned burgundy. The other was dilated as it projected a holographic display.

"Major Lars, I'd like to properly enjoy my Sunday afternoon," said the golden-bearded man in the display.

"I'm aware, King Vitio," Lars said with a bow. "I wouldn't press this so suddenly if it wasn't urgent."

"Make it quick."

"You're familiar with Olethros, sir?"

Vitio paused for a moment. "The sector that was crushed by one of the Archaic Mountains' avalanches? Tragic loss of hundreds of people."

"Yes, milord," Lars replied.

"What about it, then?"

"It wasn't an avalanche, milord. It was a person."

"And what is your source?"

"The parents of the one who did it."

Vitio cocked an eyebrow. "Why would someone betray their child, and after so many years of silence?"

"They feared King Itta. Now that he's locked up and no longer in the picture, they felt it was the right thing to do—to expose a dangerous individual responsible for roughly four hundred murders."

"And who is capable of such a feat? I don't even think the generals have such power."

Lars hesitated. "Milord, it was Lita Rhyparia."

The Intel King's face froze. Lars could hear the thrumming of the king's fingers.

"That's a bit unbelievable, Major," Vitio said quietly.

"I thought the same thing, milord."

"That had to be … almost a decade ago."

"February 7, 1491," Lars recited.

"Eight years ago—so that would have made her what?"

Lars sighed. "Seven. Almost eight, milord."

"Preposterous." Vitio shook his head. "A seven-year-old. Are you out of your mind? Why bother me with such nonsense?"

"Sir, you saw what she could do during Generals' Battle weekend. She flattened a restaurant and killed dozens."

"She was also fifteen years old, and it was only a building—not a damn *sector.*"

"There was a reason for that. Her parents were there. They know how to hold her back."

Vitio rubbed his eyes. "I'm not listening to any more of this, Lars. I want to enjoy the rest of my Sunday with my family."

"Milord … All I ask is that you question King Itta. According to Mr. and Mrs. NuForce, he was the one who covered this up."

"Good day, Major Lars."

"I think this may be a first," Flen said, "but I'm going to have to agree with Vitio on this one. It sounds a bit absurd."

"And that's why it's been hidden so easily."

*　　*　　*

"Is that all, sir?"

"Yes," King Vitio said. "Thank you, Vistas."

The king yanked open the door handle and stepped into the hall. He heard footsteps in the distance. He looked to his right and caught the hem of a dress slipping around a corner.

"Shelly!" he bellowed.

A couple seconds passed before a pale face with a green pixie cut peeked around the corner.

"Come here." He watched as his daughter guiltily walked down the long hallway. "How much did you hear?" he asked.

"Nothing, Father."

"Evasion of eye contact," he said. "Obvious lie."

"I'm sorry."

The king paused, then sighed. "What do you think I should do?"

Shelly smiled. "I think you were correct," she replied. "No way could a child do such damage."

He nodded. "A logical mind knows this."

Shelly looked at Vistas. "And you, Vistas?"

"I think your compassionate heart is playing you for a fool, milady."

Shelly's eyes narrowed, so the Dev servant explained himself: "Intelians are logical beings. But here you're using logic as an excuse to protect Rhyparia. My mother used to tell me, 'The compassionate heart shields the logical mind, but in doing so, blinds it.'"

Shelly frowned. "So you're implying there was merit to what Major Lars said?"

"I'm saying you cannot dismiss his accusation without investigating it. A real Intelian relentlessly besets a problem until an answer is found. I believe that's the mindset this kingdom's success was derived from."

Vitio stared at his adviser for a long moment. "Should I address Itta when I visit the Archaic Kingdom?"

"That is entirely your decision, sir," Vistas replied. "But I witnessed first-hand what Rhyparia could do in Necrosis Valley. And I believe you have a method of extracting the truth from Itta."

Vitio nodded. "Marcus."

* * *

Chief Arbitrator Grandarion Senten gazed down the bridge of his nose through his tiny spectacles at a table seating five others: Spy Pilot Ophala Vevlu, Chief Merchant Toth Brench, Chief Senator Rosel Sania, Chief Officer Wert Lamay, and Prince Sigmund Archaic.

"So it is settled," Grandarion said. "By a vote of three to two, the five teenage boys accused of disabling two Adren soldiers will be sentenced to ten years in prison."

Chief Wert let out a grumble. Chief Toth didn't look pleased either. Ophala closed her eyes and relaxed her shoulders. The two men had been pushing hard for the death penalty. Ophala and Rosel had pushed for time served. After a long and bitter dispute, Grandarion eventually came down near the more forgiving path.

The Amendment Order and the Archaic Prince gathered their belongings and left the meeting room. While Ophala was pleased with her victory, she was disturbed by Toth and Wert. Why would they be so adamant about killing teenagers? They attacked a couple officers. They didn't take a life.

"Mrs. Vevlu."

Ophala turned to see an olive skinned boy of nineteen. "Prince Sigmund," she replied with a sweet smile. "How did you enjoy your first trial?"

"I learned a lot," he said. "Not that I particularly enjoyed it."

"That's usually the case," she replied.

Sigmund turned to look behind him before returning his attention to Ophala. "Can we walk?" he asked.

"Sure."

The two of them exchanged small talk as they strolled through the Archaic Palace. But when they stepped onto a small stone balcony that looked out over the grounds several hundred feet below, Sigmund turned to more intriguing issues. "Unlike the others I trust you, Mrs. Vevlu."

"And why is that?"

"You're an Archain, native to this kingdom. And you've served this kingdom for many years as a top officer—the pilot of our most skilled silent killers."

"Don't fall victim to the same thing your father did."

"Revenge?"

Ophala shook her head. "Pride."

"But that's a good quality," he pointed out.

"Not in excess. Don't make decisions based off which kingdom someone comes from. That's a narrow-minded view. I could be against you."

"But you're not. I can tell. You see the good in me." Sigmund paused. "You see the good in most."

Ophala smirked. "That can also be detrimental in excess. One of my frustrating flaws. It's why this kingdom is in the state it's in now."

"What do you mean?"

A black starling landed on the balcony railing. "The event at the Generals' Battle never should have happened, but I didn't put my ancient to effective use. Itta always showed traits of being a terrible human, and I ignored them."

"That touches on what I wanted to talk to you about," the prince said. "I think you're making that mistake once again."

Ophala closed her eyes. "You mean Chiefs Toth and Wert."

"They talk to me more than any of you," Sigmund said. "They show empathy for my situation. They don't say anything forthright, but they hint at things. Things like getting my father out of the mess he's in or turning me into a more powerful man than even King Vitio. And with the way they carried themselves today, I fear they're as power hungry as my father."

Ophala gently caressed the starling's beak with her finger. "All right then, Prince Sigmund. I will take this as an order from my future king."

The prince smiled and drew himself up to his full height. "Spy Pilot Ophala Vevlu, I command you to discover the true motives of Chiefs Toth Brench and Wert Lamay."

Ophala laughed and bowed. "Yes, milord. I will not fail you!"

21
The Science of Weaving

Bryson returned to the Bricks for the first time with real trepidation. Shaking the image of the roasting bodies was impossible, and he could still smell the burning human flesh.

His shoes were off as he sat on the low brick wall and wiggled his toes in the fake grass. The fire was ablaze at the center of the little indoor courtyard, illuminating the Bricks and the enormous bookcases that surrounded them.

Agnos sat on the grass next to Bryson with his back against the bricks. Several books were sprawled around him and one was open in his lap. They each pertained to obscure languages that had either been dead for centuries or existed only in tiny, isolated villages. He occasionally glanced at the parchment with what Bryson had managed to remember so far from his dream—a whopping two characters. And he wasn't entirely sure how accurate those were.

Bryson stretched his back. "What's taking her so long? She's been a guide for years, so she should know this place like the back of her hand."

"I too have been a guide for a long time," Agnos said without ungluing his eyes from his book. "I may know my way around, but that doesn't mean this place shrinks on my behalf. There's a strange magic to the Warpfinate. They say the library expands according to how much you've explored, meaning that it's impossible—and I mean that quite literally—to see it all."

That caused Bryson to look up—no ceiling in sight, only a void of black.

"Not just up," Agnos said. "All the years I've spent in this place, yet I've never seen a wall. The floor seems to be the only boundary."

Two Passion librarians in crimson robes stood outside the grassy area. Their jobs were to tend to the fire and make sure it was under control. A few other students sat along the brick wall. They would quickly glance away every time Bryson made eye contact.

"How many of them do you reckon already know about weaving?"

Agnos looked up, brushing strands of black hair from his eyes. He observed the faces around them. "I'd say some of them know a good amount, more than you. Some of them look too young, however."

"Embarrassing," Bryson muttered.

"You care entirely too much."

"Let's sit somewhere else."

Agnos chuckled. "So insecure. Let them see you learn. It'll be comforting for them to know that a Jestivan has a weakness—that you're just like them in a way."

"You're a smooth talker, you know that?"

"And you're a smooth runner. We all have our specialties."

Bryson glanced at the book. "Making any progress?"

"Not at all," Agnos said. "For whatever reason, my glasses won't interpret what you've given me so far."

"I probably drew the letters wrong. They're not exactly simple designs, and by the time I wake up, I've forgotten the specifics."

"That's possible. I have other theories though, which is why I've been spending all of my nights in this place."

Bryson sighed. "You know you don't have to work so hard for me."

Agnos smiled. "I'm gaining something out of this too. Don't you worry; I just have to find the right book."

Bryson looked up at the sound of wheels. Lilu stepped onto the grass with a wheeled chalkboard in tow.

"I'm sorry," she said. "Quite a journey."

"It's okay," Bryson said. Agnos smiled at the pages of his book.

Lilu placed her hands on her hips and took a deep breath. "We'll start with a few key terms …" She looked back at Bryson as she wrote. "What are you doing?"

"Paying attention."

"That won't help. You need to take notes."

"I didn't bring any materials."

The royal daughter turned scarlet. Agnos handed Bryson a stack of blank parchment, quill and ink, and a large leather-bound book to serve as a surface.

"Thank you, Agnos," Lilu said sweetly as she stared down Bryson. "At least someone is responsible."

Bryson rolled his eyes—then hated himself for doing so. He'd picked up that habit from her, after all.

Lilu stepped away from the chalkboard. Four underlined terms were written on it: *Energy, Current, Weaving, EC Chain.* She pointed at the first word. "What is energy?"

"It's something that flows through a person's body, and it's what creates an ability, depending on the specific type of energy. For example, Intel Energy makes electricity."

"Eh … kind of. Energy itself doesn't do anything. It requires a reactant."

"Huh?"

"You didn't think that energy just magically turns into an ability, did you?" She pointed at the next word. "What's a current?"

"I'm going to go out on a limb and guess that it's the reactant."

"Correct," Lilu said, ignoring the sarcasm. "While energy is found in your body, currents are found in nature. For each type of energy—Intel, Passion, Spirit, Adren, Archaic, Dev, Still, Cyn, Prim, and Power—there is a corresponding current with the same name."

Bryson hunched over his parchment as he wrote that down. Agnos smiled while focusing on his own task. Lilu wore a smug look, clearly pleased with herself. "What's weaving?" she asked with a new air of confidence.

"It's the process of weaving your energy in different ways to create varying effects of your ability."

"Not quite. It's the process of weaving a strand of energy with a strand of current. Weaving energy with energy does nothing." Bryson resumed scribbling as Lilu continued: "A woven chain of energy is pointless if a current isn't present. An EC chain is what you call a successfully woven chain of energy and current."

Bryson looked up from his notes. "So energy and currents are the reactants, and the EC Chain is the product."

"The EC Chain is a transitional state, but we're getting ahead of ourselves." Lilu erased the board. "Let's ignore currents, weaving, and EC chains for a moment. Now Bryson, can you control your energy?"

"Yes."

"That's good. That's the first step toward weaving. Most students at Phesaw can too. Though energy constantly flows throughout your body, you can manipulate it to become highly concentrated in certain areas."

She began writing on the board again: *Step one: Control your energy*. "Do that for me," she said.

Bryson did just that with little effort, though it would have taken all his focus a year ago. Shelly's words entered his thoughts: *like flexing a muscle.*

Lilu put chalk to board: *Step two: Send your energy to your fingertips*. "Of course you can send your energy wherever you want, but for now we'll focus on the fingers since that's the easiest method."

Bryson emitted jolts of electricity from his fingers—another sign of the progress he and Shelly had made over the past year.

"All this time you've thought that was your energy creating those sparks?"

"Basically," he said. "And if what you say is true, then why is it working for me if I don't even know how to weave?" He gazed at his hands again. "I'm just pulsing my energy through my skin with no thought."

She grinned. "Because of clout." *Step three: Use your clout to propel your energy from your body and into nature.* "Clout is the force at which one expels their energy into nature. Some have greater clout than others. That comes with practice and genetics." She watched while Bryson scrunched his face as he tried to emit his electricity farther. She giggled. "Cute."

"So my clout is weak," Bryson sighed.

"You haven't practiced enough."

"Okay, but how does that explain how I can do this without actually weaving?"

"Who said you weren't weaving? When you use your clout, the energy propelling from your body collides and tangles with random currents in the air. And the stronger your clout is, the more intense those accidental collisions become, allowing you to deal immense damage without having any knowledge of weaving."

"So I'm weaving, but by luck."

"Exactly," Lilu said. "Who do we know that relies greatly on their clout?"

Bryson thought for a second. "Jilly."

"Good. Luckily for her, she possesses such incredible clout that she can still wreak havoc. The downside? She can hurt people. And unlike weaving, it quickly drains her stamina because she's using her energy instead of nature's. Got all that?"

"Yes."

Lilu wrote down the next step. *Step four: Detect currents.* "This is when it becomes difficult. Ever wonder why you can't emit your energy for more than maybe twenty seconds? It seems to dissipate instantly. It's because the currents swarming your energy are too overwhelming. There are billions upon billions of currents in nature, and when you don't know how to detect and pinpoint individual strands, all of them hit you at once. And that leads to what?"

"Complete energy exhaustion," Bryson said.

Lilu clapped. "Yay! You're learning the terms and properly applying them."

Bryson was genuinely excited to be learning about a realm of knowledge that was so foreign to him. Debo had never taught him any of this. Olivia didn't use her energy either, so why would they discuss it? And his only other friend was Simon, who was too young and focused on archery anyway.

"We'll stop here for today," Lilu said.

"What about weaving?"

"You need to learn how to detect currents before we go any further." She grabbed her bag and pushed the chalkboard out of the Bricks.

"Thank you, Lilu."

She stopped and looked back with the sweet, infectious smile he hadn't seen in months.

"You're welcome."

*　　*　　*

Bryson and Agnos exited the library a short while later. The sun had set. With the end of October upon them, Bryson's typical chill was now accompanied by nature's cool bite. Agnos removed his glasses as they entered Phesaw Park—a more peaceful route to Wealth's Crossroads. He let out a sigh of frustration and handed the parchment that he had been studying all day back to Bryson.

"Should have snuck some books out," Bryson suggested.

"That would be against Phesaw's policies."

"Jeez, I was only kidding," he lied. After walking for a short while in silence, Bryson said, "We're never going to figure out what those letters mean."

"A mindset expected from someone who doesn't spend much time around books."

Bryson gave him a quizzical look. "A bit harsh."

"Apologies. What I meant to say was there's a book suited for every question you can think of. Some are just harder to find than others."

"I wish I had that thirst to gain knowledge," Bryson confessed. "Maybe I would've tried to learn about weaving when I was younger."

"Weaving was one of the first wonders of this world that I taught myself," Agnos replied. "From books, of course."

"You can weave?" Bryson scoffed.

"The other Jestivan may know how good I am at weaving, but you wouldn't, seeing that you had your first lesson on it today. It's somewhat disheartening to know that you've thought of me as some broken, useless piece of a puzzle this past year."

"I just thought—"

"You thought I can't weave since I wasn't able to fight."

Bryson didn't say anything.

"How else would I be able to use an ancient?" Agnos asked. "And not just an ancient, but a relic, and one that requires high-level weaving. These glasses won't work unless you're able to weave some of the most complex EC chains. And the more obscure the language, the more intricate your chains must become. These glasses would be useless if Rhyparia owned them. Truth is, the only other Jestivan who can come close to my weaving is Lilu. If anyone has a question regarding it, they come to one of us."

"I'm sorry," Bryson apologized. "That's amazing."

They exited the other end of the park, and the Intelights of Wealth's Crossroads opened up in front of them.

"So what about Grand Director Poicus?" Bryson asked. "His ancient allows him to replicate the appearance of another human. Is that more weaving or clout?"

"Weaving. Tactical ancients tend to require it."

"And Rhyparia is clout?"

"For the most part, but that's because she's still learning. Her ancient is versatile. It can achieve astonishing feats in the possession of a proper weaver. When she crushed the restaurant, that was all clout. When you saw her practically flying through the sky during our first exam, that was weaving."

Bryson's mind was running at full speed as they walked into Lilac Suites. But then he was distracted by a rumble in his stomach as the smell of food wafted over from the kitchen. Himitsu was frantically waving at him from one of the tables. He was seated across from … *Yama*? Odd pair.

Bryson and Agnos took a seat. Yama took one glance at Agnos and stood up without a word.

Bryson watched as she walked out the front door. "I think I've said a total of ten words to that girl since we became Jestivan," he said. "And all ten were over this past summer."

"You have no idea," Himitsu moaned. "I was minding my own business, enjoying a beer … then she just sits down right there. Just sits down and says nothing! My life flashed before my eyes."

"She's lonely," Agnos said. "Jilly has been treating her differently."

"Why all the empathy?" Himitsu asked. "She hates you."

"I've seen her go through something similar to this before, when we were younger."

"Toono," Bryson said.

Agnos cocked his head. "How do you know that?"

"Overheard her talking about it once." It was during a heated conversation she was having with Agnos last year, but Bryson didn't want Agnos to know he'd been snooping. He looked at Himitsu, wanting to change the subject. "So what about your mom? What does her ancient rely on?"

"Your mom is an Archain?" Agnos asked. "What's her ancient?"

"Some sort of staff that allows her to enter a bird's vision," Himitsu said, tilting his mug of ale.

Agnos's eyes widened. "Unbelievable," he said. "Your mom is Spy Pilot Ophala Vevlu?"

Himitsu burped. "So much for secrecy."

"That's why nobody knows your last name."

"I think you mean 'knew,' till you started shouting."

"I need to meet her," Agnos said.

Himitsu gave him an uneasy look. "Slow down there, buddy. First of all …" He paused, then corrected himself: "Actually there is no first of all. It just wouldn't happen."

"Please. She has information I need."

"And what information is that?"

"I need to know who possesses the ancient that allows you to communicate with sea life."

"Strange request, but I'll see what I can do," Himitsu said.

22
The Diatia

It was approaching eight A.M. on a cool November morning as Bryson ran out of Dinny Diner with a buttery pastry stuffed in his mouth and Olivia's wrist in his hand. Even though it was a Saturday, he had to be at Telejunction's hill in three minutes. Special guests were arriving today.

Olivia passively allowed him to pull her along. Bryson glanced back at her as he ran. "Don't you care that we're going to be late?" he asked around the pastry.

She gave him a placid look. "I don't."

"Why can't you run?"

"I'm tired."

Bryson laughed. As they curved around the north side of Phesaw's main building and past the slums—so politely named by the students—he nearly tripped as a massive tremor shook the ground.

He felt bad that his mind instantly went to Rhyparia, but that was the only answer that made sense. Phesaw wasn't known for earthquakes. The ground shook again.

"What is happening?" he asked.

"That would be Power Warden Feissam."

"Who?"

"Do you research anything?" Meow Meow retorted.

"He's the leader of Ipsas's Power Wing," Olivia explained. "A warden is the Ipsas equivalent to a director at Phesaw. The Diatia have arrived."

Bryson let go of Olivia's hand and bolted toward Telejunction. He had to see what kind of person could cause this.

Feissam was a mountain of a man who cast an equally massive shadow on the hillside. He was built with sheer muscle, and not the lean kind seen on Debo, Buredo, or Toshik. He could have picked Bryson up with one hand. The Power Kingdom had been a faithful ally of the Light Realm for centuries, but it was hard not to see menace in the man.

Doors and windows began to open from the school buildings and dorms as curious heads poked out. Warden Feissam had to be thirteen feet tall, and that wasn't an exaggeration. He was an edifice of a man, a gigantic slab of marble.

"If it was possible, I'd piss myself," Meow Meow muttered.

The giant looked down at the Jestivan and the directors with a grouchy curl to his lip. "Hello," he grunted. His voice sounded like a dull thunder in the distance. His skin was sandpaper brown from the sun, and he wore black robes that draped over his shoulders. They were similar to the directors' robes.

"Power Warden Feissam, pleasure to meet you," Grand Director Poicus said as he extended his hand.

The warden raised his hand as well, though he balled it into a fist. Poicus gently placed his hand on top of it.

Strange handshake, Bryson thought.

"Likewise," Feissam thrummed. He spread his arms to his side, and a teenage boy and girl stepped forward. "Bruut Schap and Vuilni Gesluimant, the Power Diatia."

Poicus went down the line of Jestivan and directors, introducing them one by one. The Powish trio exchanged the same odd handshake with each person.

Upon reaching Bryson, Feissam paused with narrowed eyes as he looked down. "Mr. LeAnce," he said as he extended his fist. "Pleasure."

Annoyed, Bryson silently placed his hand on the man's knuckles.

Bryson shared the same exchange with the two Diatia. Bruut was strongly built—much like his warden, though his height was definitely more along the normal side of things. Vuilni was also bulky—more muscular than Bryson, in fact. Bruut's complexion was fair, and Vuilni was dark-skinned like Ophala. She wore a hood over her head, and her black hair fell in braids down her chest.

Olivia was the last to be introduced. Feissam stuck out his fist, and she extended an open hand as if to give a normal handshake, but she didn't make contact as she looked up at the warden with a blank stare.

A deep rumble of amusement rolled up from Feissam's chest. "That would be ill-advised, young lady."

Olivia silently continued to hold out her hand. Feissam stared at her hand for a few moments before finally opening his fist and locking his hand with hers.

"My, my," Feissam grumbled. "What was your name again?"

"Olivia Lavender."

"Your bones didn't break from the pressure of my grip … That is worthy of Powish respect."

Bryson smiled, proud of his best friend. Even the directors hadn't taken that chance.

"All right, young ones," Poicus said. "Bryson's team will spend the day with Vuilni. Olivia's team gets Bruut. Learn about your new friend."

After their dismissal, Bryson's team formed an awkward huddle. Vuilni stood quietly off to the side and gazed at Phesaw's school building in front of them.

Jilly was first to speak up. "Your name is pretty."

Vuilni smiled. "Thank you."

Jilly paused, then added, "Your braids are pretty."

"Thank you …"

"Your muscles are—"

"Shush, Jilly," Toshik cut her off.

Vuilni might have stifled a giggle. "Care to show me around?" she asked.

Bryson, Jilly, Himitsu, Toshik, Rhyparia, and Vuilni took a stroll around the campus. They showed her the school's lobby and the auditorium it circled. Then they visited the library but didn't go in. Bryson had spent enough time in that suffocating cave the past couple months. Vuilni seemed happy throughout most of the journey, but her smile faded when they entered the slums.

"Is that seriously what this place is called?" she asked, scanning through the crudely constructed wooden dorms.

"Eh, that's not the official name," Himitsu said. "It's just what the students call it."

"Tasteless."

"Whoever chooses to live here is tasteless," Toshik said. "No offense, Rhyparia. Besides, your life in the slums is a thing of the past now that you're a Jestivan."

Jilly reached up and flicked him in the ear. "Be nice."

Vuilni gave Toshik a cold stare. She pulled her hood farther over her face, concealing it in shadows.

"Don't worry, we're not all like Toshik," Bryson said. Vuilni didn't reply.

They stepped into Phesaw Park, under the pink canopies of cherry blossoms. "You like it?" Bryson asked after walking for a while.

"It's beautiful," Vuilni replied. "When we arrived at Telejunction, these trees were the first thing I noticed. But these trees only bloom in the spring, don't they?"

"These aren't normal cherry blossoms," Jilly said. "They're from the seeds of the Spirit Kingdom's Cherry Forest. They stay in bloom for an average of five years before meeting a permanent death."

"Interesting. I'm guessing the Spirit Kingdom is a beautiful place."

"It is!" Jilly exclaimed.

"What about everyone else's kingdom?" Vuilni asked.

"Adren Kingdom is very plain," Toshik said. "Buildings constructed of wood and drywall. Even the capital's palace is smaller than our school. In fact my home is the biggest building in the entire kingdom."

"My home—the Passion Kingdom—is beautiful and wild," Himitsu said. "Volcanoes and dangerous forests. And Fiamma, the capital, is basically an artist's dream."

Rhyparia, who hadn't said a word the entire morning, gave a dry response: "Bare, desolate, corrupt: Archaic Kingdom."

"I'm sorry," Vuilni said. "I can relate."

"No … no, you can't."

"The Intel Kingdom is wealthy, innovative, and filled with buildings of steel," Bryson said.

"That must come at a cost," the Diatia said.

"Yes, lots of money."

"Not exactly what I meant," Vuilni said.

Rhyparia pursed her lips. "Maybe you can relate."

They sat down at the lake's edge. "So what wins: speed or strength?" Toshik asked.

Vuilni laughed. "Both. Strength can create speed, and vice versa. The faster you're traveling, the more force you can strike with. The more force you use to push off, the quicker you'll accelerate."

Toshik gazed across the lake. "I guess I never thought of it that way."

Students who had come to enjoy their Saturday morning at the park were staring, which was normal. But this time they were staring at the Power Diatia. Most of them had probably never seen someone from the Dark Realm in their entire life. Bryson wondered if they looked at her as some sort of monster. They wouldn't know real monsters, like Storshae and Fonos.

"What's the Power Kingdom like?" Bryson asked.

"Depends on the perspective," Vuilni replied. "It's fantastic for some people, like Bruut and Warden Feissam."

"And you?"

She forced a small laugh. "Could be better. I live in a place called Cascade Closure."

"I'm sorry," Rhyparia said.

"You've heard of it?" Vuilni asked.

"I've read about it."

Vuilni pulled at her braid as she looked out over the water. "The name sounds pretty—*Cascade Closure*—but it's nothing of the sort."

*   *   *

Vuilni spent most of her afternoon with Rhyparia. The two girls seemed to have a lot in common, so this wasn't a surprise. Bryson had tracked down Olivia, who had decided that Bruut was not to her liking.

Bryson and Vuilni were seated in the Lilac Suites lobby as the orange sky of dusk splashed through the windows. Olivia was at the bar ordering drinks. Vuilni was gazing at the massive chandelier.

"I suppose it's not something you'd see in Cascade Closure?" Bryson asked.

She looked at Bryson with her black eyes. "Is that an attempt at small talk or to fish information out of me?"

"An attempt at getting to know you better."

"We're not there yet."

"Do you always wear a hooded jacket?"

She nodded. "Do you?"

"All the time," Bryson said. "We have our own similarities."

"And what is that supposed to mean?"

"You and Rhyparia connected on certain points. We can do the same."

She arched an eyebrow. "If you want to discuss our choice of apparel, then go ahead. Just don't mention my home life."

Bryson shrugged. "Fair enough. Deflecting topics that exacerbate your insecurities; I can relate."

"Oh, really?" she teased. "What does Mendac's son have to be insecure about?"

The look of consternation must have showed on his face because Vuilni addressed it immediately: "His shadow swallows your existence." She paused, then said, "A shadow swallows my home … maybe there are some similarities."

A pair of mugs slid across the wooden table, interrupting the conversation. Olivia plopped down next to Bryson and took a loud sip while giving Vuilni a dead stare.

Vuilni laughed. "You're an odd one."

Olivia calmly lifted her mug to her mouth.

"She's not much of a conversationalist with strangers," Bryson said.

"I see that."

The lobby's front door opened, and Tashami and Agnos walked in. Bryson gave them a friendly wave as they headed upstairs.

"I'm interested to see what they're like," Vuilni said as she watched them climb.

"Tashami is as nice as they come, gentle and kind-hearted," Olivia said. Vuilni's eyes widened at her eerily dry voice. "He was the one with the white hair. Agnos is also nice. However there's a certain snarky arrogance that can peek through at times. Yama is a lone wolf, standoffish. Then there's Lilu—Bryson likes her."

"Really, Olivia?" Bryson sputtered as Meow Meow cackled.

Vuilni giggled. "You may not show emotion, but that doesn't mean you're void of a sense of humor, however deadpan it may be."

"Only at my expense," Bryson sighed.

The door opened again—this time to reveal Rhyparia, who immediately headed up the stairs. Vuilni stood up. "I'll be leaving now. It was a fun day, Bryson."

"Where are you going?"

"Bruut and I were given the choice of who we get to room with, and I chose Rhyparia. I'm going to go check out the room."

Bryson frowned. "Oh …Well, good night."

As Vuilni chased down Rhyparia, Bryson turned and said, "At least I still have—"

"Good night, Bry," Olivia said. She tossed back the rest of her juice and stood up.

"… you." He watched as his best friend marched toward the front door. "Dammit," he muttered.

Bryson was still hungry for some company, so he decided to head up to his dorm room and summon Thusia. A lot had happened today, so there was plenty to talk about. Hopefully she wouldn't bring up his dream. He had enough of that with Agnos.

He unlocked his door and threw his keys on the desk. Then he froze. Seated on top of a sleeping bag on the floor was a burly boy of about eighteen.

"Hello, roommate," Bruut said with a smile.

23
Puppeteers

The maximum-security chamber of the Archaic Palace held a single cell. The chamber was a grand circle, but the cell gated off on the far side was of a more modest size. The room's ceiling was tall and domed with wooden support beams that stretched across at varying heights. Bats hung from the beams, hidden in the midnight darkness.

One of the bats opened its orange eyes as the chamber door swung open. Two people walked in: a muscular man with blond hair and a lanky brunette with a sword sheathed at his hip. The door swung shut behind them as they approached the gate.

"Toth and Wert, good evening," the prisoner wheezed.

"King Itta," they both said with a bow.

"How goes the Amendment Order?" Itta asked.

"It's serving its purpose for now," Chief Toth Brench said, "granting us a sort of diplomatic immunity. We can achieve things without fear of being investigated."

"That Ophala woman is insufferable, however," Chief Wert Lamay added.

Itta laughed weakly. "Ophala can be manipulated. Her need to see the good in people blinds her to the more pressing threats. Why do you think I gave her the position of Spy Pilot?"

"Because you could misguide her attention," Wert replied.

"Exactly. I used her ancient as an excuse for her to be perfectly suitable for such a job. And while she resided in Rim for five years, aimlessly flying her birds above the mountains, I set plans into motion."

"We no longer have the benefit of her residence being hundreds of leagues away," Wert pointed out.

"Are you being careful?" Itta asked.

"Of course," Toth said. "In fact Prince Sigmund is keeping her busy right now—chatting her up about some kind of nonsense."

A silence followed. "I'm proud that my son has not given up on his old man," the king muttered.

"He's a great asset," Toth said.

"He isn't an asset!" Itta snapped, then doubled over as coughs racked his body. "You may be a famous businessman, Chief Brench, but you won't speak of my son that way."

"Forgive me, Itta. I must break such habits."

"Have you been keeping in touch with … *him*?" Itta asked.

"Yes," Wert said. "A plan is in motion. Albeit a slow-developing one."

"Good. It's a shame this kingdom must rely on that man once again, but he's all we have. Goodnight, gentlemen."

As the two chiefs exited the chamber, the bat that had been watching from above closed its eyes …

Ophala opened her eyes to her candlelit office. Prince Sigmund was gazing out at the city of Phelos with both hands on the windowsill. Ophala leaned her staff against her desk and stared blankly ahead. After a little thinking, she finally said, "They're making plans with Dev King Storshae."

Sigmund snapped his head around with a baffled look. "There is no way. That man screwed us over once. Why would they trust him again?"

"Because they're relying on you," she said. "You have your Branian. Storshae's Bewahr is dead. The Archaic Kingdom would have the upper hand in such an arrangement."

"They don't have me."

"Don't let them know that," she replied. She closed her eyes and sighed. "I will not fail this kingdom again."

* * *

Spy Pilot Ophala was having breakfast with Chief Arbitrator Grandarion Senten at a vast table in one of the palace's formal dining rooms. Grandarion was shoveling potatoes and eggs into his mouth while staring at a stack of parchment next to his plate through his tiny spectacles. He tossed a sheet to the side and grabbed another from the pile.

"Another morning of petty crime," he said as he chewed.

"Considering the crimes that were reported when our group first started its tenure, I'd say that's a good thing," Ophala replied.

"I suppose you're right," he grunted. They ate in silence until Grandarion's fork froze halfway through its ascent to his mouth. "Oh, no…"

"What?" Ophala asked.

"An Adren soldier was killed as he patrolled 43rd Street."

"By whom?"

"A twelve year-old girl," he muttered with a slight shake of his head. He continued reading out loud: "According to soldiers who were first-hand witnesses, Cornilia Selim, a twelve-year old girl, had approached a group of Adren soldiers with bright eyes and a friendly smile. She was an unassuming girl, simply asking for a hug and thanking them for their service. One of the soldiers picked her up …"

"Don't tell me," Ophala said.

"She pulled a concealed blade from her waistband and sliced open his neck."

"How could she do such a thing?"

"The report says she instantly began to cry in hysteria." He glanced at the parchment again. "She claimed her mother forced her to do it, which according to past records would make sense. Ms. Selim has a history of protesting the stationing of foreign military on her kingdom's soil. And digging even deeper, she was once a radical supporter of Archaic King Itta."

"That's not going to be an easy one to handle," Ophala said.

"We were doing so well, too … It had to happen just a few days before the royal heads arrive with Marcus."

"What do you think of Chiefs Wert and Toth?"

Grandarion lifted his gaze and looked at Ophala from above his spectacles. "You're worried about what they'll want to do with this girl."

"I believe it's a valid worry."

"Understandable. They are … unforgiving men, to put it nicely. In this case however … She took a life, Ophala."

"It didn't seem to be her choice."

Grandarion sighed. "You are too forgiving—to the point of being reckless. Where do you draw the line?"

"It sounds as if the girl's verdict is already in," she snapped.

"Of course not. A proper trial will be conducted. The Amendment Order doesn't cut corners, nor does it make rash decisions without the gathering of evidence and the acts of healthy debate between the chiefs. What I was getting at was that I may be an Intelian, but that doesn't mean I bend corners on behalf of the guilty because I sympathize with their traumatic pasts or reasons."

"Was that a jab at your king?" Ophala asked.

"King Vitio has been guilty of such antics, so yes."

She leaned back in her chair. "So what's your take on Rhyparia NuForce?" she asked after a moment.

"The Jestivan girl who flattened the restaurant during the Generals' Battle? She should have been executed."

*   *   *

Toono was lying on a sofa in Fiamma's suburbs while Kadlest was cooking in the kitchen. The home had been sitting on the market for months, and they had crept in after the owners had moved out. The life of a criminal was an exhausting one—a life cloistered behind curtains over windows until you were driven from your hideout to search for a new one.

"I need you to go to Phesaw," Toono said while staring at the ceiling.

Kadlest poked her head around the corner. "Sooner than expected," she said. "We haven't even finished our business here."

"I need to know what's happening on Storshae's end."

"That's not my fault. I told you Illipsia should stay here with us. She's our only means of communication with that foul man."

Toono frowned. She wasn't wrong.

Kadlest gave him a warm smile. "Just focus on preparing for your duties in a few days."

"I can't."

Kadlest walked into the living room, pushed Toono's legs aside, and took a seat on the sofa next to him. She smelled of crushed herbs. "Let's go over the reasons why you shouldn't be worrying, shall we? We know the Jestivan took out three of the Dev Assassins as we planned. They have no idea about the other three. Storshae is establishing a relationship with Brench and Lamay. And Mr. and Mrs. NuForce leaked the information about Olethros. I'll admit that we got kind of lucky there, but everyone needs luck. Now we no longer have to infiltrate the palace since the royal heads will be heading to Phelos with Marcus in tow. Chaos is spreading, leading the focus away from us. Pieces are moving precisely how we need them to and at the right time."

"And what if Storshae botches things with Toth and Wert?"

Kadlest placed her hand on Toono's knee. "We must focus on us. We are the farmers. We've planted the seeds. What happens next is up to nature."

"Terrible analogy," Toono muttered. "Farmers tend to their plants by watering them."

Kadlest laughed. "The point is, control what you can. And as of right now, that's yourself. So what are you going to do in a week?"

Toono released a deep breath. "Eliminate Passion King Damian."

"Good man."

24
Extraction

Four royal carriages, each draped in a different color, traveled down the widest road in Phelos. Adren soldiers stood guard as the crowds watched the Light Realm's powers make their way through the city.

The first carriage was a blood red, and it was surrounded by horses and soldiers dressed in the same color. Passion King Damian and Marcus were inside. Second in line were Spirit Queen Apsa and her Dev servant in their blue carriage. Adren King Supido's was silver. His carriage was closer to the ground, longer and sleeker. Intel King Vitio's gleaming carriage was plated with gold.

The royal heads had come to Phelos for two reasons: to evaluate the Amendment Order and how the Archaic Kingdom was responding with them in power, and to use Marcus to extract truths from the deposed King Itta, such as his dealings with Dev King Storshae and the purpose of their alliance.

Vistas sat alongside Vitio in his carriage. The king had ordered Princess Shelly to remain in Dunami and govern the country with the help of General Lucas.

It had been an exhausting journey. The Intel Kingdom's teleplatforms sat right on the border of the capital, but the Archaic Kingdom had placed theirs several hundred miles from Phelos, which wasn't really their decision. Mendac had created them that way.

"How are you feeling?" Vitio asked.

"I'm all right, milord," Vistas replied. "And yourself?"

"My mind is racing."

The servant peeled back a curtain. "I wish these carriages were racing."

Vitio chuckled. "I'll never stop being surprised when you make a joke."

"What's on your mind?" Vistas asked.

"I'm worried Marcus will refuse to ask the questions we want."

"Valid concern. He doesn't serve you."

"But you still have connections with him, yes?"

"We've kept in touch over the years, milord. But that doesn't mean he'll choose friendship over his king."

Vitio rubbed his temple. "Damian would be displeased if he found out I used Marcus for my own purposes. I'd be running his servant dry."

"But if what we were told about Rhyparia ends up being true, the other royal heads wouldn't be able to ignore the magnitude of what we learned. And if we learn that the accusation was false—"

"We pretend nothing happened."

"HALT!" someone yelled from outside. A chorus of neighs followed, signaling their arrival.

"Time to stretch these legs," Vitio said as he rose from his seat.

Sunlight splashed into the carriage as its side door opened. Vitio refused the help of a soldier as he stepped down to the pavement and shielded his eyes from the sun. "I haven't been here since I was a teenager, and the sun is just as painful as I remember."

"It is very hot, milord," Vistas agreed.

The other parties had already disembarked from their carriages. Vitio squinted at the dirty-blond hair of Marcus, who was dressed in the same burgundy robes that Vistas wore. Six people stood at the top of the stairs:

Chief Arbitrator Grandarion Senten, Chief Senator Rosel Sania, Chief Merchant Toth Brench, Chief Officer Wert Lamay, Spy Pilot Ophala, and Archaic Prince Sigmund.

Vitio had to stop himself from frowning at the sight of Grandarion, whom he despised. Eager to be rid of Grandarion's constant resistance to his proposals, he had sent the elder to the Archaic Kingdom. Now Vitio had come to pay the bill for the peace that decision had brought him.

The royal heads climbed the steps with their Dev servants at their side. The palace was exactly as Vitio remembered it from so long ago, a building prided on its history—much like everything in this kingdom. Archains didn't believe in renovation when it came to design. The stone walls, the Archains claimed, were more than a millennium old. How they hadn't eroded to dust was a mystery.

"Good afternoon, kings and queens," Grandarion said with a bow. "I hope your journey wasn't too exhausting."

"It's not as if we used our own feet to get here," thrummed the voice of Adren King Supido.

Grandarion smiled. "We'll have lunch in thirty minutes, where we'll discuss the rest of the day's events. Follow me."

The sixteen of them traveled through the palace, using the time to catch up with each other. Vistas had a friendly conversation with Marcus, as instructed by Vitio. Each royal head discussed current events with their respective member of the Amendment Order. This meant Vitio had the displeasure of Grandarion at his side, and their conversation was extremely short.

They entered the dining hall and sat as they pleased at the table. Vitio, Vistas, and Marcus sat in a row. Passion King Damian sat next to Marcus. While everyone was getting settled, someone took a seat to Vitio's right. He glanced at the stranger.

"Hello, King Vitio. It's an honor to finally meet the one man who's as rich as I am."

"You must be Toth Brench."

The man smiled. "You know of me."

"I do. Brench swords are some of the finest in this realm."

"*The* finest."

A fake grin lingered on Vitio's face as he said, "That's nice." Then he pointedly turned away. "Marcus!"

"Good to see you again, King Vitio."

"How's that big ol' guy treating you?" Vitio asked as he nodded at King Damian.

Marcus smiled. "Very well."

Archaic Prince Sigmund rang his glass with a fork. "Before we get to the matters that you all are really here for," he said from the head of the table, "I want to express my gratitude. To be at a table of such esteemed individuals is quite a privilege for me. I've come a long way under the wings of the Amendment Order. Grandarion, Ophala, Toth, Wert, and Rosel have taught me what it takes to properly run a kingdom, and I thank the royal heads for putting them in such a position." Sigmund paused. "You could have easily given up on me, but you didn't."

Spirit Queen Apsa raised her glass with a gracious smile. "Cheers to that, young man."

"Hear, hear," the others said in unison.

"After lunch, the Dev servants will be dismissed," Sigmund said. "The royal heads, the Amendment Order, and I will remain here to discuss the state of Kuki Sphaira. At nine o'clock we will reconvene at the maximum-security chamber to interrogate my father."

Vitio turned to look at Marcus. His eyes were closed, and there was a look of focus on his face. Extracting truths was one of the most difficult feats of weaving for a Devish. There were probably less than a dozen of them capable of such a task, and most of them never revealed the ability in fear of being caught by criminals who sought out their skills. Then there was the fact that all royals were taught how to shield their minds at a young age.

Lunch eventually concluded, and the servants left the dining hall. "What should we discuss first?" Grandarion asked.

"Toono," King Vitio instantly answered.

"So far as I'm aware, there has been no news of him since he killed that Cyn Diatia nearly eight months ago," Grandarion replied.

"What about Damian's teleplatforms?" Vitio asked on behalf of the mute Passion King, who nodded in agreement.

"But that attack was made with ice," Apsa said. "A Stillian must have been guilty of the crime."

"Toono could have been involved," Vitio said.

"Well there's no way of determining that," Grandarion declared. "The Still Kingdom has isolated themselves from the rest of Kuki Sphaira for centuries."

"That doesn't mean we dismiss Toono," Chief Senator Rosel Sania said. Heads turned, for she rarely spoke. "Grand Director Poicus has informed us Toono stole the Anathallo from the Archaic Museum. This means there are still eight more targets he intends to sacrifice—assuming he hasn't already killed people that we don't know about."

"That load of crap?" Wert spat. "Nobody's coming back from the dead. And even if such a tall tale were true, there's supposedly another piece missing to it."

"Skeptics tend to be fools, Chief Wert," Rosel replied.

"Unfortunately there's not much we can do about Toono besides keeping an eye out," Supido said. "We have no idea where he is."

"Spy Pilot Ophala could assist with such a mission," Chief Toth suggested.

"I'd prefer to focus on Prince Sigmund," Ophala said. "He is my prince and future king, and I want to help make him into a respectable royal head."

"I agree," Queen Apsa said. "The boy needs a bit of a woman's touch." She smiled at Rosel. "No offense."

Rosel shook her head. "None taken."

"Anyone else perturbed by the fact that Grand Director Poicus invited the Power Diatia and Warden Feissam to Phesaw?" Supido asked. "I thought the Diatia were enemies of the Jestivan."

"Apparently they're supposed to be beacons of peace for Kuki Sphaira's future," Vitio said. "Praetor wants to connect the Light and Dark Realms in harmony."

"The Sphairian Summit in the 800s was supposed to accomplish that," Prince Sigmund said.

"And the plan was to hold such a summit every fifty years," Rosel said. "Now tell me, how many times has that happened since?"

Sigmund seemed offended by her short rebuttal.

"None," Rosel continued when the prince didn't answer. "But I agree with the Grand Director that peace is possible, so long as the efforts are made by young elites invested in the future rather than stubborn old minds."

"What about King Storshae?" Queen Apsa asked. "Has anyone heard anything recently?"

"Outside of the Dev Assassins who have been taken care of at Phesaw, it's been quiet on his end," Vitio said. "Which is to be expected, with his general and Bewahr dead."

"That's still a head scratcher," Apsa said. "One of the Energy Directors eliminating a Gefal …"

"Well it was at the expense of his own life," Supido replied. "Still, don't underestimate the directors."

Vitio grinned. "You shouldn't have to tell yourself that, with your brother being one of them."

Supido smiled. "Speaking of family, Gondha is pregnant."

Vitio smacked the table. "Congratulations! The Adren first-born is finally on its way!"

* * *

Vistas gazed over the crumbling stone edge of the tower's roof while Marcus sat on the ground, focused on the ball of yarn, quill, and parchment that he had brought up from his room. Marcus was practicing his weaving in preparation for extracting truths later that night—a similar routine to an Adrenian stretching before a run.

Yarn unwound from its ball, curling and rising on its own—or what looked to be on its own. The quill was standing at an angle and scurrying across the parchment with no hand to guide it. Marcus was manipulating both with his Dev Energy, his weaving resulting in telekinesis. To be doing two highly intricate tasks at once was a testament to his talent as a weaver.

The yarn formed the outline of a butterfly, its wings fluttering gently as it danced through the air. The parchment also had a butterfly drawn onto it, and the quill continued to sketch patterns in its wings.

Vistas shook his head. "Extraordinary."

Marcus looked up at his friend while the objects continued to move. "I'm sorry about Tristen."

Vistas's eyes fell for a moment as he was reminded of his brother, who had been killed at the hands of Dev King Storshae for espionage.

"Ever wonder why we've accepted this fate?" Marcus asked.

"I have moments, yes. But then I recall who was responsible for our misery during our early years as servants of King Vitio."

The quill and yarn fell to the ground. Marcus sighed. "Mendac."

Vistas nodded. "King Vitio is a flawed man, like any of us. But he is kind."

"I agree. And since I was sent to the Passion Kingdom, King Damian has treated me just as well."

"How long have we known each other?" asked Vistas.

"Since we were children, playing in the streets of Tames. You, Flen, Tristen, and me … Good times … Humble times."

"If I were to ask you to do something for King Vitio and me, would you do it?"

Marcus's eyes narrowed. The parchment flipped over and his quill began moving again. Then the parchment lifted off the ground and hovered next to his face. Marcus gave an evil smile as the page flipped to reveal his answer: *In a heartbeat.*

* * *

King Vitio and Marcus strode through a dark corridor an hour before the scheduled time for the royal heads to meet. They were silent and cautious, checking every hallway that turned off in a different direction. When they reached the turn they were supposed to take, they stopped and peeked around the corner. Four soldiers were standing guard outside the steel door to the chamber that housed Itta.

"Dammit," Vitio whispered. "I was hoping we'd get lucky."

"The percentages were low," Marcus said.

If they had been guards from the Archaic Kingdom, Vitio could have easily gained access. But Adrenians prided themselves on their sense of duty. They followed their orders to perfection—or died trying.

Vitio leaned back against the wall. "This would be easy if you or Vistas could make them hallucinate."

"Even we're not that good," Marcus replied. "And stop worrying. We'll be fine."

Spy Pilot Ophala and Archaic Prince Sigmund approached with focused looks in their eyes. Ophala carried her staff and Sigmund wore his scarf—their respective ancients.

"It's about time," Vitio said. He gaped as the pair marched straight past him and turned the corner toward the guards without a response.

"Sigmund, where are they?" came the mocking voice of Ophala.

"Beats me," Sigmund replied. "Perhaps they're running a little behind."

Marcus snorted. Vitio ignored him and hurried after the Archains.

"Spy Pilot Ophala Vevlu, Archaic Prince Sigmund," announced one of the surprised guards. Then he noticed the others. "Intel King Vitio and …"

"Marcus," the Dev servant said.

"We weren't expecting to see anyone this early."

"It was decided to have Marcus ask Itta a few questions as a warm-up prior to the scheduled interrogation," Ophala said. "That way he can get a feel of how he needs to weave."

"Is that true, King Vitio?" the soldier asked.

Ophala's eyes narrowed. "Since when do you need reassurance from others? I've seen the guards allow access to certain chiefs countless times."

"Excuse me, ma'am?"

"Don't act dense. As a member of the Amendment Order, I am one of five people who hold sway over you—even if you're Adrenian. I ask that you let us in."

The man froze. "My apologies, Mrs. Vevlu," he said as he pushed open the steel door. The group entered the hollow chamber, the door slamming shut behind them.

"Who were you referring to, Ophala?" Vitio asked.

"Not now."

Moonlight spilled into the circular room from the small windows in the domed ceiling. The wooden beams that the bats hung from cut the bluish light into irregular patterns. Vitio gazed into the lone cell. The smell was ghastly. He could barely recognize Itta's emaciated body that sat in the back of the cell.

Itta looked up with disinterest. Then his eyes widened at the sight of his son. "Sigmund …"

The prince responded with a cold, emotionless, "Father."

"Go for it," Vitio instructed Marcus.

"I would have expected all of the royal heads to be present for such a matter," Itta said. "This seems a bit odd. Suspicious, even." Nobody responded, which didn't seem to bother him. "You aren't going to learn much from your yes-or-no questions."

Marcus stood in front of the cell with his eyes closed, facing away from its prisoner.

"What is it you want to know?" Itta continued. "My purpose with Prince Storshae? I have nothing to hide."

Marcus's eyes opened to reveal only the whites. Itta smirked, feeling the Dev servant's presence in his head. "All for naught."

"Do you know the name, Rhyparia NuForce?" Vitio asked.

Itta sat in a frozen shock, his face a blank mask as Marcus answered, "Yes."

"Was it an avalanche that wiped out the sector of Olethros in the city of Rim?

"No."

Itta's breathing grew heavy, and Marcus panted at the same rhythm.

"Was it Rhyparia NuForce?"

A mighty roar bellowed through the chamber as Itta rose from the floor. He slammed his fists and forearms against the stone wall. This was the easiest, most effective method for resisting a truth extractor. The pain overwhelmed the nervous system—the exact spot Marcus was targeting.

Marcus screamed in agony, for he felt everything that Itta did.

"Was it Rhyparia NuForce?" Vitio shouted over the mix of Itta's roars and Marcus's cries.

"Yes!" Marcus shouted through strands of saliva.

"Were you responsible for covering it up?"

"Yes!"

"Was it to keep Rhyparia for your own gain?"

Itta punched the stone, and the bones in his hand gave way with the sound of a handful of twigs being snapped in half. Marcus howled as blood poured from his eyes and down his cheeks.

"Stop!" Ophala commanded.

What were your plans for Rhyparia?!" Vitio shouted, forgetting that this wasn't a yes-or-no question. He was about to correct himself, but then Marcus did the unbelievable …

As Itta mashed the bones of his fingers with his other hand, Marcus shrieked, "A secret weapon to eliminate your kingdom!"

The clamor stopped as the servant listlessly collapsed to the floor. Itta also lay motionless on the ground. Ophala rushed past the frozen Intel King and grabbed hold of Marcus. She frantically smacked his cheek a few times.

"He's barely breathing!" she shouted.

Vitio stared at nothing, his mind racing elsewhere. Rhyparia was a weapon of mass destruction. Did she know?

The chamber door slammed open. The rest of the royal heads and chiefs entered. Curious looks turned to confusion, then to worry. Damian, the round Passion King, wobbled toward his servant. After taking a look at Marcus's face, he turned back to Vitio with livid eyes. He may have been a mute, but that glare spoke a thousand words.

"I'm sorry, Damian," Vitio said. "I fear I've made many mistakes."

"I'd say so," Apsa said. "Get Marcus to a doctor."

Damian and Ophala picked up the servant and carried him out of the chamber. King Supido gazed into the cell before looking back at Vitio. "So what information was so important for you to find out?" He gazed at Itta's trembling body. "And so important for that man to go to that extent to protect?"

"Olethros," Vitio croaked. He cleared his throat. "The sector that was flattened several years ago, killing hundreds … It was Rhyparia. She isn't just a girl who lacks control. She is a weapon being trained to kill on a large scale … to completely annihilate populations."

"I recall everyone telling you that she should be locked up for good," Supido said. "You were the one who convinced Apsa and Damian to give her another chance."

Vitio shook his head. "I was wrong."

The Adren King's response was dry and flat: "Let's go get her then."

25
The Battle of Lake Kaloge

Agnos and Bryson journeyed through the deserted late-afternoon school halls. Bryson had already spent enough of his Monday in this building, and he couldn't hide the annoyance on his face. To make matters worse, they were in the Morality Wing. As an Intelian, it was basically engraved in his mind to despise Archain thinking.

"Why can't we go over this stuff in the park, where everyone else is?" Bryson whined.

"Because I think things will come easier to you where we're headed."

"This is the last place to help me think."

Agnos stopped as they reached a door. "I think you'll recognize this place."

Bryson's eyes widened as they stepped into the classroom that had been haunting his dreams.

"I talked to Director Senex today," Agnos said as he began writing on the chalkboard. "I didn't ask him about the characters because you've only drawn what looks to be a single character and half of another one. And I doubt they're accurate, seeing that you've redrawn them countless times."

"It's hard, okay?"

"I know that. But I did ask him which classroom he held lectures for the first Jestivan." He put the chalk down and turned to face Bryson, who was slowly walking between the rows of desks and examining the room.

"Dreams are manifestations of your subconscious," Agnos continued. "They're involuntary reactions to experiences you may have gathered from not only your own deep past or memories, but of someone else's you may have been related to. Most of the time these are things you cannot willingly force yourself to visualize while awake."

"Great, a lecture."

"Have a seat."

Bryson picked a desk and sat down.

Agnos smirked. "Do you realize where you sat?"

"The same spot as my dream?" Bryson deducted after gazing around. "Coincidence, I guess."

"That decision came from your subconscious. It's widely believed that a person can trigger specific dreams by manipulating what's happening around them in the real world at the time of falling asleep."

"Don't tell me you brought me here to sleep."

"I brought you here to sleep."

Bryson got up. "I'm leaving."

"Fine, but then it's goodbye to your weaving lessons with Lilu."

The Intelian paused halfway out the door. "What?"

"We decided a while ago that if you don't cooperate with one of us, you lose us both."

Bryson stared at Agnos for a few seconds then slowly returned to his chair.

"I situated everything for you," Agnos said. "You're in the same classroom, and I've written the characters you've given me on the board."

Agnos walked over and took a seat next to his friend. Bryson raised an eyebrow. "You're going to sit there the entire time while I try to fall asleep?"

"And while you sleep."

"Creepy."

A couple minutes of silence passed, which Bryson spent staring at the writing on the chalkboard as he waited for his eyes to grow heavy. He glanced at Agnos to tell him what a colossal failure this was, and nearly laughed when he saw that Agnos was silently mouthing nonsense.

Then it finally clicked. This wasn't funny; it was serious. Agnos was going to this extent for Bryson while he treated it like a joke. Finally his eyelids became heavy and he rested his head on the desk …

… Bryson opened his eyes, fingers numb as he exhaled clouds of white. The temperature had dropped significantly. Agnos was to his right, inaudibly moving his lips. The strange man sat to his left, and Director Senex stood on a stool at the front of the room next to the foreign writing on the chalkboard. This time the writing was clearer. The haze had cleared, making the characters easier to decipher.

While Bryson intensely studied the board, someone screamed to his left. The temperature plummeted further as he stared into the expanse of shadows where the wall had been. Along with the screams, echoing thuds carried from its depths … and he heard a song again, but he couldn't tell what it was.

Then something new happened. Bryson rose from his seat and walked toward the shadows. The screaming grew louder, almost inhuman. The distant thuds became loud bangs.

He was at the cusp of the unknown when the cacophony peaked, making his head spin. Then he stepped into the darkness, and it was as if he had left the classroom. Black swallowed him whole, and the noises were replaced with a deafening silence. His body was paralyzed from the neck down as his head swiveled in every direction. He could have sworn he was breathing harder than he ever had in his life, but he couldn't hear it. It was like he entered a vacuum of sound and light.

Finally, a gentle, distant sound made itself heard. Someone was humming a melody. He strained to make it out, but his efforts were useless. The tune was just too obscure for him to decipher …

When Bryson awoke, Agnos was staring at him with a satisfied grin. "How'd it go?" he asked.

"Your idea worked."

"I know." Agnos tapped the parchment on Bryson's desk. "Look."

It was the first two characters of the word in his dream—perfectly drawn. "I did that?"

Agnos nodded. "This is a great start."

The two friends gathered their bags and headed out of the room. It was dusk, so Bryson must have slept for a couple hours. "What were you humming by the way?" Agnos asked.

"Was I? Someone was humming in my dream, but I couldn't hear it."

"It's definitely important."

"How'd it go?" Bryson asked.

Agnos pondered on it for a moment, but he eventually repeated what he could remember.

Bryson frowned. "That's 'Phases of S.'"

*   *   *

Several of the Jestivan and one of the Diatia had gathered in the open fields by the High Sever. Olivia, Rhyparia, and Vuilni formed one group; Himitsu, Tashami, and Jilly another; and Bryson and Lilu made a pair.

Bryson had been getting better at sensing currents over the past couple of months and was now able to muster up longer strings of electricity, and more consistently. Lilu, who stood several feet away from him, leaned to her right in order to dodge one of his electrical strikes. The flower in her hair was a chocolate cosmos—one of her more frequent choices.

"I think it's time I teach you the rest," she said.

"About time," Bryson replied, using his clout to fire his energy toward a specific cluster of currents, which resulted in another electrical strike.

"You have control of your energy and your clout has increased, allowing you to create more powerful and farther-reaching attacks, and most important, you have gotten a grasp of sensing nature's currents surrounding you. But now we focus on weaving … and I mean conscious weaving, not accidental. This is the hard part."

Bryson shrugged. "I can feel it when it's happening—the weaving, that is."

"You're feeling the reaction that occurs from the weaving and creation of an EC chain," Lilu explained, rolling up the sleeves of her blouse. "The proper terminology for it is *thrust.* Clout is your body's propulsion of energy, while thrust is nature's propulsion of your energy through the use of currents. Just as you can dictate the movement of your energy through your body, it's the same thing with weaving. You spin your energy around a current in order to dictate the movement of an EC chain. Controlling your energy becomes more difficult the farther it travels from your body. And the only way you can make it travel far is through weaving and the thrust that results."

"I prefer just using my clout. Work on strengthening that aspect."

"And that's the attitude of someone who's lazy," Lilu snapped. "Don't be like my sister—all power, no control or stamina."

"Well, stamina and control don't matter if you're strong enough to take your opponent out in the first few strikes."

Lilu stared at Bryson with an exasperated look. "That's not very Debo of you."

"What's that supposed to mean?"

"I'm going to put this in a way that makes sense. Remember my first one-on-one speed percentage lesson with Debo in your backyard?"

Bryson laughed at the image of Debo's hairy legs in a pair of high heels. "Of course."

"I thought speed was all about just that … *speed.* But it wasn't. There is a technique to it. You run using the balls of your feet and your toes, which is the first step to creating balance and agility. Someone can run as fast as Yama, but if that person has no balance or agility, they're useless in battle."

"So you're saying speed is like clout. It's the power. And balance and agility are like weaving. It's the technique."

"Yes."

Bryson nodded. "Hmm. I see."

"But weaving will take a year or two, at least, to get good at."

"Not for me." he declared.

Lilu shook her head. "Don't underestimate—" She looked over Bryson's shoulder. "What is she up to?"

Bryson turned around. Rhyparia was pointing her open umbrella. Vuilni, Olivia, Tashami, Jilly and Himitsu were loosely scattered around her. Rhyparia waved Bryson and Lilu over.

"I'm not perfect at this," Rhyparia was saying. "But I've gotten good enough to show you what I've been working on. Besides, a certain someone has been begging to see what my ancient does since she's gotten here." She smiled at Vuilni, then began to twirl her umbrella. "Ready?" she asked.

"Don't crush us," Himitsu said.

But that wasn't what they felt at all. Instead their bodies felt lighter as they started to lift into the air. A moment later they were floating just a few inches above the ground.

Each person reacted differently as their bodies inched higher. Himitsu smiled and casually leaned back as if he was lying on the air. Olivia stared blankly while Meow Meow was trying to blow away the strands of Olivia's bangs that had floated in front of his face. Jilly was laughing uncontrollably while swimming through the air.

"Kind of happy I put my hair in a bun," Lilu said.

Vuilni's reaction was the most priceless. A loud thud caused everyone to spin in her direction. She was upside down with a look of sheer horror, her legs dangling in the air with her hands and forearms in the ground.

Tashami was dumbfounded. "Did you just punch through the ground … then grab onto it like it's a handle?"

Laughs erupted from the Jestivan as they rolled in the air—except Olivia, of course. Then their euphoria was cut short as they smacked the ground without notice.

"How about a warning next time?" Lilu asked.

Jilly shot up from the ground. "Encore!"

"No!" the others shouted.

* * *

The royal carriage rolled away from the Passion Kingdom's teleplatforms with Fiamma in its sights. Marcus lay across a bench with bandage wrapped around his eyes. Though the bleeding had long stopped, even the faintest ray of light brought sharp stabs of agony through his temple.

After a few hours the ride went from smooth to bumpy, alerting them to their arrival at the bridge that stretched across Lake Kaloge.

King Damian was happy to be returning home. No crises had erupted while he was gone, and he was thankful to escape the smoldering Archaic Kingdom and its dingy capital. He loved Fiamma's beauty.

He glanced down at the parchment that listed all known murders and injuries committed by Rhyparia NuForce.

Olethros: 142 injuries, 389 deaths.

Generals' Battle Restaurant Incident: 4 injuries, 16 deaths.

Total: 146 injuries, 405 deaths.

Damian shook his head. There was no excusing this.

Lulled by the steady clatter of the wheels against the bridge's wooden span, Damian was only on the verge of sleep when he was jarred awake by a loud bang. The carriage flipped on its side and tumbled off the bridge's edge, crashing into the lake below.

Marcus had already swum toward the surface, and the Passion King tried to follow his lead. Then something elastic sent him plummeting toward the lake's floor.

Damian glared up at his assailant, who was covered from head to toe in thousands of tiny bubbles. Damian knew what this was. Toono had marked his next target.

* * *

Toono crashed into the water, his bubbles flattening as he swam. Swimming was something he had forced himself to master at a young age. It was necessary for his original goals—goals that now belonged to Agnos.

He knew that this fight would be a more daunting test. Damien wasn't a boy like the Prim Prince, or a young Diatia like Chelekah, or an old woman like the Still Queen. This was a first-born king in his forties—too old for a Branian, but that was because he didn't need one anymore.

Toono plunged into the lake's depths, ramming Damian's massive midsection with his shoulder. Damian tossed him aside and shot toward the surface for air. Toono couldn't allow that to happen. This whole plan hinged on his success to keep the king submerged, for it gave him a massive upper hand. Toono could breathe because of the bubbles molded around his body while Damian couldn't. And since flame was useless in water, Damian couldn't weave.

Passion soldiers had come to their king's aid, recklessly splashing into the lake without a thought for the disadvantages they faced. And though they weren't a threat to Toono, they were definitely a nuisance as they plunged down on top of him and tried to force him back down to the lakebed.

Toono smacked a soldier in the face with Orbaculum as he brought it to his mouth. He blew into it, creating a larger bubble. It thudded dully as the soldiers punched at it with their weak, water-logged blows.

Damian had reached the surface as his men pulled him up to the bridge. Toono grit his teeth and surged upward. He grabbed hold of Damian's ankles, but the king was too strong. Toono's grip began to slip, and he realized that he would fail, that this was an early end to a very long road.

Then Damian abruptly let go and crashed back into the water. The skin on his hands had eroded, exposing raw muscle and white bone. Only one person could corrode someone's skin like that: Kadlest and her acidic ancient, Baldum.

As Damian gaped at his hands, Toono sent him tumbling through the water with a kick to his torso. The king roared, but only a flurry of air bubbles escaped his mouth. Then his expression changed—to something like sadness, or pity, and Toono felt a surge of guilt.

Toono took a deep breath and blew into the lone bottom hole of his staff. The bubble expanded until it could fit ten Damians inside. He raised his staff above his head and hacked downward with all his strength.

The steel bubble descended at a speed like an arrow shot from a bow, and a cloud of sand billowed up from the lakebed. Toono stared at Damian as the sand slowly dispersed. He thought for a moment, then swam down and grabbed his victim. He was exhausted and starting to breathe in water as his suit of bubbles began to burst one by one. It took a lot of effort, but he eventually reached the surface, which was thick with the bobbing corpses of soldiers dressed in red.

"Kadlest!" he yelled.

A face covered in blood and burns gazed over the bridge's edge. "Do you bring good news?" she asked.

He allowed Damian's bald head to bob above the water.

She smiled. "Very good." She disappeared for a second. "Here," she said as she tossed a heavy sack down to Toono. It was filled with rocks from the lakeshore, and a rope was tied to its end.

Toono tied the rope around Damian's torso and sent the king's corpse down to the lakebed. Then he swam to one of the bridge's wooden beams and climbed up. Collapsing onto his back, he stared at the cloudless, bright blue sky and the crusted underbellies of the two islands that floated high above the Light Realm. With this being his fourth murder of an elite, he was beginning to wonder if the Bozani would intervene—or if that was even how they operated. He had no clue.

"We have a new friend," Kadlest announced.

Toono rolled his head to the side. Kadlest stood next to a man with bandage wrapped around his eyes. "I'm guessing that's the truth extractor."

"Sure is," Kadlest replied. "And it looks like they did quite a number on him over in Phelos."

"Well get rid of him."

Marcus stammered, "Please don't—"

His plea was cut short as Kadlest thrust a blade across his neck. She bent down and tied a bag around the Dev servant's burgundy uniform. "Now we return to Apoleia," she said.

26
The Winter Festival

The grounds of Phesaw Park were blanketed by the fluffy white snow that continued to gently twist down from the night sky. Fat snowflakes glittered in the Intelights that illuminated the festivities. Booths and attractions were scattered throughout the park. It was an atmosphere very reminiscent of the first night of the Generals' Battle weekend thirteen months ago, when the Jestivan explored the Intel Kingdom's capital of Dunami.

Despite its name, the Winter Festival wasn't held every year, but only to celebrate momentous occasions such as the original Jestivan's formation thirty years ago. This year it honored the first-ever visit of students from Ipsas, the school of the Dark Realm. It was a big step in a mission for peace and the annihilation of bigoted ignorance.

If there was one member of the Jestivan who didn't need a festival to remind her of those values, it was Jilly. The joyful girl—her cheeks an extra red in the cold—was making her presence known at a target booth, where stuffed animals hung from the wall as rewards. Her huge sunhat rested on her back to make room for earmuffs. Toshik and Yama stood on either side of her, both occasionally glaring at the other with looks that lacked appreciation of the other's company.

Jilly eyed the many targets that covered the booth's far wall. There were roughly thirty of them, and the goal was to hit the one in the center. The trick was that each row of targets moved from side to side in alternating patterns. She frowned, mustering up a deranged glare of concentration, before waving a hand toward the center bull's-eye.

Every single target was blown over by a formidable wall of wind. Even the man running the booth was knocked to the ground. As he pulled himself up, he blinked a couple times and said, "The objective isn't to hit all—"

"She knows that," Yama interrupted. "She has a little trouble controlling herself."

The man said nothing. He probably knew Yama's reputation and didn't want to provoke her. Toshik had become distracted by a girl in the distance.

"So who is your victim tonight?" Yama asked. "You look like a hawk scoping the field for prey."

Toshik smiled. "No one. I was watching the kids playing in the snow over there."

"We want the big purple stuffed emrok," Yama said to the man in the booth.

"You didn't win it," the man replied with little conviction.

"Then I'll give it a go."

The man pointed at the sign that hung above the booth: GAME ONLY FOR INTEL, PASSION, SPIRIT, OR ARCHAIC ENERGY (DEPENDING ON THE ANCIENT). NO ADRENIANS.

"No big deal," Toshik said. "We'll try a different booth." Jilly followed him with a skip in her step.

While Yama remained at the booth, Jilly and Toshik walked farther into the park. Jilly gazed up at the tall Jestivan. "Would you rather find a different girl to spend tonight with?"

"No," Toshik answered. "I have a habit of wandering eyes. I'm working on it."

"That's okay," Jilly said with a bright smile. "I have a habit of a wandering brain."

Toshik laughed, causing his charge to blush.

Yama ran up and handed Jilly a stuffed emrok. She squealed with joy. "Thank you!"

Toshik smirked and shook his head. "You either stole it or harassed that poor man until you got it. Either way, I respect your efforts."

Yama ran a finger across her throat while Jilly embraced her in a hug.

* * *

Bryson sat in the snow, shivering despite a scarf and two layers of clothes. Agnos and Tashami sat next to him. Agnos had a book in his hand that he had gotten from one of his professors. It had something to do with the Sea of Light. Tashami and Bryson were more focused on the hilarious snowball fight unfolding before them.

It was two against two: Simon and Himitsu versus Illipsia and Lilu. The two little ones focused on each other while Himitsu and Lilu made it their mission to annihilate the other. The battle was full of narrow misses and playful banter. Then as Himitsu loaded up a massive ball of snow with a sinister smirk, a cluster of snowballs pelted him in the face from the side and knocked him off of his feet.

Rhyparia and Vuilni were dying of laughter, pleased with their ambush. While Lilu congratulated her fellow litas on their success, Himitsu approached the zanas with a sour look.

"They ganged up on me," he said, rubbing his jaw as he sat down. "I think I know which one was Vuilni's too."

"It's a shame Olivia couldn't stay past dark for this," Tashami said.

Bryson looked down. Even after all these years, Olivia's strict curfew bothered him sometimes.

"I'm going to Phelos to bring the new year in with a bang," Himitsu said.

"Going to see your mom?" Bryson asked.

"Yes. Unfortunately my dad is occupied with his job …" Himitsu refocused on Agnos. "Oh yeah, I'm going to talk to my mom about that ancient."

"I appreciate that," Agnos said.

"What was it about again? Talking to fish?"

Agnos's lip curled down a bit. "Communicating with and controlling sea life—just like what Ophala can do with creatures of the sky. It's called Marigium."

Bryson watched Lilu, who was wearing a long slim-fit coat that reached her shins. She was laughing with Vuilni and Rhyparia. Perhaps it was all the time he had spent with her this semester, but his feelings for her were creeping back. He couldn't remember their last argument—which had to mean it was long overdue.

The Intelights in the park cut out, casting an ominous blanket over the festivities. Confused murmurs carried through the cold air as students tried to make sense of what was happening. Then bright lights ignited in the distance, and people began heading in that direction.

"What do you think's going on?" Tashami asked while excited students hurried past them.

"Probably some type of ceremony," Himitsu said. "This school loves its ceremonies."

Agnos sighed. "I was enjoying my book."

As they got closer, Bryson saw bleachers wrapping around the open field. Students were rushing up the steps, laughing and shouting as they took their seats. Blinding Intelights flashed on, all of them directed at the field. A voice boomed through the air:

"All students take a seat! I need the Jestivan and Diatia to report to the silver tent in the far corner."

Agnos squinted. "That's the Archain who hosts the Generals' Battle."

Bryson's stomach dropped as he suspected what was to come. He nervously entered the tent. It was big, roughly half the size of the Lilac Suites lobby. Candles kept it illuminated instead of Intelights.

"Is everyone in the crowd ready to end 1499 in a big way?" a voice boomed outside the tent.

A thundering roar shook the tent. Bryson thought he might puke.

"All right! We'll get things started in ten minutes!"

As the cheers continued, the tent's curtain opened up to reveal a short man with a bullhorn in his hand. Agnos had been right. This was the same person who had commentated at the Generals' Battle. The man smiled with delight at the elite students' faces.

"Who's ready to put on a show?"

No one answered.

"That would require them to know what show they're putting on." The Jestivan turned to Grand Director Poicus, the five Energy Directors, and Power Warden Feissam. Feissam was hunched over with the tent's ceiling pressed against his shoulders.

Poicus smiled. "I told you at the beginning of the school year that there would be a tournament down the road, but I never laid out the specifics." He paused. "I wanted to keep it a surprise. Now we'll really get to see who has been serious about training, and I don't just mean with your respective directors or warden. I mean everything you've done on your own time too."

Passion Director Venustas unraveled a massive scroll and set it down on a table.

"That parchment shows the bracket," Poicus said. "You will see who faces whom, and what day and time each round takes place. Obviously the first round is tonight."

The Jestivan and Diatia exchanged glances. This was supposed to be a night of carefree fun.

"You'll notice that four people have a bye in the first round," Poicus continued. "Olivia is one of them, so her absence tonight won't be an issue. Do not confront any of the directors about the bye selections; you will be disqualified immediately. And do not fight with the intent to maim or kill. That should be obvious. Keep all attacks in the vicinity of the field of play. Nothing should put the crowd's safety in jeopardy. No one is allowed to disclose this bracket to *anyone*." He paused and scanned their faces. "All clear? Good. We'll be watching from the stands. Now put on a show."

Poicus left the tent while the students rushed to the bracket. As Bryson waited for some of them to disperse, he saw Rhyparia stop Archaic Director Senex at the tent's entrance. There was worry on her face, and Director Senex looked to be trying to calm her.

A hand smacked Bryson on the shoulder. "Looks like you have nothing to worry about, Mr. Captain," Himitsu said. "You got a bye. Vuilni and Bruut too. Looks like they gave it to the captains and the Diatia."

"A bit unfair if you ask me," Toshik said. He smirked at Himitsu. "I'm gonna make you wish I'd let that spunka finish you off."

Himitsu sighed as the lanky swordsman walked away. "Outside of Yama, he's the hardest for someone like me to fight. Why did I have to get him first?"

"It's time to begin!" the host boomed to more roars. "The first match of the night is between two litas! One is a member of the royal Intel Family and the other is a speedy, ferocious swordswoman of the Adren Kingdom! Make some noise for Lita Lilu and Lita Yama!"

Lilu seemed nervous, even afraid, while Yama looked adamant and focused. Both girls had tied their colorful hair up.

"Good luck," Bryson mouthed to Lilu with a thumbs-up and a smile. But on the inside he felt as stricken as she looked. The only person who wasn't intimidated by Yama was Olivia.

They stepped out of the tent and stood on the sidelines to watch. Lilu and Yama faced each other on the field. Yama held up a wooden sword.

"Ready?" the host yelled.

They raised their hands, and the match commenced. Yama transformed into a blur of colors that streaked toward Lilu. But Lilu was prepared for it, and wove a three-tiered wall of electricity in front of her. Yama hit the first one, then hopped to her right, pausing as she searched for a clear line of attack.

As she pushed off again, one of Lilu's walls morphed into a vicious curling bolt of lightning that struck Yama in the side. The swordswoman fell to a knee with smoke curling up from her tunic and breeches.

The crowd cheered. Surely they were just as surprised as Bryson was. Agnos wasn't kidding when he said that Lilu was a spectacular weaver. She was putting up a fight without even moving—proof that her lack of speed didn't mean much. She wasn't even using her hands. Everything she was doing was with her mind.

Yama rolled to the side as a ball of electricity shot past her. It fizzled just in front of the bleachers. She rose to her feet, studying Lilu in the distance.

Yama circled around Lilu, picking up speed as she ran. To the people in the crowd, she had disappeared, but Bryson could see a giant smear of color surrounding Lilu. Yama was going to randomize her angle and timing. Lilu stood dead still with an austere gaze.

Yama broke off from her path and lunged at Lilu. Bryson cringed, then widened his eyes. Lilu was standing safely inside of a voltaic sphere. Yama stumbled backward, her limbs twitching from the high-voltage contact.

The audience's roars became thunderous, and Bryson found himself on his feet. The other Jestivan were also standing in shock.

"Let's go Lilu!" Himitsu shouted.

Then something took over Yama. Instead of determination, there was rage. And knowing her, it was anger at herself. Once again she disappeared, and even Bryson couldn't follow her. Lilu managed to throw up a few walls of electricity, but then she was tackled to the snow. Yama stood over her with her wooden sword pressed against her heart.

"That's it!" the host announced. "We have our first winner of the tournament—Lita Yama!"

Lilu trudged to the sidelines with her head down.

"This means Yama will move on to face Vuilni, the Power Diatia, in the second round!" The crowd began chanting Yama's name.

"For our next match, we have a battle of the quieter Jestivan. They may keep to themselves, but that doesn't mean they can't dish out some power! Let's hear it for Zana Tashami and Zana Agnos!"

Tashami strode out onto the field. Agnos remained seated in the snow, reading his book.

"Zana Agnos!" the host shouted. Agnos didn't acknowledge it, and boos erupted from the audience.

The host hurried over. "We're waiting for you."

Agnos looked up from his book. "I forfeit."

"What?"

Agnos snatched the bullhorn from the host and put it to his mouth. "I'm forfeiting."

After a short pause, laughter rang from the fans. Himitsu was laughing so hard that he had to wipe tears from his eyes. Bryson wondered why the directors had even bothered including him in the bracket. What else were they expecting?

Agnos returned the bullhorn, and the host shrugged. "Tashami has won by default and will advance to the second round, where he'll meet Olivia Lavender!"

Bryson had no doubt that Olivia would win that matchup. Now his side of the bracket was next—Toshik versus Himitsu, and Rhyparia versus Jilly.

He had to admit that when Himitsu and Toshik stood out on the field—their six-and-a-half-foot frames sizing each other up—he was excited for what was to come. They were undoubtedly talented, but it was their relationship that made this interesting. They were rivals, and though they had learned to tolerate each other during their escapade in the Rolling Oaks, there was still animosity. Beyond all of that was the simple fact that they were two young men with a point to prove.

Himitsu had several disadvantages working against him. He wasn't very good at this style of combat, for one thing, and the white snow and the glare from the Intelights would make it impossible to conceal himself with his black flames. But that snow was also a hindrance for Toshik, whose agility and acceleration would suffer.

Toshik was easier for Bryson to track than Yama as he bolted from one spot to another, and Himitsu, whose speed and reflexes had significantly improved from Rhyparia's gravity sessions, was able to dodge all of Toshik's initial attacks. Himitsu was doing a lot of sidestepping, and he would occasionally wave his hand with a blast of black flames. Their fight was more of a dance than the first—a testament to Yama's ruthless, straight-line approach.

Unfortunately the fight didn't last long, as Toshik overwhelmed Himitsu with his superior close-range skills. His sixth blow struck Himitsu on the shoulder, knocking him to the snow.

Toshik stood above Himitsu with his wooden sword pointed at his opponent's neck.

"It was a good match," Toshik teased.

A sharp intake from the crowd caused Toshik to falter. Himitsu pushed himself up into a seated position. "You're lucky this is a tournament, so I'm refraining from fighting with gimmicks. Otherwise you'd be in a world of pain right now."

Toshik turned to see a wall of black fire. He leapt back and stumbled over Himitsu, falling to the snow. Himitsu stood up, using one arm to help Toshik to his feet—his other arm hung limp.

"Solid victory, Toshik," he said with a wink.

The last match of the evening was between Rhyparia and Jilly, the two Jestivan more notorious for their clout than their weaving. As the host called the two girls to the field, Jilly frolicked to her point, clutching her hands into a single fist and pumping them up and down above her head like a prizefighter. Rhyparia trudged to her spot, shuffling her feet in the snow.

"Many students seem to think only a few can match Lita Yama's talents," the host said. "Lita Rhyparia is one of those few! Ladies … BEGIN!"

Chaos immediately ensued. Spiraling gusts of wind and snow erupted and enclosed the two girls, making it difficult for spectators to see. The wind's howls drowned out any sounds. Jilly wasted no time, instantly releasing her clout all at once without any regard for bystanders. Bryson tightened his hood around his face to keep the freezing winds from stinging his skin.

Rhyparia opened her umbrella and allowed the wind to lift her high into the air, where she floated for a few seconds, readying to pounce. She then intensified the gravity around her, causing her to plummet at an unnatural speed. Poor Jilly had no clue that Rhyparia was about to strike from above her.

But then the whirlwind of snow disappeared, and a vertical gale exploded upward from Jilly's hands, knocking Rhyparia off course. A collective *ooh* escaped the crowd as Jilly sent another strike of wind at Rhyparia, which sent her flying into the ground. Precision attacks were something Bryson had never seen from Jilly. She was getting better, just like the rest of them.

Rhyparia hopped to her feet and blocked the next gust with her umbrella. She crouched low in order to hide behind her shield. The umbrella flapped wildly and the wind whipped her hair, but she stayed in that position until the stream finally ended. Spectators roared with excitement.

"Why isn't she making proper use of her ancient?" Vuilni asked.

"I think she's scared to," Bryson replied.

"Why is that?"

He thought about it for a second. "She thinks she'll hurt her." That was as specific of an answer that he'd give. Clearly Rhyparia hadn't told Vuilni about her deadly accidents.

Jilly lunged at her opponent with a fist raised. Punches, kicks, elbows, and knees were exchanged—along with the occasional block or attack with an umbrella. This was more like the team training sessions when the Jestivan would spar for five-minute rounds before switching partners. Bryson marveled at their improved speed and reflexes.

Suddenly Jilly's feet lifted off the ground. She clawed and kicked at the air as she floated higher and higher. While Rhyparia's refusal to increase the gravity around Jilly proved that she didn't trust her ability to control her clout, it was clear that she was perfectly comfortable with a bit of weaving.

"If she's not going to crush her …" Vuilni said.

Bryson finished her thought: "Then she'll drop her from a great height."

The same conclusion dawned on the announcer. "It appears as if Rhyparia is about to let Jilly fall out of the sky!"

But Jilly had other ideas. She snatched herself out of the up-current with her own burst of wind, tossing her sideways. As she tumbled, she thrust out her palms. A heavy barrage of wind collided with Rhyparia, walloping her into the snow.

Rhyparia lay motionless as a silence bathed the field. Jilly landed and instantly ran toward her friend. Vuilni and Bryson also ran across the snowy expanse. Bryson's heart was pounding.

Thankfully Rhyparia's eyes were open as Jilly pulled her up to her knees. Bryson stopped and stared at her snow-covered face. She was fine, but Bryson was amazed by the power of Jilly's clout.

"Lita Rhyparia is okay!" the host shouted. "We have an upset, folks! Lita Jilly will advance to take on one of the Power Diatia, Bruut!"

And that was the end to the frenetic night. Round two was set: Bryson versus Toshik, Bruut versus Jilly, Olivia versus Tashami, and Yama versus

Vuilni. Bryson was determined to spend the winter break working his body even more rigorously than he had before.

* * *

A young girl with long black hair slipped out of the Jestivan's abandoned tent. She crumpled some parchment into her pocket and briskly walked away from the crowds toward the library. She would sleep there until morning. Even though she was disappointed to leave Simon without a goodbye, Kadlest was waiting for her at the Passion Kingdom's teleplatforms.

She had obtained everything she needed to satisfy Toono and Kadlest. She recorded tonight's fights between the Jestivan, which would prove more useful than the training sessions she'd watched over the course of the semester. She also jotted down the times and dates of the tournament's future rounds, figuring that might help Toono out. She wasn't exactly sure why she was doing all of this, but Illipsia didn't ask questions. She simply did as she was told—just like she was raised.

27
Blinded

Toono arrived at a wall of clay that jutted from the ground with Kadlest following behind him. He kicked his feet until he found the makeshift vent in the ceiling of Olivia's room, and they dropped into the cave. They walked down a long tunnel lined with sputtering torches. It never ceased to amaze Toono that Apoleia and Olivia had lived in this dreary place for so many years.

"I had enjoyed my time away from this woman," Kadlest whispered.

"Don't be like that."

"I suppose you're right." She paused for a moment. "It's freezing."

Toono's eyes narrowed. "Stop."

Kadlest stood still as Toono crouched low and examined the floor. "Tripwires," he said.

"Do you want to see what they do?"

The question came from a shaky voice that sent a chill up Toono's spine. He slowly lifted his head to look at the woman standing in the shadows of the tunnel.

"Not particularly," Toono said.

She giggled momentarily before maniacally laughing with delight. "I'm gonna throw something at it!" It wasn't a bluff. A rock was hurled from the shadows, hitting the wire with enough force to make it snap.

Toono and Kadlest flinched, but nothing happened. The woman giggled again. "They're not tripwires, silly. I just wanted to mess with you."

"Well this is a lovely welcome, Apoleia," Toono said.

"You've finished your business in the Passion Kingdom?"

"I have."

Her dark silhouette began walking toward Toono and Kadlest, snapping through the wires. It also sounded like she was smearing something against the wall.

She stopped directly in front of them, and the temperature plunged drastically. Her violet hair was a stringy mess, and tiny icicles hung from her ears, chin, and nose. Her face was layered in a thin sheet of frost, and her bloody hand had left a trail of red along the dirt wall. The skin on her forearms had been mutilated with a zigzag of deep cuts.

She smiled and let out a sigh of satisfaction that caused Toono's nose to crystalize. "Then I suppose it's my turn," she said, her voice eerily steady.

Toono nodded. "Let's prepare."

* * *

Boisterous shouting echoed throughout a vast sunbathed chamber. "It has been two days!" a woman exclaimed. "Three scouting units have yet to return, and the other two came back empty-handed!"

"Major Paltie, I ask that you calm down," Passion General Landon said.

"How am I supposed to remain calm, sir?"

"At least lower your voice," Landon suggested. "You know how Prince Pentil likes to sneak around. He doesn't need to find out his father has vanished—not like this."

Paltie took a deep breath. "What are we supposed to do? Both of the boys are worried. They know that something's wrong."

Landon waited a moment before answering. "He could still be alive. And that's why we're not telling anyone yet. I refuse to allow this kingdom to go into an unnecessary hysteria."

"And if King Damian doesn't return by mid-January, will you still do what the royal heads asked of you?"

"No," Landon replied. "I wouldn't leave a kingless Fiamma without its general too. Sending four generals after that girl is preposterous in the first place. It's overkill."

Paltie frowned. "That they're being so careful is telling, no?"

Landon shrugged. "I have my own issues to attend to. Rhyparia NuForce isn't one of them."

* * *

Chief Merchant Toth Brench stood off to the side of a training field filled with Archaic and Adren soldiers. They were going through drills, sweltering under the Archaic Kingdom's merciless December sun. At the head of this mixture of brown uniforms and slim-fitted silver cloaks stood Chief Officer Wert Lamay, who wore a magnificent blue uniform reserved for officials of his high rank. It was a strange squad of soldiers—a Spirit Major leading Archains and Adrenians.

"Adrenians, spar in pairs!" Wert barked. "Archains, run until I'm satisfied! Some of you lot are a disgrace!"

"Yes, sir!"

Toth laughed while Wert turned and headed his way.

"How does it feel when soldiers from other kingdoms follow you without question?" Toth asked.

Wert splashed cold water over his face from the barrel Toth was leaning on. "It feels right."

"It's amazing how nearly all of them use swords that my company has crafted."

"A successful monopoly."

"A monopoly that will run itself into the ground if Toshik doesn't get his head out of his rear."

Wert chuckled. "It's not like much is being asked of him. Don't lose Jilly to that girl … that's it. We aren't putting them in the thick of our operations here. They're allowed to live their lives and enjoy Phesaw."

Toth shook his head. "They're the benefactors of all the hard work we're putting in here."

"Exactly! Selfish is what that boy is. But we already know that. Jun's death is a constant reminder."

The mention of Toth's wife pulled his attention away from the present. Memories swept through his thoughts as he stared up at the sky.

Wert didn't seem to notice. "These Archains and their ancients are some of the most desirable tools for an army I can think of. That lady there—" Wert pointed— "is an elastic woman."

The two men fell silent. The only sounds were the grunts and clashing steel of sparring swordsmen in the distance. Watching only reminded Toth of Jun. She was amazing with any sort of blade, which was why he handled the business side of operations while she did the hunting. And all of Toshik's talents in life were physical, making him more of his mother's son than his father's. Toshik didn't care about his father's business savvy.

Heavy footsteps and breathing approached from behind the two chiefs. "Chief Wert, sir."

They turned to see an Archain soldier hunched over from exhaustion. "And what do you need?" Wert spat.

"I promised my family I'd be home tonight for supper. Training was supposed to stop an hour ago, sir."

The chief's eyes widened with rage. "Get back to running!" he bellowed.

The man flinched. "Yes, sir."

As he sprinted away, Toth said, "Go see your wife, soldier."

The man stopped, his back facing them as if he was contemplating the idea of defying his Chief Officer's orders in favor of the Chief Merchant, who had no jurisdiction over him. Wert whirled around and glared at his counterpart.

Toth repeated himself with more sternness: "Go see your wife."

"Thank you, sir." Without looking back, the soldier dashed off of the field.

Toth picked up his sword, which was leaning against the barrel. "Wert, do me a favor."

"What's that?"

"Instead of focusing on bashing my son and reminding me of my dead wife, concentrate on useful matters—such as developing an army that wants to fight for you. I see a bunch of strong, talented men and women here, but I see none willing to lay their life on the line for what you represent. If we are to overtake the Amendment Order and make the Archaic Kingdom our own, we'll need all the faithful troops we can get."

Wert grunted. "Smooth-talking is your job."

Toth started walking toward the castle. "Wrap this up, please. We have a broadcast with an important friend in thirty minutes."

* * *

Toth stood in the palace's kiln cellar, a dingy room that pumped hot and cold water throughout the building's skeleton. His hand gripped an overhanging pipe as he waited for his comrade, who was running late.

There was one other person already in the room with Toth—a woman wearing an elegant burgundy cloak. Her hair, eyelashes, and irises were a deep blue, and her skin was a dark brown. These were all telling characteristics of someone born in Prayoga, a city in the Dev Kingdom's southwest corner—a city very similar to Brilliance. If not already evident by the wealth of her outfit, she was a Dev servant of the Brench family, given to Toth five years ago by Adren King Supido.

"Tazama," Toth said. "How is he doing?" he asked. "I'm assuming he's lost his patience by this point. Let him know it's Wert's fault."

Tazama closed her eyes for a short moment. "I'm told he's fuming."

Toth impatiently tapped the pipe and glared at the stairwell. Eventually heavy footsteps grew loud enough to be heard over the basement's machinery.

"Let's go, Wert."

The Chief Officer made a motion with his hand as if to imply to get on with it.

Toth looked at Tazama. "Connect us."

A holographic display lit up the room. A man with rustled charcoal hair and a glare of pure annoyance sat at a desk in his office. While the sun had set in the Light Realm, it was now shining in the Dark Realm, and the light from the display was blinding.

"Hello, Prince Storshae," Toth said, who had drawn himself to attention. Wert was still hunched in the shadows.

"Mr. Brench. Mr. Lamay."

"We don't have much time to discuss things," Toth said.

"And who's to blame for that?" Storshae fired back.

A noise of disgust came from Wert. Storshae ignored it. "Was Itta able to hold his tongue during the truth extraction?"

"Luck was on our side," Toth replied. "They weren't able to interrogate him about the matters that were originally intended. Instead Intel King Vitio pressed his own agenda, depleting Marcus's energy."

"And what did Vitio want to find out?"

Toth smirked. "Apparently Itta has had a secret weapon of mass destruction up his sleeve for a very long time."

"Are we speaking along the lines of a technological breakthrough?"

"More like a person," Toth said, causing Storshae's eyes to widen. "There is a member of the Jestivan—a girl known as Rhyparia NuForce. She manipulates gravity."

The Dev King laughed. "I've run into that girl. I wasn't aware she was a product of Itta!"

"Yes, she would be a great tool for us. Her body count is north of 300. And she defeated a couple of your highest officers with ease."

"Well then go get her!" Storshae exclaimed.

"The generals are doing that for us. Wert and I will have to convince the other members of the Amendment Order that she shouldn't be executed."

"And how is our mysterious friend?" Wert asked. "Are we any closer to Dev King Rehn's rebirth?"

"The Passion Kingdom doesn't know it for a fact," Storshae said, "but King Damian is dead. So we're not only one step closer to resurrecting my father, that's one less threat opposing the rebirth of the Archaic and Dev Kingdom's alliance. Excellent work, gentlemen. Good night."

The hologram disappeared, and the two chiefs exchanged satisfied looks, but Tazama appeared skeptical. "Have you ever wondered why you've never met or spoken with Toono?" she asked. The two men stared in silence. She let out a small laugh. "Fools," she muttered.

"What did you say?" Wert snarled.

She stared him down with her blue eyes. "You have strength and Toth has wealth, but that's a self-destructive equation when you're missing a key variable—intellect."

Toth listened carefully, as he always did when Tazama spoke. Wert, on the other hand, was ready to pounce. "You're implying we're being played."

"More used than played, but I'm not completely sure," she said. "All I can go on is my intuition. You're making friends with people prided on their brains. Storshae, a Devish. And Toono, an Archain."

"They don't scare us," Wert retorted.

"Hmm …" She smiled. "In Prayoga, we say that a person is blind if their judgment is clouded by their might or their money. They're so focused on tangible, materialistic gains that they ignore what's most powerful of all because they can't see its worth."

"Knowledge," Toth said.

Tazama nodded. "There's a saying in Prayoga. 'In a game of minds, money and might serve only as blinds.'"

"Stop with the riddles and get to the point," Wert snapped.

"The strings of your blinds are waiting to be pulled closed, Chief Wert, obstructing your vision and purpose and replacing it with another's. I could grab them in an instant. Would you like that? To have your strings pulled? To have such a surplus of money and might, but be fighting for someone else's cause? You're a puppet of Storshae, who is a puppet himself."

Wert's face was boiling red. "*How dare you mock me!*" he roared.

He threw a heavy fist, but it was stopped mid-flight. He gaped at his hand, unable to move it in any direction.

Tazama smirked. She glanced back at Toth, who wore a contemplative expression.

"Get out," Wert commanded, his fist still frozen in the air.

She glided toward the exit and stopped at the foot of the stone steps. "Be careful in this game of minds."

28
1500 K.H.

The Archaic Kingdom's Phelos Palace was bustling with people eagerly awaiting the arrival of the new century. Groups were scattered across a vast stone patio that overlooked a gentle hill. Some danced under the moonlight to the instruments in the background while others simply mingled. There was also a grand buffet right inside of the open doorways.

Himitsu danced with his mother. Though quite tall, Ophala was a full head shorter than her son.

"How's dad?" Himitsu asked.

"He's fine, sweetie."

He sighed. "I guess that's all you can say."

"You know that."

While they continued to sway in one spot, slowly spinning in a circle, Himitsu noticed a bird perched on one of the patio's low-rising walls. "There's a bird staring at us."

"Don't worry. It's mine. It doesn't want to eat you or anything."

"But you don't have your ancient. How are you controlling it?"

"I'm not. It's called loyalty … trust. If you took a good look around, you'd see them everywhere."

Himitsu looked more carefully as they danced in a circle. Sure enough, he saw different species of birds every which way.

"If someone were to approach me from the back, they'd alert me with bird calls because they know I can't see through their eyes without my ancient. Honestly, it's a bit unfair to them. They do too much for me."

Himitsu smiled. "I guess you don't need me or Dad."

"Correction. Your father needs me."

They both laughed, then he remembered something. "Mom, how much do you know about all the different kinds of ancients?"

"Depends on the classification," Ophala said. "I know a lot about the tactical and stealth ancients, such as mine. Director Senex could help you a lot more with that."

"I told one of my fellow Jestivan I'd try to get some information from you."

"Well, as the Spy Pilot, it's my job to not only siphon information from highly secure targets, but to protect what I already know."

Himitsu nodded. "Trust me, I told him to not get his hopes up."

"Then shoot."

"Do you know anything about an ancient that allows someone to control sea life?"

She stopped dancing and looked up at her son. "What a peculiar question."

"Hey, I'm simply the messenger."

"There is such an ancient," Ophala said.

"And who has it?"

"That I will not answer."

Himitsu shrugged. "Oh well. Was a shot in the dark anyway."

He was abruptly pushed to the side as a sunhat bounced through the lower part of his vision. Blond hair swayed back and forth as a girl bolted toward the buffet's dessert section.

Ophala giggled to herself. "That girl … my goodness. Every time I see her, she takes me back to being a kid at Phesaw with how much she reminds me of Thusia."

"Someone needs to keep her away from all of that sugar," Himitsu groaned.

*   *   *

Jilly's wide-eyed look of awe as she took in the endless variety of cakes, cookies, and pastries would have made any baker shake in their boots. She rubbed her hands together, then picked up a monstrous serving platter and began scooping up desserts by the handful.

"I'll take you and you and you and ..." She paused and scanned the selection before spotting a jelly-filled powdered doughnut. "And you!"

Finally she turned and stared at the esteemed guests while stuffing the pastry in her mouth. She chewed viciously, and then bits of doughnut sprayed everywhere.

"Toshy!"

Toshik towered next to her with a glass of wine in hand. His face was flat from boredom.

"Aren't you happy to see me?" she asked.

"My dad just wants people to see us together—two Jestivan and the offspring of two chiefs of the Amendment Order. I like to put on shows, but not like this. Put on a talent show or beauty contest and I'll dazzle any woman who's in eyesight."

She crammed a slice of cake into her mouth. "Dazzle is my new favorite word."

Toshik looked up to see his father, who was staring at him through the crowd. A laughing pair cut in front of his vision. It was Himitsu and Ophala.

"Hey, guys!" Jilly shouted.

They both turned and waved, but continued going their own way. Toshik turned back to see his father still casting an occasional glance in his direction while he talked to Chief Arbitrator Grandarion Senten. Someone tugged at the gold chain that adorned Toshik's vest pocket. He looked down to see Jilly, who wore a rare solemn expression. She nodded toward the patio floor, instructing him to follow.

As they wended their way between aristocrats and royal family members, Jilly reached backward and grabbed Toshik's hand. Eventually they stepped off the patio and onto the grassy hill that sloped downward toward a small pond in front of the palace's exterior wall. The music and conversation had waned as they stood at the top of the hill and stared at the city skyline.

"Your mom would be proud of you," Jilly said, causing Toshik to shoot her a stunned look. "When I became your Charge, you were so mean to me—a total bully. But you'd stick up for me when anyone thought they could mistreat me. It took me a few years to understand why. I was too young at first to make sense of the million emotions that come from losing your mother since I never knew mine.

"You were sad because your mother was gone—the one parent who could connect with you. You felt guilty because you thought it was your fault. You were angry that your dad made you my protector—just days after you proved, in your mind, that you couldn't protect anyone. You took that anger out on me. But you made it your duty to not let history repeat itself.

"Agnos likes to talk to me sometimes. He called it 'counseling.' When I told him your story, he said to me, 'Rage makes him mistreat you; guilt makes him protect you.' You've shown less of that anger over the years; especially the past seven months. You can see it not just with me, but Himitsu and Bryson. And that's why your mom would be proud."

Jilly gave the brightest of smiles to her friend. "You've protected me from the bad guys all my life, which has allowed me to keep the innocence I have. I know I'm not normal, but it's a good kind of not normal. You have proven to me that, while a mother is a blessing, a person can still grow up strong and happy without one. And I thank you for that."

"Where did that come from?" Toshik asked.

"I saw how you looked at Himitsu and Pilot Ophala."

Toshik's eyes narrowed. "I've never heard something that deep come from you."

"It's not on purpose. It usually only happens when Yama's around. The fact that you were able to pull it out of me is a sign …"

Toshik smiled. They turned to stare at the city once more. She leaned her head against his arm as the countdown to the new year was chanted behind them.

"Remember when we were kids, hanging out at your house?" she asked.

"Mmm."

"And we'd roll down those ginormous hills that it sat on?"

"Yuh—"

Jilly tackled him, and her body wrapped around his as they tumbled down the hill.

"Five!" the crowd shouted behind them. "Four!"

Her soft, golden hair brushed against his face. Then her shoe struck him in the groin as their speed increased. He didn't care. It was the pure, unbridled joy in her laugh that brought him back to childhood. They came to a stop near the pond's edge, Jilly gazing down at Toshik as she sat on top of him.

"*Happy new year!*" the crowd erupted from beyond the hill.

Their lips connected. A feeling ignited inside Toshik that he had never felt before … Was he falling for her?

But their bliss made them blind to their surroundings, as Yama watched from the roof of a tall building just beyond the wall. The look on her face was as unreadable as Olivia's. She turned and dashed across the rooftop, then leapt to the next one.

* * *

Olivia marched through the Archaic Desert, undisturbed by the night's blistering cold temperatures. Her time in the Still Mountains as a child had inured her to the cold—not to mention the arctic tantrums her mother would throw, which would turn their entire cave in the Lallopy Forest into ice.

Illipsia walked beside her. Unlike Olivia, her teeth were chattering. In an attempt to shield herself from the cold, the tiny girl had wrapped her long black hair around her body from her shoulders to her ankles.

She looks like the world's biggest furball, Meow Meow thought with a shudder.

Olivia also gave her a look. They had walked in silence over the past day and a half through brutal country, subsisting on the waterskins and fruit they'd bought from the lodge at the teleplatforms. Toono, Kadlest, and

Apoleia were already waiting for them, not wanting to arouse the suspicion that a large group traveling toward the desert would attract.

"I saw you on the last day of the semester," Olivia said, finally breaking the silence. "You and Simon were walking toward Phesaw Park for the Winter Festival."

Illipsia mumbled something inaudible.

"If you were there the entire semester," Olivia said, "I'm impressed that you managed to avoid my eye."

"I was only following instructions."

Olivia didn't respond. Instead she and Meow Meow had their own conversation.

Toono and your mom are planning something.

I know.

Meow Meow hesitated. *Do you think it's along the lines of … that?*

Yes. And they didn't tell me, fearing I'd back out.

Would you have?

I'm dedicated to my mother, so no.

The kitten's carefulness with his words was noticeable. *But after all these years? Don't think this will be easy, Olivia. She will expect your cooperation without question.*

And that is what she'll get, Olivia replied. *Mental and emotional fortitude are not something I struggle with, and that is thanks to her. I am with her.*

The tone of your thoughts is wavering … That is very unlike you.

Olivia ignored him. After a couple more hours, she finally found a patch of dirt that was a slightly darker brown than the rest. She bent down and brushed it away to reveal a steel plate with holes. It looked like a sewage lid. She put her fingers through the holes and dragged the chunk of steel to the side, revealing a pipe with ladder rungs bolted to the metal. Illipsia entered first, and then Olivia followed, sliding the lid back on above.

When the two girls stepped off the ladder, an even harsher cold swept over them. They had landed in a tiny space, barely big enough for the two of them. There was a door just ahead, and Olivia knocked on it.

There was no response. Olivia knocked again.

A playful voice came from the other side: "Password, please."

Meow Meow racked his memory. *They didn't say anything about a password.*

Olivia punched through the door, which was made with wood that was several inches thick, and unlatched the lock on the opposite side. They stepped through to see Apoleia dying of laughter.

"Hello, baby!" she squealed, grabbing Olivia and lifting her into the air.

Olivia gazed emptily over Apoleia's shoulder as she was twirled around. Toono and Kadlest were nowhere to be found.

She's not looking good, Meow Meow thought when Apoleia finally placed her daughter on the ground.

The woman was completely covered in frost. And Olivia could tell that it had been a while since she had hurt herself. Patches of ice stained a dark crimson shade ran across her neck and up her forearms. Her blood had frozen.

Apoleia gave her daughter a kiss on the cheek, and a frostbitten chill spread through Olivia's face and down her neck.

"And hello again, Illipsia," Apoleia said with a sweet smile.

The girl gave her a nervous look. "Hi, Ms. Apoleia."

Apoleia paused and gazed deeply at the little girl. "Toono and Kadlest are through that door over there."

Illipsia hurried toward the door, eager to escape.

Apoleia smirked. "It's a bit warmer where they are." She turned and headed down a hall. "Follow me, baby."

Olivia did as she was told. The chill only intensified as they walked deeper into the tunnel. *How do we always end up living in some kind of cave?* Meow Meow whined.

They eventually reached a small room with a mat lying on the floor. Apoleia took a seat and patted the spot next to her. "I haven't spoken to you about this yet," Apoleia said.

Olivia gave her mother an empty stare. "I already know what you're up to."

"Of course you do, silly. You're a smart girl. I meant I know that you've been breaking my biggest rule."

Meow Meow gulped.

"I'm sorry," Olivia said.

"You must forgive me for this unexpected question, but the news that Toono gave me months back caused me immense pain." Apoleia gently turned Olivia's head, and whispered into her ear, her lip grazing it: "Must I worry about my own daughter's loyalties?"

A coat of ice slithered over Olivia's ear. "No," she replied.

"Because you know what's next. You know the time has come. Why else would I have trusted Toono? Why else would I have started leaving our home in the forest? Why would I return to the Still Kingdom? All these plans set in motion."

"To bury your demons," Olivia said.

"No. To *conquer* my demons," Apoleia hissed.

*　　*　　*

Bryson had stayed home for the first week of winter vacation, allotting that time to Thusia since they hadn't seen much of each other while he was at Phesaw. But once she returned to the Light Empire, he decided to stay in Dunami Palace for the remainder of the break. He couldn't stand the thought of being alone in that house for too long.

Bryson stared at a slew of wooden pallets in the northwestern courtyard, which were spaced out at varying distances and angles. He swiped his hand in front of him, and a stream of electricity shattered the pallets into splinters. His attack also struck the marble pillars holding up a patio roof in the distance. Fortunately they were a lot stronger and merely cracked.

Princess Shelly clapped. "Well done! Well done!"

Bryson faced her with a smile, giving her a deep bow of gratitude. "I appreciate your—"

His sentence was cut short as Lilu smacked the back of his head.

"That was pathetic," she spat.

"What are you talking about? I just annihilated everything in my path!"

"Including your friendlies!" she shouted, pointing in the direction of his carnage. "You were supposed to spare the red ones!"

Shelly was holding back laughter as Lilu ranted at Bryson. "I don't care how much clout you have if you can't even weave a strand of your overgrown bangs around your damn finger! You almost collapsed the patio! You have no ability to control what you're doing! You're just brainlessly using as much clout as you can muster up!"

"Works for me," Shelly said.

"*Shut up!*"

"Let's go again," Bryson said. "I'll fix it."

Lilu's mouth dropped open. "You— What—" she stammered, enraged. "No! You're wasting my time!" She took a deep breath. "We're done until you can create an Intelight—the most basic example of being able to weave and exercise delicacy when it comes to clout."

Lilu stormed off as Bryson watched her long white coat flutter behind her.

"Oh man," Shelly sighed, wiping tears of laughter from her eyes. "That was great."

"I beg to differ."

"Don't worry. We'll still have our little sessions, and I won't bother trying to dampen that promising clout of yours."

"Can you get me more pallets?"

Shelly stared at him with her ivy green eyes. "So adorable," she said, pinching his cheeks. "We're celebrating a whole new century tonight. And the beginning of the second half of this millennium. I have to prepare for the celebrations. Princess stuff. You wouldn't understand." She winked. "I'll see you tonight. Don't forget to bring your pal."

The princess exited the courtyard, stepping over the broken pallets. As the guards left their positions and filed behind her, she raised a hand and snapped three times. A group of servants materialized and began picking up the mess. Bryson watched them, amazed that someone could hold such power over other people.

Eventually he sighed, joined the servants, and began helping them clear up the mess that he'd made. It's what Jilly would have done, and he had decided a long time ago that everyone should be a little more like Jilly.

* * *

Bryson grabbed the ridiculously ornate knocker on the mahogany door and knocked three times. As he waited he observed the luxurious quarters he was standing in. Like everywhere else in Dunami Palace, the space was practically a solid gold box. The palace always seemed strange to Bryson, considering most of the wealthy buildings in Dunami were constructed of steel—something that made this city stand out from the others in the Light Realm.

The door opened, and a lanky man with sleek black hair stood in the doorway. He smiled. "Good to see you, Bryson."

"Vistas! How are you?"

"Can't complain." Vistas motioned for Bryson to come in.

The Intel Jestivan stepped inside and gawked at what he saw. It was the bookshelves that caught his attention first. Hundreds of books lined each row. It was enough to make him nauseous.

"How have your friends been holding up?" Vistas asked while he poured a glass of water from a pitcher and handed it to Bryson.

"Everyone has been great. Olivia has fully recovered. I suppose you remember the disaster of a relationship between Himitsu and Toshik."

The Dev servant laughed. "Oil and water, those two."

"Well they've become closer—not that that means much, considering how far apart they were originally. Jilly is … well, she's Jilly. And Rhyparia is amazing. She's really learning to rein in her Archaic Energy."

Bryson walked to the fireplace, where a holographic portrait perched on the mantle caught his eye. He poked his hand through it.

"Fascinated by my holopic?" asked Vistas.

"How is this possible?" Bryson muttered. "Is it a memory?"

"Something like that," Vistas said. "It's pulled from my memory, created by Dev weaving. It's a special type of weaving called permanence."

Permanence. Intel Director Jugtah had introduced it as a master-level class at Phesaw this year. Lilu was taking it.

Bryson paid closer attention to what was actually in the portrait. There were four young boys—probably around the age of eight—standing together and laughing in a reoccurring loop. Three of them were identical. They must have been Vistas, Flen, and Tristen.

"Who's the fourth boy?"

"That would be Marcus," Vistas said. "The truth extractor Princess Shelly told you about. Of course, at that age, he was merely a boy—as were the rest of us."

"It looks so real."

"Perhaps too real for its own good."

Bryson took a seat in a cushioned leather armchair. "Thank you for keeping my secret," he said.

"Are you speaking of Thusia?"

"Yes. I'm ashamed to say I was apprehensive about you knowing."

Vistas gazed down at the fire. "Secrets can weigh a person down—and I bear many of them—but I can still shoulder that burden."

Bryson nodded. He did trust Vistas, which was odd since people with Dev Energy were typically conniving, like Dev King Storshae … or at least that's what he was taught as a child.

"How many people have trusted you with their secrets?"

Vistas looked up from the fire. "Too many. And I try to not allow myself to learn any more after what happened several months back."

Bryson started to ask for a more detailed explanation, but Vistas waved his hand. "I will not speak of it. All I know is that I was told to release the memory at the proper time. The dilemma I face is whether to follow those instructions. Some things are better left unseen."

The crackling flames occupied the quiet of the room. Vistas picked up the holopic and stared at it. "Although our circumstances are different, Bryson, we are both victims of the same man."

* * *

There was a lot weighing on Bryson's mind as he walked out of the dining room with Shelly. What had Vistas meant when he had mentioned Mendac?

Shelly led him into the royal quarters, where he had never set foot before. The vast hallways were empty. Unless you were of royal blood, there was no entering this section of the palace. But who would want to live in this place anyway? Bryson felt like he must have climbed thousands of stairs to get here.

"That's Lilu's room," Shelly pointed out as they passed a pair of golden doors. "You know, in case you ever want to sneak back in here in the middle of the night."

Bryson ignored her remark and the teasing smile on her face.

The sun had set hours ago and Intelights illuminated their way. Eventually the space opened into an enormous circular room with no doors or windows. Portraits lined the curved wall. Bryson walked over to Princess Shelly's. He had almost mistaken her for Lilu because of the long hair.

"I had to cut it off once Lilu hit puberty," Shelly said. "Turns out she can flaunt long hair better than me. I needed to distinguish myself somehow."

He glanced back at her. "As if being the royal first-born and possessing a Branian wasn't already distinguishing enough."

Shelly's friendly expression was replaced by a thin scowl. "You watch yourself. I most definitely did not ask for this."

Bryson paused. She was right. "Sorry."

He looked at the painting next to hers. "This must be a much younger King Vitio."

"Prince," she corrected. "That was long ago. I think he was fifteen."

Bryson examined the painting. It was weird seeing Vitio without any facial hair, just a full head of golden locks. All of his fat-layered muscle was just muscle—lean muscle, much like Debo's.

"Let's go," Shelly said.

"Where to?"

"Up."

Bryson looked up at the ceiling.

"Stand next to me," Shelly said. "Step here," she added, hovering her foot over a section of the floor that looked no different than the rest.

As Bryson did so, the marble floor gave way a tiny bit. The center of the floor dislodged itself from the rest and lifted into the air. He glanced upward with wide eyes. The ceiling had opened.

He had witnessed this before. At every opening ceremony at Phesaw, the Energy Directors would rise from underneath the stage on platforms. In fact Bryson and the rest of the Jestivan had used those platforms to sink below the stage a year and a half ago.

The platform lifted them into a room of pure glass. It looked like it had been shaped all out of one piece, even the ceiling. Only the floor was carpeted.

"Welcome to my sanctuary," Shelly said.

Bryson walked toward the glass wall. A balcony encircled the room, but he didn't know how to get to it. Was there a door disguised somewhere in this glass? He gazed back up at the sky. Stars punctured the darkness, as did both of the moons. He had never seen a clearer sky in the Intel Kingdom.

"Where are the clouds?" he asked.

Shelly stepped toward the other side of the room and pressed against the glass. A doorway opened, and a blast of freezing air rushed in. "I'll show you," she said.

Bryson followed her out onto the balcony. Besides the cold, the first thing he noticed was the thinness of the air.

Shelly leaned over the rail. "What you seek is below us."

Bryson gazed over the edge to see a vast blanket of cloud roiling beneath them. They glowed a deep blue in the reflected starlight. Not a single manmade building joined them above the clouds.

"You're welcome to literally freeze to death out here if you want," Shelly said. "I'm heading in."

Bryson followed her inside and studied the center of the floor, looking for any sign of machinery or energy. "How does this thing work?" he asked.

"That's a question better suited for Lilu. She's left her mark all over this place. This is all weaving. And not just weaving, but permanence."

"Are you ready to do this?"

"If you are," she replied. "But I'm not promising you anything. I told you, he's not happy with you."

"That's what Thusia is for."

Shelly studied him for a moment. "Very well, then."

Two orbs of light manifested in the room, and Bryson shielded his eyes. The lights took the shapes of humans. Soon a woman with straight blonde hair and a white neckband and a redheaded man with a scimitar strapped to his back were standing at the center of the room.

The two Branian stared at each other with slight frowns. "What is the purpose of this?" the man asked Shelly without removing his gaze from Thusia.

"What a lovely greeting, Branian Suadade," Thusia replied. She turned and glared at Bryson.

He smiled. "Hi. I missed you."

Suadade's eyes flickered to Bryson. "I'm leaving," he said.

"No!" Shelly shouted. She quickly added, "I'm in danger …"

Her Branian slowly turned to look at her. "Based off a quick assessment of the situation, I'd disagree. However, I'll stand over there just in case an assassin flies out of the clouds." He walked toward the windows and stared at the sky.

Thusia sat down on a sofa and closed her eyes. Bryson and Shelly stared at her in silence. Finally, she opened her eyes. "It's nice to meet you, Princess Shelly."

"You know me?" She smirked at Bryson. "I'm flattered."

Thusia shook her head. "He's mentioned you once or twice, but I've known you since you were a child."

"How?"

"You don't think Bozani talk in the Light Empire? Suadade has spoken of you many, many times."

"About how amazing I am?" she asked. Her tone was sarcastic, but this was Shelly. Deep down, she meant that.

Thusia smiled. "About how pompous you are."

"False," Suadade said, belying his pretense of not paying attention.

"I'm kidding—kind of," Thusia said. "He speaks highly of you."

Shelly frowned. "It sounds like the two of you are friends, but by the looks of your faces when we summoned you, it seemed like you wanted to kill each other."

Thusia rolled over, putting her legs over the top of the couch while her head hung toward the ground. "He's mad at me. I just like to mock him for fun—see if I can match his grumpy face."

"I know why he hates *me*, but what did you do?" Bryson asked.

"Well the first thing you must know about Leon is that he's sensitive."

"I'm not," Suadade protested.

Thusia started kicking her feet. "And he's almost always mad at everything."

"Untrue."

"And he's stubborn."

"Liar."

"See what I mean? But besides that, he's mad about a little dust-up with our team."

"Our team?" Bryson repeated.

Thusia nodded at Shelly. "Explain it to him."

"I have no idea what you're talking about," Shelly said.

Thusia curled herself onto the top of the sofa to face Suadade. "You haven't told her anything, have you?"

He finally turned around. "The Light Empire is irrelevant to commoners."

"Okay, I'll tell you," Thusia said as she spun forward again.

"You're a fool," Suadade pronounced.

"It's not like I'm breaking a law. They are allowed to know basic things, so long as I avoid giving specific names of people."

"Let's hear it then," Bryson said.

"Let's start with the beings like Leon and me. We are Branian, the lowest tier of the Bozani hierarchical chain. There are fifteen of us."

"I thought there were only five."

"Five *active* Branian. Depending on the collective ages of the royal first-borns, anywhere from zero to five of us are active."

"What do the others do then?" Shelly asked.

"They're dormant. For example, I was considered dormant before Bryson summoned me for the first time."

"How many are active right now?"

Suadade's head snapped around, but Thusia replied just as quickly: "I cannot divulge that information. But you obviously know that there are at least us two."

"Okay, but what did you mean by 'team'?" Bryson asked.

"Do you remember what Debonicus was called?"

It took him a moment to recall the term. "A Pogu."

"Pogu are the second of the Bozani's four tiers. There are five Pogu. There's no such thing as active or dormant for this class since they don't hold assignments to royal first-borns. As you've learned, they're executioners. But the need for them outside of the Light Empire is astronomically rare, so their true role is to serve as teachers to the Branian."

"Teachers? What exactly do they teach?"

"Not for you to know," she said. "The point is there are three Branian for each Pogu, and that each group forms a team. Leon and I are on the same team, and Debonicus was our leader."

"So who's the third member?" Shelly asked.

"Can't say. The only names I'm giving to you are ones you already know."

"So what are the two tiers above Branian and Pogu?"

This made Thusia hesitate. "I'll hold back on saying anything about that," she mumbled. "There are some gray areas when it comes to her."

Bryson didn't bother asking who the "her" was. Obviously it was someone with great sway.

"And anyway, Suadade's upset about the new Pogu who took Debonicus's place."

"And he blames me for Debo's death," Bryson said.

Suadade slowly turned from the window. "How was that your fault?" he asked with narrowed eyes.

Bryson gave Shelly a baffled look. "The princess here said that you told her you didn't want to be around me."

"Yes, I did say that. But not for reasons of anger—at least not directed toward you. That anger is focused elsewhere, such as Vitio and Debonicus. My problem with you lies in something more shameful than spite."

"It's spite, however you try to mask it," Thusia said.

"I was—"

"Am," Thusia corrected.

Suadade sighed. "I am jealous of you."

Princess Shelly scrunched her nose. "Quite a disreputable feeling for someone of your stature."

"Exactly why I said it's shameful, but it's hard to shake. Debonicus and I knew each other for a long time. We spent hundreds of years together in the Light Empire—I even knew him when he was a Branian like Thusia and me … before he was promoted."

"Before my time," Thusia added.

"I also knew him when we weren't Bozani at all, when were just normal people like you and Shelly. We died on the same day, nearly 600 years ago."

"So when he left the Light Empire to raise me—a five-year-old boy he had just met—it rattled you," Bryson concluded.

The Branian gazed at Bryson with thoughtful eyes. "More than that. It rocked the very foundation of my persona. You wouldn't understand. That fairy tale—*The Third of Five*—mentions me just once, and only as an afterthought. It doesn't even use my correct name … it says 'Leo.' You don't know the real story. Only the people of my hometown know that."

The room became quiet. Thusia walked over and placed her hand on Suadade's shoulder. He took a deep breath and looked at Bryson.

"Those weren't easy times for us. It wasn't like it is now. But I've always known what you were to him. Biological or adopted—it didn't matter. You were a son, and that man loved you."

Bryson felt his grip of his own composure loosening. Thusia must have noticed, for her consoling eyes had settled on him.

Suadade's eyes were fixed on him too. "Thusia has told me you've taken a liking to *The Third of Five*. Whenever you're ready to hear the real story—the one that wasn't tampered with—let me know."

Shelly, who seemed to be the only one unaffected by all of this, gave her Branian a curious look. "Were you and Debonicus … *in love*?"

Suadade was gone in the blink of an eye, replaced by a momentary cluster of white lights that quickly fizzled out. Shelly blinked a couple times. "I guess that's a yes."

Thusia glared at the princess. "You couldn't have kept that conclusion to yourself?"

The blankest of looks sat on Bryson's face. No wonder Debo had always been alone.

29
Taken

With two days remaining before the beginning of Phesaw's second semester, the school was empty except for the professors and directors who were spending the weekend preparing for the long four and a half months approaching.

The lone student wandering the halls was a frail zana of the Jestivan. Agnos had just left the library, where he had spent countless hours ever since Bryson approached him about his reoccurring dream. After another hopeless hunt for answers, he knocked on a rickety wooden door.

"Come in," came a frail voice.

Agnos stepped into the office. A very short man stood behind his desk, his shoulders hunched to reach the parchment he was scribbling on. He gazed over the top of his crooked spectacles. "Zana Agnos, good morning."

"Good morning, Director Senex."

Senex set his quill in its holder. "My wife could pack a full load of groceries in those bags under your eyes. Perhaps I wouldn't be wrong to speculate that you spent the entire night at the library again?"

"Not at all."

"And you've struck gold?"

"I think my odds would be better if that's what I was hunting."

Senex chuckled. "When it comes to figuring things out on your own, you've always been stubborn, Zana Agnos."

The young man looked away. "I concede defeat."

"It's about time," Senex replied. "One's genius only expands to its fullest potential when they are accepting of other's perspective."

"So you knew I would come," Agnos said.

"I did. During your last visit, I caught a glimpse of what was on the parchment you had in your hands."

Agnos tried to hide his wounded pride as he placed the parchment on the desk. "So you know what language this is?"

"I do," Senex answered.

"And you can interpret it?"

"I cannot—not in its current state at least."

"Why not?"

"For the same reason your ancient can't. What you have written there is a very old and elusive language—Technous. You won't find anyone who can read that, and I doubt you'd ever find a book that translates it into any modern language."

"So all this time I've put into this was a waste."

Senex shook his head. "Now, now. You know better than that. There is always an answer. Your relic is that answer. You just have to complete the word before your glasses can decipher it."

"What?"

"In Technous, a specific character does not represent the same thing every time."

Agnos scowled. "I don't get it," he admitted.

"A character's meaning is determined by the characters that precede and follow it. And what makes it worse is the fact that Technous has over one hundred discrete symbols compared to our twenty-six. In other words, it is impossible to guess what a word is unless it's been entirely written out." Senex smiled. "Kuki Sphaira's hardest puzzle. Practically impossible to crack, really. Luckily for you, you possess a rare relic capable of doing the impossible."

"Shouldn't you know the word?" Agnos asked, inwardly cursing Toono for never having warned him of what he'd be up against. "Since you taught the class and wrote it on the board, according to Bryson's dream."

"I don't know why or how Bryson is seeing Technous in his dreams. An accidental gift from his subconscious, perhaps? But I know that I've never written anything in Technous in my life. It died out 1,500 years ago, when the Known History timeline began."

Agnos extended his hand. "Thank you, Director Senex."

Senex leapt onto his desk, making himself eye-level with his student. They shook hands. "Thank you for allowing me to expand your mind. Maybe now you'll be able to venture deeper into the Warpfinate."

Agnos smirked. "Do you think there's an end to the library? I feel like I've gone farther than most."

"You certainly have. I assure you of that. But I don't think that place has a limit outside of one's mind. They call it the Warpfinate for a reason. The building warps and grows simultaneously with an individual's knowledge."

"Speaking of growing, sir …" Agnos glanced around the office. "Why didn't you ever get furniture more appropriate for your size?"

The director just winked. "Have an ethical day, Zana Agnos."

The frustration that Agnos had felt for the past few months fell away, replaced by satisfaction that there was something in this world that was too complex even for his mind. A challenge he looked forward to conquering.

As Agnos reached for the door, the room shook ferociously. He fell over, one hand still clinging to the doorknob. Archaic Director Senex had fallen off of his desk and was trying to regain his feet on the bucking floor.

"Is this Power Warden Feissam?" Agnos shouted.

Senex shook his head. He looked … *scared.* "We must hurry!" he shouted. "Get out of here and exit through the nearest side door!"

As the two of them staggered through the hall, Agnos tried to determine what was happening. This wasn't the Power Warden. Then it clicked, and the horror set in. He had felt this countless times before.

They finally reached an exit and burst into a giant courtyard that separated the Morality and Courage wings. They ran toward the scattered buildings that sat between the slums, Phesaw Park, and Wealth's Crossroads. Everything was collapsing. Buildings crumbled to rubble, crashing to the ground below. Trees that sat on the outlying areas of the park were ripped from the earth.

As Agnos got closer to the chaos, the weight of the air intensified. It was subtle, but it was enough to weaken his breathing, and the shift in gravity only worsened with every step he took. He collapsed to all fours and clutched at his chest, grabbing a handful of thin robes with it. His refusal to participate in any combat or gravity training sessions over the past year had come to haunt him.

Agnos managed to lift his heavy head and scan the area in front of him. Director Senex was still going. *Such a small man, yet a force of will that not even a giant could match.* It was too difficult to see much of anything else through the blizzard of debris. Agnos tried to inch backward, but he lacked the strength. Why had he blundered into this?

Then something gripped his ankle and tugged him backward. He bounced across the cobblestones until he could feel gravity's hold on him lessen. After a good fifty feet of bumps and bruises, his foot hit the dead grass as whoever it was let him go.

Agnos rolled onto his back and flinched at the fury in those blue eyes. An instant later they disappeared, and Agnos felt the pull of the speed at which his friend moved, for it must have dragged him across the ground a few inches. Bryson LeAnce was entering the fray.

* * *

Grand Director Poicus sat in his sun-drenched office with Tally, the school's Dev servant. A holographic display flickered between them.

"I thought the royal heads had decided to pardon her," Poicus said.

Inside of the moving picture was King Vitio's scruffy face. "That was before the recent information we've gathered."

"Such as?" the director prodded.

"The disaster in Olethros wasn't caused by an avalanche or earthquake. It was Rhyparia."

"You're saying a little girl annihilated an entire sector of a city?"

"I also didn't believe it at first. Trust me. It wasn't until Major Lars followed a breadcrumb trail of clues that forced me to investigate it." Vitio hesitated. "I had Marcus extract truths from the former Archaic King. He was planning to use her as a secret weapon of mass destruction for their kingdom."

Poicus nodded, paused, then nodded again. "So what will be done about it?"

The king took a deep breath. "Before I contacted you, the generals had just arrived at Telejunction. They should be seeking her—"

"How could you do this without approaching me first? This is my school!"

"Good to know the old Praetor is still in there somewhere. After all these decades of playing the docile Grand Director, I had begun to think you were no longer acting."

The vein in the middle of Poicus's forehead throbbed. "Don't patronize me, Vitio."

"Rhyparia may be a Jestivan, but above all she is a subject of the Archaic Kingdom." The king's stare turned to stone. "And I shall claim my prerogative."

"At least give me a warning! Do you not trust me enough to fold?"

"None of the royal heads do."

Poicus stared at Vitio.

"I advise you not to try anything reckless, Praetor. Your battle with Storshae has permanently damaged you. And this isn't the 1440s … You aren't Spy Pilot Poicus anymore."

The Grand Director drew himself up to his full height and walked toward the window behind his desk. He gazed out of it and saw three people strolling past the library.

"You're a man short," Poicus said.

"What do you mean?" Vitio asked.

"I see Minerva, Lucas, and Sinno, but no Landon. Did King Damian back out of your arrangement?"

Vitio fell silent. Poicus turned back toward him and said, "This was a terrible way of going about things, Vitio. Don't you realize that this could explode in your face?"

The king's distracted eyes refocused on Poicus. "Which was why we were extra cautious in sending four—or three, apparently—generals to handle her. Also, we came during Phesaw's emptiest days."

"So is this about the hundreds of lives that she's taken, or are you scared that she'll be used against the Intel Kingdom?"

The two men glared at each other.

"I have to contact Marcus and Damian," Vitio said, "so I'll cut this short. But remember that if you try to stop the generals, you'll have a lot more to worry about than just Rhyparia—such as all five of the Light Kingdoms. So let's see you exercise that wise Archain mind of yours."

Poicus signaled for the broadcast to be cut off before Vitio said his goodbye. He sat in his chair and twirled the ends of his hairy eyebrows. There was nothing he could do. Everything that Vitio had said was correct. Even if he was the young Spy Pilot he once was, that wouldn't mean anything against the combined will of all five Light Kingdoms.

The room rattled as sounds of destruction began to boom through the walls. He sighed at the realization of his fears. He grabbed his cane and limped out of the office.

* * *

Bryson had never run so fast in his life. His calves threatened to rip free from the bones as he ran across the cobblestones. Rhyparia's gravity fluctuations threatened to tear his heart free as well. It was like he was in the restaurant she'd crushed before the Generals' Battle fourteen months ago, but Bryson was stronger now.

His eyes darted in every direction, absorbing every detail he could manage. Buildings continued to cave around him, the ground violently shook with each impact of heavy debris, and people lay motionless on the ground.

At the middle of this mayhem, a few hundred feet ahead of Bryson, were three individuals strategically spaced in a triangular formation. He recognized them from the Generals' Battle, for they were the ones who participated in it: Spirit General Minerva, the brutish lady in blue; Adren

General Sinno, the long, lean man in silver; and Intel General Lucas, the man with the battle-worn face and uniform of yellow.

They each held a point of the triangle, each pressed against the ground. In the center of that unfathomable well of gravity sat Rhyparia, her hands placed on the ground as she screamed in agony toward the sky.

Bryson's legs buckled mid-stride and he pitched face-first into the cobblestones. The ringing in his ears was pierced by Rhyparia's ghastly screams. As he pushed himself onto his knees, the ground cracked in a thousand different directions, then suddenly dropped a couple inches. The sinking continued as Rhyparia morphed the ground into a funnel with her body as the epicenter.

Bryson and the generals began to roll toward her. He yelped as the bones in the fingers of his left hand snapped. Where were the directors?

As if Bryson had summoned him with his thoughts, a helping hand—an unbelievably massive hand that could have flicked Power Warden Feissam clear across Phesaw's campus—scooped him up as delicately as if he were a butterfly and lifted him high into the air.

It was Archaic Director Senex, enlarged to ten times his normal size. Spectacles sat errant on his nose, and his wiry brown and gray hair seemed to stretch for hundreds of feet every which way.

As Bryson stood on the director's palm, he noticed a pair of people on a rooftop. One was a plump, stiff woman and the other was a scrawny and feeble man. Rhyparia's parents. They, Bryson knew, were somehow responsible for this.

Rage boiled inside him as he prepared to strike. He raised his uninjured hand in the air, then swung his outstretched arm downward in a violent motion. A concentrated whip of electricity flew across the sky and smashed into the roof's shingles, sending up a whirlpool of splintered debris.

Bryson collapsed, limply rolling off the director's hand and onto the ground. His body was completely numb, and he didn't know why. It was a surreal feeling, like his insides were drying up.

The sounds of disaster had come to a stop. He heard crying somewhere close by, and though he was too weak to tilt his head in that direction, he knew it was coming from Rhyparia.

"What did Bryson do?" asked a weak voice that Bryson recognized as Grand Director Poicus's.

"Massive electrical attack—all clout," Director Senex answered. "His energy canals are likely withering into nothing."

"Get him to the clinic," Poicus mumbled.

"I'll take care of it," thrummed a deep, grating voice. A pair of arms scooped Bryson up and carried him away from Rhyparia's cries. Bryson peeled open his eyes to see Power Warden Feissam's grim face above him.

* * *

Grand Director Poicus watched as the two generals limped toward Rhyparia, engraving every detail of her in his memory as he willed himself not to intervene. Senex knelt next to his crying student's slumped body with her ancient in his hand. If the director thought that there was still hope for the girl, he was about to be disillusioned.

Tashami and Agnos hovered over the motionless body of Intel General Lucas. Bones from his mangled skeleton protruded from the thick golden material of his uniform. Poicus felt nothing. This was King Vitio's fault, and he alone would bear responsibility for the death of his general.

Vuilni and Bruut lingered in the outskirts of the rubble. Like Tashami and Agnos, they had remained on campus during the break. As for Bryson, someone must have tipped him off.

"Don't touch her!" Senex shouted at Generals Sinno and Minerva. He had a mix of fury and guilt on his dirtied face. The director looked at Poicus, who shook his head. Rhyparia and her ancient were pried from the Archaic Director's grasp.

A man in a burgundy coat picked his way through the rubble toward the scene.

"Get word to King Vitio that Lucas is dead," Minerva said. "Someone needs to retrieve his body. You stay here until help arrives."

The Dev servant nodded and closed his eyes, telepathically sending a message to whoever was on the other side of it—likely Vistas or Flen.

Minerva slung Rhyparia over her shoulder and Sinno picked up the umbrella. Vuilni started to sprint after them, but Bruut grabbed her by her hood. The two Power Diatia struggled for a moment in the dusty air.

"Let me go!" Vuilni demanded.

"No! This is not our realm! If you interfere, we'd be trapped here with the whole Light Realm against us!"

"That wasn't her!" Vuilni shouted after the generals, who were already ascending Telejunction's hill with Rhyparia and her parents. "She isn't that person!" Vuilni stopped struggling and collapsed to the ground in tears.

Poicus carefully descended into the crater and extended a hand to Senex. "We've grown old, Mynute," Poicus said as he helped his friend to his feet.

Senex watched as the generals climbed the Telejunction platform. "I've nearly had my fill of life."

"A fulfilling ninety-three years."

"Not quite," Senex replied. "I have one more thing to take care of. She needs a voice in court."

"That will be a lengthy process."

"I know, so please accept my resignation as Archaic Director."

Poicus smiled. "Retirement sounds a bit more endearing."

"You won't fight me on this?"

Poicus hesitated for a moment. "No. That they didn't take you into custody as well tells me that Vitio doesn't care about the lives that were lost in Olethros or the restaurant. This was done out of selfish fear. That young girl has him shaken. He sees her as that wretched Itta saw her: an object, a weapon."

"Praetor, I saw who Bryson attacked. Rhyparia's parents. And though I'm sure he attacked them out of an instinctive rage, I saw what the woman was doing. This is a bigger issue than Rhyparia lacking control of her clout. I believe I can serve a believable defense for her."

"You know the odds are against you."

The two men fell silent as the wounded groaned and sobbed in the distance.

"I'm ancient. The odds are against me every night when I go to sleep—a gamble that I seem to frustratingly win every time."

"Let's say your eyes don't open," Poicus mused. "Instead of seeing daylight, you see Rhyparia's head in the gallows."

"We're Archains, Praetor. My mind will force my eyes open to an array of possibilities. And I will do whatever it takes to reach the desired one—no matter how unlawful it may be."

"Rather un-Archain of you."

Senex shook his head. "You've never been a typical Archain in the way you handle yourself, but you still know that law and morals aren't mutually inclusive."

"I've never been big on classifications of personalities based on energies or kingdoms," Poicus said. "I am my own person, regardless of the energy flowing through me."

"You don't have to tell me that. While you've fooled these young ones with your elderly, fun-loving charm, I know what's hidden beneath."

Poicus felt insulted. He *had* changed over the past few decades. The person he had become wasn't a role. It was a transformation.

But never mind that. Those were selfish, petty thoughts. He joined the school medics combing the wreckage. Passion Director Venustas would have been helpful during a time like this, for she was a gifted medical mind. Alas, Venustas, Neaneuma, and Buredo had yet to return from their winter breaks, and Intel Director Jugtah had just arrived to observe the scene from a safe distance.

Jugtah was such an odd individual, socially awkward and annoyingly arrogant—the complete opposite of Mendac, or at least the younger, charismatic Mendac whom Poicus had met when the boy first entered the school.

But he could still see the similarities in Jugtah that would have drawn someone of Mendac's intelligence to him. Neither was shy about flaunting their minds. And since Jugtah had always been known as a man with answers, Mendac—an eager boy with too many questions—was a perfect disciple for him.

"Let me help you with that, sir," Tashami said. Together they heaved a concrete slab off an unconscious woman. Agnos bent down and held his ear to her mouth, then tilted her head back so she could breathe more easily. Vuilni and Bruut crouched a few feet away, frantically sifting through a collapsed building. Through all of this disaster, fear, and hate surrounding them, these young students displayed camaraderie, generosity, and love. Poicus had been a bit rougher around the edges when he was younger, but what he was seeing right now was proof that he had changed for the better since taking over as Grand Director. He was going to lead this younger generation into a future filled with unity—not just between the Light Kingdoms, but throughout both realms.

The formation of the first Jestivan was a mistake, done for the wrong reasons—not that Poicus had a choice in the decision. He had learned much from its destruction decades ago, and when he decided to form it a second time, he did so with the exact opposite objective. Widely divergent personalities and backgrounds were thrown together to become a family and inspire that same mentality in all the students who looked up to them.

30
Politics and Family

King Vitio slowly circled a golden coffin in the vast throne room. All eyes watched as their king's muddled mind came to grips with who occupied it.

General Lucas's face was grotesquely disfigured. His cheekbone and temple had been caved in while his mutilated right arm had been sewn back to the shoulder.

Vitio ran his fingers across the casket's lip. "That will do," he said softly.

Eight men lifted the coffin and carried it through the massive doors. Vitio waited for the doors to shut before gazing to the side of the room, where his daughters and wife stood. Delilah and Shelly looked calm if pale, but Lilu was distraught, and understandably so. She had never been informed of the plan to capture Rhyparia.

Vitio returned to his throne and took a seat. He leaned his head back and stared at the cavernous ceiling of elaborate decorative panels.

The doors opened once again, this time to the friendly face of Vistas.

"Have you been able to contact Marcus?" Vitio asked him.

"I have not, milord."

The king corkscrewed his mouth. "Same as before? He's sealed off his Dev energy, blocking communications with him from the outside?"

"Yes, sir."

"What's the longest time Marcus has done something like this?"

"I don't recall him ever doing something like this, milord, but I'm not the most reliable of sources. We spoke sparingly throughout the past several years."

Vitio scratched his beard. Obviously something was off. It wasn't like Damian to distance himself from the other Light Kingdoms, and he was a particularly close ally of the Intel Kingdom. It had been over a month since Vitio had heard from his fellow king—and to raise more concern, there was Passion General Landon's unexplained absence from the mission to capture Rhyparia. Was Damian angry because of the incident with Marcus and Itta?

"Milord, there is another possibility," Vistas said.

"Yes?"

"To put it bluntly, the only other way of sealing off one's energy would be to die."

"We would have received news," Vitio said, almost as a question.

"I'm simply providing alternate theories."

Vitio thought of the incidents at the Passion Kingdom's teleplatforms over the past eight months. Were Damian and Marcus ambushed on their trip home from the Archaic Kingdom? But if that were the case, news would have reached him by now.

"Milord, we could send someone to Fiamma as a scout," an adviser suggested.

Vitio shook his head. "No. At least not right now. We're already spread too thin. Vistas, have you spoken with anyone from the Amendment Order?"

"With Ophala Vevlu this morning, milord. Her birds show the unit transporting Rhyparia to be roughly a hundred miles outside of Phelos. It will be another day and a half at the least."

"Any word from Phesaw?"

Vistas nodded. "Mynute Senex has retired from his position as the Archaic Director."

"Peculiar timing."

"I wouldn't worry. He plans on fighting in court—nothing reckless."

Vitio snorted. "I'll be interested in seeing the defense he tries to put up in the face of hundreds upon hundreds of murders, including a general. Nobody will want to send their children to Phesaw with students who can't control their powers running loose. Have you heard anything from any other Devish about Toono? Any leads?"

"No, milord. Nothing since the attack on Chelekah."

Vitio thanked and dismissed Vistas before returning to his thoughts. There hadn't been a reliable sighting of Toono in a year and a half, when he robbed the Archaic Museum of the Anathallo. That he had assassinated the Prim Prince and the Cyn Diatia seemed likely, but there was no concrete proof.

But at least that speculation was *something*. Toono was proving to be a slippery man, and this silence made him all the scarier. If he was really hunting down an elite from each kingdom, who could say that he hadn't already added a couple more to his tally?

Vitio glanced at the three most important women in his life. As long as he knew that the three of them were safe, he could endure this. He sighed and lifted his great bulk from his throne, then walked toward them with a smile on his face. He spread his arms, and the four of them embraced each other in a family hug—one head of gold and gray, the other three a grassy green.

* * *

Chief Senator Rosel Sania opened the doors to a circular grand room with rich mahogany walls and tall windows. Archaic Prince Sigmund stepped inside with her. Directly in front of them was a small staircase that traveled down to the carpeted floor. Several curved rows of pews surrounded the space, sectioned into four triangular corners by staircases that cut through the middle of each side.

"Your father and his father didn't believe in trials by jury," Rosel said from the top of the stairs. Her rigid posture demonstrated—perhaps theatrically—the propriety incumbent in the office of Chief Senator. "They took the power of judgment into their own hands, and so this room has sat empty for decades. It took a few weeks of renovation, but now it's ready."

The prince observed the space. Trials held in the judgment room were ones of momentous and consequential significance. Rhyparia's case would mark the first one under the Amendment Order's reign.

Rosel descended the stairs and gestured toward the pews that stretched to the right and left. "These are for the audience. The only people allowed will be family members of the accused, potential witnesses, and royal guests. By royal decree there will be Dev servants stationed throughout this room, all of whom will be recording and broadcasting to the major cities across the kingdoms."

"This is sort of a public progress report then?" Sigmund asked. "The royal heads demonstrating to their subjects that our kingdom is under stable control?"

"Exactly," Rosel said, placing her stack of parchment on a wooden table. "This is where we will sit—the Amendment Order and you. Ms. NuForce, will stand at the center."

"But I don't have a say in the verdict."

"Yes, but when all is said and done, the entire purpose of this is to make sure that you don't follow the same path as Itta, so you will spectate from the floor."

Lone candles occupied each table that curved around the floor. Considering the copious amount of candles placed throughout the room and in the chandelier that hung above, they seemed unnecessary to Sigmund. "Is there any significance behind those?" he asked, a bit ashamed that he had to ask so many questions about his own kingdom's traditions.

Rosel smiled apologetically. "That is still new to me too. Every kingdom has its own customs, after all. But from what I've studied, each member of the jury has the freedom to blow out their candle whenever they see fit, thus extinguishing the life of the defendant's case in that juror's eyes. And with Rhyparia's case, it is very likely that those candles will be a literal representation of her life."

"You expect her to be executed?" Sigmund asked.

"Don't you? And it would likely be an effortless decision if we weren't dealing with a Jestivan … that pesky matter of elite privilege."

"The exact thing I've benefited from."

"Not at all, Prince Sigmund. You are not to be held responsible for the actions of your father. You are your own person. The royal heads saw that you were an impressionable young mind that was led astray by someone you trusted and loved, and that there was still a chance for that to be corrected."

"I appreciate that, ma'am," Sigmund mumbled.

Rosel gathered her papers and clasped them against her chest. "Best we get going, Sigmund. A lot of studying and preparation to be done. You might have more of a say in this young girl's future than you might think you do."

"What do you mean?"

She twirled her hand for him to take a seat in a pew. "The Archaic Kingdom's approach to legal hearings has always been unique—before your grandfather came to power at least. It was the only kingdom to use a jury. Every other kingdom used one juror—the royal head—and it's still that way to this day."

"Isn't that the same method as my father then?"

"No. Your father didn't hold trials. The entire concept of a legal proceeding was wiped away. In the other kingdoms, though the final say may lie with the royal head, they still go through litigations that involve the participation of witnesses, gathering of information, and debates between prosecutors and defense attorneys. This allows them to make a wise, informed decision. We will conduct that process here, and the jury will decide Rhyparia's guilt or innocence by a popular vote. There are always an odd number of jurors, but there can still be a tie when it comes to determine the punishment if there are more than two options.

"According to Archain tradition the judge would break that tie. But in our case, Grandarion Senten will serve as both judge and juror, and the responsibility of breaking a deadlock would fall to you."

*   *   *

Bryson was inside the classroom again. Nothing had changed. Director Senex held his inaudible conversation with Agnos, who was seated to

Bryson's right. The same eight characters were written on the chalkboard, and when he looked to his left …

Wait, this wasn't right. Instead of the wall of shadows, a young man was seated at the desk next to him, a soft blanket of calm on his bronze face. Bryson had seen him in the dream once before. Long ago, before Bryson had asked Agnos for help, and he had forgotten about him in the months since then.

Bryson rose from his seat, the chair's feet making no noise against the wooden floor as they slid back. This was also fairly new. He couldn't move the last time this mysterious man was in his dream.

Instead of walking toward the pitch black that stretched into infinity and the screams that clashed with the melodic humming of a song, Bryson stopped in front of the man, whose bald head glistened with an oily substance. The ear on the far side of the man's face was badly burned, a withered mass of skin and cartilage. The skin on his cheek and halfway around his eye had been scalded.

Bryson turned and saw another presence toward the back of the classroom. It was a boy on the verge of crossing into manhood. Even from where Bryson stood, he could see that the boy's face was sutured together like a patchwork quilt.

Bryson approached the back of the classroom to get a closer look, but an ear-shattering shriek caused him to stop abruptly. He stared into the black and noticed a sheet of ice slowly crawling across the floor out of the darkness as if it was trying to run from the source of that scream.

But Bryson found himself walking toward it for some inexplicable reason. He felt the ice soundlessly crunching beneath his shoes. He turned back to see that the classroom had disappeared. His breaths became audible, along with a piano's melody in the murky distance.

The piano and his breathing stopped. Anticipation was all he felt. Then it was the hairs on the back of his neck and arms standing at attention. Instinct told him to turn around, and so he did …

*   *   *

Bryson bolted upright in his bed. He groaned as he fell onto the mattress. After a moment he lifted his heavy arm and examined the thick, awkward cast that encased it. Metal rods poked out in all directions.

"Crap," he groaned.

He heard a familiar laugh. "Look at the bright side—it could make a formidable weapon. Who wants to get beat by my spiked club of an arm?"

Bryson rolled his head to his right. Sure enough, Himitsu was sitting on the empty bed beside him, watching his friend with a teasing smile that had the slightest curl to one side.

Bryson smirked. "Do you?"

"Olivia has beaten me senseless enough, thank you."

Bryson sat up and looked around the room. He was in Phesaw's medical building, and the sterile scent gathering in his nostrils reminded him of his trips to Dunami Hospital when Lilu was in a body brace and Rhyparia was in a coma.

Bryson nodded at the window, hearing the laughter of children from below. "That sounds like a lot of activity for winter break."

"What do you think today is?" Himitsu asked.

"Sunday."

"It's Wednesday."

"I've been knocked out for four days?"

"Eleven."

"What?" Bryson exclaimed, trying to push himself out of bed.

"Not a wise decision," Himitsu warned.

Cringing in pain as he staggered to his feet, Bryson wobbled across the giant rectangular room lined with the same plain beds.

"You mean to tell me that these people are just going about classes and training while Rhyparia has been taken from us?" Bryson ranted as he approached the door.

Before he could reach the handle, the door swung open to reveal Grand Director Poicus. He stood quietly in the doorway, looking down at the impulsive Jestivan. Even with a slight lean on his cane, the director was still taller than the average person. The two stared at each other for a few seconds while Himitsu watched from his seat on the empty bed.

Poicus spoke first: "Why so hasty, Zana Bryson?"

Bryson's eyes narrowed. "Why so calm, *Grand Director* Poicus?"

Poicus simply extended an open hand toward Bryson's bed without breaking eye contact. "Lie down, Bryson. You have recovered nicely over the past week and a half, but you're not ready to leave yet."

"You're stalling, trying to make sure I can't try to rescue Rhyparia before she gets to wherever it is she's going."

"Actually the doctors made the decision to put you in a medically induced coma. You were suffering from energy depletion, and the procedures to recuperate your body are extraordinary painful. But I will say that chasing after Lita Rhyparia would have done you no good—not to mention impossible in your condition."

Bryson slumped. Poicus placed his hand on the Jestivan's shoulder and gently guided him back toward his bed. He pulled up a chair and gingerly sat down while Bryson stared at the tile floor from his seat on the edge of the bed.

"You must understand, this was difficult for me to come to grips with too," Poicus said. "I didn't know that any of this was happening until those three generals were marching down Telejunction's hill. ... Resistance was entirely too late by then and would have been considered treason by your king."

Bryson didn't respond.

"This hurts," Poicus said. "The Jestivan is your family, and it feels like you just lost a sibling. Heh, it feels like I've lost a kid. But we must remember that her fate has not yet been decided. Senex is with her right now, getting ready to fight on her behalf."

A hint of life returned to Bryson's face. "Is he really?"

Poicus smiled. "Yes. And let me tell you, he has a hunch that can very well get our friend out of the mess she's in."

Bryson looked up at Himitsu, who wore an optimistic smirk. He tried to remind himself that this wasn't the same as it had been with Olivia. Rhyparia wasn't being held captive, beaten, and starved by an evil king. Himitsu's mother was a member of the Amendment Order, and she would fight on Rhyparia's behalf. Presumably Toshik and Jilly's fathers would as well.

Bryson managed the weakest of smiles. "I understand, sir."

"Fantastic," Poicus said. "Now I want you to know that things are still a mess where the incident occurred. The debris has been cleared, but nothing's been rebuilt. And a lot of parents are holding their kids out of school."

"Was there a memorial service?" Bryson asked.

"No need. Everyone is alive." Poicus gave a side-eyed glance to Himitsu. "The rest of the Jestivan are in classes, I believe. Except for this one, who is apparently playing hooky."

"Break period, sir."

The old man ignored the comment. "The tournament will go on," he said to Bryson. "The next round is in three weeks."

Bryson studied his cast. "How am I supposed to fight anyone like this?"

"The doctor told me that the cast can come off in two weeks. You'll be limited in what you can do, but that's what your other limbs are for. And based off the attack you unleashed on Mr. and Mrs. NuForce, I'd say you have more weapons than your limbs now. Just don't unleash all of your clout at once again, or you'll end up right back in this bed."

The door opened and Jilly rushed in, followed by Olivia, Lilu, Toshik, Agnos, Jilly, Tashami, and Vuilni.

The Grand Director grabbed his cane and pushed himself to his feet. "Well it seems the rest of your family has arrived."

Bryson looked up at him. "I'm sorry, sir … for how I acted earlier."

There was a twinkle in the old man's eyes. "No need, Zana Bryson. I've always admired your willingness to fight for your family. Jilly might be the Jestivan's engine, but you're both the shield and the sword."

Bryson blushed. "Thank you," he mumbled.

The director smiled. "I'm giving you three days, and then I expect to see you patching up that roof you destroyed."

Himitsu started laughing as Poicus walked away. Lilu approached with a look of relief and everyone else sported smiles. The lone exception was the expected one.

Olivia's blank blue eyes held steady on Bryson, while Meow Meow was in the middle of one of his random naps. Knowing she wouldn't initiate contact, he stood and hugged her. She didn't bother returning the embrace—she never did. That's who she was, and he was okay with that.

Everyone caught Bryson up to speed. But there wasn't much to go over, and they quickly fell into an awkward silence.

Jilly stood up with her hands on her hips. "What does pouting achieve?" she asked. "She's not dead. No one died. We're not falling! We may have fumbled with the ladder's rung, but our fingers are still holding on!"

Himitsu stood up and squeezed Jilly against his side. "Jilly's right. We need to lean on each other here while Senex and my mother work to bring Rhyparia back to us."

"Can I start by telling you that there's a hole in the crotch of your pants?" Toshik asked.

Himitsu looked down. "*Heh*, slightly embarrassing."

Vuilni was the first to burst into laughter, followed by most of the others. It was moments like these that made Bryson appreciate his team. Sure, Olivia may have gotten the superior fighters—supposedly—but he had the personalities. For someone who had spent his entire life mocking qualities such as spirit and optimism, he found himself appreciating them in his teammates more than anything else.

31
A Slave

Bryson gratefully returned to the daily student routine a week later. The cast that encased his hand was smaller and the rods had been removed, and his energy was back to normal.

He held a textbook in his uninjured hand as he walked outside after the day's classes. Professor Warwig, Bryson's instructor for both of his weaving classes—Introduction to Weaving and The Science of Weaving—had loaned him the book.

Bryson had grown fond of Professor Warwig. Unlike Director Jugtah, who refused to help him with any topics that were ahead of his curriculum, Warwig was always excited to see her students take initiative and jump ahead. And the book she had given Bryson was for an entirely different class.

Once in his dorm room, he dropped the textbook on his bed. He stared at his wardrobe, annoyed that Bruut's wreckage of a suitcase was spilled in front of it. He stepped through his roommate's pile of clothes and reached into the wardrobe to grab a heavier jacket. As he poked his arm through a sleeve, something caught his eye among Bruut's clothes. He knelt down and picked it up. It was a letter from Bruut's grandfather.

Bryson stared at the door handle, contemplating when his roommate would arrive. Then he looked back down at the letter.

Bruut,

During your visit to the Light Realm, you are to keep this with you as a reminder of what is expected from you. The Power Kingdom does not break, so as a Powish, neither do you. You are far stronger than anyone in that realm. Your Power Energy grants you that gift.

I want you to show the Jestivan, and anyone else who knows nothing of you, the unimaginable force you are. You are to beat every bit of nonsense out of your opponents that is possible without killing them—after all, they are our allies, and we should treat them as such.

But—perhaps more important than anything else—don't let that pile of filth girl from Cascade's Closure show you up. Be a constant reminder that she is below you and everyone else—just like the garbage town she lives in. You are a man of the Power Kingdom, a Diatia, and the grandson of a general. You live at Stratum 9 of Ulna Malen. A girl from Stratum 0 deserves to eat our waste, and don't let her ever forget that.

Fight with might,
Granddad

Bryson read through the letter twice more. It was appalling. The man who wrote this was the Power General? It made him question Bruut's character and the moral values of the Power Kingdom. Bruut had never spoken about his life at home—now Bryson knew why. And now he wondered about Vuilni even more.

But that would have to wait for another time. He was running late, so he zipped up his jacket, threw on his hood, and returned the parchment to its home. Passion Director Venustas would be waiting at the construction site. She had volunteered to keep an eye on Bryson, and he was insulted that they didn't trust him.

Director Venustas was dressed all in red, the color of her kingdom: a thick layer of red lipstick, a fluffy red frock coat, and her long dirty-blond hair was tucked behind gigantic red earmuffs. She stood off to the side, speaking with a student as the two of them looked over a stack of parchment.

With his mangled hand, Bryson couldn't do any of the physical repairs to the roof, so he was relegated to carrying heavy materials from the ground level up to the building's third floor. It was monotonous, tiring work. As he passed through the modest dorm building, it struck him how lucky he had been to have lived in places like Lilac Suites and Dunami Palace for the past two years.

The afternoon dragged along, and Bryson was lathered in dirt and cold sweat when they knocked off for the day. He walked downstairs to see Olivia, who shoved a mug of water into his chest.

"I spoke to Agnos yesterday," she said. "He said that he's been helping you with a dream, although he wouldn't give me specifics. Why haven't you told me?"

"I figure you had enough to deal with. And there's nothing to it anyway. It's just a stupid dream."

"Liar," Meow Meow scolded.

"If you're hurting, tell me," she said.

Bryson stared at her for a moment, then smiled. "Trust me, I'm fine. If I were in trouble, you'd be the first person I'd go to."

Olivia glanced toward the Intelights that hung above the street as they began to ignite. That was a sign that she was on campus past her curfew. "I must head home," she said. "Good night, Bryson."

Bryson pointlessly mumbled a goodnight to her back as she marched toward Telejunction's hill. Then he headed in the opposite direction toward Wealth's Crossroads until entering Lilac Suites.

The familiar pair of Agnos and Tashami sat at the bar in the lobby. Vuilni also sat with them, her braids crashing down her back. Bryson was reminded of Bruut's letter. He walked over and joined them.

"Glad to be getting back into the thick of things?" Tashami asked.

"Never thought I'd miss school so much," Bryson replied.

Tashami laughed. "I wish I could relate."

Agnos shook his head. "At this point school is nearly pointless for me. I was going to leave Phesaw at the end of last year, for what I seek is elsewhere now."

"Then what's keeping you here?" Vuilni asked.

"My friends."

They all smiled, including Agnos. "I can't believe that's my truthful answer," he said. "Younger me would be ashamed of what I've become."

"Younger you wouldn't have been able to understand what you've become," Tashami said. "You made friends with books. Now you make friends with humans."

"The same could be said for all of us," Bryson said. "I'm pretty sure if you stood any of our younger selves in front of us right now, they'd either be disgusted or pleasantly shocked."

"What would it be for you?" Vuilni asked.

"The latter."

Her eyes shifted to Tashami. "And you?"

"Same."

"Has the Diatia changed you?" Agnos asked.

She frowned and admitted, "The Diatia doesn't operate like the Jestivan. We're very segmented."

"Seems like it's a reflection of the realm it belongs to," Agnos said with a nod.

Bryson glared at Agnos. "Hey. You don't know that."

Vuilni gazed emptily at the wine bottles that lined the wall behind the bar. "Agnos is right. This visit has been eye-opening for me. When I first saw how you interacted, I was in disbelief. I thought for sure that you all were putting on an act since we were new, that the cracks would eventually show over time. But you all are truly a family."

Agnos raised his mug. "Hear, hear."

"Once I realized this, I attributed it to the fact that Phesaw was a school of unity between kingdoms, and thought that such a family could thrive only in a place like this. I was certain that the kingdoms themselves couldn't coexist on such terms. But even that misconception fell away when I saw three generals, each from a separate kingdom, marching in unison on the same mission. Such cooperation is unimaginable in the Dark Realm."

"It's not all roses and rainbows over here," Agnos said. "My kingdom feels like the Light Realm's unwanted stepchild. Look at the Amendment Order—they treat us like they're our last chance at being a proper country."

Vuilni and Tashami said their goodbyes not long after, and Agnos moved over a stool so he and Bryson could talk privately.

"How's Tashami doing?" Bryson asked.

"He's gotten better. He needed closure, and I think seeing the Unbreakable helped. Of course, he'll never be able to fully shut the door. He is his father, after all. And what about you? How's that dream coming along?"

Bryson reached into his jacket pocket and handed some scrap paper to Agnos.

"Two more characters," Agnos said. "We're making progress. How many more are there?"

"Four."

"What you're doing is impressive," Agnos said, placing the parchment in his pocket. "This is a lot of detail, and most people can't remember their dreams at all."

"Yeah well, when you continuously have the same one, it tends to stick."

Agnos raised his eyebrows. "Something in your dream changed. I can tell by your tone."

Bryson sighed. "Nothing gets past you. There were two new people in my dream. Well, one of them had been in my dream once before, but I had forgotten about him. Both of them looked like older students—our age. One had a burned ear, cheek, and eye. The other guy in the back of the classroom had his face stapled together."

"Do you remember anything else?"

"The burned one was tan-skinned like Himitsu, and he was bald with an oiled down scalp. I can't remember anything about the second guy outside of the damage to his face."

"Do me a favor. Meet me at Director Senex's office tomorrow morning."

"What's there?"

Agnos downed his juice and stood up. "A hunch. Good night."

Bryson spent the next ten minutes debating whether he should join the girls at their table. Ultimately he decided against it. He was on good terms with Lilu, but he was still ashamed that he wasn't at the level of weaving she expected of him. Every time he was around her, he felt like he was being judged. Then there was Yama, whom Bryson had almost no relationship with at all. Jilly and Vuilni would have been fun to pass time with, but he wasn't going to try to pull them away from the others. So he headed up one of the spiraling staircases to the fourth floor. Himitsu's door was cracked open, and violent yells came from within.

Bryson peeked inside to see what was going on. With swords in hand, Himitsu and Toshik were quickly alternating sparring stances, Himitsu mimicking Toshik. Normally Bryson would have either joined in or made fun of them, but he didn't want to ruin this moment. Slowly and carefully, he closed the door.

When he arrived at his own room, a blast of body odor assaulted him. Bruut was hammering out one-handed push-ups like a man possessed.

Bryson covered his nose with his jacket collar and took a seat on his bed. He opened the textbook that Professor Warwig had given him, but he couldn't concentrate. He could never get over how stout this guy was. Veins popped out from Bruut's muscles, and his arms were as thick as Bryson's head.

Refocusing, Bryson read through a paragraph and turned the page. There was a diagram depicting the more popular methods for weaving energy and currents to make an Intelight. The Intel Energy was gold and the Intel currents were black, and they sort of came together in a random scribbled mess of looping lines. He shook his head. It looked like a toddler had drawn it.

He thought back to what Lilu had told him: Focus on how the lines are moving. Don't just look at the whole. You must follow individual EC chains before trying to understand the shape of the cluster.

Bryson buckled down, and after a few minutes, recognized the pattern. The Intel Energy was looping around strands of Intel currents—and they were big loops, which signified that a loose EC chain was being formed. And those EC chains were then curving inward on themselves, almost as if they were making a circle. Instead of a scribbled cluster of EC chains, Bryson now saw a ball of looped rings.

He sent his energy to his fingertips, then focused on using a sparse amount of clout to expel his energy. Sparks emitted from his fingers. He sensed the currents around him and began weaving chains by loosely spiraling his energy around a current, then trying to fold the resulting chain back in on itself.

Though a complicated, layered process, it happened in a split-second, which was why weaving was so difficult. There were many steps involved that required flawless finesse, and they had to be carried out instinctively. It took Bryson several tries, but then he saw it. For a brief moment a soft light glowed at the tip of his finger.

"That's the kind of stuff you're planning on defeating Toshik with?"

Bryson looked down at Bruut. "Not everything is about combat."

Bruut stood up and removed his sweat-drenched shirt. Bryson worked his core a lot, but Bruut's torso looked like a lobster's. Bryson watched as his roommate threw the shirt into the hamper, where it hung halfway over the lip.

"You only throw your clothes in the hamper when I'm around," Bryson said. He nodded at the mix of clean and dirty clothes on the floor. "Otherwise I end up stepping on them."

Bruut ignored the comment, grabbed a towel, and wiped down his chest. "What's the point of using your energy if it isn't for combat?" he asked.

"You've been here forever now. I'm sure you've seen an Intelight."

"That's what a candle is for."

"They're not as bright."

"Still pointless."

Bryson rolled his eyes. "What about teleplatforms or broadcasting?"

"Don't need either," Bruut said. "All I care about is my kingdom. I don't need to travel or communicate between the others."

"What about for trade?"

Bruut laughed. "Do you really think kingdoms trade via teleplatforms? They use the river system and the sea. Very big ships capable of transporting mountains of product." He shook his head. "Aren't you supposed to be smart, Mr. Intel man?"

This angered Bryson. He usually didn't care about his average intelligence, but it was a lot more insulting when it came from a slab of meat like Bruut.

Bruut's smirk grew into something sinister. "Your energy is for imposing your superior strength onto others, not gimmicks."

Bryson narrowed his eyes with menace. "That's not how we operate here at Phesaw, and if you try to bring that mindset into your fight with Jilly, you'll be slurping your chicken through a straw for the rest of your miserable life."

Bruut's smile disappeared as he matched Bryson's intensity. "That girl can take care of herself. I saw her fight Rhyparia. I'm not going to hold back."

"I'm surprised you show her respect, considering how you treat a girl like Vuilni."

"People of Stratum 0 don't deserve my respect," Bruut snarled.

"Why not?"

Bruut yanked the door open. "Because they're our slaves."

As the door slammed shut, Bryson sat back down on the bed. He had gotten bad vibes from Bruut from the start, but now it was official. Bruut was a vile man.

32
Musku Rao

"Time is running short," Ophala said, "and you've yet to find a way to prove your hypothesis."

A vase of extravagant flowers sat on the desk that separated Spy Pilot Ophala Vevlu and former Archaic Director Mynute Senex. Neither Archain appeared relaxed or happy.

"If only there was a way to get her mother to show her cards," Senex said as he leaned back against the headrest of the chair he was standing on. "If I were Praetor, I'd know a few ways."

"But neither of us are that kind of person. We are every bit of what an Archain represents—no matter how much it may hinder us at times."

"I know you've done some heinous deeds in the past—or at least been the initiator of such deeds."

"To bad people," Ophala clarified. "And only after I've gathered enough evidence to prove that the target is indeed a threat to the Archaic Kingdom. Then I send the assassins. I'm simply a spy, nothing more."

"And my word isn't proof enough?"

"No."

"We need to think of something," Senex said as he hopped off the chair.

"My advice is to wait. Rhyparia's parents won't be discharged from the hospital until after the first trial. Then we can try to figure something out for the next two."

Senex didn't reply. He stood out of sight behind the desk.

"Bite your tongue until then," Ophala warned. "For Rhyparia's sake."

She heard footsteps. Then she finally saw the stringy gray and brown hair bobbing its way toward the door at the room's exit. Ophala shook her head, picked up the vase, removed the flowers, and grabbed a cup from a drawer. They were fake flowers, carrying no scent—the perfect disguised prop.

She poured some of the vase's liquid into the cup, then took a swig. Her smile brightened as she leaned back in her chair with a sigh. *Nothing beats the taste of alcohol.*

*   *   *

Bryson stepped into Senex's old office. Agnos stood in front of a bookcase with a book open in his hand. His relic sat on the tip of his nose. "Good morning, Bryson."

Bryson made a pathetic whimpering noise in return. He had never spent so many weekend mornings and weekday evenings inside of this building. For once he just wanted a day without the stress of a dream, studying, training, or classes.

Agnos laughed and returned the book to its rightful spot while putting his glasses in his robe pocket. "Can you summon Thusia?"

"Thusia? Why?"

"She'll be of help."

Bryson was too exhausted to question him further. A few seconds later, Thusia morphed out of a white light.

"Hello!" she shrieked.

"Can you not?" Bryson wailed.

The blonde bundle of joy squeezed him tight. "Awwww, ish wittle Bwyson cwanky?"

"Get off me!"

"Hi, Agnos." She let go of Bryson. "Well this must be important if you're here."

"I was wondering if you knew who that is," Agnos said, cutting right to the chase.

They turned around to see a small portrait. Bryson's eyes widened. It was the guy from his dream—the one with the scalded face. Except in this painting his skin was intact and as smooth as his shiny head.

Thusia giggled and clapped. "Wow, that's Musku! I miss him so much!"

"I thought so," Agnos said.

"One of the gentlest people I had ever met in my life," she said while stepping closer to the portrait and examining it.

"With one of the gentlest smiles, according to Director Senex."

"Definitely."

Bryson stared at the painting. Somehow he felt the tranquility they were describing just by staring at the original Archaic Jestivan's face.

"Do you know why Bryson would be dreaming about him?" Agnos asked.

Thusia whirled around. "I do not." She looked at Bryson. "You don't tell me anything."

"You have more important matters to attend to," he replied, nodding at the ceiling.

"It's boring up there. What's he doing in the dream?"

Bryson explained everything to her from beginning to end—the foreign language on the chalkboard, the younger Senex at the front of the room, and Agnos in the chair. Thusia frowned when he mentioned Musku's presence and the damage to his face.

"I don't ever remember Musku being burned," she said. "As for everything else, I'd assume you're in a warped perception of Mendac's memory."

"We've come to that conclusion," Agnos said.

"Anything else?" she asked.

Bryson told her about the student at the back of the classroom with the mangled face.

"That's Saikatto," she murmured.

"The original Adren Jestivan." Agnos sighed. "Why didn't I guess all of this?"

That made sense. Bryson remembered the story Thusia had told him in the Rolling Oaks about Mendac, how he had mauled Saikatto for yelling at Thusia. "So the Saikatto I'm seeing in my dream is the guy Mendac attacked?"

"I'd say so," she softly replied.

Bryson's stomach did a flip. *That's* what his dad did to someone for yelling? When he had heard the story, he hadn't imagined it had been nearly so brutal.

Bryson forced himself to say it: "Maybe my dad also hurt the Musku in my dream."

Neither Agnos nor Thusia answered. Bryson looked into Musku's light brown eyes until all he saw was the Jestivan's face. Then he felt heavy rain drenching his body at it smacked the ground around him. The face of Musku was no longer a painting, but sopping wet and alive.

"You don't have to leave!" Musku shouted, holding his hand to his forehead to shield his eyes from the rain.

"You're too optimistic!" Bryson responded, but not in his voice. It was the same voice as his father's from his dream a year ago. "You're all useless to me!"

"You don't feel that way! You're scared that we're only a reminder of Thusia!"

"*Shut up about her!*" Mendac bellowed.

Musku didn't waver. "We want to help you, Mendac! You've made so much progress!"

Bryson looked up to the candlelit window in the small house that sat just behind Musku. "That's why they're trying so hard to keep me around, eh?"

"They're—"

Mendac finished the sentence: "Scared!"

Musku paused, allowing the storm to dominate their silence.

"You're scared too!" Mendac shouted.

"Entirely not the case. You're a brother! The Jestivan is a family!"

"That was Thusia's motto," Mendac scoffed. "She's gone! It's time for me to go my own way and put the fear I strike in others to use! There are so many wonders in this world ready to be discovered—theories to be tested!"

"Didn't you learn from Director Senex or Thusia?" Musku asked. "What would they think?"

There was another pause. Then Mendac's hand rose and gently placed itself against the side of Musku's head, as if he was caressing it. "You're right, Musku. Let's head back. I don't want to disgrace the love of my life."

There was a masked coldness in his voice, and Musku must have noticed it because his eyes widened. An instant later there was a flash of light as an electric charge emitted from Mendac's hand. Musku's face burned, and he yelled as his body convulsed.

When Mendac removed his grasp, the entire left side of Musku's face and scalp had been scorched. His ear was a wad of shrunken cartilage.

"I could have killed you," Mendac said. "I guess maybe you're right … Maybe I'm not a monster."

Bryson awoke to a pounding headache and blurred vision. He was still in Director Senex's office, but seated against the wall on the floor. Thusia and Agnos stood at the desk, heads down as they studied something.

"Hello, sleepy head."

Bryson turned to see Thusia watching him. "How long have I been out?" he asked.

"Fifteen minutes, give or take. You were breathing so we left you alone. What'd you see?"

"I witnessed a memory of my dad's … and I saw what he did to Musku."

"You don't have to say anything," Thusia said after a long pause. "None of it would be a surprise to me."

He wasn't going to. The vision was already overwhelming enough. He had spent his entire life hearing about how great of a man his father was. But he had never really thought about what "great" meant. He was starting to realize that they weren't referring to his generosity or kindness. People just assumed that he was a wonderful human being because of the story of his death—how he sacrificed himself to protect the Intel Princess. But

Bryson had learned the real story. Mendac was executed by a Bozani. *The Fifth of Five* was a lie.

Tears formed in Bryson's eyes. He was the offspring of a monster. Now he understood why Thusia and Ophala had tried so hard to stop him from killing the Dev Assassin in the Rolling Oaks.

"Why are you crying?" Thusia asked.

A tear fell down Bryson's cheek. "I'm thinking about all of the children out there who grow up idolizing Mendac. About the silence from Debo, how he never told me the truth. How our realm treats a terrible, evil human as a flawless icon of what you should grow up to be, and how King Vitio was this man's friend. Storshae has a right to be angry, as does the entirety of his kingdom and likely the whole Dark Realm."

"There is no such thing as an impartial arbitrator in the moral litigation of good versus evil," Agnos said, "for perspective is subjective and therefore unjust."

Bryson shook his head. "I don't agree. My father was an evil man—plain and simple." They didn't respond, so he pushed himself up to his feet. "I'm going for a walk."

With a heavy mind, Bryson strolled through Phesaw's building. Part of him wanted to run to Telejunction, transport to the Intel Kingdom, and bombard King Vitio with questions. He stifled the impulse.

The halls were empty—to be expected on a Saturday. The angle at which the sunlight shined through the windows of the exterior halls told him that it was probably an hour or so before noon. Up ahead of him, Intel Director Jugtah stepped out of his office and carried something to the classroom right next door.

Bryson crept down the hallway and peeked through the door's window. For some reason he felt nervous, though it was hardly suspicious to see a teacher in the building on a weekend. Most of them lived in it.

Lilu was standing next to Jugtah, their backs to the window as they huddled over a large wooden table. She looked to be hammering at something while Jugtah held it steady. It made a loud clanking noise, and Bryson could hear the occasional "careful" from the director.

Just as Bryson turned to walk away from boredom, Jugtah's shout of "No!" was followed by an explosion. The room was a mess as Bryson pressed his face against the glass. Overturned and broken tables were strewn across the floor, and everything was blanketed with soot. Lilu was covering her head while the Intel Director was curled up on the floor.

Lilu looked up at the window. The back of her hair was blown out, making her look like a green-tailed peacock. "Bryson!" she shouted.

Bryson finally entered the room.

"What are you doing here on a Saturday, Mr. LeAnce?" Jugtah asked as he pushed himself to his feet.

"I walk into this, and you're the one asking me questions?"

The director dusted himself off. "Let me rephrase, Mr. LeAnce: what can I do for you?"

"I'm pretty sure that explosions are a safety hazard, sir."

"You wouldn't understand," Lilu said. "This is beyond anything in your curriculum's scope."

"What? Permanence?" Bryson caught a glimpse of the material Jugtah had been carrying earlier. Lilu slid it behind her back.

"Yes. Can you make an Intelight yet?"

"Yeah."

"Let's see it then."

"Fine," he replied with a shrug. He lifted his hand and concentrated on the weaving pattern. He knew he had a stupid look on his face, but it was worth it when an orb of yellow light sat at the tip of his finger. And for the first time it wasn't disappearing.

"Congratulations!" Lilu exclaimed. "Now I want you to try to tighten your EC chains—not too much though. Otherwise it'll turn into an attack. I can tell by the softness of the light that your chains are too loose."

Bryson focused on weaving his Intel Energy around the currents with a tighter grip while making sure he was limiting the amount of clout he was using to force the energy out of his body.

Astonishingly, it worked. The Intelight grew brighter, casting shadows on their faces. Lilu clapped. "Very good!"

He laughed—and then the light fizzled out. But Lilu didn't seem discouraged. "All right, try it again," she said. "You've learned to control the light's intensity—now you must learn how to make it last without the constant influx of your body's energy."

She stuck her finger in the air, and a pulsing light formed on its tip. But unlike Bryson, she was able to take her finger away from it, leaving it suspended in midair.

"How …?"

"In the book Professor Warwig gave you, what did the weaving patterns look like in the diagrams for an Intelight?"

"The EC chains looped backwards onto themselves," he recalled. "But that's what I'm doing."

"But are you connecting the tails of your chains back to the original chain or are you just letting them hang loosely in a loop?"

Bryson paused, confused by what she was asking. "I'm not connecting anything."

"Well that's your problem. You must actually make a connection. That's what allows the reaction—the *thrust*—to occur without you constantly pumping your energy into it."

"So it's an infinite thrust."

"Not quite," Lilu said. "It's just a long-lasting thrust that doesn't require constant input from the user. It can be left unattended and still work. The proper term is a self-feeding loop."

"Makes one wonder," Jugtah said with an air of boredom, "did you read the text that went along with the diagram or just look at the picture?"

Bryson hated him for being right. There was nothing more boring to Bryson than dense text loaded with scientific lingo. He liked visuals—just another trait of his that was completely embarrassing for someone who was supposed to be an Intelian.

"I don't expect you to learn all of weaving's finer details," Lilu said, "but certain aspects and terms are a must. Now try again."

Bryson tried to weave a self-feeding loop, but what resulted was a highly concentrated ball of electricity that popped and nearly singed his eyebrows.

Lilu giggled. "That's what happens when you weave too tight. You're not disciplined enough to handle highly concentrated EC clusters."

Bryson smirked and waved an arm to encompass the wreckage that was the classroom. "And what do you have to say about this?"

"You'd kill all of us if you tried doing what she's doing," Jugtah said. He gazed upward, his gleaming golden glasses crowding his face. "And I do mean that literally, Mr. LeAnce."

"Are you going to show me what's behind your back?" Bryson asked.

"All in due time," she replied.

"Fine I'll see you later. Have fun cleaning up."

33
The Gravity Trials: Day 1

Rhyparia stood outside a closed door with two Adrenian soldiers in silver flanking her. Chains bound her wrists together behind her back, while the muffled murmurs of her audience seeped through the cracks.

A Dev servant stood in front of her. She was dark-skinned with blue hair and blue eyes—a combination Rhyparia had never seen before. "All right," the woman said. "They're ready."

The servant opened the door, and the soldiers led Rhyparia into the judgment room. The murmuring stopped, for all eyes turned to the girl. She hung her head low as she descended the steps, her bandana nearly covering both eyes. She was in rags once again—as she had been for most of her life before becoming a Jestivan.

After positioning her at the center of the room, a soldier yanked the bandana away from her eyes. She lifted her head and gazed around. When she saw the elderly face of Archaic Director Senex standing on his seat in the curved pews, a morsel of hope fluttered inside of her.

Four curved tables stood on the room's floor—the chiefs of the Amendment Order, she surmised. And Archaic Prince Sigmund, the man who was much younger than the rest.

Long minutes passed as the chiefs exchanged whispers and shuffled through the parchment in front of them. Occasionally a Dev servant would walk down the stairs and lean close to a chief to listen to whispered instructions before retreating up the stairs.

Finally one of the chiefs—a heavyset man with his glasses on the tip of his nose—raised his hand. "Start broadcasting," he commanded.

The eyes of the Dev servants at the top of the stands turned a burgundy color. The woman who had opened the door to the judgment room stood on the main floor. Her blue eyes were now burgundy like the others.

The hefty man stood up. "We convene here, the eighth of February, 1500 K.H., to commence the first hearing of the Gravity Trials. The Amendment Order has been given the reins of this case by the royal heads of the Spirit, Adren, Intel, and Passion Kingdoms. The jury consists of Spy Pilot Ophala Vevlu, Chief Senator Rosel Sania, Chief Merchant Toth Brench, Chief Officer Wert Lamay, and myself, Chief Arbitrator Grandarion Senten."

As Rhyparia listened to the names, three of them stood out: Ophala, Toth, and Wert. They were the parents of three of her fellow Jestivan.

"The trial will be held on three separate days, each a week apart. On this day we will discuss the events that took place nearly nine years ago—the destruction of Olethros, Rim at the footholds of the Archaic Mountains. On day two we will discuss the destruction of Gourmet Filet, the restaurant in Dunami, last year. Day three will focus on the murder of Intel General Lucas.

"Before we bring forth witnesses, allow me to explain the candles placed in front of each of the chiefs. As of now, they are lit. At any time throughout these three trials, a chief can extinguish their candle, which would signify a guilty verdict in his or her eye. Even if all five candles are extinguished before the conclusion of the third trial, the trial will still go on since the degree of punishment will need to be decided. With that said, for our first witness we'd like to call down—"

Grandarion paused as Chiefs Toth, Wert, and Rosel blew out their candles, calling the room to order as the audience gasped and chattered. Then Grandarion followed suit, leaving one tiny ember that flickered in front of Spy Pilot Ophala. No more than a couple minutes in, and a unanimous verdict was declared when Ophala reached out and pinched the flame into nothingness.

Rhyparia gazed up at Director Senex. He appeared undisturbed.

"By unanimous decision," Grandarion declared, "Rhyparia NuForce has been found guilty of the destruction of Olethros, Gourmet Filet, and areas of Phesaw's campus; the slaughter of approximately 350 civilians; and the murder of Intel General Lucas Golding."

More muttering rose from the pews. The Chief Arbitrator held up his hand and commanded them to be quiet. "With that said, the chiefs will now judge each trial with the focus of determining the degree of punishment." He sat back down. "The Amendment Order calls down Guinea Trolk, mayor of Rim."

Trolk was as large as Grandarion. His hair was gray and thin, and he wore robes that reminded Rhyparia of Agnos.

Grandarion gazed at his colleagues and extended his arms, as if offering them the floor. Chief Senator Rosel jumped right in: "Mayor Trolk, recount for us the events of the day that the sector of Olethros perished."

Trolk dabbed a napkin against his forehead and cleared his throat. It was clear he was nervous. "I'll never forget that morning. I was going through the paperwork typical of such a position—as you very well know, Chief Rosel—and I felt tremors shake the building. Now this was nothing out of the ordinary. The Archaic Mountains are legendary for their frequent earthquake-induced avalanches, and we experience the destruction at least six times a day. It did feel slightly more violent, but I simply waited for it to pass."

"And how long does that typically take?" Rosel asked.

"Around thirty seconds."

"And on that morning, how long did you have to wait for it to pass?"

"Seven minutes." The audience quietly reacted again before Grandarion's hand silenced them. "But eventually my curiosity got the best of me. Something was clearly wrong, so I got up and looked out of my window. It was an ugly morning—stormy and dark—but the demolition of Rim's most outer sector, Olethros, was plain. Buildings were collapsing. Panicked and screaming people fled through the streets, and the very crust of the land crunched like bones in the mouth of a hyena.

"I was rushed into the saferoom by my guards—against my will, mind you, but that was the protocol." Something told Rhyparia that was a lie. "From there I received occasional updates … the scope of destruction, the number of injuries, and the rising death toll." He sighed. "Worst day of my life."

Chief Wert withstanding, the Amendment Order was feverishly jotting down notes. Rosel looked up. "Continue. When did you visit the site?"

"Later that day, when the sky cleared," Trolk said. "I vividly remember exiting my carriage upon our arrival and stepping into a thick pool of mud. But it was wet with blood, not rain, and the air was thick with its iron-like scent. Bodies were grotesquely contorted within the rubble. I had never seen anything like it, and I was beginning to wonder how an avalanche could cause such injuries—"

"What about natural debris from the mountains?" Rosel interrupted. "Surely if an avalanche caused it, there would have been rocks and boulders strewn throughout the wreckage, correct?"

Trolk shook his head. "Not a single piece of evidence that it was an avalanche." More mutters from the pews. "However, it was explained to me that it was the earthquake that did the damage."

"An earthquake that struck both the mountains and Olethros?" Rosel asked.

"Yes, and I had every reason to believe the report, for there was evidence of such a disaster."

"Such as?"

"There were giant cracks in the ground, splintering in hundreds of different directions. Bodies were lodged in some of the gaps."

"Which very well could have been from increased gravity at the hands of Rhyparia," Rosel said.

"An awfully rash conclusion, considering the girl was seven years old at the time," Ophala retorted.

Rosel looked across the floor at her counterpart. "You extinguished your candle, so why are you defending her?"

"I never said she was guilty of Olethros. As for the restaurant and the Intel General, those are different stories. But if you expect me to believe that a seven-year-old flattened a sector that stretches miles across and killed north of three hundred people in the process based off word of mouth, then you are out of your mind."

"But she did," Trolk insisted. "And there is evidence, which was covered up by King Itta."

"What evidence do you have?" Rosel asked.

Trolk nodded his head at a Dev servant recording the proceedings from the top of the stairs. "I would need Flen to be able to show it."

Grandarion raised his hand. "The Amendment Order calls down Flen Araba, Dev servant of the Intel family."

The man casually made his way down the steps.

"Any day now," Grandarion grumbled. "And you can stop recording."

Flen's eyes returned from burgundy to black. He stopped next to Rhyparia, a few arm-lengths away.

"You may present the evidence," Grandarion said.

"May I approach Flen?" Trolk asked.

"Go ahead."

"Rim is a poor city—a very poor city. Thus Olethros was left the way it was. To this day, our homeless live there, making homes out of the wreckage. Itta never wanted Olethros to be cleaned up. He would visit from time to time to see the destruction. I always noticed a childlike glee in his eyes when he'd look upon it. Truly terrifying. But enough rambling. The point is, the proof of Rhyparia's guilt is in the debris." Trolk mumbled something to Flen, and the servant's eyes dilated to project a holographic display that hovered under the chandelier.

"It's just wreckage. What are we looking for?" Ophala asked.

"I had Flen record this a couple weeks ago. Look at the remnants of some of the taller buildings. See how every single one of them lies in the most unnatural of ways. When a building collapses in an earthquake, part or all of them fall over. But every single building in Olethros looks to have caved directly in on itself. Even the tallest building in Olethros, a very popular inn for the poorer citizens, was reduced to a mountain of rubble that sits directly on top of its original foundation. With a building that is five floors high and the way the ground was cracked and shaped around it, at least part of it should have fallen to the side.

"And if those recordings aren't damning enough, how about these?" Trolk gestured to the display as it changed to a different image. Gasps escaped the audience. Ones with weaker stomachs shielded their eyes. "I'm sorry, but bones don't break like that because of an earthquake. What you are seeing is the result of immense and unimaginable pressure."

A long silence followed.

"That doesn't mean Rhyparia is the culprit," Ophala said. "If anything, you proved how much more ludicrous the idea of this is … the amount of clout needed to do that?" She shook her head. "Unfathomable."

"I agree," came a new voice. Ophala's head whirled in its direction. Toth was leaning forward, his elbows resting on the table. "I've never heard of such a thing. Not even the stories of the fabled legends from the *Of Five* were documented to achieve such power at that age. Gatal, Sephrina, Ataway, Qualeen, Mendac—not a single one."

All eyes turned to a sweating Trolk, eager to hear his counterstatement. "I understand the absurdity, but it's the truth," he said. "It's why Itta rushed to Rim just days after the accident. He specifically sought out the NuForce family—and more specifically, this young girl here. Rhyparia had been discovered by medics, unharmed but unconscious. She was checked into Rim's medical facility and was determined to have suffered from a rare incident where someone enters a coma from near-complete energy depletion. And I have the documents to prove it."

Rhyparia closed her eyes as Rosel gestured for Trolk to hand over the papers.

"She stayed in that coma for a month," Trolk said. "When the king had arrived, he requested three things: to visit Rhyparia, her parents, and the site where Rhyparia's body was discovered. Of course I granted all three.

"I was never told the truth. Itta held his meetings with the NuForce parents in private. Also, I never understood why he wanted to visit the spot where Rhyparia had been found. But now I do. The day he came back from that visit, he concluded a meeting with Mr. and Mrs. NuForce at the end of the night before his journey back to Phelos. The next time I saw the parents?" He paused and took a deep breath. "They were placing the umbrella next to Rhyparia's hospital bed."

There it was. All of it was enough to doom the girl's first day: the documentation of her admittance into the hospital while being in a coma for energy depletion and the story of Itta's retrieval of her ancient. As the crowd conversed with nobody bothering to silence them, the chiefs scribbled away. Ophala slumped back in her chair. Trolk appeared to be relieved, and Flen looked bored.

A quiet sadness swept over Rhyparia as tears rolled down her cheeks. Ophala had fought for her and Toth seemed to do the same, but it was hopeless. The look on Ophala's face said as much.

More witnesses were brought to the floor to discuss Olethros, and each one made Rhyparia's case worse. Intel Major Lars explained the reasoning behind her parents' sudden betrayal of their daughter. How they were threatened by Itta to keep it quiet. The penalty would have been their lives. They had come forth when Itta was no longer in power. Then the doctor from Rhyparia's hospital stay confirmed Trolk's testimony.

After the hearing's conclusion, Rhyparia was escorted up the steps by the Adrenian guards. The somewhat gentler nature they had exercised earlier that afternoon was gone, proven when Rhyparia tripped and banged her knee on a step and they yanked her back up and dragged the rest of the way. Part of her wanted her life ended now … to get it over with. But most of her wanted her friends—her fellow Jestivan. But even that left a sour taste in her mouth. None of them would ever look at her the same—not after all of this. They'd judge her, condemn her. She was sure of it … and at this point, she couldn't even believe in herself.

* * *

Ophala stormed through the hall with Toth Brench in her sights. She grabbed the back of his suit, and he whirled around in astonishment.

"What's the matter, Ophala?"

"I know what you're doing. You're defending her in efforts to soften her punishment. You don't want her executed."

"Hmm, that's odd. Isn't that what you want as well?"

"Your reasoning does not align with mine," she hissed. "Yours is selfish and malicious."

His eyes narrowed. "I'm not sure what you mean, Mrs. Vevlu, but you should be happy that there is someone else also fighting to keep the girl alive."

Scowling, Ophala watched the lanky man walk away. Why had she confronted him? Now he would only be more careful in the future.

34
A Brute

Bryson sulked as he strolled beneath Phesaw Park's pink canopy. Olivia and Himitsu walked with him. The two of them carried a conversation while he was off in his own world, thinking about how miserably Rhyparia's hearing had went.

The Jestivan had watched in the Lilac Suites lobby, which proved to be a mistake. The space was crammed full of students and staff. Bryson had stomped out halfway through, enraged by how the students laughed with each other and noisily ordered drinks and food like they were at a party.

"You ought to be focused on what is to come, Bryson."

Olivia's voice snapped him out of his thoughts. He looked up at the branches and sighed. "Rhyparia is more important than some exhibition fight with Toshik."

"Rhyparia is out of your control."

Bryson didn't bother arguing, and they walked in silence to their destination. Once again, grandstands had been set up on the field. They walked around them and entered the tent. Bryson sat in a corner, threw his hood over his head, and stared down at the grass, his arms folded across his knees and forehead pressed against them.

His mind was still on Rhyparia. Director Senex hadn't done a single thing to help her. What happened to the big talk from Director Poicus about Senex having her back? And then there was Intel Major Lars. He was being tricked by Rhyparia's parents—Bryson was certain of that.

He looked up as someone tapped his shoulder to see Jilly's smiling face and rosy cheeks. "Let's go, Captain," she said. "Olivia and Tashami are first."

He got up and headed toward the exit, but someone stopped him. "Zana Bryson." He turned to see Adren Director Buredo.

"I need you to beat Toshik."

Bryson's eyebrows rose. "Shouldn't you be rooting for him, sir?"

"He needs to taste a loss on a stage like this."

"Well, I'm definitely not fighting to lose," Bryson glanced down at his cast. "No matter the hindrances."

Buredo nodded. "Good luck."

As Bryson stepped out of the tent, a cheer erupted. His eyes adjusted to the sunlight as he gazed toward the field.

Tashami was attempting to keep Olivia at bay, throwing blasts of wind at her as she marched forward, her arms shielding her face. It would take more than wind to overpower someone with Olivia's strength. Tashami understood this, but he was using it as a stalling tactic. A punch or kick from Olivia had the ability to splinter bone. But this was precisely the problem for Tashami. Olivia was his worst possible matchup. Since his wind was unable to uproot her, he'd be forced to engage her in close-quarters combat. It was only a matter of time.

Olivia must have understood this because she stopped and stood her ground as Tashami threw countless attacks. Finally, both Jestivan came to a standstill as the arena went quiet. She stood with a face of stone while he breathed heavily.

The ground under Olivia's foot sunk as she pushed off and sprinted at her friend. Then a whistling sound cut through the audience's cheers. Olivia looked down at a hole in her sleeve. She looked up at Tashami, who stood about a hundred feet away. He flicked his finger and another invisible projectile struck her other shoulder, causing her to twitch backward.

"Looks like he's gotten the hang of it," Agnos said.

"What's he doing?" Bryson asked.

"He's weaving tightly packed clusters of even finer spun individual Spirit EC chains, creating tiny bullets of heavily concentrated wind. He has turned himself into a marksman."

Bryson watched Tashami with astonishment. It seemed that every type of energy had limitless creative potential if someone knew how to weave.

Olivia was forced to duck, turn, and stumble backward as Tashami released a flurry of air bullets, most of them striking home. He had her retreating, and the crowd was on its feet.

Though patches of blood dampened her clothing, her face remained expressionless. And then she recollected herself and moved forward again.

She marched through the pellets. An arm or shoulder would occasionally jerk backward from the impact of Tashami's attacks, but her feet never stopped moving. They started to spar once she was in grabbing distance. The audience roared as the fight looked to be hitting its climax. Tashami backpedaled with two long strides to create distance, and Olivia planted her foot with a bang before lunging through the air with a vicious punch. He bent backward, his back parallel to the ground as she thrust her knee down into his sternum. The crowd let out a collective *ooh!* of delighted sympathy as Tashami's back slammed into the ground.

Olivia pinned him in the grass with her knee against his throat, and he tapped her leg. She stood and helped her friend up.

The crowd roared while Bryson gawked at Olivia. Cuts wept through her tattered clothes. She was gripping her shoulder with the plainest of looks. Her face was unmarked. Tashami had probably avoided it on purpose.

"It's unnerving to think about how easy it is for some of us to take a life," Agnos said. "Both Tashami and Olivia were holding back, and the same can be said for the first round. Everyone's too scared to give it their all."

The next match was called for, and the spectators practically quivered in silent anticipation. It was a battle of speed against strength—Yama vs. Vuilni.

The two girls eyed each other until the commentator commanded for them to begin. Yama instantly disappeared, but Vuilni didn't move. Then there was a loud crack, as Yama stood in front of the Diatia, staring in shock at the splintered remains of what used to be her wooden sword. It felt like the entirety of Phesaw's campus was swallowed by the Sea of Light—there was nothing but an awed silence.

Vuilni bent and threw an uppercut that connected with Yama's chin. The swordswoman was sent flying high into the air, a trail of blood marking her path. Her body was limp as it started its descent, and Vuilni rushed under. Miniature tremors shook the field as she ran, and her thighs and calves bulged as her strides grew in distance. She stopped and threw another punch at Yama's descending body, but the swordsman had regained control of her flight and landed with one foot precisely on Vuilni's fist. To be able to land perfectly on such a small surface area was incredible. The punch's vigor had to be immense, but she bent her knee at the perfect time, allowing most of the impact to be absorbed and used as a springboard. This time she would have complete control over her flight.

She was shot out of a cannon at a speed that Bryson could barely keep track of. Usually when Yama moved, he could see a solid streak of color; but this time he only saw momentary glimpses as she rebounded off of the arena's walls. She wasn't touching the ground at all, making it from one side of the field to the other just by bouncing back and forth. Each time she'd hit a wall, a blast of wind would cause the crowd to scream.

"I can't see her," Himitsu said. "Can you?"

"Only glimpses," Bryson replied.

Vuilni looked around, then flexed, and her arms bulked up again. She punched both hands into the ground and grabbed hold. She then did the same with her feet. A moment later there was a sickening sound of popping bone. Yama rolled across the grass and stopped on a single knee, gazing back at her opponent as the crowd let out gasps of revulsion.

Bryson, Himitsu, Jilly, and Lilu ran onto the field. Vuilni's muscles had shrunk to normal. She lay still, her eyes bulging as her lower left leg jutted to the side, blood beginning to course down the exposed white bone. Her clenching hands tore at the grass, bringing up handfuls of black soil.

"What did you do?" Bryson shouted at Yama.

She wiped the blood from her chin. "She's strong. That was the only thing I could do without an actual sword. I wasn't trying to break anything."

"Well, you did!"

"Stop!" Vuilni gasped. "It was my fault. I'm the one who rooted into the ground. I knew the repercussions if my body wouldn't hold up to the impact."

Two medics carefully lifted Vuilni in a stretcher while the Jestivan surrounded her. A third medic tried to assist Yama, but she shook his hand away. As she passed the group, she looked at Jilly and said, "I didn't mean to do that."

Jilly's usual smile was nowhere to be seen as she shook her head and looked elsewhere. Yama's face hardened and she looked down at the ground.

"That's the Yama I know," Agnos murmured.

As they watched Vuilni be carried off the field, the commentator boomed into his ancient: "Is it even possible to top what we just witnessed?" Bryson scowled when the crowd cheered. "I think it's possible! The next fight features the son of one of the *greatest men* to ever live—the Fifth of Five! Zana Bryson against Zana Toshik!"

As Bryson took his spot in the center of the field and glared at the commentator, the man's eyes widened before looking away. Then Bryson turned to Toshik as the swordsman strolled to his spot.

"*Fight!*"

Toshik unzipped his coat to reveal a black suit and tie, provoking laughter from the crowd.

"Are you kidding me?" Bryson shouted.

"This is a big event. I have to look good." He brushed off his sleeves and chest, then gave Bryson a sinister look. "And wearing black to your funeral seemed fitting."

Toshik dashed toward Bryson—painfully slowly in comparison to the otherworldly Yama. Bryson smirked and swept his arm forward, releasing a wall of sparks that coursed through Toshik's now-convulsing body. As the swordsman stumbled forward, Bryson threw a punch with an electrified fist. Toshik was able to narrowly lean away from the blow, but the electricity scorched his face.

Bryson planted his foot and chased after his opponent. Toshik darted to the side and took a long arching route across the field, and Bryson changed his angle of attack. A long game of cat-and-mouse ensued. Bryson could have ended it at any time but he was determined to win solely by weaving.

Toshik ran at Bryson at his highest speed percentage and swung wildly with his sword. Bryson stepped to the side, cleanly grabbed the weapon with his good hand, and shoved the back of Toshik's shoulder with his cast. Toshik skidded across the turf, and though he almost instantly leapt to his feet, Bryson had already disappeared, intercepted his path, and was waiting for him with an electrified round-kick to the stomach.

Toshik made a pathetic gagging noise as his body folded forward. He fell onto his rear, his eyes wide with shock. Bryson quickly grabbed his tie to hold Toshik upright instead of letting him fall onto his back. Bryson loosened the knot of his teammate's necktie with a smirk. He patted his chest and said, "There. That should open your windpipe."

As the medics swarmed Toshik, Bryson noticed for the first time just how loudly the audience was cheering.

"Was that Zana Bryson or the Sixth of Six?!" the commentator bellowed. "Either way, he's moving on to the semifinals! Who will be his opponent? The next match will answer that!"

A woman touched Bryson's arm. "Come with me to the medical tent," she said. "You seem to be all right, but we'll need to check your energy levels to be on the safe side."

As Bryson followed the woman, Jilly and a shirtless Bruut stood across from each other in the center of the field. It was a wonder that Bruut's skin could contain his bulging veins.

Bryson slowed down as the announcer yelled for the match to begin. The medic turned back with a look of impatience. "Come on now, Zana Bryson."

"I need to watch this. I promise I'm okay." Bryson assured her.

The woman gazed hopelessly for a few seconds. "Very well then."

It began like Jilly's last fight—with a furious windstorm that was quickly becoming her signature move. Vicious gales ripped at the field, but Bruut's statuesque figure didn't budge. His face was rigid with concentration.

As the fight progressed, it became obvious that Jilly didn't have a chance against the type of opponent Bruut was. In the fight between Olivia and Tashami, Tashami had been able to affect Olivia—someone with strength like Bruut—because he could weave wind into bullets. Though Jilly's weaving had improved, she still wasn't anywhere near that level. Bruut was absorbing her gusts of wind as if they were nothing more than a refreshing breeze.

Jilly had worn herself down and was breathing heavily. Bruut ran with powerful strides as the ground shook beneath his bulging thighs. Jilly swept her arms forward, and a burst of wind scooped her off her feet and into the sky. But this didn't faze the stampeding bull. He finished a stride by planting two feet into the ground—the frozen sod cracking beneath his feet—and jumping high into the air toward the Spirit Jestivan.

Jilly tried creating another gust to change course, but Bruut grabbed the collar of her tunic with a single fist and flung her toward the ground. She plunged at a blazing speed—somehow even faster than Debo plummeted off the cliff of Necrosis Valley.

Bryson sprang forward, hoping that he would be quick enough to catch her. But he was knocked out of the way and sent flying across the field and into the arena wall with a bang.

His vision spun as he staggered back to his feet. The audience was raining down a deafening mixture of cheers and boos. Standing with Jilly thrown over her shoulder was Yama, a piercing rage rippling her face.

Bruut matched Yama's glare from his indentation in the frozen ground. "I want to fight you," he declared.

"To avenge what I did to Vuilni?" she asked. "That wasn't my intention. But this, this was deliberate. You tried to kill her!"

"And that's it!" the commentator roared. "Lita Jilly has been disqualified for outside interference! Bruut is your winner!"

Boos and howls shook the grandstand as the students threw trash onto the field. It took a long time for the arena to settle down and empty.

Over the course of an hour, the Energy Directors and Power Warden Feissam sat with each Jestivan and Diatia individually and then as a whole. They attempted to explain that while Bruut was in the wrong, the source of his reckless assault was his sincere concern for Vuilni.

Bryson dismissed the rationalization out of hand. "It had nothing to do with her broken leg," he insisted. "He was just mad that Yama embarrassed the Power Kingdom."

"That's extremely unfair," Grand Director Poicus said. "I've witnessed Bruut's kindness and selflessness. When Rhyparia was taken, Bruut spent hours excavating the rubble and rescuing survivors."

"You know how they run things in Ulna Malen," Bryson seethed. "Vuilni is from Stratum 0! Bruut lives in Stratum 9! He doesn't see her as a person, but a slave!"

"I've never seen Bruut reflect such an attitude, Mr. LeAnce," thrummed the deep voice of Power Warden Feissam. "He's a great young man who has the upmost respect for the journey Vuilni has had to travel to get to where she is."

"I bet you think my dad was a great man too!"

"You may get away with talking like that to me, Zana Bryson," Poicus warned, "but I will not allow you to speak like that to our guests."

Bryson ignored it and instead looked at the other Energy Directors, who had sat idly by with nothing to say. "What about everyone else? Are we on Yama's side or Bruut's?"

"There are no sides," Poicus replied.

And that was the end of it. Bryson debated telling them about the letter from Bruut's father, but he didn't know how the Power Warden might react. Better to show it to Poicus in private, he decided.

Later that night, Bryson searched through Bruut's belongings. He wasn't careful about it, tossing clothes across the room like Bruut would do when he wasn't around to object.

"What are you doing?"

He turned to see Bruut standing in the doorway. "I misplaced something," Bryson replied.

Bruut stared at him for a moment before kicking off his shoes and lying in his pile of dirty clothes. He rested his head against his hands and stared at the ceiling, then after a contemplative moment released a large belch.

"You're scum," Bryson said.

"Is that so?"

Bryson didn't reply.

"Your Grand Director doesn't seem to agree."

"He doesn't know what I know."

"Because he doesn't spend his time snooping through someone else's things. Didn't think I knew you were a dirty little sneak, did you?" Bruut stood up and retrieved the letter from his pocket. He held the parchment over a candle on the desk until it dissolved into ash.

"Why'd you choose to be my roommate?" Bryson asked.

Bruut smirked. "Because of your last name."

35
Senex, The Critter

A flickering glow illuminated the dark room. Toono sat transfixed by what he was witnessing in the holographic display. Its source was the tiny frame of Illipsia. He had commanded her to return from Phesaw after every round of the tournament and rebroadcast her recording of every match.

He had learned a lot about the Jestivan—tendencies, weaknesses, and strengths. He would cross paths with the Jestivan eventually. So would Apoleia, but she had no intention of watching the fights. He couldn't blame her … she had her reasons.

Toono watched as Yama's fight against Vuilni unfolded, thinking back to his two-month visit to the Power Kingdom before traveling to the Void. It had been a hopeless scouting mission. The way its capital was constructed—the layered stratums separated by vast differences in elevation—made it impossible to penetrate the highest levels where the Powish elites lived.

Toono's eyes narrowed. To see Yama struggling was odd, but he didn't give it too much thought since she lacked her sword. He smiled at her improvised technique of ricocheting off the walls. It was a tactic that he had practiced with Orbaculum a lot recently.

Bryson's fight intrigued him—mostly because of the ease of which the young Intelian disposed of the swordsman, Toshik. But once again, the Adrenian didn't have his sword.

When the final match began, Toono leaned forward upon noticing the girl with a sunhat and blonde hair. When he watched the first round a month ago, Kadlest informed him of Yama's playful interest in this girl … Jilly was her name. Since learning this, he had spent most of his time thinking of a way to turn this into an advantage.

He watched the match unfold, and when he witnessed Yama's dashing rescue, a part of him became excited. She was even faster than he remembered. And now he saw how he could make use of her.

The broadcast cut off, leaving a few candles to light the space.

"Thank you, Illipsia."

"You're welcome."

"What do you know about that Power Diatia—the male?"

"His name is Bruut Schap," Illipsia said.

Toono knew that name. He'd heard it while scouting Ulna Malen. Apparently this young man was related to the Power General in some way.

"Anything else?"

"Not much," Illipsia replied. "He seemed like an all right person to me, but Bryson is convinced that he's bad."

Toono's head tilted slightly. "After watching what he did, you don't feel the same way?"

She shrugged. "I saw a lonely person in a strange place lash out because his friend got hurt."

"I disagree. I'd say his name suits him."

* * *

Himitsu was awoken by tapping on the window. He tried to ignore it, but it only grew louder. What the heck could even be tapping on a fourth-floor window? He lifted his head from his pillow to see a blue and white barn swallow pecking a crack in the glass.

He stumbled out of bed and yanked open the window. The bird flew in and perched on one of his bedposts. A parcel was attached to its leg. While he carefully untied it, he looked into the bird's eyes in search of his mother's iris pattern, but it wasn't there. Not that she could control a bird from this distance. This little swallow was simply doing as Himitsu's mother asked of its own free will.

He smiled and kissed its head before reading the note. It was a letter requesting his appearance at Rhyparia's second trial, which was only four days away. Apparently his mom wanted him to testify about the Generals' Battle.

He hurried to his desk, scribbled out his reply, and tied it to the swallow's leg. Then he started throwing some clothes into a bag. There wasn't any time to dawdle since the trip to Phelos would take two to three days. As he looked around the room to make sure he hadn't forgotten anything, he spotted a few white blotches on his sheets and laughed. *Damn bird*, he thought as he ran out the door.

* * *

It was high noon, and the halls of the Phelos medical center were crowded. Unlike Dunami Hospital, where everything was white, squeaky clean, and buzzing with Intel Energy-ran technology, this institute was constructed of stone and wooden floors, and the only source of light was the sun spilling in through the windows.

In the midst of this chaos crept Senex, who had shrunken his body to less than two inches tall. The recently retired Archaic Director scurried down the hallway, veering left and right as gargantuan feet stomped by. All the while he had his eyes on two individuals in front of him: a heavyset woman and a thin man. He followed them all the way out of the building, narrowly missing being squashed under the sole of someone's shoe several times. Once outside and in the hot Archaic Kingdom sun, he scrambled down the stone steps toward the driver standing next to the open door of his carriage. Senex sprinted past the couple and leapt for the first step, then pulled himself up to the wooden floorboard and ran under the seat. He swiped his forehead, smiling at the ridiculousness of a man of his age on such an adventure.

"Good day, Mr. and Mrs. NuForce," the driver said.

"Good to see you again, Jakob," Mr. NuForce replied. His wife said nothing.

The carriage started moving, and the couple sat in silence for a long while. As the ride neared the hour mark, Senex started to worry that the effort to remain at this size would exhaust him. But as he was debating whether he could scramble out of the window unseen, the clopping of the horses' hooves finally ceased.

After a few tense moments of silence, occasionally interrupted by the sniffling of a nose, the door opened.

"Hello, Chief Toth," Mrs. NuForce said.

Toth rested his sword against the bench and took a seat. "I hope you don't mind guests," he said. A fourth set of feet walked in. "I need her for a presentation, for what I'm about to ask of you will be alarming."

The NuForces said nothing.

"It has been well over a year since you last had contact with Itta," Toth added.

"*King* Itta," Mrs. NuForce said.

"Yes, my apologies. I'm here to tell you that not all hope is lost. Tazama, please."

There was a hum of a holographic display and shadows flickered in the carriage.

"King Itta!" Mrs. NuForce exclaimed. "It has been—"

"Pointless," Toth interrupted. "It's a recording."

"Vliyan … Preevis …" Itta wheezed. "I'm sorry I left you with such abandon and no return, but I've been in no condition to reach you. The most recent truth extraction took quite a toll." There was a long break as violent coughs racked his body. "I'm dying. And if time isn't my executioner, then the likes of Ophala, Grandarion, or Rosel will take its place. Either way, there is no more for me.

"But that doesn't mean all is lost for the Archaic Kingdom … or the two of you, for that matter. Chief Merchant Toth Brench is worthy of our trust. Plans are in motion to take our kingdom back, and the two of you will play your part. In turn you'll be rewarded with aristocratic status. But first … Vliyan, I need you to hand over your ancient to Mr. Brench until the conclusion of Rhyparia's trials. I trust you'll do the right thing. Goodbye, Vliyan and Preevis."

"Don't look at me like that," Toth said after the display cut off. "I heard what happened at Phesaw. It was reckless—done in front of too many suspicious eyes."

There was a long silence. Toth was simply waiting the woman out, as any good negotiator does when he trusts his adversary to acknowledge the inevitable.

Finally Vliyan let out a huff. A moment later her husband stood and his feet walked across the carriage.

"I appreciate that," Toth said. "Now is there anything I can do for you?"

After another silence—a short one this time—Toth stood up and grabbed his sword. Senex scurried out from under the seat and climbed the back of Toth's clothes and hid himself in the pitch black of the man's cloak.

"How'd you think it went?" Toth asked as Senex heard the carriage behind them roll away.

"You did well," Tazama replied.

Senex stuck his hand in a pocket, searching for the ancient. Green and purple spots swirled in the darkness as he fought to keep from passing out from exhaustion.

Suddenly the cloak was removed and tossed away. It and Senex landed on something soft and cushioned.

"Don't leave it in your cloak," Tazama said. "We have this box for a reason."

Fighting panic, Senex searched for a way through the folds of cloth. He pushed partly free and realized that he was on a couch. He squeezed into a crease between the cushions right as the cloak was lifted away. After waiting for a few seconds, he cautiously poked his head up from the cushions, then hopped down to the floor. Toth had his back to him, and was dropping a silver necklace into a black box in a satchel. Senex slid under the bottom of the door and allowed his exhausted body to warp back to its normal size. He covered his mouth to block the heavy breathing and crawled down the hall and around a corner. He took a seat against the wall and sucked in great gouts of air.

He looked around and realized this wasn't a functioning building. Huge heaps of cobwebs hung from the ceilings—years' worth of them. The air was rank with mold. He stood up and crept down to the window in the wall at the end of the corridor. A desolate dirt road lined with decayed buildings lay three stories below, and the skyline of central Phelos stood in the far distance.

Senex sighed. It was going to be quite a journey back to the palace, which was where he'd have to steal Vliyan's ancient. He couldn't do it here. He had run his energy dry, and it'd take him several hours to recover.

* * *

"I don't understand."

Spy Pilot Ophala was tending to her birds while the young Prince Sigmund watched from a few steps away, his hands gripping a low-hanging beam above him.

"I don't expect you to," Ophala said as a trio of starlings pecked seeds from her cupped hands. "But I do expect you to trust me. That is what you said all those months back, correct? That you trust me."

"Yes, the lady who seemed to hold the most morally correct heart in the Amendment Order."

She looked back at Sigmund with sad eyes. "Chiefs Rosel and Grandarion have good hearts; they just don't know the truth about Rhyparia."

"The truth you're seeking doesn't matter. It doesn't negate the fact that she's killed hundreds of people."

Ophala held her prince's gaze for a few moments longer before turning back to the birds. "When Senex returns, you'll change your mind."

There was a pause. "You have a lot of faith in him."

"Did you know that Senex was supposed to be the Archaic Spy Pilot many decades ago?"

"No …"

"Well he turned it down, which was how Grand Director Poicus—or just Major Poicus at the time—came to be in the position instead."

"Quite the credentials," Sigmund said. "Leading candidate for Spy Pilot of the Archaic Assassins, then an Energy Director at Phesaw."

Ophala tossed the seeds across the floor, causing a swarm of wings to converge. "Senex was supposed to be the Grand Director too. The point is, he knows what he's doing."

"I see."

"When he comes back with the necklace, we'll plant it on Mrs. NuForce before the trial. She won't even know it. That evidence will be enough to sway the tides in our favor."

"And if there is no necklace?" Sigmund asked. "Or if there is a necklace, but you can't plant it on her? Or we do plant it, but it doesn't affect the opinions of anyone? The only thing being gained would be Mr. and Mrs. NuForce also being charged."

"I'm hoping it doesn't come to that," Ophala said. "But if it does, we're still in good shape. I'm the only juror who wants Rhyparia's freed; Rosel and Grandarion want her executed; and Toth and Wert want life in prison. That would make a tie, which would null everyone's vote and make you the sole judge. Toth and Wert wouldn't mind that outcome because they believe they have you in their pocket."

"Why wouldn't they just side with you and gain the majority that way? If they want Rhyparia alive so desperately?"

"Because her freedom would gain them nothing. She'd return to Phesaw under the watchful eyes of the other Jestivan and the Energy Directors, making it that much harder to retrieve her in the future."

Sigmund followed Ophala down the spiral staircase that led from the bird tower. "Why aren't you telling anyone about Toth and Wert?" he asked. "I thought you learned from your mistake with my father."

"You don't understand the power that someone like Toth Brench has—even more than Itta had when he was king. His last name holds weight across both realms. Outside of the Intel family, he is the wealthiest man in Kuki Sphaira. We'll have to take care of those two ourselves, within our own kingdom. But we'll focus on that after Rhyparia. We're not going to let an innocent girl die—or just as worse, become a weapon in the hands of others."

36
The Gravity Trials: Day 2

Himitsu stepped into the entrance hall of Phelos Palace, relieved to have finally arrived after a long journey cooped in a rattling carriage by his lonesome. The guards who had escorted him refused to sit inside and give him company, no matter how many times he begged. They just stayed on their horses, their silver coattails sweeping down the horse's backs. Adrenians were always so strict about their orders. So he had gotten drunk, lapsing in and out of consciousness, occasionally waking with a bang when a bump in the road knocked him to the floor.

The sunlight from the tall windows told him it wasn't time for bed, no matter how much his pounding headache begged otherwise. A door opened across the barrel-vaulted foyer, revealing his favorite person in the world: his mother. He ran toward her and they embraced in the kind of hug that only a parent and child could know.

"Someone needs a shower," Ophala said. "You smell like a distillery." She walloped him on the back and threw her arm around his shoulder. "That's my boy!"

They ended up on a stone patio next to a garden. There was a table set with silverware and plates, and a massive umbrella provided shade. A waiter came over and poured them a glass of red wine, then returned a moment later with their meal.

Ophala lifted her glass. "A toast."

"To Rhyparia's freedom," Himitsu said.

They clinked their glasses together and he took a gulp. "Is this what royals drink? I was expecting brandy."

"It's a bit delicate, but it will do for now," Ophala said. "You must be lucid for the trial tonight."

"Can I see Rhyparia before the trial? It's been a long time since I've spoken to her."

"I'm afraid not. Nobody can speak to her—including the chiefs. But when you're called to the floor as a witness, you'll be able to stand next to her. Hopefully that counts for something."

"Can I say hi?"

"No."

"I'm gonna say hi," Himitsu declared, tearing a leg off of a duck.

Ophala smirked. "I've been retrieving information about the ancient your friend, Agnos, was curious about. I've made progress, and I think I know where it might be."

"Why would he even want such a thing? What's the use of controlling fish?"

"It's deeper than just controlling. Depending on how the wielder treats the animals, relationships can be built—to the point that you don't even need your ancient to ask favors of them, just like me and my friends."

"What would he do with it?" Himitsu asked.

"Who knows? I've never even met him. But based off what you've told me, he seems like a very intelligent individual with esoteric goals that most people wouldn't understand."

"Give me an ancient that produces champagne."

"It exists."

Himitsu looked at his mother with the duck leg between his teeth. "No …"

She laughed. "Yes."

"Where is it?"

"Why would that matter? You can't make use of it." She winked. "Thank your father for that."

She was right. Curse that wretched law of nature where the offspring of two different energies would possess only one or the other. Himitsu had ended up with Passion Energy from his father.

"Are you prepared for tonight?" Ophala asked.

He nodded. "I'm assuming I'm just answering some questions."

"They'll be simple. Probably won't last more than a few minutes."

A waiter came and cleared their empty plates. Himitsu wiped his mouth with a fancy napkin. "I'm gonna be honest," he said. "It doesn't look good after the trial last week."

"We're in a better spot than you'd think," Ophala said. "Senex has provided us with groundbreaking evidence that we'll be put into play tonight."

"You really think she's innocent?" Himitsu asked.

"Well, not innocent exactly. But what do you think?"

"She's a good friend. And she's come a really long way with restraining her clout, and learning to weave. The incidents seem so out of character. Maybe Bryson's right to blame to her parents. The only times she had lost control was when they were around. But he's defending her out of blind loyalty, not evidence." Himitsu thought for a moment. "The evidence Senex collected is about her parents, isn't it?"

"Shush. We can't discuss specifics outside of the hearing." She threw back her wine and grabbed her staff. "I have business to attend to." As she walked past, she leaned close to him and whispered, "That doesn't mean the birds can't."

She exited the garden with a smile. He squinted at one of the hummingbirds feeding on a flower's nectar. The tiny beauty turned to him and answered his question with a twitchy nod.

* * *

"Himitsu arrived an hour ago," Ophala announced as she entered her office.

"You know …" Senex said in a shaky voice from atop her desk, "… I stood here for hours trying to figure out where that scent of ale was coming from."

"To be fair, it's not meant to be found."

"Then I noticed that the flowers in this vase look exactly the same every day. And they smell like ale." The old man picked up the vase and gave it a sniff. "Keep this up and I might outlive you."

"Is everything done?"

Senex sat on the edge of the desk, legs dangling. "All set."

Ophala grabbed a glass from under her desk and poured herself a portion from the vase. "Can I fancy you some poison, old man?"

"Talking to your liver again, eh?"

"Touché."

*   *   *

Chief Officer Wert Lamay sat with Chief Merchant Toth Brench in the latter's office in Phelos Palace. Dozens of plaques plastered the walls, testifying to Toth's prestige and wealth. Decorative blades of all sizes and makes also adorned the room, and the gold figurines on his desk each represented one of the many ships in his merchant fleet.

Toth reclined in his chair with his feet crossed on the desk. His eyes were on the little black box that sat next to his polished shoes.

"You've thought about selling it, haven't you?" Wert asked.

"It's crossed my mind."

"How much could it get you?"

Toth glanced up at his colleague. "A town … a city."

"Not quite a kingdom."

Toth pressed his fingers together. "Not quite," he quietly replied. "Our goals, though difficult to attain, will bring us far more than what that necklace could."

"Can I see it?"

Toth studied him briefly before grabbing a book from a shelf behind him and sifting through the pages. He pulled out a key and put it into the box with a quick twist.

"Is this some kind of joke?" Wert asked.

Toth turned the box around. It was empty. A wave of dread crashed over him.

There was a jarring knock on the door. "Chief Toth, Chief Wert! The trial is starting in ten minutes. You must be escorted to the Judgment Room."

* * *

The large audience in the Judgment Room sat in absolute silence. Dev servants lined the outer ring of the room, observers sat in the pews, and Rhyparia stood at the center of the main floor. But two chiefs were missing, and the litigation couldn't begin without them. With the royal heads watching, this was embarrassing for the Amendment Order.

Finally a door swung open. Ophala smirked as the two chiefs hurried their way down the stairs. Wert's face was glistening with sweat. Toth appeared calmer, but there was still a hint of concern hidden in the slight downward curve of his lips.

After Chief Arbitrator Grandarion's brief admonishment of the two men, the trial carried on without any hiccups. The usual introduction was given, followed by the details of the day's topic, which was to be the incident at Gourmet Filet—the restaurant that was crushed during Generals' Battle weekend. Some statistics, such as death tolls and property damage costs, were presented. All of it sounded bad for Rhyparia, if not quite the massacre at Rim.

When it came time for calling witnesses, Ophala was the first with a request.

Whispers crept through the pews as Himitsu Vevlu made his way to the center of the room. Most of the audience was elite in wealth or rank, but in all the history of the world, there had been only fifteen Jestivan.

Himitsu stopped a couple arm-lengths away from Rhyparia. "Hi," he said to her, siphoning a smile out of Ophala.

Grandarion Senten gazed up from his parchment, over his spectacles. "There will be no talking to the prisoner, Mr. Vevlu."

"*Zana* Himitsu will do," the young Jestivan replied.

Senten set down his quill. "Excuse me?"

Himitsu cocked his eyes to the left with feigned confusion, then snapped his finger. "I'm sorry—Zana Himitsu will do, *sir.*"

There was chuckling from the pews, and even Rhyparia was failing miserably at muffling her own laughter.

"Zana Himitsu," Ophala said. "You, along with three other Jestivan—Bryson LeAnce, Lilu Intel, and Olivia Lavender—were present with Rhyparia NuForce during the restaurant collapse?"

"Yes. We were all seated at a table for dinner."

"Can you give us an account of what happened during the dinner?"

Himitsu proceeded to tell his story of that devastating day. He recalled the unexpected visit from Rhyparia's parents and their sudden departure the moment the building had begun to shake.

"You said everyone escaped, but didn't give specifics," Chief Rosel said. "Was Rhyparia able to walk or crawl out?"

"Bryson and I had to drag her," Himitsu replied.

"Was she too weak? Too frightened?"

His voice dropped: "She wasn't conscious."

"Seems very much like her condition in the wake of the Olethros collapse."

"We've already come to the conclusion that Rhyparia is guilty of the restaurant incident," Ophala said. "My interest in the witness's testimony is her parents' involvement."

"And why is that?" Grandarion asked.

"I don't think it's by mere coincidence that all three times an incident occurred, her parents were there. Why has she never lost control of her clout when they're not around?"

"I don't remember anyone claiming that her parents were around during the Olethros collapse," Rosel pointed out. She flipped through pages of her notes. "In fact, during Mayor Trolk's testimony last week, he said—and I quote—'There were no records of Mr. or Mrs. NuForce's admittance into any medical center that day or any day thereafter.' Surely if they had been anywhere near Rhyparia, they would have required medical care."

Ophala combed through her own notes, then read out a couple numbers: "North of 350 dead and 500 injured … It wouldn't be a stretch to say a lot of patients slipped by without being documented."

"Fair point," Rosel agreed with a slight nod.

"Zana Himitsu, you may return to your seat," Ophala said. "Thank you."

While Himitsu left the floor, Ophala glanced at the table occupied by Chiefs Toth and Wert.

"I'd like to call Vliyan NuForce to the floor," Ophala said, and the two men froze.

Vliyan seemed unsurprised and unbothered as she strode down the stairs. When she reached her spot, Rhyparia purposefully looked away.

"How would you describe your relationship with your daughter, Mrs. NuForce?" Ophala asked.

Vliyan seemed to give it some thought. "Shattered."

"Use of such a word would imply it's irreparable."

"Not from a lack of trying."

"On whose end?"

"Ours. She hates us."

Ophala looked at Rhyparia. "Is this true?"

"Yes," Rhyparia mumbled.

"Mrs. NuForce, why would your own daughter hate you?" Ophala asked.

"The poverty … the lack of food and basic necessities. And that was when there were only four of us—Preevis, my husband; Sal, our eldest son; Rhyparia, our eldest daughter; and I. It wasn't until I was pregnant with our third child that Rhyparia's disdain grew to a point where it was scary—which is strange to say about a three year-old. Then, of course, came the fourth and fifth child within the few years that followed.

"Needless to say, food became even scarcer with seven of us to account for. Rhyparia became distant and unresponsive. She'd disappear for entire days. A six year-old roaming the streets of Olethros alone—"

"Rhyparia, is this accurate?" Ophala interrupted. "Her reasons for you hating her?"

"Not at all. We actually had a good relationship before the Olethros collapse. I loved my parents and siblings." She paused before elaborating, "I *still* love my siblings, even if they'll never love me back again."

"According to documents, you had six children, Mrs. NuForce," Chief Merchant Toth Brench said. "Maybe I'm mistaken, but I recall you mentioning only five."

Vliyan looked down at the floor. "She died a newborn."

Tears streamed down Rhyparia's cheeks as Toth asked, "Cause of death?"

"The Olethros collapse."

Murmurs flooded the Judgment Room and drowned out Rhyparia's sobs. Chief Arbitrator Grandarion held up his hand for silence.

Vliyan stared hard at her daughter. "A sixth child was too much for her, and she released her clout in rage … She murdered her baby sister."

"If she was such a danger," Ophala said, "why were you allowing her to possess an ancient?"

"We didn't know it was an ancient. She had found it a few months prior, during one of her escapades through the city—or at least that's what she claimed. I never thought much of it—we certainly couldn't afford toys, so she had to fashion one out of the trash that littered the streets of Olethros … It wasn't until King Itta visited after the collapse that we found out."

Ophala bit the feather of her quill. "That leads me to another question. Have you ever had an ancient of your own?"

Vliyan's eyebrows rose. "If we couldn't afford food, how would we buy an ancient?"

"Some can be found—as you pointed out. Some go missing for years … decades … centuries. Maybe you stumbled upon a very rare one."

"Was never fortunate enough to be lucky. If I had ever found a 'very rare one,' I would have sold it to provide for my family."

Ophala leaned forward, resting her elbows on the table. "Have you ever heard of the Cloutitionist's Necklace, Mrs. NuForce?"

"No, I haven't," Vliyan answered without hesitation. Unlike Wert, who had been sweating puddles, she showed no signs of worry.

"Don't tell me this is your argument, Pilot Ophala," Rosel pleaded. "It has been what? One hundred and fifty years since its last sighting?"

"Why is it that you hate your parents, Rhyparia?" Ophala asked.

"Nobody would believe me."

"I suggest you do your best to convince them."

Rhyparia looked around the room with the lone green eye unhidden by her bangs. She paused on her mother. "Because when these incidents occurred, it never felt like it was me. I mean … I felt the power. I felt my energy expelling from my body, but I never triggered it, I swear. It always felt as if someone was forcing it out of me against my will."

"And you think it was your mother," Ophala concluded.

"Yes."

The audience stirred from the trial's sudden turn, and Grandarion silenced them once again.

"The Cloutitionist's Necklace is a relic that allows its user to gain control of someone's clout," Ophala explained. "It's a string of silver. In order for it to work, the user must possess a strand of their victim's hair. And that strand of hair is what ties the two ends of the silver string together, turning it into a necklace. Each time the relic is used, the hair that connects the necklace burns out, requiring another strand of hair to be plucked before it can be used again."

"Relics require masterful weaving skills," Toth said. "Are you suggesting that this Mrs. NuForce is capable of such a thing?"

"Your wealth is unimaginable, Chief Toth, so you may not be able to grasp this concept, but the poor often possess talents of their own." Ophala looked back at Vliyan. "I know you possess the necklace."

"We don't just make accusations like that, Pilot Ophala," Grandarion warned.

She waved him off. "Chief Rosel, can you approach Mrs. NuForce and remove her jacket?"

Rosel eyed her suspiciously, but she eventually did as she was asked.

"Check the inner pocket, and there should be a small torn hole. Pull out what you find."

Rosel rummaged through the pocket as the audience leaned forward. After several seconds, she pulled something out. The audience whispered as a silver chain hung from Rosel's fingers. She examined it closely.

"Well?" Ophala prodded.

Wert's face was a bright red and Toth was leaning back in his seat with a look of defeat. Rosel walked to Ophala and placed the necklace on her desk. "I'm guessing you've done some spy work the past few weeks, but this is fake silver, Pilot Ophala."

"What?" Ophala stammered as she picked it up and studied it. Brown spots leaked through, exposing a copper undercoat. The silver paint was chipped … Rosel was right.

"I promise you …" Ophala mumbled. "She has the relic."

Rosel gazed down at her colleague with stern eyes, but had an empathetic tone when she said, "It doesn't even have the latches for the strand of hair."

The Chief Senator returned the necklace to Mrs. NuForce while Ophala looked for answers elsewhere. Her sights went from a smiling Toth to a relieved Wert, then to Preevis NuForce in the pews. She looked for Senex, and found him with an expression equally as baffled as hers.

"I had no idea it was a fake relic," Vliyan said. "Growing up poor and uneducated, there was no way for me to learn about ancients. I would have tried to sell it if I thought it had any real worth." She paused and looked at Ophala. "But what would anyone pay for a bit of costume jewelry?"

Ophala wanted to jump the table, incensed by the smugness behind Vliyan's theatrical surprise.

Grandarion called a recess and Ophala began to gather up her notes. There were no more arguments for her to make, at this trial or the next. Rhyparia had killed a general, and she'd be wasting her breath trying to defend that to the people. The girl's last hope was a 2-2-1 vote for death, life in prison, or freedom, leaving Sigmund to break the tie.

Ophala looked around the room for the Archaic Prince. Toth and Wert had the boy sandwiched between them as they exited the room.

* * *

It was late, and Chief Toth was tipsy, having spent the night celebrating with Wert. They still had no idea what had happened or how, and there was a tiny voice in the back of his mind warning him that the relic could be anywhere, but he had downed enough drinks to ignore that fact until morning.

He opened the door to his room and saw a woman in a silk nightgown seated on the edge of his bed. Her deep blue hair was wet, and the skin on her legs glistened like bronze in the candlelight. Her blue eyes were transfixed on him as he closed the door.

"Tazama!"

No response.

"You look ready to celebrate too," he said while fumbling with the buttons on his vest. "Let me just get all of this off."

Toth was starting to kick off his pants when a finger pressed into his chest. He stopped and looked at the seated Dev servant. She took his hand and gently opened his fingers, then dropped a silver necklace into it. He stared at it in wonder. She had saved him and his mission—no, *their* mission. She was every bit a part of it.

Tazama touched his chin and smiled sweetly. "Now we can celebrate, love."

37
The Verdict

Rhyparia's final hearing would be held today, and a punishment would be given.

Bryson sat on his bed with his legs crossed while Bruut snored on the floor, oblivious to the constellation of Intelights floating throughout the room. Bryson had learned how to weave multiple self-feeding loops of EC chains. More important, he had held up his end of the bargain with Lilu, so she had to start teaching him again.

Ordinarily this would excite him, but he was preoccupied by Rhyparia's trial. Anxious of what tonight's verdict would be, he hadn't even tried to sleep.

He turned and looked out his window, where Telejunction's massive hill loomed in the distance. Himitsu had yet to return, likely choosing to stay in Phelos until all was said and done.

A groan interrupted the snores. "Turn those things off," Bruut said in his sleep before rolling over.

The floorboards outside the room creaked. Bryson cut his EC chains, and the Intelights fizzled out. He stood up, slowly approached the door, then took a deep breath and yanked it open.

Nothing. Just the empty balcony that circled the building's interior and looked down to the lobby three floors below. Must have been the settling of an aging building. He'd heard similar noises throughout this week.

Bryson looked over the banister. Two girls were seated on a sofa in the lobby. A crying Yama was slumped in Jilly's embrace.

The frightening Adrenian swordswoman Bryson had once known had morphed into something softer since Jilly's sudden allegiance to Toshik. And at this point he wasn't sure what could snap her out of it.

*   *   *

Spy Pilot Ophala sat nervously at her desk in the Judgment Room for the final trial. Archaic Prince Sigmund had spent a lot of time with Chiefs Toth and Wert over the past several days. The prince had reassured her that he wasn't wavering, and the good in her wanted to believe him, and perhaps it was only the anger in the room after the testimony about the Intel General's death that made her anxious. Either way, her hands fidgeted with the urge for a stiff drink.

The hearing ended after testimony by a contractor outlining what it would take to rebuild the section of Phesaw's campus that had been destroyed in the collapse. Then there was a lull in the proceeding while the chiefs compiled their papers. As always, Rhyparia was fixated on the ground.

"As the Gravity Trials come to an end," Grandarion said, "the Amendment Order would like to thank everyone for their cooperation—the Dev servants who broadcasted these proceedings to the Realm, the audience who watched with minimum disruption, the witnesses who assisted greatly in making sure we make the right decision, and the royal heads from the Spirit, Intel, Adren, and Passion Kingdoms for trusting us with this process. One by one, the Amendment Order will stand up and state their desired punishment." Grandarion extended his hand toward Chief Officer Wert Lamay.

Wert stood tall, chest and chin out. "Life in prison."

"Life in prison," Toth seconded.

"Death," Chief Senator Rosel Sania voted with a cold malice in her voice.

"Freedom," Ophala said.

There was an outcry from the pews—surprised shouts and gasps quickly followed by jeers and curses.

"And I also vote for death," Grandarion said. He shook his head, while Rosel's stare was harder than ever. "This means there is a tie. By Archain law, all votes cast are voided, and a decision will be made by a single juror. Archaic Prince Sigmund, please stand and give the realm your verdict: life in prison, death, or freedom."

The anger in the room was sucked away by an absolute silence as everyone stared at the young prince. Even Rhyparia was watching him with one sad green eye.

The prince paused for at least ten seconds, a single muscle twitching below his grim mouth. Finally, he spoke:

"The Amendment Order was established to properly guide me down a moral path. With hundreds of lost lives on your hands, I simply cannot allow you to walk free. Ms. Rhyparia NuForce, I sentence you to death."

Cheers erupted from the audience as Rhyparia fell to her knees. Despite her young age, she would go down in history as one of the deadliest criminals to ever walk the Light Realm.

Himitsu sprinted onto the floor and hugged Rhyparia. He was crying while he held onto his friend. Adrenian guards in silver cloaks pulled him away.

"I love you!" he yelled back at Rhyparia. "You're a sister to me!"

Ophala marched over to the guards. "Stop it," she said to her son. "You're going to get yourself in trouble." She took him under his arm and helped him to his feet. Once they were far from the room, she hugged her only child, muffling his sobs in her hair.

38
The Realm Responds

Intel King Vitio stood on a balcony in Dunami Palace. He watched as crowds cheered in the shadows of the buildings while the sun set beyond the skyline. Intel soldiers flooded the streets as the frenzied celebration turned to rioting. Mobs were flipping over carriages and looting market stalls.

Princess Shelly came to her father's side. They stared in silence for several minutes.

"Will Bryson ever forgive us?" Shelly asked.

"It will take some time."

"And Lilu?"

"She realizes what Rhyparia has done," Vitio said. "In her mind there is nothing that needs to be forgiven."

A billow of black smoke rose from one of the market squares just out of sight. "You should get your people under control, Father," Shelly said. "We aren't barbarians."

Vitio ran his fingers through his blonde and gray hair. He let out a deep breath. "Get Vistas. We need to find out what's going on with King Damian."

"What about not spreading our resources too thin?"

"I think the Amendment Order has proven that they don't need us to hold their hands. It's time to start gradually pulling our units out of the Archaic Kingdom. Sigmund has made great progress, and soon he'll be a proper king."

* * *

Grand Director Poicus limped his way through Phesaw's Emotion Wing in search of Passion Director Venustas. He turned a corner and saw the youngest of the directors walking down the hall with her head bowed over an open textbook.

"Good morning, Felli," Poicus said. "What are you reading?"

Venustas snapped the book closed and flashed him the title: *The Human Skeleton.*

"Quite a novice read for someone of your standing."

"Since Vuilni broke her leg, I've been reading up on accelerating the healing process—and why not try the basic curriculum too?" She frowned. "I've been disappointed with how out of date a lot of the information is. This is the exact same book I used when I was a student."

"Well, you're what—28, 29?" Poicus laughed. "It wasn't that long ago for you."

"I was ten when I took this class. Technologically speaking, it's a whole new world now."

"Phesaw has never been hailed for its medical studies."

"Let's change that," Venustas pleaded.

"What do you suggest?"

She looked back at the book. "A larger curriculum. Classes on science and medicine—maybe even technology." She started to grow excited. "We'll hire experts to write new textbooks, and I'll help. I learned a lot when I transferred out of this place."

"Why not?" Poicus replied. "I see Intel Director Jugtah has rubbed off on you. He's completely sculpted the Intel Weaving curriculum into his own."

"Yes, he's been quite productive. Anyway, did you want something of me?"

Poicus laughed. "Have I already forgotten? Oh yes! Passion General Landon contacted me. He requests your presence in Fiamma. Apparently King Damian's wife could use the advice and comfort of an old friend."

"And that's okay with you?"

"Very much so."

"What about the tournament?" Venustas asked.

Poicus closed his eyes. "I'm calling it off."

"I was wondering when you'd come to your senses. You speak of uniting realms and kingdoms, but you have them fighting each other."

He shook his head. "Shameful. I thought the adversity would make their bonds stronger, but I think that was my mind tricking me into my old ways."

"Adversity should be naturally occurring, not manufactured."

Poicus grinned. "Senex retired, yet his words are still here to haunt me."

* * *

With a torch in one hand, Toono marched through a crude tunnel in the deepest part of their cave underneath the Archaic Desert. He didn't visit this part of the cave that often—maybe twice before. It was best to leave her alone.

But the time had come. With Rhyparia's execution scheduled, he sensed an opportunity.

He followed the wails—a sound he had grown accustomed to. His eardrums were aching by the time he reached the curtain that covered the opening to a room. A bitter cold pierced his skin as he pushed the curtain aside.

"Apoleia."

The hysterical cries stopped, replaced by a few sniffles. After a moment Apoleia heaved herself off of the frozen floor. She looked miserable, and her bluish-white skin was encrusted with crystals of ice.

"We leave in one week," Toono said.

The ice on Apoleia's face cracked and crumbled as a deranged smile abruptly appeared. Ice popped as she bit her lip, and a trail of blood ran down her chin.

* * *

Bryson sat at the edge of one of the lakes in Phesaw Park with Lilu by his side. She was supposed to be teaching him more weaving, but he wasn't in the mood. There was a bitter look on the young man's face as he stared into space. All of Director Poicus's words of comfort had turned to ash. Rhyparia was on her way to Olethros to be hanged, and Directors Neaneuma and Buredo were guarding the teleplatforms to make sure none of the Jestivan attempted what Poicus had deemed "suicide missions."

The end of March had brought more bearable temperatures, but it still wasn't warm enough to warrant anyone taking a dip in the lakes. Yet a head surfaced far from the shore. His white hair sopping wet, Tashami gasped for air and wiped his face. He laughed and slapped the water.

"Show off!" Tashami shouted.

A second head popped up several feet away. This one belonged to Agnos. They had been doing this routine for hours. They'd swim down to the lake floor and sit there for minutes at a time. Agnos always lasted longer.

Bryson finally caved. "What is the point of that?" he asked Lilu.

"Fun fact about Agnos. He's fascinated with water. He practices swimming nearly every day and trains his lungs to hold more oxygen. Then he'll up the difficulty by doing those things in the deepest parts of a lake, where the water pressure is at its greatest."

"For fun?"

Lilu shrugged. "Knowing Agnos, I'm sure there's a purpose. He told me it's something he's practiced his entire life. I guess Tashami tagged along."

There was a silence before she added, "He's fascinated with the Sea of Light. I think that's probably his ultimate goal—his greatest challenge."

The two Jestivan dove under the surface once again.

"There isn't any chance of your dad helping us go after Rhyparia like he did with Olivia, I'm guessing," Bryson said.

"Zero."

"You think she deserves it."

"I think the victims and their families deserve to see her punished for her acts. I think Rhyparia owes them her death."

Bryson stared at her in disgust, then shook his head.

"Of course I feel terrible for her," Lilu said. "To be hanged above the very disaster she caused. But the Archains believe her death will bring peace to the souls wandering the wreckage of Olethros. Perhaps that's true."

Bryson rose to his feet and slowly walked away.

"Where are you going?" Lilu called after him. He didn't answer.

*   *   *

A young man stood behind a burgundy throne with his hands placed on its back. He didn't sit in the chair, for it wasn't his—at least not in his mind.

The doors opened, and three women approached him and bowed. One of them was an older woman with black hair. She wore an extravagant robe embroidered with bluish holographic designs that hovered over the fabric. The other two women were on the brink of adulthood. Both of them were redheads with freckles.

"It's an honor to be in your presence, Prince Storshae," the older woman said.

He smiled. "The Dev Warden and her two Diatia … I hope the three of you are as good as advertised."

"We can be your greatest asset."

He laughed. "I am my own greatest asset, but I admire the spirit. We'll see what you can do when we depart. In the meantime, you'll have to be caught up on everything." He paused, then sneered. "Have you ever crossed realms?"

*　　*　　*

A line of royal carriages made their way toward the city of Rim. A unit of cavalry led the caravan, followed by an uncovered carriage. Rhyparia was seated on a bench in the hot sun, her ankles bolted to the floor and wrists shackled to the seat.

Somewhere farther down the line, in the middle of the pack, Himitsu, Senex, and Ophala shared a carriage. Himitsu had come along unbeknown to the rest of the Amendment Order, who were under the impression that he'd headed back to Phesaw.

None of them had spoken for nearly the entirety of the ride as they collected their thoughts. But it felt like an understood silence—like each of them knew what the others were thinking.

The execution was to be held the evening of their arrival at Rim. That would be tomorrow. And come that time the sun would cast Olethros in its dying light, just as it presently fell upon the plains as Himitsu peeked out the window and looked at the Archaic Mountains in the distance. Itta had banished Ophala to those mountains while he had worked his machinations in Phelos, but she had learned many valuable things in those years.

39
Rhyparia's Past: Atychi NuForce

Through the dirt streets of a rundown sector that sat at the foot of the Archaic Mountains, a young Rhyparia laughed and ran about with her older brother, Sal. Her long brown hair bounced against her back, and the bottom of her dirty, overgrown t-shirt—a hand-me-down from her brother—rustled around her knees. She ran at full speed, her tiny legs doing everything they could to keep up with the boy who was only a few strides in front of her.

Just ahead, a shop owner was pushing a wheelbarrow full of vegetables across the street. Her brother ran around it, but Rhyparia leapt over it, snagging a turnip as she flew over.

"Dammit, Rhyparia!" the man shouted as she fled.

She giggled and waved behind her, taking a giant bite of her stolen turnip. She planted the heels of her bare feet in the dirt, her eyes watering as she bent over and spit out the burning onion.

She sat on her knees in the middle of the road, snot leaking from her nose. She laughed and tossed the onion away. She'd deserved that. She hopped back up and ran through the narrow, unsanitary streets of Olethros.

When she finally reached her home that sat on the edge of Olethros under the shadows of the Archaic Mountains, she saw Sal leaning against the fence around their tiny chicken pen. It only housed two roosters, and with no hens around to induce egg laying, Rhyparia's mom insisted that they should be eaten. But her father would never agree to such a thing. He tended to them like they were their pets. The whole neighborhood loved them, even if they complained that they woke the entire street at the crack of every dawn.

"Did you trip and fall or something?" her brother asked.

"Onions are gross," she replied. She hopped the fence and hugged Preevis Jr.—the rooster she had named after her dad. They were practically the same height—she was only four years old, after all.

"You and Momma are gonna go downtown tomorrow morning," Sal said. "Time to learn how people like us get by."

"I thought we don't do that anymore." Rhyparia got up and brushed the dust off her scabbed knees. "Is Daddy home?"

"When isn't he?"

She ran inside. "Daddy!"

Her father was sitting at the broken wagon wheel that served as their table. His eyes were red.

"What's wrong?" Rhyparia asked.

"Nothing, honey," he said with a smile. "I'm cutting onions."

"I ate an onion today!"

"Did you?"

"Bleh!"

He laughed. "That sounds about right." He looked at her daughter for a moment. "Go outside and play with your brother."

She returned to the hot sun. "I think we're having onions for dinner."

"Just onions?" Sal asked. "Sounds rancid."

"Daddy was crying. He said he was cutting them."

Sal sighed. "That's cause we're gonna have a baby brother or sister. Momma's pregnant."

"Wow!" Rhyparia exclaimed. "That should make him happy!"

"Uh, no. We can't afford another kid. It's already hard enough as it is. Why do you think Mom is taking you into Rim tomorrow?"

The words were lost on her. She was in her own world, dreaming about a baby sister. She knelt next to Preevis Jr. and beamed. "Are you ready for another NuForce, PJ?"

* * *

Rhyparia woke to the roosters announcing the start of the day. She whimpered and rolled over, but her mother grabbed her wrist.

"Get up, girl."

She lay still with a stubborn pout.

"Or I will drag you out of this house."

Rhyparia stood up on the rickety wooden floor, then hissed with pain as a splinter pierced her big toe.

"Stop the whining and let's go."

She followed her mother out of the house. They walked through Olethros and the other sectors of Rim in silence until they reached the central market. The eyes in Rhyparia's dirty face widened as she watched wealthy people buying things with actual coins.

"It's time for you to do what a NuForce does best," Vliyan said.

Though Rhyparia was only four, she understood what that meant. They were a family of thieves and con artists. That was just a way of life in a place like Olethros, but Sal had warned her that the people downtown would chop your hand off if you were caught.

Vliyan squatted next to her and whispered into her ear. "I want you to do something very simple. You're a runner—just like your brother." Rhyparia gleamed at the rare compliment. "Sal's grown too big for this job. He can't hide himself among the legs of the crowd."

"I'm not too big!" Rhyparia excitedly pointed out.

"You're right. I want you to steal from four different stalls. First, the meat truck over there. When you grab something, run until the owner stops chasing you. Wind through peoples' legs and make yourself hard to catch.

After that, you'll go after the fur cart, then the produce cart, then the blacksmith's stall."

"What's a blacksmiff?"

"Forget the blacksmith. How about the milkman?"

"Okay!" Rhyparia shouted.

"Let's go then."

The first three carts were easy pickings: a turkey drum, a reptilian leather satchel, and a head of cabbage. Meanwhile Vliyan robbed the vendors as they chased after her daughter.

Rhyparia stopped at the end of the square and studied the milkman. Seemed easy enough. She shrugged, then crept around the market's perimeter, then ran and swiped a bottle in each hand.

"Hey!" the man shouted. "Get back here!"

Rhyparia sprinted across the stone street, her bare feet sore against the cobblestones. She was getting tired and couldn't run as fast as she had before. She looked up and saw her mother standing in an alley. Someone stuck out their foot, and she smacked face-first into the stones, the glass bottles shattering ahead of her.

Burly hands grasped her shoulders and pulled her up. "She's filthy," the guard said. "Probably an Olethros girl. Take her to the station. We need to find her parents—if she has any."

"My momma is right down …" Rhyparia stared down the empty alley way. Her mother had deserted her.

* * *

Rhyparia lay in the rooster pen with PJ standing on her stomach. She wiggled her toes while humming a tune and gazing at her favorite sight—the crusted underbellies of the islands floating in the sky.

A shadow fell over her. It was her mom. "Why are you always daydreaming? Go find some shade—I don't want to listen to you crying about your sunburn all night."

"I'm looking at the islands!" Rhyparia said.

Vliyan said nothing for a long moment, then sat down next to her, scaring PJ away. "You can see them?" she asked.

"Can't you?"

"The stories say that only special individuals can."

Rhyparia gasped. "Am I special?"

"I guess you are," her mom replied. "Do me a favor and describe them to me."

"Hmm … They're huge, like they should fall out of the sky and squish us all."

"Interesting."

Rhyparia giggled. "What's up there?"

"Nobody really knows."

It went quiet again. "I like talking to you, Momma."

"Well," Vliyan said, "perhaps you're worth talking to after all."

Rhyparia rolled over and nestled her head against her mother's hip. She smiled. "Momma's special daughter."

She didn't see it, but her mother's grin was ear-to-ear.

* * *

Rhyparia followed her mother up a set of shaky stairs that zigzagged their way up the side of a building. The little girl was five now. Vliyan knocked three times on a door when they reached the top.

It creaked open and a face peeked outside. "Ah, Vliyan. Come in."

It was a dark, dingy room. The windows were boarded shut, so a few candles were all that lit the space. Rhyparia had to step carefully to avoid the clutter. This place was even worse than her house. While she poked around the junk, her mom and the man had a conversation.

"How's business, Karl?" Vliyan asked.

"Slow month. Nobody has a need for fossils. Everyone wants artifacts or relics."

"You probably have a relic buried somewhere in this mess and don't even know it." She gazed around the room. "As if anyone around here could even afford any artifacts or relics anyway."

Karl laughed. "Exactly. Who's the girl?"

"My daughter … my very special daughter."

Rhyparia turned and smiled. "Hello!"

"Where'd you find her?" Karl asked. "You've never mentioned a daughter."

Vliyan ignored him. "I saw something last time I was here, but I knew I wasn't able to afford it at the time." She strolled between the mountains of items to the glass cabinets on the far wall. Inside one of them was a silver necklace. She pointed at it and said, "It's calling my name."

Karl grinned. "Do you even know what it does? Or is it just the silver glint that's catching your eye?"

"Cute, coming from the man who doesn't know what any of these ancients do—ninety percent of this junk aren't even ancients at all."

Karl shrugged. "What the customers don't know won't hurt them."

"How much?"

He scratched at his beard stubble. "Everything you have in your pockets."

"You drive a hard bargain, Karl, but if you insist." Vliyan pushed aside some junk on a table and dumped out two big handfuls of her coins.

He looked like he was staring at a steak. "Let me get the key."

Once back outside and under the sun, Rhyparia had to shield her face with her arms. She looked at her mother to see a dazzling string of silver cascading between her fingers.

"It's so pretty!" Rhyparia squealed.

"I also got you this," Vliyan cooed, slipping a beautiful green glove on her daughter's hand.

"Wow! What for?"

Vliyan caressed Rhyparia's cheek, brushing her hair behind her ear. "It gives you super powers."

*　*　*

In an unusual break for the normally arid kingdom, it had rained for most of the past week. Now the sun was back and Rhyparia sat in the dirt in front of her mother, who was seated on the first step that led up to their house. Rhyparia's hair fell in clumps with each cut of the scissors.

They talked about mother-daughter stuff—things like what Rhyparia wanted to be when she grew up or whether she liked any of the boys on the street, or possible names for the fourth baby growing in mom's belly. Anything to distract Rhyparia from the fact that she was losing her beloved hair.

"The sun's burning my scalp," Rhyparia said.

"Think of what this is getting us," Vliyan said. "Some sick bald girl will get a new head of healthy hair, and you'll grow yours back before you know it. And we need the money, of course. Speaking of which …" She abruptly dropped the scissors and wandered down the street with Rhyparia's hair trailing from one fist.

Rhyparia raised a hand to her scalp. She was bald in places; tufts of hair an inch or so long stuck out in others. She hurried into the house, resolved to never go outside again.

* * *

The house became Rhyparia's world for the next two months until the birth of her new siblings. Vliyan had given birth to fraternal twins, so instead of four children, there were now five to worry about. Sal was twelve and Rhyparia was six. The other three were all less than two years old.

Babies crying constantly and Vliyan scolding her husband had become the norm. Each day grew more unbearable. Rhyparia was reduced to skin and bone, for she'd always give most of her meager and infrequent meals to the babies. And while the family slowly starved, the piles of junk grew higher.

As much as Rhyparia longed to get out of the house, her mother had cut off her hair again. And more than that she just didn't feel well. Perhaps it was her hunger, but she was exhausted and her body felt dry. The rain had returned yet again, and as always, she felt even worse while the storm raged outside.

One day her mother asked her to go to the building with the shaky stairs and the man named Karl. She said it was important and that Karl would know why Rhyparia was there. Rhyparia defiantly refused. Surprisingly, Vliyan didn't lose her temper. She had grown increasingly patient with her daughter as of late.

Sal walked in, soaking wet from his daily search for work and food. He looked at Rhyparia with soft eyes and said, "I have something for you." Then he stepped behind her and tied something around her head.

Vliyan's eyes lit up. "What a great idea," she said. "Now run along to Karl's."

Sal held up a piece of broken mirror and handed it to his sister. "What do you think?"

Rhyparia looked at her reflection and grinned for the first time in a long time at the sight of the burgundy bandana. "It's pretty! My favorite color!" she exclaimed. "Thank you so much, Sal!"

Rhyparia stomped through every muddy puddle she came across in the streets. Bystanders shrieked at her as she splashed them with the brown water. When she arrived at Karl's building, she stared at the stairs for a second before climbing. They made her nervous. Thankfully they didn't wobble as badly as the time she was with her mother.

She got to the top and rapped the door. She looked to the sky while she waited, allowing the rain to patter against her face. It had rained almost every day for the past couple months—strange weather for a kingdom that was notorious for droughts.

Rhyparia knocked again. Still no answer. She pounded her fist against the wood. "Mr. Karl! It's me, Rhyparia … Vliyan's daughter!"

She eventually gave up and retreated down the stairs. When she reached the final bend in the back-and-forth staircase, she saw something resting against the rail that hadn't been there when she arrived earlier. She looked around for whoever must have left it by mistake, but nobody was in sight. So she did what any NuForce did best—swiped it up for her own.

She put it to the test on her way home, and it passed with flying colors. Not a single droplet landed on her thanks to the massive umbrella that she twirled above her head.

* * *

Ten months later, Rhyparia was sitting on an overturned bucket behind her house, washing herself with a grimy wet rag. As she twisted it above her feet, the warm water soaking between her toes, she looked across the stretch of jagged moraine that divided Olethros and the Archaic Mountains. Her house was the very last one on their street. Beyond that, an avalanche-swept zone of lifeless desolation. No plants could extend roots through the rubble to the soil below, and even if they could, rocks poured down from the mountains as often as five times a day.

Then the mountains roared as if they had heard her thoughts. Monstrous clouds of dirt soared into the air while entire sections of the closest mountain broke apart and tumbled down the slopes, shaking the ground under her feet.

She stood up, looking on in awe. She usually wouldn't react to an avalanche, but this one looked and felt bigger. After about ten minutes, it came to a stop not twenty feet from where she was standing.

People came out of their homes to her right and left with the same awestruck gazes. Rhyparia reached into her pocket for the glove that her mother had given her. It wasn't there. She looked to the ground. Nothing. She panicked, falling to all fours and crawling around while digging through the mud. She started crying. It was a gift from a woman who used to never treat her like a daughter until the past year, and she didn't want to lose something with such meaning.

Sal came outside and watched from the open doorway. "What are you looking for?" he asked.

"My glove!"

"Ma went to go sell it … said you didn't need it anymore or something."

Rhyparia sat up on two knees with a sorrowful stare. She cried as she looked down at her muddy body.

*   *   *

"Get out! Get out of my house!" Vliyan bellowed between heavy, forced breaths. She was lying in a makeshift tub with a small amount of water at the bottom. Preevis was stationed between her legs, ready to receive child number six.

Rhyparia did as she was told; she left the house, scooped PJ up out of his pen, and ran far away. All she had done was shout words of encouragement to her mother. She was excited for another sibling.

The streets were no longer mud, but dirt. The rain hadn't shown itself in months. But Rhyparia still carried her umbrella with her. It shielded her from the sun's assault. Her beet red skin was now painlessly pale.

She slowed down to a walk, twirling her umbrella while humming a tune. Her mother's anger didn't fluster her. She understood that her mom was in pain, which was why she acted out in such a way.

Rhyparia tilted her umbrella and gazed up at the sky. She smiled, imagining that she'd finally get a little sister to play with.

* * *

Blissful tears flooded Rhyparia's eyes as she held her newborn baby sister, Atychi NuForce, in her arms. She was so quiet, so calm. Her brothers had cried constantly during their first weeks out of the womb. Rhyparia touched Atychi's nose as the infant's unfocused eyes took in what they could of this foreign world. Her little arms stretched in different directions, as if trying to grab at air.

Rhyparia laughed, then wiped her cheek. "Hello, Atychi. I'm your big sister. You've entered a crowded house filled with boys, but don't you worry. I'll protect you from our brothers!"

Atychi looked up at the sound of Rhyparia's voice, her round eyes still an ambiguous color that had yet to become their own.

Vliyan came in from the kitchen with one of her sons in her arms. "Rhyparia, sweetie, can you do me a huge favor?"

"Yep!"

"Run down to the pump and see if there's any water left."

Rhyparia handed Atychi off to her mom. She gazed at her baby sister for a few more seconds before bolting out of the house and grabbing an empty bucket from the rooster pen. She wanted to get back quickly and hold Atychi some more.

She ran through the streets, her umbrella in one hand and a bucket swinging at her side. At this early hour, there was the typically long line waiting at the pump when she arrived. She looked toward the gray sky while she waited. Rain had begun to fall in torrents.

Thunder boomed across the sky and the crowd scattered, so Rhyparia walked straight to the front of the queue. She set her umbrella aside, and rain beat down on her as she filled her bucket from the pump until it was full. She headed back home and as she went to turn the corner down her street, she collapsed to her knees. Something was wrong. Something was happening inside of her body.

A crack of thunder snapped from above while the rain drenched her. One of her neighbors rushed out to help her, then abruptly doubled over and clutched at his chest. Rhyparia gaped at him as he shrieked and smacked the ground with a splash. Then the house behind him collapsed as if a great hand had pressed down on it. No thunderstorm could do that. The other houses on the street followed, and then her own house collapsed into itself with a deafening but almost instantaneously quick snap.

Rhyparia howled. She tried to crawl toward them, but her body refused to move. She wasn't being crushed like everything around her—she simply felt drained. Her head fell to the mud, but out of one eye she could see people bent in hideous ways, most lifeless but some crying in pain and panic. The air was thick with an orchestra of thunder and buildings collapsing in the distance. Her grip on the umbrella loosened, and the destruction abruptly ceased. Only the storm raged on.

Meanwhile, in the pile of rubble that was once her home, a little baby girl lay motionless amongst the junk and splintered wood, her eyes closed shut and her few breaths of life cut short.

* * *

"Any final words?"

Rhyparia looked up from the floorboards beneath her feet. The sun was setting beyond the mountains, and a massive horde of people stretched across Olethros. They were packed together so tightly that she couldn't even see the rubble they were standing on.

The noose around her neck was loose for now, but it was heavy on her shoulders. She had been surprised by its weight, but when she thought about it, it did make sense. It had to be able to catch someone's falling body weight without ripping. It was also coarse, and there was a maddening itch on her collarbone that she couldn't reach with her hands tied behind her back.

She was about to die, and the Archaic Kingdom had decided to make a show of it. At least the royal heads had declined to broadcast the execution like they did the trials. Rhyparia didn't want her fellow Jestivan to watch her die.

A strange cry came from the distance—it sounded like it was hundreds of leagues away. The ravished sector watched as Rhyparia searched for the right words. Was there even anything worth saying?

And it hit her. It was so simple.

With great strength, she bellowed a single name: "*Atychi!*" She paused to take in a deep breath. "*This is for you!*"

A small door in the floor opened, and her heart caught in her throat as she fell. She hated herself for releasing a frightened cry.

The fall took longer than she thought it would. But the inevitable impact that would snap her neck never came. Instead her knees buckled beneath her from an unexpected landing. She was crumpled on the ground—dazed from the impact but alive. Uproar came from the masses. Guards, civilians, the whole mob swarmed toward her, their faces contorted with the rage of thwarted justice.

She slapped at a sudden itch on her face—likely a bug. But then she heard a voice in her ear. She recognized it at once.

"Lita Rhyparia, let's get you out of here."

40
Gale Thrasher

The wooden gallows shattered as Senex morphed to an incredible height. Rhyparia lay flabbergasted in the palm of his gigantic hand. He raised her toward his shoulder. "Hold on to my collar," Senex panted. "They're shooting at us, and I need both hands free."

She gripped the collar of his shirt and climbed. She ducked as an arrow whizzed past, narrowly missing her head. She looked down and was horrified to see dozens of arrows embedded in his back.

She heard the strange distant cry again—louder this time. Still she saw no source. Senex stumbled and let out an involuntary hiss of pain. Rhyparia looked down again to see at least two dozen Adrenian soldiers bounding through the rubble below, their coattails billowing from their silver uniforms. They fanned out, the fastest advancing level with Senex from the left and right.

"Adrenians approaching at your feet, Director!" Rhyparia shouted as an arrow snagged her hair, sending her tumbling down Senex's chest. He snatched her out of the air with a massive palm, and she looked between his fingers to see the semicircle of Adrenian soldiers tightening, their swords gleaming like pins in the moonlight from hundreds of feet below. They slashed gouges into Senex's ankles from multiple angles, retreated, then attacked again.

"I can't bother with them," Senex gasped. "All I can do is run." He stumbled, then regained his stride. "Besides, I'd be a fool to commit to such a mission without reinforcements."

Back on the director's collar but hanging from the front this time, Rhyparia turned her head and saw Himitsu's mammoth wall of black fire.

* * *

Himitsu watched in awe while Senex thundered past. The ground shook as if the mountain of a man were triggering earthquakes. But Himitsu had to focus. Though most of the Adrenians had died horribly in his inferno, the fastest were able to sprint through the fire, extinguishing the flames in the wind they created.

Five of them continued on after Senex, and the remaining two advanced on Himitsu. Their swords were drawn in front of them—one man, one woman. Himitsu released a calming breath. This was his chance to see how much improvement he had made. He reached within his cloak and unsheathed the long, slender blade that Toshik had given him. It was a Brench Craft made of Spunka spines, and the hilt was gilded gold.

Both Adrenians attacked at the same time. Sluggishly, it seemed to Himitsu, whose eyes had been trained from sparring with Toshik, Yama, and Bryson. He swept his sword in front of him, fending off the man's blade while simultaneously using his other hand to create a wall of flames between him and the woman.

As Himitsu parried with the man, the woman sprinted around the wall and slashed down at his back. Himitsu ducked under the man's blow and thrust upward, driving his sword through the woman's stomach. He spun, dragging the woman with him and sweeping a foot between the man's feet. Then he planted his foot against the gasping woman and freed his blade. Walls of fire sprung up about him. A sword came slashing through the smoke and Himitsu leapt backward, tumbling into a pile of rocks. He allowed himself to roll, his head cracking painfully against the moraine as he did a reverse summersault and sprang back to his feet.

The woman emerged through the smoke, her face pale from rapid blood loss but somehow still alive. Her sword slashed across his shoulder, the edge grinding against bone. He yelped, but with one cupped hand, he sent up from the ground a column of black flames that engulfed her entire body. A quick jab through her neck with the point of his sword quieted her agonized shrieks.

Himitsu heard the shuffle of a foot on pebbles and he leapt to his left as a sword whipped over his head. He inhaled as deeply as he could, his chest swelling. The soldier bounded off one boulder, then at an angle to a second, then shrieked as he flew down toward Himitsu from above.

Himitsu exhaled, meeting the man with a vast gout of fire. He stepped to the side as the soldier fluttered to ground, more ash than bone and flesh.

Heaving, Himitsu grabbed his shoulder. His cloak was soaked in blood, and he could feel the gouge. He removed the cloak and used his teeth and free hand to wrap it around the wound. He sat down and watched as Senex ran toward the Archaic Mountains. He was hopeful for success.

Then an immense wave of heat surged through him, the air buckling in the inferno. Himitsu looked over his shoulder, and his eyes widened as he saw a towering wave of broken crust and lava at its crest, beginning to curve back down to the ground below.

* * *

"Lava!" Rhyparia shouted.

"That would be General Inias's son," Senex said. "He's as talented with that ancient as his father was."

The heat climbed as the lava neared, and the remaining Adrenian soldiers parted to let it do its work. Senex stumbled forward on the gory remains of what had been his ankles, a machinery of frayed ligaments twitching in their bath of blood. The inexplicable cry from before returned, then was cut off by the roar of an earthquake. Boulders tumbled down the slopes and crashed over steep cliffs. Senex cupped Rhyparia in his hand as a stinging hail of splintered rock fell down around him. Then the Archaic

Director screamed as the lava finally caught him, a wave of molten rock that incinerated his feet and calves as it swept past. He pitched forward, flinging Rhyparia into the air with all of his dying strength.

She soared through the sky, thousands of feet above the ground. In a few seconds she would die an instantaneous death against the mountainside, spared from the lava by her teacher's last gift.

But then she heard the cry. It came from directly behind her. With such grace, a mammoth creature flew past and banked a turn between her and the mountain. Its beak was as long as its body, and pointed and narrow like a sword. Its blue and white feathers rustled in the wind. There was a second, much smaller pair of wings positioned above its talons.

It released another piercing scream as it dove to intercept Rhyparia's path. The creature swooped underneath her. She hit its back at an angle and slid through its silky smooth feathers. After a terrifyingly long instant she got a handhold that she almost immediately lost hold of as the creature arched sharply out of its nosedive. The beast flapped its colossal wings, thundering against the air like a ship's sail in a storm.

It cried out once more before shooting off into the night sky. After climbing to a height that made making shapes out on the ground impossible, it leveled out and flew toward a crevice between two mountains. To squeeze through, it rotated completely onto its side, each wing pointing to either the sky or the ground.

Rhyparia didn't know what was in these mountains, but she understood that Senex tried to get her here for a reason. There likely wasn't going to be a return for her in the future. Was a life of exile in this desolate place worth the life of the kindest man she had ever known? There were tears in her eyes, but only from the wind as the creature swooped its way between the mountain peaks. She felt empty, as drained of her emotions as she had been of her energy on that fateful day in Olethros.

They landed in a valley of rocks. The creature let out a soft cry as it set its wing flat on the ground, and Rhyparia dismounted. This took a considerable while. This thing would have dwarfed Phesaw's school building.

The beast opened its beak and dropped a note on the ground. Rhyparia snatched it before it was blown away in the winds. She watched as her majestic escort flapped its wings, then soared into the sky … leaving her stranded and alone in a mountain range where no human had ever survived.

She looked down at the note:

Someone will meet you shortly.
Good luck, Rhyparia.
—Ophala, Pilot of Spy and Sky

*　　*　　*

Himitsu arched around the receding molten sea, his right arm hanging limp. He had felt a familiar presence earlier. There was another assassin nearby.

It had been a few minutes since Gale Thrasher had carried Rhyparia into the mountains. Its departure had left a disturbing lull over the moraine.

Himitsu turned and headed toward Shanty, another outlying sector of Rim. He looked for the sector's tallest building, which stood a couple stories higher than the rest. The streets were deserted with most of Rim in Olethros for the hanging.

He entered the building and found himself in a lobby with a reception desk. Several empty offices stood behind it. He found the stairs and climbed to a door at the top floor. When he opened it, he froze. Now he understood the sensation earlier.

His mother he had expected. But the man next to her wasn't supposed to be here. Like Himitsu, he was tall. Aged scars ran down his cheek until they disappeared underneath his chin, and there was a gradient of gray hair between the white of his temples and the black hair on top.

"Dad …"

The man smirked, widening the wrinkles at the corners of his eyes. "Son."

"I thought you were on a mission somewhere."

"A greater mission beckoned me."

After hesitating for a moment in shock, Himitsu walked across the room and embraced his father in a hug. "You stink," Himitsu said.

Horos let out a quiet laugh. "In the chaos of the last couple days, bathing was quite low on my list of priorities."

Himitsu stepped back. "When do we leave?"

"Our escort has yet to arrive," Ophala said as she gazed out the window.

"Well nobody knows we're here, so we should be fine."

"They know," Horos said. "And they're on their way."

A door slammed several floors below. Himitsu shook his head. "How'd they find out?"

"We had them tipped off," Horos said.

"What? Why?"

Instead of an answer, Himitsu heard the cry of Gale Thrasher as it returned from the mountains.

"Let's go, son," Ophala said.

"Not without you."

"We'll be right behind you."

"You get on first," Himitsu said.

Horos sighed, then locked the door. He grabbed Himitsu and pulled him across the room, shoving the boy out the window while Ophala slipped something into his pocket. Himitsu crawled onto Gale's wing and offered a hand to his mother. "Come on!" he yelled.

His parents stayed put, and that's when Himitsu realized what they were doing. "You only came to take the fall for me!"

Horos smiled. "The most important mission of my life. Senex, your mother, and I know how important you Jestivan are to Kuki Sphaira's future."

"No!" Himitsu bellowed. As he started crawling back to the window, Gale's wing jerked up and sent him tumbling down the surface of feathers. Someone shouted outside the door. Ophala and Horos turned toward it and locked elbows like the wife and husband they were, blocking the view of the window. A blast of wind shattered the door as Gale shot off the ground and took to the sky.

Himitsu sat speechless as he gaped back at the building that grew smaller and smaller. His wind-whipped hair stuck to the tears that lathered his dirty face, while Gale released a cry much softer than any of its previous ones … as if it, too, understood what had just happened.

Ophala and Horos Vevlu would be convicted of the highest of treason—not only against the Amendment Order, but all five kingdoms of the Light Realm.

41
The Pianist

Once again Bryson was unable to sleep. At first he had been glad that Rhyparia's execution wasn't broadcasted, but as he stared at the ceiling, he visualized it in his head a hundred times—and in a hundred different ways. Did she cry? Scream? Accept it peacefully? Was it by hanging or a squad of archers … or something unimaginably worse? Was she granted any final words? And if so, what were they?

He tried to focus on the memories of their time together. Only one image came: the dirty, barefoot, frightened girl who stepped off the platform wearing a raggedy shirt that reached her knees. He had known her less than two years, but she had grown so much since then.

He rolled over and glanced at the folded parchment that sat on his nightstand. It was still missing two letters from the mysterious word on the chalkboard, and even Agnos had given up on asking him about it.

With a sigh, he looked at the ticking clock on his wall. It was approaching three in the morning. He had been wrestling with the idea of visiting Dunami to confront Intel King Vitio tomorrow. Now that the execution was over, Directors Buredo and Neaneuma wouldn't be patrolling Telejunction any longer. But did he really want to do that?

Perhaps he could go home for the day. He could train on the peg course or spend time with Thusia … or just sit in the living room and stare at the painting of him and Debo. Bryson missed him so much—the jokes he'd crack, the sarcastic tone—and although he hated to admit it, the fatherly censure.

What would really bring Bryson some peace of mind was his piano. Ever since becoming a Jestivan, his life had narrowed to weaving and training, and his focus on events around him that he had no control over. He couldn't even do anything about the rockhead lying on his dorm floor—and he was right there in easy striking distance!

What was the point of being a Jestivan if there was no action to take? All they did was lie dormant on Phesaw's campus, protected by countless barriers: the Sea of Light, Rolling Oaks, High Sever, Energy Directors, and the guards and assassins at Telejunction. Or was that a selfish way to think? Dormancy implied peace, which was what everyone wanted … No. He'd already had this conversation with Agnos.

"That's a naïve mindset, Bryson," Agnos had said. "Chaos can exist in a stagnant state, wedged in the nooks and crannies until the circumstances allow its release. Tricky little pest, that chaos. It's like a rat—never eradicated, but hopefully held at bay."

Maybe Agnos was right. Nobody seemed to know anything about Toono—not the royal heads, generals, or directors. Even if they had the ability to find him, they were too focused on Rhyparia.

The floorboards outside his room creaked again, but Bryson stayed in bed. Nobody was ever out there.

* * *

Poicus sluggishly opened his eyes. It took him a few moments to orientate himself and realize that someone was knocking on his office door a floor below. He sat up and rubbed his thigh while peering out the window. The horizon glowed orange with the coming of dawn. Something drastic must have happened for someone to wake him.

He grabbed his cane and pushed himself up. It had been a year since Storshae damaged his leg, but his body had apparently lost its ability to heal itself.

The pounding continued as he made his way down the spiral staircase. He reached the door and opened it. His Dev servant stood on the other side.

"Good morning, Tally."

"Good morning, sir." His response seemed rushed. "Intel King Vitio wants to speak with you."

The director's smile faded. "I don't want to speak to that man, and I'm disappointed that's what you woke me for."

"It's about Lita Rhyparia. She escaped."

Poicus stared at Tally for a minute, habitually twirling the tail of his long eyebrow. This was definitely Senex's doing. Rhyparia couldn't have done it on her own without her umbrella.

Eventually Poicus chuckled. "Didn't think the old man would have it in him. Connect me."

Poicus stepped aside, allowing Tally to enter. He took a seat as a holographic display appeared. King Vitio immediately erupted into a rant.

"I have an escaped prisoner, a traitorous chief, a criminal director, and dozens of dead soldiers. And I know that Jestivan Himitsu was involved too. How am I supposed to explain this to my citizens? That a few traitors were able to topple a staged execution under the watchful eye of the Amendment Order and high-ranking officials of the Light Kingdoms. How?"

"First of all," Poicus replied, "Zana Himitsu arrived at Phesaw last night, so there was no way he was involved." This was a lie. "As for your inability to form an explanation, it's quite simple: 'We were trying to be too cute.'"

"Cute?"

"Unnecessarily transporting her all the way from Phelos to Rim so you could put on a show for the downtrodden people of Olethros in order to win their support. Political theater of the lowest and cynical kind."

"It was for them to taste vengeance," Vitio said. "They had waited nearly a decade for such a moment."

Poicus sighed. "What is it that you want from me, Vitio?"

"I want you to tell me if you had any knowledge of this treasonous plan."

"I did not."

Vitio's eyes pierced through the hologram. "If I find out you did, there will be consequences."

The director raised an eyebrow. "Because that's the way of the Intels? Strike down anybody who threatens to topple your supremacy?"

"There is no supremacy," the king grumbled.

"I guess my memory of your infiltration of the Dev Kingdom under General Mendac is a delusion of my old age."

"That was different. Dev King Rehn was a threat to the Light Realm—not just my kingdom."

"No," Poicus said. "When I sent Mendac and Thusia after King Rehn, *that* was for the realm." There was a hardness in the director's voice that had been absent for many years.

"And it failed," Vitio pointed out. "Thusia died, and the Jestivan fizzled into nothing shortly after while Rehn lived. Thus I struck up my own mission with Mendac at the helm. It was met with success, and the Light Realm didn't have to live in fear of Rehn the Oracle."

"You also captured and enslaved hundreds of Dev soldiers and intelligence officers to threaten and intimidate anyone who dared to cross you in the future." Poicus held Vitio's gaze. "Don't worry. I have no intentions of crossing you, even if I was pleasantly surprised when I found out Senex did."

"How many times do I have to tell you it's not about crossing 'me,' it's *us*?"

"You keep telling yourself that—"

An explosion rattled the office walls.

"What's wrong?" Vitio said.

Poicus jumped out of his chair, grabbing his injured leg as a muscle seized, and gazed out the grand window behind him. A few early rising students were gazing curiously in the direction of Telejunction. Poicus opened the window and stuck his head out. Students who commuted to Phesaw every morning were sprinting down the towering hill. Some tripped over their own feet and tumbled down the slope.

Poicus hurried out of the office, leaving a confused Vitio in the broadcast before Tally ended it. Was the school under attack? If so, the timing couldn't have been worse. The Jestivan and Energy Directors were spread out and Poicus had no way of alerting them.

Once he stepped outside, he heard frightened screams from students as they ran away from Telejunction. Some headed toward Phesaw Park while others ran past Poicus and into the school. Most sprinted in the direction of Wealth's Crossroads, likely trying to reach the deepest parts of the campus before hitting the High Sever.

Poicus walked toward the hill, holding himself up on his cane when students knocked into him. He looked up and saw men and women in burgundy cloaks marching down the hill. Daggers were flung from within their cloaks toward the fleeing students. At the hill's crest stood five individuals: Dev Prince Storshae, Kadlest, the Dev Warden, and both Dev Diatia. They simply observed.

Adorned in his robes of burgundy, Storshae smirked at Poicus. The two men had unfinished business to attend to.

* * *

For the first time in over a month, Bryson sat in the classroom with the writing on the chalkboard. Agnos sat next to him, mouthing silence. Musku, the original Archaic Jestivan, sat on his other side, and Saikatto, the original Adren Jestivan, sat in the back of the room. Senex stood on a stool while pointing at the mysterious word on the chalkboard.

Bryson got up and retraced his steps from his previous experiences. He walked in front of Musku to see his burns, then made his way toward Saikatto to study the webs of scars where they'd stitched his face back together. Bryson's father had done this to them.

He turned toward the wall of shadows. As he crept closer, the temperature plummeted with each cautious step. At the cusp of blackness, he stopped for a brief second as his shoes crunched in the ice. Distant screams spilled out of the dark. Bryson was hesitant, leery of the unknown within that void. But something took over and forced him to penetrate the shadows.

The screaming ceased, and sobbing took its place. Then the tapping of a piano key joined the cries. It sounded like it came from straight ahead. Bryson stepped forward, more ice cracking beneath his feet. He couldn't see anything, but he knew to reach out and grab a handle. The hinges moaned as he pushed the door open.

The crying stopped, but the piano didn't. Instead it picked up its pace as it entered the second stage of his favorite song, "Phases of S." His mouth cast a white fog against the infinite black with each breath.

The music stopped, leaving Bryson in an echoing quiet. He felt something approaching from behind, but his body refused to turn. It took several agonizing seconds before a cold and clammy hand grabbed his shoulder and exhaled a skin-crawling giggle into his right ear.

* * *

Bryson shot out of bed. He had finally strung together more than four hours of sleep and in doing so, was able to dream again. He grabbed the parchment on his nightstand and a quill and scribbled down the final two letters. He studied them as if he could somehow understand the characters. He needed to find Agnos.

He pushed aside his blankets and realized that something wasn't right. It was too cold for this time of year. His breath was visible just like in his dream. Bruut was trembling on the floor as he slept. Someone was playing the piano in the lobby, which wasn't allowed at this early hour.

He opened the door and recognized the song. All around the circling balcony, other Jestivan stepped out of their rooms—some with annoyed, cranky looks; others were confused and dazed.

As Bryson followed his teammates down the stairs, he looked out a window and saw panicked students running toward Wealth's Crossroads. He flew down the steps two at a time, then went flying when he slipped on the sheet of ice covering the floor.

Everyone stared at the piano. Frost crept around its black body as an ice-covered woman occupied the bench, racing her fingers across the keys with a look of rigid concentration. The song was in its final part—Spite—the hardest section to execute. But she was marvelous, even better than

Bryson. There was fluidity in its harmony with just the right amount of harshness in its rage.

The woman stopped, turning her head toward the Jestivan and other students. The focused glare morphed into a maniacal smile that then became a chilling laugh that lasted for several seconds before abruptly coming to a halt. A thin, dreadful line formed in her lips as she fixed her eyes on Bryson.

With a bitter tone, she muttered, "This wretched seed too shall bleed."

42
A Reunion

Bryson's eyes narrowed as the screams outside continued. "Who are you?"

The woman rose from her seat while laughing quietly to herself. "My name is Apoleia."

"And of what relevance are you to this school?" Agnos asked.

Her eyes stayed fixated on Bryson as she replied, "I only have interest in this boy here."

"Well if you have an issue with him, you have an issue with all of us," Lilu said.

Apoleia's gaze flickered to Lilu with an annoyed curl to her lip. She flicked her finger just as Lilu leapt to the side, and a spiked pillar of ice shot up from the floor where the princess had been standing.

The disgusted curl turned into a smirk. "Quick footed," Apoleia remarked.

A barrage of attacks bore down on the ice woman: electricity, wind, and a lunging, sword-wielding Toshik. They battered against a wall of ice that appeared in front of Apoleia, cracking but not breaking its surface. Bryson sent an electrical pulse that punched a hole through it.

They heard her giggle from the other side. "Such scary children!" Apoleia teased.

"You're going to get yourself killed," Bryson warned, stepping toward the wall.

"You vile little replica!" she hissed. "Talk some sense into them, baby."

Olivia stepped from behind the wall. Bryson stared, at a loss of words. She wore the same empty look as she always did. "Everyone needs to leave," she said. "Except Bryson."

"Olivia …" Bryson stammered. "What is this?"

She ignored him, addressing the rest of them. "Go now. She doesn't want anything to do with any of you."

"We're not leaving him," Tashami replied.

"And I will not let any of you hurt my mother."

It went quiet. Mother?

"Your mother is a Stillian?" Bryson asked.

They were interrupted as a young boy burst through the door. He was breathing heavily. "My friend's dead!" He looked up and cried, "Help us!"

"How?" Lilu asked.

"There are bad people everywhere. People in cloaks. Things are flying through the air!"

"There are other people here who each of you need to focus on," Olivia said. "Dev Prince Storshae, the Dev Warden, both Dev Diatia, some Dev Assassins lurking about. And Toono requests Yama's presence. He said to find him in the auditorium."

Lilu, sensing the urgency of the situation, bolted out of the building. So did Vuilni and Bruut. Agnos and Yama hesitated until hearing Toono's name.

Bryson stared in shock at his best friend. "Get out of here," he commanded to his lingering friends. "I'll be fine."

Toshik and Tashami left without question. Jilly hesitated. As she hovered, unsure of her decision, Toshik ran back and grabbed her arm. "He'll be okay," he said.

The frozen barrier vanished. Apoleia loomed behind Olivia—a splitting image of her daughter, other than the radically different expressions. Olivia's face was as neutral as always, while a manic expression lit up her mother's face.

"Olivia," he croaked. "Why are you doing this?"

She ignored the question and instead walked past him and out the door. Baffled, he looked at Apoleia. The woman giggled and followed her daughter. The freezing temperatures bit at Bryson's skin, and when her shoulder brushed against his, he lost his breath as a woman's screams echoed through his head. He sharply inhaled. He had seen this woman before.

A little over a year ago, when Bryson had visited Debo in Grand Director Poicus's office before leaving for the Dev Kingdom, someone had interrupted their conversation by pounding on the door. When he left the office, there was a person in a traveler's cloak waiting in the hall. They crossed paths and bumped shoulders, and the same sensation resulted. Debo had known Olivia's mom?

He refocused. Olivia had mentioned Dev Assassins, and Himitsu wasn't here to counter them. Bryson summoned his Branian. They could use a Spirit Assassin in this fight … whatever fight this even was.

Thusia's smile promptly vanished when she absorbed her surroundings. Crying and shouting students burst through Lilac Suites' front door, spilling on the ice. She spun toward them with a look of horror.

"What's going on?" she shouted.

"There are Dev Assassins loose," Bryson said.

Thusia darted out of the building. Bryson ran after her. Apoleia and Olivia stood at the far end of the roundabout of Wealth's Crossroads. The quiet was as chilling as the frost that crept through the air. The chaos from other sections of Phesaw's campus sounded like it was miles away.

"What are you doing? Go find the assassins," Bryson said.

Thusia looked at him with somber eyes. "You'll never escape his shadow. It's a shame his legacy is a crooked trail of demons. I must stay here, for you can't comprehend the delicacy of this situation."

*   *   *

Vuilni and Bruut sprinted through the campus in search of their fellow Diatia among the disarray. Dev soldiers chased students into buildings. Some brave souls fought back, most dying swiftly, a few killing their assailants before being overwhelmed.

Vuilni and Bruut turned a corner and stopped when they saw that the grounds ahead of them were empty. There were sounds of combat from the vicinity of the Spirit Wing, so the two Diatia headed that way. Spirit Director Neaneuma was in the courtyard fighting a woman with brown hair.

Ground-shaking footsteps approached from behind. They spun to see Power Warden Feissam bearing down on them. He scooped them off the ground—one person to each arm—and began to run.

"What are you doing?" Vuilni shouted. "Put me down!"

"We're leaving," he rumbled.

"Why?" she yelled.

"Because we didn't come here for this. This is an irreparable rift that's forming between two sides. We came here to strengthen our bonds with the Light Realm, not choose a side between the two realms. We want both, so we will leave."

"Grand Director Poicus won't see it that way once he finds out you abandoned them," Vuilni retorted.

The warden grumbled but didn't respond. Once they could see Telejunction's hill, despair set in. Fights had broken out across the cobblestone streets and grass. Among them were Poicus versus Storshae and Adren Director Buredo versus Dev Warden Gala.

"Jina, Halluci, and Warden Gala are here," Bruut said. "Why aren't we helping our teammates?"

"Stop it," Feissam commanded as Bruut tried to break himself free.

As the giant reached the hill's crest, ready to step onto a cross-realm platform and depart Phesaw, his two students simultaneously threw their elbows into his stomach. He keeled over and groaned while they escaped his grasp and flew down the hill.

*   *   *

Toshik and Jilly ran side by side through Phesaw Park, looking for higher-value targets than the Dev soldiers they ran past, though from time to time Toshik would veer aside to run his sword through one of their stomachs.

A thick branch snapped from its tree and was telekinetically tossed at Jilly. She knocked it away with a swift gust.

Toshik scanned his surroundings for the culprit, even looking toward the canopies to see if there were any soldiers hiding above. No luck. Then he heard a slight rustle of the leaves above him. He looked up again. Branches shook, but nobody was there.

He heard a faint footstep behind him, and as he stepped aside, a blade grazed his lower back. They had run into a Dev Assassin. Toshik thought back to the advice that Thusia, Ophala, and Fane had given during their preparation for the Rolling Oaks.

"You want to engage Dev Assassins in open spaces," Thusia had explained, "Typically you'll have to lure them out. Otherwise they'll hide among the trees."

Why do they need to hide if they're invisible?" Jilly had asked.

"It's harder to track them," Ophala replied. "Their footprints can be spotted in the grass. And when they're in the trees, it doesn't matter if they make noise because they'll just telekinetically manipulate branches elsewhere, which will make it seem like there are ten of them."

Toshik spun in circles as the lecture replayed in his head. Pink petals fluttered to the ground as they were violently shaken from their homes. He had no idea which tree was currently housing the assassin. The pain from the cut on his lower back grew more insistent, and he felt the blood running down his leg. How deep did the assassin manage to cut?

He noticed the grass flatten just a few steps from Jilly. She saw the look on his face and twisted her body, and a gash ripped open in her shoulder. He screamed her name as he ran to her side, but he was nearly swept off his feet by a powerful blast of wind. He fell back with his hands shielding his face while Jilly squatted low to the ground with her blond hair whipping in every direction.

Instead of playing hide-and-seek, he realized Jilly was trying to force the assassin out of hiding. He observed the branches breaking in the wind, looking for a pattern among the chaos. Jilly nodded from within the funnel of her tornado, and Toshik turned to see a Dev Assassin appear upon a violent collision with a tree.

The windstorm dispersed, and Toshik bolted toward the plummeting assassin. He leapt at his enemy, his sword pulled back at his hip, and impaled the assassin against the tree.

The man hacked up blood, his head hanging down as the sword pinned his limp body to the tree. Toshik grabbed a dagger from his waistband and jammed the blade into the brain stem. He pulled his sword free then turned his attention to Jilly, who was holding her shoulder and wincing in pain. He crouched next to her and assessed the damage. It was a deep cut, and she'd need medical care soon.

He sheathed his sword and scooped her up. He felt the blood dripping from his own wound down his leg. In the heat of the moment he thought it had been a graze, but that was clearly not the case.

"Put me down, silly," Jilly said. "I can walk."

He gave her a stern glare. Somehow she was smiling through the pain. "No can do," he replied.

"We need to find the others and help," she said.

Toshik watched as groups of students took on Dev soldiers in the distance, circling them in hopes of using their numbers to their advantage. He could have gone to help, but Jilly's wellbeing was more important to him—a selfish quality he had gained from watching his mom and sister be shredded to pieces as a child.

He jumped to the right as a tree caught fire. The flames were a dense black, and Toshik looked around, searching for their source.

"Is Himitsu here?" Jilly asked.

"How about you put the girl down and let her fight?" The question came from a deep scratchy voice. "She's awfully good."

Toshik turned to see an older man with a red cloak approaching.

"Fane!" Jilly shouted.

He put his hand up and shook his head. "Pay attention. There are two more in the vicinity."

* * *

Dev King Storshae marched down Telejunction's hill, hurling a relentless assault on Grand Director Poicus. One hand would throw a ball of Dev Energy, then the other, then he'd flick his finger to fling a blade, rock, or whatever was disposable. Poicus was a blur of defense and evasion. A year of training with his cane had done him good, but he was completely on the defensive, and that needed to change fast.

Spy Pilot Ophala had given Poicus this cane a few weeks after his grand return from the Dev Kingdom a year ago—when he had collapsed on this very same hill, bloody and beaten. It was a powerful ancient. And Poicus had refused to use it up until now.

He swung his cane at an incoming ball of energy, and it solidified and burst into fragments. With a quick rap against the ground, the cane shot a deep trench toward Storshae, whose feet unbelievably tripped over each other before he sidestepped the trench.

"Quite a surprise, old man," Storshae remarked as the director hobbled toward him. "I thought you were more of a tactical combatant ..." He smirked. "Hiding in the skin of other people and such."

"I am whatever the situation calls for me to be," Poicus replied.

"I think it calls for you to be a little faster," the king remarked. With a subtle twitch of Storshae's finger, a dead soldier's shield flew across the grass, then shattered into pieces as Poicus's cane swung down.

Storshae's eyebrows climbed higher. "Though you definitely have my attention."

* * *

Agnos sped through the grand lobby that circled Phesaw's main auditorium. Yama was likely already inside. Even though they both left Lilac Suites at the same time, no one could match her speed. Toono's face had been in his mind for the entire sprint. Agnos understood that the Toono he was about encounter was a vastly different person than the one he'd called his best friend as a child. He was prepared for all the changes—his face, his demeanor, his build … or at least he hoped he was.

Agnos slammed open one of the doors that led into the auditorium and came to a stop. He gazed down at the stage where Toono stood. The brown beard and short dirty blonde hair was a far cry from the baby face and mop of waves. And he was taller than average. But even with all of that, there was still the bandage that circled the top of his head.

Agnos made his way down the steps in silence as Toono watched. He tried to read the masked look on Toono's face. Yama's eyes were glazed and red. The bubble wand, Orbaculum, was strapped to Toono's back. When Toono had given Agnos his glasses years ago, he claimed that he didn't need them anymore, that he had a new ancient that better served his new goals.

Agnos began to cry. He didn't think this reunion would have such an effect on him, and he was disappointed by his reaction. Toono was a terrible person now, so Agnos shouldn't have missed him so dearly.

"I'm glad you still share my sentiments," Toono murmured.

"All of the nefarious crimes you have committed," Agnos said, "yet an aggravating piece of me wants nothing more than to grant you clemency."

"I would expect no such thing," Toono replied. "Like a stalker in a young lady's hedges, there is a cruel fate waiting for me in earnest." He paused with the same passive gaze and quoted, "If man can be forgiven of any and all sin …"

Agnos finished the quote: "… then why would man not repeat that cycle?" He sighed. "Gatal Accus, *First of Five*."

They studied each other for a few seconds before Toono's eyes grew stern. "I am not forgiven of anything I've done over the past several years. My cycle isn't infinite. There will come a time when my reckoning dawns, but that time is not yet." His gaze switched to Yama. "So what's the verdict?"

Yama slowly shook her head. "The nerve of you," she muttered.

Agnos studied her, then looked back at Toono, then back to her. He frowned. "No, Yama," he pleaded. "You're not like him, no matter how much he tries to convince you otherwise. Stay here with your friends."

Toono didn't bother countering, allowing her a moment to think. Yama finally looked at Agnos. "*Friends?* I don't have to stay here with the Jestivan."

"Friendship isn't an obligation," Agnos replied.

"I barely know any of them. They are too different from me." Yama paused. Her voice shook with her next words: "And Jilly … she wants nothing to do with me."

"She'd be heartbroken if you left. Toono and Kadlest aren't your friends. I assure—"

"*Shut up about friends!*" she shrieked. It was a miracle that the glass window in the ceiling didn't shatter. She collected herself. "This decision isn't about that. I have no attachments to any of you, and that includes *him*." Her eyes pierced at Toono. "He isn't my charge anymore. That ended a decade ago. My decisions are made based solely off how I'll benefit."

Now Agnos joined Toono in his silence. Yama continued ranting: "The nerve … to think you could show up and ask for my assistance—like I'm a sidekick. You really think I'd just join and follow you wherever you go? What makes you think that?"

"I don't think that," Toono said. "I *hope* that. However, I can provide incentives. If you come with me, your skills will flourish at an unprecedented rate, for the path I journey is treacherous—the enemies unyielding."

Toono was a master of discourse—even more so than Agnos, who had to put a stop to this. "Don't fall victim to his—"

"Is that all you can offer?" Yama asked, cutting off Agnos as if he wasn't there.

"Not at all," Toono said. "I've heard there's a certain Diatia roaming this campus that is in need of a vengeful disposal."

"If you're suggesting you'd take him out for me, then no thanks. I can do that myself."

Toono nodded. "There is no denying that." He stepped off of the stage and onto the floor. "I remember the day I met Kadlest. After that day, I slowly grew distant from you."

"I think you're forgetful of one other," Agnos chimed in.

Toono turned toward Agnos and corrected himself: "The both of you." He redirected his attention to Yama. "The day I left for good, after weeks of treating you like an acquaintance rather than a friend, you broke the hand of the orphanage's most vicious teacher in my defense—the hand he'd use to paddle any child who dared to cross him. He had paddled me that day as I left class for what would be the final time in my life, for Kadlest was waiting outside to take me on a new journey."

Toono rested his hand on Yama's shoulder. "I remember hearing his screams. And you did this even though you knew I was abandoning you, and it was likely you'd never see me again. As I left the orphanage and walked down the road with Kadlest, I looked back and saw you staring at me from afar, your sword sheathed at your hip and hands casually tucked in your pockets. You didn't give chase. That was your way of saying goodbye … a selfless act."

Yama's eyes were now open in awe. Toono's hand slipped off her shoulder as he turned and headed up the stairs. "Now let me return the favor."

As Agnos watched the two of them climb the staircase, he wanted nothing more than to stop them. But that was foolish. Toono and Yama were both elite fighters, likely able to topple any of the royal heads.

A door at the top of the auditorium swung shut as the pair left. Agnos took a deep breath and slowly made his way up.

The good that man could have done.

43
A Helping Hand

Yama marched toward the fight between Lilu, Tashami, and Vuilni against the two Dev Diatia and Bruut. They had broken off into three dueling pairs. Yama's sights were focused on Bruut. Toono wasn't with her at this moment. They already had a plan in motion, and it required his presence elsewhere.

Vuilni and Bruut were in the midst of exchanging heavy blows. Yama was nearly swept off of her feet from the impact of the colliding Powish fists. When they briefly separated, Yama took the split-second to squeeze between them.

Bruut smiled. "Of course someone like you would want a taste of the action, Lita Yama."

"You've always said you wanted to fight me," Yama said, "and now we are treated to a fight to the death."

Bruut's eyes lit up with glee. "How it should be."

"I have one condition," Yama said. "We can't involve anyone else on campus."

"Lead the way."

Yama turned in the direction of Phesaw Park with Bruut eagerly on her heels. This was about as easy as she'd expected, knowing the kind of person Bruut was. Their taste for domination was very similar, but not exactly the same. Yama fought to see progress while Bruut fought to see blood.

While walking through the park, Yama spotted Toshik, Jilly, and a man she'd never seen before in the midst of a fight with an invisible force. Trees were ablaze and Toshik was hacking at air. She figured they had run into a Dev Assassin, but she continued on her way. Their fight had no relevance to her cause.

She stopped as she heard a strange cry far in the distance. Bruut also paused as he looked toward the sky.

*　　*　　*

"This would be a lot easier if I had another assassin helping!" Fane yelled as he jumped to avoid a flying blade. He threw a ball of black fire toward a spot where the Dev Assassin had to be, and it fizzled out just like his other attacks.

"Why can't Jilly do the wind thing again?" Toshik asked as he looked for footsteps or broken branches while being wary of telekinetic projectiles.

"They're not complete idiots," Fane said. "The other two aren't going to succumb to the same fate. Do you know of any open spaces nearby?"

Toshik nodded. "Follow me." He took them to the space that had hosted the tournament battles between the Jestivan this year. They sprinted to the field's center. The assassins had followed them, according to Fane.

"Shouldn't they be uncloaked by now?" Toshik asked.

"Normally, yes. I'd say these two are higher ranks, considering their stamina. I will try to give direction, but be alert. Listen for movement and look for footprints."

"And shadows?" Jilly asked.

"And shadows," Fane confirmed with a smile. "I don't know why the others question your wit."

Toshik winced. "We have to end this quickly. I've lost a lot of blood."

"How quickly will be up to you two," Fane said.

Then they were off. Fane managed to singe an enemy at times. Toshik and Jilly were nearly blind in this fight, though Jilly proved to be of some help. With her wide-stretching attacks, there were times she'd make contact.

"I hit him!" she'd shout each time.

And Fane would then respond with words of encouragement: "Good on you, Jilly!"

A shadow swallowed the field, announced by a tremendous shriek. It was as if the sun had set, bringing an overcast night sky.

He looked up to see the underbelly of a gigantic winged beast. This was Gale Thrasher, and there was only one of its kind. Centuries old and hidden for most of that time, it was a legendary bird fabled to break mountains apart with its mighty wings. A part of Toshik smiled as he gazed up in wonder, imagining the reaction of his mother if she had witnessed this.

Gale Thrasher descended upon the center of the open field, its wings toppling a few trees on the periphery. Himitsu had returned in the most extravagant way possible.

*   *   *

Himitsu had felt the presence of Dev Assassins from afar. He ignored Jilly's shouts and approached a wide-eyed Fane.

Gale Thrasher took off behind him, flattening the grass with the wind shoved from its wing.

"Remember my dad's favorite technique?" Himitsu yelled over the gale.

"Of course!" Fane shouted.

"Do you know how to do it?"

"He said it was only for the Vevlu family to know!"

Himitsu groaned. They were still shrouded in darkness, as Gale Thrasher rose and fell above them, slowly flapping its wings as she remained above the field. One last favor to the son of Ophala.

"All right!" Himitsu said. "Make use of Gale Thrasher! Use your flames however you see fit. Toshik, Jilly! Get out of here!" They didn't move. "These winds will make our flames impossible to tame, so leave! The Dev Assassins will make use of this chaos if you stay here!"

"And if they chase us?" Toshik shouted back.

"If they do, we will follow! But that's unlikely! Just get out!"

Himitsu turned and caught an invisible fist. Then he ignited his own body in black fire, serving as a cloak to conceal himself in Gale's shadow. The Dev Assassin's body ignited in flame and became visible. The woman screamed in agony.

He punched her in the gut, then drew his sword and swung. She collapsed as her chest was cut open and the fire swallowed her whole. He looked for Fane, but all he saw was an inferno of black that twisted to great heights.

A pain cut through Himitsu's heart … *For everything you've taught me, Mom and Dad.*

*   *   *

Yama reached one of Phesaw Park's two lakes. There was a small grassy clearing that turned into dirt that led to the water. She turned and looked at a grinning Bruut.

"This is it?" he asked.

"Shall we start?"

He didn't bother with a response. He charged at her, thighs and calves bulging with each step. She stood still and looked her attacker in the eye. He was lead-footed, but immensely powerful. And as much as she wanted to step out of the way, she wouldn't. This was a test of Toono's reliability.

Bruut threw a punch, and just before it connected with her face, a bubble blasted him to the side. He grabbed his head and pried his body from the divot that he had carved into the ground, then staggered to his feet. Rage painted his face as he looked for the source of the interference.

Yama watched as he turned to the lake. He cautiously approached the water's edge and peered across. "Where did that come from?" he asked.

"Not sure."

Without moving his eyes from the lake, he said, "I'm disappointed that you'd commit to something so cowardly."

"Resourceful is a better word."

Another bubble burst from the lake's surface and hit him in the chest. His feet slid in the grass, but he kept his balance. He even managed to grasp its sides with both hands. As he came to a stop, his biceps and forearms bulged to a size that Yama had never seen from him. He released a mighty yell as he squeezed the elastic material as durable as steel until it burst into nothing.

Bruut panted as a man strolled out of the lake's depths.

"That was something," Toono said. "No one has ever been able to puncture one of my bubbles."

Bruut didn't respond. He marched forward with fire in his eyes. "And who are you?" he asked as his feet splashed in the water.

Toono stepped back into a fighting stance with his ancient at the ready. "I don't think that matters."

Yama heard heavy breathing approaching from behind, and recognized the familiar wheeze. Agnos was also curious of the outcome. For one of these two young men, this would be the final fight of their lives.

44
Blood and Water

Bryson was at a loss for words as he stared at Olivia and Apoleia. How did Olivia know so much? What was her role in all of this? The thought of having to oppose her was beyond comprehension.

He finally managed to muster up a few words: "Olivia, what's going on?"

She didn't respond.

"My daughter doesn't need to answer to you," Apoleia said. "Men don't deserve answers from women. That is the Stillian way."

"Olivia always talks to me," Bryson replied.

Apoleia's frozen lips pursed. "A despicable fact that I learned recently. But she will atone."

For years Bryson had wondered what Olivia's family was like, never having the opportunity to visit her home. He had only asked why once, right after Debo's memorial service. Her answer?

You are my darkest secret.

Thusia stayed in her ready stance. Bryson shivered, his eyes on Apoleia as she leaned over and whispered something in Olivia's ear, which gathered frost with each syllable.

Olivia charged at him. He didn't know what to do. A bone-crunching punch connected with his chin. He was knocked back, his feet not lifting more than a few inches from the ground until he crashed into the main door of Lilac Suites several hundred yards behind where he had stood. He lay there in a haze, concussed and flabbergasted. He looked up to see the chandelier that hung from the ceiling four floors above. Then he saw the hundreds of frightened faces that peeked over the banisters of each floor. Students were watching the two captains of the Jestivan turn on each other. What were they to think?

Bryson pushed himself up to a knee. He spit out a tooth, along with a good amount of blood. Olivia waited for him outside. There was a wall of ice next to where Thusia had been standing. Apoleia must have thrown it up to stop the powerful Branian from interfering with Olivia's attack.

"*What are you doing?*" Bryson cried to his best friend, surprising even himself with the outburst. The desperation and confusion behind his voice was enough for Meow Meow to slip a pitiful look.

Olivia made no response. Her mother burst into a fit of maniacal laughter. "Fight back, young man. Put those merciless genes on display."

Bryson shook his head and stood up. Just a year ago he was risking his life and many others' to save the person who was trying to kill him now. And that same desire to save her was as strong as ever—but from what? Did she want saving, or was this who she was—her mother, but better masked as an impassive girl?

She rushed forward once again, leading with her foot and sending him flying into the bar. He staggered up from the pile of bar stools and was hit with a fist that bent him back over the countertop. The pain in his tortured spine nearly matched that in his face as she punched him again and again.

Something was holding him back. Maybe it was Meow Meow's somber expression, as if he was teetering on the verge of tears while Olivia's face was as blank as always.

Is that Meow Meow's sadness or Olivia's?

"Olivia," he slurred, "… please."

She grabbed him by the collar of his hood and slung him back toward the missing front door. He slid across the hard cobblestone, ripping his jacket and shredding away the skin on his shoulder and forehead.

He looked up, expecting to see Thusia pulverizing Apoleia in his defense. But even as she evaded piercing icicles and massive pillars of ice, she never bothered to parry. Was she not attacking because of her respect for Bryson's friendship with Olivia?

Apoleia's forearms and hands became coated in a thick sheet of ice that formed two spears. She engaged Thusia in a close-quarters fight, swinging and thrusting wildly with her frozen weapons. Thusia jumped, rolled, and skipped back in the most nimble of ways. She seemed to glide and float when she moved—the traits of a skilled Spirit Assassin. It was a little surprising to see the effort in Thusia's face, however miniscule it might have been. It spoke to Apoleia's skills in battle.

Bryson felt a heavy boot press into his back. Only Olivia walked with such weight on her feet. The pressure released, and his confusion was briefly replaced with fear as he realized what she was doing. Pain was one thing, but he couldn't allow himself to be paralyzed or killed.

So he rolled to the side, and there was a powerful crunch as Olivia stomped a dent into the ground. Thusia screamed as ice pierced her shoulder. A boot smashed into Bryson's ear, the second concussion just as disorienting as his head hammered against the ground. The ringing in his ears turned into a steady high-pitched scream. He blacked out.

Then he heard conversation. His eyes began processing the sunlight again. Fuzz turned into shapes, which became people and objects. Wealth's Crossroads looked as if it were slowly tilting toward the sky.

"You mean to tell me you can't kill him?"

The question sounded like it came from Apoleia.

Bryson didn't hear anyone respond.

"I wouldn't allow that anyway," Thusia said. "This is a waste of time, Apoleia."

"How dare you label this as such a thing?"

"He is not who you're angry at."

"He is *exactly* who I'm angry at! Look at him!" Apoleia shouted. "That blond hair! Those blue eyes! That thing between his legs!"

The temperature plunged, and frost inched across Bryson's skin. He released small surges of electricity to counter it.

"I guess I'll take care of this," Apoleia sighed.

Bryson was shoved off the ground by a column of ice that rose from below him. It carried him to Tabby's Gift Shop and pinned him against its wall as he screamed. The same thing happened to Thusia, though she remained calm.

"What happened to not letting me die?" Bryson asked.

"Nothing happened."

"Why haven't you done away with her yet?"

"Why haven't you?" Thusia asked.

"I'm not killing Olivia's mother."

"That's your reason? At least mine is good. I understand what she's doing, and I feel for her."

Apoleia walked toward them with Olivia trailing. Apoleia was a magnificent figure of ice and frost that glimmered under the sun. Ice crumbled from her body as her joints bent, creating a sparkling trail of crystals.

"Hum the tune," Thusia said.

"Huh?"

"'Phases of S.' Hum it for her to hear."

Bryson began to hum the first phase of the song: Seclusion. Apoleia's face soured. "Stop that!" she hissed.

Confused, Bryson kept going, transitioning into the second phase: Sorrow.

"Do not sully my story!" The rage continued to twist on her face as he continued, and it boiled over once he reached the final phase: Spite. "That is *my* song!"

She was sobbing, tears of anguish rolling down her face. "There are no differences!" she ranted. "Every bit is the same! It makes me sick to look at you!"

Spikes of ice grew from her arms, legs, and head. Bryson's blood began to crystallize. Why did Thusia tell him to do that? He looked over and saw that she was staring at Olivia, and at first he couldn't tell why. But then he saw something he had never seen before. Olivia's eyes were glistening.

"The next block of ice is going straight through your heart!" Apoleia yelled.

"*Stop it!*" Olivia roared. Even her mother's head slowly turned in awe. Olivia's eyes began to flood as she shook her head and screamed even louder: "He's your *son*! He's my *brother*! He's our *blood*!"

A single tear ran down her face and clung to her chin before plummeting toward the ground. It hit the stone with a splash, instantly transforming into a gigantic wave that entrapped Olivia and Apoleia.

The shafts of ice pinning Bryson to the wall melted, and steam rose from the water.

Thusia grabbed Bryson by the wrist. "We need to get out of here!" she yelled over the roaring waters.

He didn't move. The crest of the wave defied gravity and curled back to create a perfectly vertical cylinder. Then it twisted, forming a tornado of scalding hot water. Bryson flinched as droplets seared his skin, but he couldn't tear himself from the scene.

He had just met his mother. Olivia was his sister.

The geyser receded as it crashed back down to land, morphing into a dome that trapped the two women inside. Bryson could only see shapes through the water … wait, there was a third person. As he walked closer, a mass of darkness erupted within the dome. Black fog whipped with the water's current, and an inexplicable and overwhelming sense of despair swept over him. Someone yanked at his collar.

"Get away from that," Thusia snapped.

"Why? What is it?"

She didn't answer. The dome disappeared, but only Olivia and Apoleia stood where it had been. Bryson could have sworn there was a third shape.

Apoleia was unmasked of the ice that had blanketed her, exposing her fair skin and violet locks that were now sopping wet. Olivia's cheeks were wet with tears. Her head hung low as she sniffled. Meow Meow's gaze was solemn as he too stared at the ground.

Apoleia slowly turned her head toward Bryson. There was a dull fire in her eyes, as if she recognized defeat but couldn't stomach it. Her daughter had turned on her. And in all likelihood it had happened years ago. She pressed her fingers against the front of her neck, then sliced across her throat. She didn't break eye contact or even flinch. Instead she smiled as the blood coursed down.

Something told him not to, but he said it anyway: "You're my mother?"

"You're my mistake."

Bryson looked over at Olivia. "And you're my sister."

"*Twin* sister," Apoleia corrected. "You're probably wondering why you have no recollection of me. You've seen me before, but you were too young to remember. Where else would you have learned such a song?"

"But you use ice."

"That seems to be the conundrum, doesn't it?"

"You and Mendac were—"

"Nothing. Everything you are, everything you have is credited to me. That Branian standing by your side is a product of me. But none of that matters since you look exactly like that man."

This got Bryson's mind reeling. "I thought only royals could have a Branian."

She laughed. "*You* are a royal. At least by definition."

"You … You're the Queen of the Still Kingdom—the royal first-born?"

"Making you and Olivia the Still Prince and Princess."

"But I have Intel Energy."

Apoleia walked toward him. Thusia stiffened, but Bryson obstructed her with his arm. Apoleia gazed at him with cold eyes, then leaned in close to his ear and whispered, "I suppose you've wondered why you've always suffered from a chill."

She pulled away and glared at Thusia with a wide smile. "Thusia, is it? So you're the one I have to thank."

"I'm sorry," she replied.

And that was it. Apoleia turned and walked in the direction of the slums, and Olivia followed.

"Olivia!" Bryson shouted.

She turned around. "Stop," she pleaded. "My mother is leaving, but I will be back."

"Don't worry about Olivia. She has made her choice," Apoleia barked. "I will not take her with me."

"Let them go," Thusia said. "We have to go into Phesaw Park and help the others."

He looked back down the winding road. With everything he already knew about his father, this incident only made it worse. What had happened to Apoleia Still?

* * *

Apoleia walked in silence with her daughter. After nearly eighteen years of raising her, she had chosen the boy who looked so much like the man who had ruined Apoleia's life. The only reason why they were still together at this moment was because their business wasn't finished. They needed to find Toono.

Tears streamed down her face. She couldn't believe that Bryson had hummed her song. It angered her. It wasn't made for a man to sing or play. It represented a transformation she experienced during those dreadful years from so long ago. And *that* day—the worst day of her life.

45
Partition

Toono stood over Bruut's motionless body. He stuck a glowing gem into his cloak pocket, satisfied with an accomplished mission. The fifth of ten sacrifices had been completed.

He looked toward the sky above the canopies of cherry blossoms. During his fight with Bruut, there had been a couple strange distractions in the distance that nearly caused him to falter. The first was the shocking appearance of Gale Thrasher, a beast he had never believed to actually exist. With its presence Toono was forced to question the truth in much of what he had read.

Yama and Agnos were studying him from afar, but his interest was in only Yama. It was a waiting game of who would move first. Toono had never really envisioned what would follow this battle. Had he expected Yama to leave with him without hesitation?

"Let's get out of here," a voice said from behind.

Apoleia and Olivia stepped out of the park's wooded area. They both seemed unscathed, but there was something wrong with Olivia. He could see it in her eyes—a foreign sadness.

"A success?" he asked.

"Not at all," Apoleia said.

Toono looked at Olivia, then back at Apoleia. "Did you tell her?" he asked.

"No."

He sighed and rubbed his temple. His deal with Apoleia was supposed to be kept secret from Olivia, but he had hoped that she would have told her daughter sometime today. How was he to word this?

"Olivia," he said softly, "I'm going to need Meow Meow." He felt silly using the name, but he did it out of respect for her.

Olivia looked up from the grass as another tear slipped down her cheek. "You're out of your damned mind," Meow Meow spat.

"Do not make this difficult, Olivia."

They held each other's gaze for a full minute. Meanwhile, the kitten hat was hissing and spitting, undoubtedly wrestling with Olivia in their thoughts. Toono understood this, so he granted them the time. But there wasn't much time left.

"It's growing too quiet," Apoleia warned. "We must leave."

Olivia reached up and grabbed Meow Meow's fur. "Stop it, Olivia," the kitten begged.

His pleas were hopeless, and he was lifted off of her head, exposing all of her violet hair. Meow Meow's face went blank. His eyes slowly refocused, then darted every which way. "Where am I?" he asked. "Who are all of you?"

Olivia sniffled while Toono held Meow Meow in his outstretched hand. Folds of extra fur had unraveled down the back, and there was a strange five-point star engraved into its back. She must have had it tucked in the entire time. This wasn't a hat, but Toono had already known this.

Words failed him. The significance of what he was holding … the massive story behind it … what Olivia had named Meow Meow was actually an even more legendary icon in Kuki Sphaira's lore than a beast like Gale Thrasher. Its story was just so deeply lodged into the most obscure parts of the timeline that nobody really knew about it, for this "cat" was a unique kind of beast, part of a civilization that thrived before the Known History timeline began 1,500 years ago—or that's what Kadlest's book had taught him.

Toono felt the gems vibrate in his pocket. He squeezed them tight. *Not yet.*

He looked at Apoleia, then walked away. She followed. After a moment, so did Yama. He glanced to the side and smiled. "I'm glad this is your choice," he said.

Yama didn't answer or look back. Meow Meow, who was now resting on top of Toono's Orbaculum and facing backward, its coat of fur crashing down the staff's length, drooled as he asked, "How many fish do you think that lake holds?" With no mind to latch onto as a home, he was oblivious to everything.

*　　*　　*

Night had fallen. Hundreds of injured students had been transferred to Dunami Hospital while the Jestivan rested in Phesaw's medical ward. This building had become all too familiar to them this year.

Himitsu climbed out of bed, wincing in pain as he touched the bandage on his chest. He gazed around the room where his fellow Jestivan either slept or conversed with each other. It had been a day of fear and sorrow.

He saw Olivia and Bryson in quiet conversation several beds down. Bryson was in bad shape. Swollen and bruised fleshed bulged between the few gaps in the bandages on his face. He also had a metal contraption fastened to his torso nearly identical to the one Lilu had during her stay in the Dunami hospital a year and a half ago. Olivia sat next to his bed without any injuries at all, her face as expressionless as always. Somehow she always managed to escape disaster unscathed.

Himitsu walked down the open space between the beds, looking left and right. Finally he spotted Agnos, who was propped against pillows with an open piece of folded parchment on his lap. He seemed okay, just some minor bruises and scrapes.

Agnos removed his glasses and set them on the nightstand. "You made quite the entrance today," he said. "Based off how soon you arrived here and the method of delivery, I'm curious as to what exactly happened over there in Olethros."

Himitsu removed a crumpled note from his pocket, unwilling to entertain any sort of discussion. It had been folded neatly by his mother, but he'd balled it up and nearly thrown it away when he read its contents while Gale Thrasher carried him back to Phesaw.

"My mother wanted me to give you this," Himitsu said. "All … Well, *most* of the information you need to track down that ancient you've been asking about."

"Thank you." Agnos retrieved the parchment and studied it.

Himitsu returned to his bed, lying down with the upmost caution for his wound. Staring at the ceiling, he spent the rest of the night picturing his parents' smiling faces. They kept being pushed away by the image of Jilly's father looming in the background.

* * *

Jilly sat by Toshik's bedside. There was an unfamiliar demeanor of gloom carved into her face.

"Go to bed," Toshik said. "You've been wounded."

She shook her head. "Yama's gone."

"She was headed for a wrong path her entire life. Today ended up being the day she found it."

"It's my fault."

"Never! Nobody can blame you for something so foul. You're as pure as they come."

"If I had loved her a little bit more …"

"And that's selfish of her!" Toshik hissed. As heads turned in their direction, he lowered his voice to a whisper. "How can anyone expect more love out of you? Do they want your heart to rupture?"

"She warned me," Jilly said. "Maybe not directly, but she dropped hints. Sure I'm not the smartest, but I should have recognized that." She wiped tears from her cheeks with the back of her hand.

"Do you love her more than me?"

"I don't know," she mumbled.

Instead of feeling angry or jealous, in that moment he wanted nothing more than to comfort her. He placed his hand on Jilly's knee. After a moment, she put her hand on his. As their fingers interlocked, he pulled her into his embrace. Her tears darkened his gown as her head nestled into his chest and he pressed his lips into her hair.

* * *

Olivia pulled her chair closer to her brother. Bryson hadn't said anything since she arrived, and she didn't blame him. She sensed his feelings of loss and confusion. She wanted to be careful with what she said, which was why she had barely spoken in the past hour.

It was painful, the silence. She used to have the company of Meow Meow's thoughts. The two of them were constantly in a discussion, to the point that they didn't realize they were speaking to each other most of the time. But with that intimacy gone, she finally understood the solitude her mother had felt all those years before Mendac entered her life, and how she could become so vulnerable. Maybe that's why her mother had given her Meow Meow, so that she would never experience that isolation.

"Bryson," she said. He didn't respond, but she saw him blink a couple times. "I understand if you don't want to talk to me, but I need to tell you a story … our mother's story. This way you know how she came to be the way she did, and why I followed her for so long." She sighed. "Will you listen?"

"Yes," he replied in a scratchy whisper.

46
Seclusion

An eleven-year-old Apoleia lay in her four-poster bed. It was an ocean of mattress, and when her mother and father walked into her room and approached her bedside, she had to roll over several times to reach the edge.

This had been the most exciting—and scariest—week of her life. Her body had gone through its first cleanse. She had officially become a woman. She was also happy that the pain was gone—at least for another few weeks. Her mother had called them "cramps."

Her dad leaned in close and kissed her forehead. "Do you need me to grab you anything before you sleep?" he asked.

"I'm good."

He smiled and wished her a good night. "Good night …" she replied. She hesitated, but the stern glare of her mother forced her to finish the sentence properly. "Gennaio."

Gennaio was her father's name. Now that she was a woman, that was how she had to address him. In the Still Kingdom, once a girl had her first cleanse, they no longer used any labels such as dad, father, or papa. Such terms would give the man power over her, and in this kingdom no man had power over a woman—no matter the age or relation.

It hurt her so much to use his name. She had slipped up several times the past five days, which only led to punishment from her mother. And there were countless moments when she had cried her eyes out over the past week, but that was shameful for a Stillian woman, so she'd reserve such a cowardly display for the washroom.

Her mother, who had stayed a few steps back, stepped closer with the same austere eyes. "You must wipe off that smile, young lady," she demanded.

Apoleia's lips straightened as if a spell was cast on her. That was the type of power a woman like her mother had.

"Your celebratory week is over now. Your persona should return to what it was. Like the ice-capped Diamond Sea, we are rigid, undeterred by emotion."

The young girl gave a firm nod. "Yes, Mother."

"You're excited, and I understand that. There is no greater euphoria than a cleanse … that feeling of your body killing off any of your male eggs. Our bodies naturally reject them."

"I don't like the blood."

"Embrace it," she replied. "That's the soiled blood of male eggs. That means the cleanse is working."

Apoleia looked at a picture of her and her father on the wall. She didn't want men to die. They had never wronged her. On the contrary she had spent her entire life witnessing the opposite. She wanted a son, but she could never say such a thing.

"Do not forget what you've been taught," the Still Queen said. "You save your emotions for times that call for them—such as grand events for the public. You use them for showmanship, nothing else. Now roll over and get situated." Her mother laid the covers neatly over the girl. "You are a woman now, so you act like one. And then when Ropinia's time comes, you'll be able to guide her through it like the royal first-born that you are."

She leaned in and pressed her hand against Apoleia's forehead, for mothers and daughters didn't kiss. "No hesitation," she whispered.

Apoleia watched as she blew out the candles on her table near the door and walked out.

*   *   *

At age fifteen Apoleia was a near perfect embodiment of what her status demanded of her. She strutted out of a classroom carrying an Advanced Business Calculus textbook against her chest. The other women had to wait for her to exit before they could even think about rising from their seats.

Part of this was because she was the Still Princess, but the main reason was that she was their teacher. Though everyone in the class had at least two years on her, her knowledge surpassed their own.

Apoleia walked through the educational wing of the palace with long strides and straight posture. A soldier opened a door as she approached. She suppressed the urge to thank him with a smile since men were not deserving of gratitude, according to Stillian culture.

She crossed the congested floor of the Icebound Confluence at the palace's epicenter, passing the towering Statue of Gefal before reaching another wing's entrance.

Four soldiers stood erect at this door, for it led to the military control wing. No questions were asked as they permitted her access. They knew that Still Queen Salia would be unhappy with this visit, but Apoleia was their superior as well.

As she journeyed through the gloomy corridors, soldiers would turn their heads away or duck into a room. They all knew that if Apoleia was here, Salia would be chasing after her soon enough. And they wanted no part in their queen's relentless questioning.

Apoleia reached her destination and she stood patiently, awaiting her host's arrival, a bit confused by why they were supposed to meet here. Why choose somewhere in plain sight?

Something creaked above her, so she looked up. A rope ladder fell to the floor from an opening in the ceiling. That made a little bit more sense. She removed her heels, tucked them under her arm, and climbed. After she pulled herself into the ceiling, she retrieved the ladder and closed the door.

It was a modest space lit only by a few candles. There weren't any windows, but grated openings on one end of the room allowed natural air to flow in, if not much sunlight.

Apoleia watched as her friend rummaged through a massive pile of junk at the far end of the room. The slits of sunlight exposed the powder blue color of his recruit jacket, the four-pointed snowflake crystal embroidered on its back signifying his status as a trainee in the Stillian army. Of course there was no such thing as a snowflake with four points, but that was the idea. Like that snowflake, he was incomplete. A real soldier wore the traditional six-pointed snowflake.

"Good morning, Titus."

He turned and smiled with all of his uneven teeth. "Princess Apoleia, morning," he replied before scouring the mess again.

Apoleia walked around the room, taking notice of certain things that caught her eye. The space wasn't big enough for a desk, only a thick plank of wood placed on top of two cinderblocks. She looked down at some parchment that littered the surface. Blotched all over it were musical notes. She picked one up and studied it. She smirked. What a mess.

"Why are there six lines in your staffs?" she asked.

"I thought I was being creative."

"You're being a butcher." She paused. "Five lines, Titus."

But that wasn't the only error in his musical notation. There were plenty of visual errors that were simply displeasing to the eye, such as bar lines being placed unevenly and notes not properly sitting between two staff lines, which would lead to confusion as to what pitch was supposed to be hit. But that was her fastidious mind at work. The more glaring issue was his lack of harmonization. As Apoleia read through the song he had been working on, she played it in her mind, and it sounded awful.

"I found it!"

Titus was holding up the most beautiful thing she had ever seen—a lyre, one of the most ancient instruments in Kuki Sphaira. It was made of aged wood that bowed upward. At the top a horizontal rod connected the tails of the bow. Six strings stretched from the rod to the bow's base.

"Frost of Francine," Apoleia swore. "I didn't think your big surprise would actually be a big surprise."

Titus flicked his eyebrows up and down. "I don't disappoint." He approached her with the instrument extended in front of him. "For you, milady."

Apoleia held it like a newborn baby, with careful and gentle hands. Who knew how long this masterpiece had languished in a pile of junk occupying a forgotten storage space? She stared closely at the foreign characters engraved on the handles. She had never seen such a language.

"Teach me," Titus said.

Apoleia laughed—something she only allowed Titus to see. "You're not ready for this. Besides, I'm not even sure I could play it."

A clattering sound came from the grate in the wall. Hail had started to fall, sending pellets of ice into the room.

"Look," Titus said. "Nature has even provided us with sound to drown out the music, so we can't be heard from below."

Apoleia thought for a moment, considering the lyre with narrowed eyes. She looked up. "All right. Let's get a feel for where we need to start with you." She handed him the lyre and took a seat on a broken chunk of a cinderblock.

He stood there, quite awkwardly, the lyre dangling from one hand. Apoleia sighed. "Sit down, Titus. Now place it on your lap and play."

Titus began to pluck at the strings. Right away Apoleia knew the problem, one she anticipated. "It isn't a harp," she said. "You don't use your fingers."

He stared at her briefly before bringing the lyre to his face as if he was going to bite at the strings. He thought he was funny, but Apoleia kept the straight face her mother had instilled in her.

"There's a plectrum hanging from the bottom," she said. "Put it in your right hand and pluck at the higher strings with it, while your free hand holds the unused strings at the bottom to keep them from accidentally making noise."

He tried to do exactly that, but his face soured from the unorthodox combination of finger movements.

"The lyre, according to material I've read about them, is easy for amateurs to learn to play, and a master can do wonders with it. But you've never practiced with a stringed instrument before."

He stared at the bowed contraption with a frown, then handed it back to her. "Let's see the master at work."

"I'm not flawless," Apoleia said as she placed it on her lap.

"In my eyes, you are."

She hesitated with the plectrum between her thumb and index finger, her eyes glued to the lyre as she took a moment to absorb his words. She wasn't supposed to fall for a man—men were supposed to chase her. But every ounce of her being wanted to be proactive. And the urge swelling within her wasn't because of the natural desire to procreate, which was supposedly the only purpose of a man in the Still Kingdom, but the love she had for him.

She plucked at a couple strings. As for how Titus reacted to the momentary silence following his bold statement, she didn't know, for she never looked up from the lyre.

Apoleia tried playing a song that she remembered from her grandmother, who was a magnificent harpist when she was alive. She was disappointed by what she was able to coax from the instrument, but if she were to judge her skill based off the look on Titus's face when she looked up, one would have thought she had composed a song suited only for the Gefal. He wore a dumbfounded smile, his lips somewhat apart. And there were tears sitting in his eyes.

She placed the lyre on the floor. "Don't cry on me, Titus."

He wiped his eyes. "I'm not crying … I have sensitive eyes."

"A sensitive soul, you mean."

"I love when you address me by my name."

She paused, taken aback once again by his forward approach. She stared intensely into his eyes, "Is that so … Titus?"

The trapdoor banged open. Startled, Apoleia lunged forward into Titus's arms. He quickly slipped away and cowered in the far reaches of the room. Apoleia turned around from where she lay on the floor to see her mother's expressionless face flickering in the candlelight. No matter how enraged she might have been, she was still able to mask it in a man's presence.

"Out," Queen Salia commanded.

Apoleia glanced back at Titus, who appeared to be staring death in the eye. She had no choice. She crawled to the trapdoor and dropped into the hallway, where General Garlo stood patiently, waiting to discipline the boy above. Salia followed her down a few seconds later.

"I will take care of him, Queen Salia," Garlo said.

"I expect so."

He bowed and then climbed the ladder.

"Let's go, Apoleia," Salia commanded as she walked away.

Their journey through the palace was one of stiff silence, for Salia wouldn't make a scene in front of the countless people crowding the halls. When they reached Apoleia's room, Salia opened the door for her, then walked in and slammed it shut.

Apoleia placed her textbook on her desk and took a seat on her bed. Her mother stood at the door. "I'm going to make this quick," Salia said. "Women do not pursue men, and we most certainly do not play music for them. Music is our way of releasing bottled-up emotions, and it is for the privacy of our bedrooms. And worst of all, the song I heard you playing was one of love. We don't fall in love, Apoleia. We use."

"Men are simply here for procreation," Apoleia replied.

"That's right."

"Please don't punish Titus for my misdeeds."

Salia shook her head. "Of course there will be repercussions. And if I ever catch you with him again, I will have him killed."

The door slammed shut, leaving Apoleia by herself just as she always was.

* * *

It was the end of the night on Apoleia's little sister's eleventh birthday, and the two girls had decided to accompany each other in the recreational wing's ice rink. While Ropinia slid her tiny feet into her skates, Apoleia, not much of a skater, tuned her violin.

Three years of forced distance between her and Titus. Just a few stolen moments of eye contact. But at least Titus was still alive.

"Did you see the traveler who approached the wall today?" Ropinia asked.

"For a brief moment."

"Who do you think he was?"

"I don't know."

For the first time in decades, someone from a foreign kingdom had traveled to Kindoliya. How he managed to traverse the Diamond Sea and its deadly hailstorms was a mystery. Even more confounding, the man had been granted a private meeting with Queen Salia and eight of her financial partners. What did he have to offer for them to ignore the Stillian tradition of women not handling business with men?

Ropinia took a few practice laps, picking up speed as she circled the rink. Apoleia would glance at her from time to time as she fussed over her already tuned violin. She wanted to sit in her thoughts for a little while longer, but her little sister was keen to interrupt that.

"Are you ready?"

Apoleia tucked the violin under her chin and gave her sister a gentle smile. "Which routine?"

"I'm eleven now, so play 'To Blossom in Winter.'"

Apoleia went quiet before explaining, "Just because I had my first cleanse at eleven doesn't mean you will too. Some girls don't get it until they're thirteen."

"I don't want to be a girl anymore," Ropinia said. "I'm a woman at heart."

"Enjoy it while it lasts."

"Just play the song, please," Ropinia pleaded.

Apoleia placed her fingers on the violin's neck and raised the bow. She tapped the ball of her foot on the floor, then began the song with one long draw of the bow across the E string.

As magnificent of a musical talent as Apoleia was, Ropinia was just as good of a dancer—especially figure skating. And when the two of them joined their talents, they could create masterpieces. Ropinia jumped and twirled in perfect unison with the flutter of Apoleia's bow, making sure to land with one leg extended straight ahead right on time with the lengthy, drawn-out notes.

They had performed for close to an hour when Apoleia removed the violin from her chin. "Time to study," she said.

"Ah, something I could actually be helpful with," a deep voice said.

Apoleia turned, confused. What kind of man would so recklessly approach the two daughters of the Still Queen? Unlike Ropinia, Apoleia held a straight face when she saw the answer. It was the traveler from this morning. He had blonde hair and blue eyes, and a peculiar waistband adorned with metal rods that hung like chimes.

"Ice skating and music are definitely not my areas of expertise, but I can definitely find my way around a textbook or two."

The two sisters continued to stare at him.

"Forgive me," he said with a bow. "I am Intel General Mendac LeAnce. It's an honor to meet you both."

* * *

Apoleia was frustrated. Two months had passed since her run-in with Mendac LeAnce, and now she saw him every day for some reason or another. He always managed to find her. And no matter how many hints she dropped that she wasn't interested in speaking to him, he was annoyingly relentless.

"Why is he always around the palace? And why won't he leave me alone?" she asked as she sat in the dining hall table with her family.

"We are businesswomen," Queen Salia said. "And when we are offered such a deal, we don't refuse. Besides, this is your chance to use your greatest asset as leverage. If he's falling for you, allow it—for the greater good of our economy."

"My body, you mean?" Apoleia asked.

"Your mind—both the creative and rational components of it. Mendac isn't like the Stillian men who thirst for physical beauty and nothing else. He's drawn to skill and intellect. More important, he's drawn to depth. You provide all those qualities. Like most foreign men, he's intrigued by the complexity of your being—the lack of bodily and facial expression, which means you're hiding things in his eyes."

"I find *him* to be the fascinating one," Ropinia said.

"Eat your dinner, Ropinia," Salia said. "This is a conversation between women."

Ropinia's eyes dropped to her plate. "Yes, Mother."

Apoleia wanted to feel sorry for her little sister, but she only felt jealousy. She hated her role in this conversation.

"He is the general for the Intel family," Salia said. "The wealthiest family in all of Kuki Sphaira. So you can understand why I'm doing everything in my power to keep him satisfied during his stay?"

"I can."

"And if you're going to be the Still Queen one day, you need to learn to do the same. And what better time than to start now?"

Apoleia glanced at her father.

"Don't look to him for advice," Salia said. "He isn't going to give you any."

"So you want me to entertain him with my attention?" Apoleia asked.

"It's already taken care of. He'll be waiting for you in the Icebound Confluence at dawn tomorrow."

"So you scold me for my actions with Titus, but you have me throwing myself at a man not even from this realm."

Ropinia's eyes widened in disbelief, though she had the discipline not to look up from her plate.

"You will give him a proper tour of the palace," Salia responded. "You will show him our living quarters."

"Our living—"

"You'll answer his questions and treat him as if he was a fellow Stillian woman—with respect. You'll teach him anything he wants to know about Kindoliya so long as it doesn't compromise our safety. You'll even play him music if he so requests."

Apoleia had been holding her composure fairly well, but that last sentence nearly made her burst into tears. She could tell that Mendac wasn't a man of music, and if he were to ever make such a request, it would only be to flatter her. And there was no greater insult to Apoleia.

With angry eyes, she looked at her mother. "And if he desires something a little more intimate?"

"No," Salia answered. "Procreation between realms? We would never break a law created by beings even greater than us."

Apoleia got up from her seat, leaving an untouched plate of food behind. "So that's how much it takes to cross the line for you—an Untenable."

* * *

The ice on the door held Apoleia's reflection perfectly. She gazed into her own blue eyes, questioning everything about what this day would bring. When she opened the door she would step into the Icebound Confluence on the other side, leaving the safety of the royal residential quarters.

She took a deep breath and crossed to the other side. Mendac stood at the room's center, hands entwined behind his back as he gazed up at the Statue of Gefal. As she approached him, he didn't bother turning to look. There was a calm, studious expression on his face. She followed his eyes to the top.

They stood there in silence for quite some time before Mendac broke it. "Magnificent work of art."

She didn't respond, for she wasn't going to entertain his false interest in art as an excuse for small talk. Mendac didn't seem to mind.

"I don't care much for the beauty of it," he said, "but the history it represents is intriguing to me. Outside of postures and items some of them seem to be holding, there isn't much to distinguish who each person is. However, I could guess at a few."

He walked around the ice sculpture. She followed. "For instance," he droned on, "it's likely that this figure represents Francine Still, the ruthless Still Queen who reigned from 731 to 784."

Once again, Apoleia stayed quiet. Was he expecting some kind of recognition for his knowledge of the Still Kingdom's history?

Finally he turned and locked eyes. "It's strange that every single figure is that of a woman." His eyes narrowed. "I understand this kingdom's belief that women are superior, but you really think the same applies to the Dark Empire's Gefal?"

"Some think that way," Apoleia softly replied. "But I am not so blind. This statue is a farce in more ways than one."

He stared at her for a moment. "There's something different about you. I see it in your actions around the palace, and now I hear it in your words."

"And why are you here in the first place?" she asked.

He looked around. "It's not fit to discuss this here."

She looked back toward the door she just came out of. She had to show him the royal quarters at some point. Better to get it out of the way now and get some answers in the process.

Mendac was fascinated with Apoleia's weaving of her Still Energy to guide the ice through the door's engraved maze. "Weaving is something I specialize in," he said as he watched. "It's part of the reason why I'm here."

The door opened, and the two of them stepped through. "Welcome," she said. "I can't remember the last time anyone who wasn't a royal visited this area of the palace."

"Thank you for the opportunity," he replied.

"Thank my mother."

As they walked, Mendac frowned. "What is it about me that bothers you?"

"Your 'charm.' It's fake, and it irritates me."

"Your opinion will change."

"That's doubtful. I am a Stillian woman, unwavering and unclouded. When I see the truth, I stand by my convictions."

"I have seen otherwise."

Apoleia didn't give him a response. She continued with the tour, showing him rooms that were rarely, if ever, put to use. The vast halls echoed as they walked down their empty lengths.

"And where is your room?" Mendac asked about an hour into their journey.

"You don't need to know. What is your purpose in Kindoliya?"

"Well that's a secret. But you too seem to have a secret. I'll tell you mine when you show me yours."

She almost frowned before she caught herself. "And what would mine be?"

"The location of your room."

"Such a request is delusional. And disturbing."

They stared at each other for quite some time. After a few moments, he asked, "When do you teach a class again?"

"Monday morning."

"I'd like to attend—not as a student, but as an observer."

"No. Only women take my classes."

"Come on now, Apoleia." Again she almost frowned, irritated by the audacity of him to address her so informally. "Your mother told me about Titus. I know you're a woman who believes women and men are no different. Both can be intelligent, powerful, or skilled. Prove that by showing your students a man in the classroom. I'm not an evil person."

"Titus has a genuine nature," Apoleia snapped. "You do not."

Mendac's face grew grave. "I will show you my genuine self."

"Be yourself with me, and I will call you a friend—provided I like what I see."

47
The Untenable

Apoleia stepped into her class. The students stood behind their desks while their princess settled in. Once she took a seat, the women followed suit. Apoleia withdrew her glasses from a drawer, put them on, and scanned the room. Mendac sat near the very back. He had dragged one of the chairs to the far corner as to not draw attention to himself, but she could tell that her students were itching to turn around and stare.

"We have a guest today," she announced as she stood up. "He is a visitor from the Intel Kingdom and wants to prove that men are as intelligent as women." A few of the students snickered into their hands.

Apoleia looked at Mendac as she finished addressing her students: "So he is your motivation to excel at a level that your exam results have not reflected as of late. You can't have a man show you up, correct?"

"No, Princess," they said in unison.

She looked down and flipped through some parchment. "We'll see, I suppose." She turned around and placed her finger on the chalkboard. A trail of frost swirled across the surface until it spelled the name Francine Still. She took a moment before turning toward the class.

"What do you know of this name?" Apoleia asked as she addressed the students.

Most of them raised their hands. Apoleia called on one.

"She was the Still Queen for the majority of the 700s," the woman said.

"Correct, but I expect everyone to know that. Answer me this …" she said while placing her finger on the board again. This time she drew a circle was with a line cutting it in half. On one side the number fifty-one appeared; on the other, forty-nine. "How is this relevant to Francine Still?"

Overwhelming silence lay in her question's wake, which disappointed her. She knew that they knew the answer, but lacked the critical thinking to come to the conclusion with the prompting she'd provided.

A hand slowly rose in the back of the room.

"Yes, Mendac?"

Every head turned in his direction as he answered. "It's a pie graph depicting the Stillian male-to-female population in 731 K.H.—the first year of Queen Francine's reign. Fifty-one percent female, 49 percent male."

Apoleia watched Mendac for a moment, expecting a smirk or some show of arrogance, but he looked back at her intently.

"Not the best of starts for the women," Apoleia said. "Now that Mendac has cleared things up for you, what do these percentages have to do with Francine Still?"

She pointed at a raised hand. "The Still Kingdom saw its largest growth in the gender gap in its history during her reign."

Apoleia nodded. "And what was the female-to-male population in 784 K.H.—the year of her death?" More hands shot into the air. "Yes, Rona?"

"Seventy-six percent female, 24 percent male."

Apoleia was about to correct her, but Mendac did instead: "Seventy-eight percent female, 22 percent male."

"Right again, Mendac," Apoleia said, her voice betraying a hint of surprise. "Francine was heralded for her accomplishment, and she still is to this day. You can see her standing tall, stiff, and proud on the Statue of Gefal in the Icebound Confluence. Stillians even use her name as an obscenity—'Frost of Francine.'"

Apoleia ignored the nervous, darting eyes, as if someone would sweep into the room and take her away for using such a phrase in front of them. Women—especially a royal woman—were frowned upon for using harsh language.

"Where did the phrase come from?" Apoleia asked.

Once again she had plenty of hands to choose from. She pointed at Lucianne.

"Queen Francine could weave her Still Energy into fine particles of frost instead of chunks of ice like most. Once a month, during her cleanse, she'd visit a different area of the city and climb its tallest tower. She'd blow a storm of frost into the sky, which would then rain down on the city streets below, where women waited to shower in the white dust."

"And what was the thinking behind such a ritual?" Apoleia asked.

"Queen Francine had six children, all of whom were daughters," Lucianne continued. "There was something special about her cleanse, how it flawlessly killed off all the male eggs, and that ability could be transferred through her frost. Baby boys became few and far between."

Apoleia stared at Lucianne. Everything she had said was correct according to what was taught in history classes during their younger years or in the fairy tales told to children before bed. But it was a lie contrived to hide an ugly truth, one that Apoleia only knew because of her grandmother, who regularly told her stories that her mother would frown upon … stories that shined an unflattering light on the women of the Still Kingdom.

Apoleia desired nothing more than to tell these women the truth, but that would only get her in trouble. "Seems like too pretty of a story for such a nasty swear, so why the contradiction?"

A stunned silence swept across the room. Apoleia shrugged and turned to the board. "Anyway—"

"Because the Eighth Century Stillian Cleanse wasn't a cleanse—it was a massacre."

Apoleia froze in shock as she stared at the chalkboard. She heard every chair slide across the floor as the students undoubtedly turned to stare at Mendac, their placid glares burning holes through him. She forced her mouth closed and pivoted so that she was leaning against the wall as Mendac further explained:

"The idea that Queen Francine's frost could cleanse a woman's body of her male eggs is ludicrous. It was more of an omen: people were going to die. Queen Francine didn't have six children—she had ten. She killed her four sons immediately after birthing them. She also killed every single man who impregnated her. Why? Because the Stillian way is that men are only there to procreate, and she took that ethos to the extreme.

"But that wasn't the extent of it. She created the mandatory labor wards that you still see in communities across Kindoliya to this day. In this day and age they're harmless. If you give birth to a boy, the only repercussion is higher taxes. But in Queen Francine's day they were execution chambers. Queen Francine would visit a different labor ward every few days and kill the boys personally, freezing them solid with her frost. I suspect she enjoyed it."

"We Stillians don't simply die when we freeze," Lucianne said. "Everything you've said is a lie. Isn't that correct, Princess Apoleia?"

Apoleia was leaning against her desk with a look of intrigue. She didn't confirm or deny the story; she didn't say anything at all.

Mendac wasn't done. "Those gavels you carry around? They represent the maxim you've come to live by: No hesitation? Queen Francine carried a massive gavel strapped to her back. But for her it wasn't just a symbol of a silly motto. She'd smash those babies into pieces with her gavel."

"You're disgusting!" Lucianne said. "Only a man could come up with such a perverse lie." She turned to Apoleia and repeated, "That's a lie, Princess."

Apoleia looked at her coldly. "One point two million."

Lucianne's face twisted into confusion. Apoleia gazed at Mendac.

"Estimated body count," he said. "Who knows if it's accurate? I haven't found anything about it since arriving in Kindoliya. The Eighth Century Stillian Massacre is quite a popular subject for scholars in the Light Realm, as you can imagine, and they've arrived at a consensus of around 1.8 million. Calculating it would be a simple matter if we had your total population numbers from 731 and 784, but unfortunately we don't."

The women of the class kept their eyes glued on Mendac for a moment. Apoleia doubted that they believed him, but they certainly weren't about to contradict their princess if she was going to support his claim.

Class was carried out as usual from that point forward, and Mendac was silent throughout the rest of the session. At the hour's end, Apoleia left the room, leaving her students and Mendac behind. She waited outside to see what Mendac would do. Would he chase after her, or would he follow protocol and wait for the other women to file out? Her face remained a mask as the students exited the room and headed in different directions after stopping briefly to give her a curtsy. Quickly she turned and started down the hall.

Hurried footsteps grew louder from behind. She didn't bother turning to see that it was the scruffy, sculpted face of Mendac.

"Tell me," she said as they walked, "how is it that you know so much of Kindoliya?"

"I must be honest here," Mendac said. "There was a point in my life when history wasn't of importance to me—unless it pertained to scientific, mathematical, or weaving theory. The culture where I grew up didn't care much for what people consider knowledge for its own sake."

"And where was that?"

"The city of Brilliance, on the northern edge of the Intel Kingdom."

"Never heard of it."

Mendac gave her a side-eyed glance. "No offense, Princess, but when you live in a place as secluded as this, you're not going to hear of a lot of things."

"Back on topic," she warned.

"I had a friend once," Mendac explained. "His name was Musku. He's to blame for me getting into the history of Kuki Sphaira—all of its kingdoms. Unlike him, I don't do much with it except enjoy it. He was the philosopher."

"Well I'd like to meet this Musku fellow," Apoleia said as she weaved open the lock to the royal wing. "Philosophers, musicians, artists, authors—I consider them all to be in a similar category of mind."

"Scientists and musicians can get along just as well," Mendac murmured.

Apoleia abruptly stopped, realizing that she had come dangerously close to accidentally guiding Mendac to her bedroom. She turned and faced him. "You aren't clever. We're heading back."

The man's blue eyes flickered around the corridor, as if he was absorbing every detail. "All right then," he replied, stepping to the side and allowing her to lead him back to the Icebound Confluence.

*   *   *

A week later, Apoleia was strolling through one of the palace's snowy gardens. Mendac was on her mind. He was the most frustrating of men. With each passing day, the pair spent more and more time together, and she was finally experiencing a rare bit of solitude outside of her bedroom.

Apoleia cursed the fact that she wasn't like her mother, and the irony wasn't lost on her. She had spent all these years wanting to trade places with her little sister, to be a child again. Now she wanted her mother's dispassion. She was developing feelings for an egotistical man from a foreign realm, and she hated herself for it.

A hand tugged at her sleeve as she passed a small gap in the walls of ice that lined the walkways.

"Frost of—"

They stood in a small area surrounded by ice walls on all sides. Only a bench occupied the space. "Hello, Apoleia," Titus whispered.

"What are you doing? This is reckless."

He put his finger to his lip. "Yeah, and you're making it worse with your shouting."

"Can you blame me?"

Titus grinned. "You're the Still Princess … act like it."

She stared at him, unsure of what to say.

"You may not notice it, but I keep an eye on you," Titus said. "And you've spent quite a lot of time with that stranger from the Intel Kingdom lately."

"You don't exactly have to be some great spy to know this. It's not like I've been hiding it."

"He's dodgy, Apoleia. General Garlo has been gathering intelligence about who he is exactly. This isn't his first trip to one of our realm's kingdoms. The Dev Kingdom has already been a victim of his wrath. And it's likely there have been others."

“From the mouth of Garlo? Really, Titus? I don’t care about what that man says, and you shouldn’t either.”

“I think you should tell Queen Salia,” he pushed. “General Garlo won’t approach her for obvious reasons.”

“Because she won’t listen,” she groused. It felt weird to show such emotion, to vary her tone like this. She had forgotten how it felt—more important, she had forgotten how Titus brought this out of her with such ease. “All she cares about is his money. Still, I don’t think you need to be concerned. What can one person do against an entire capital?”

Titus looked down at the snow. “I’m just asking you to be careful,” he said while dragging the toe of his boot to make a heart in the snow.

Apoleia kicked a pile of snow on top of his sign. “Stop that. You know it can’t happen.”

His gaze dragged up to hers. “I know,” he croaked. He reached into his powder blue cloak and pulled out the lyre from three years ago. He handed it to her with a weak smile, then walked past her and through the entranceway. The snowflake on his back had six points. He was no longer a recruit.

*   *   *

“Thank you, Tria,” Apoleia said as an elderly woman placed a plate of rabbit stew in front of her. Even the cold-bodied Stillians enjoyed warmth on rare occasions.

The chef took a bow and left the small dining room. Unlike the dining hall, this was a room for more intimate meals. The table was much shorter, and the room was softly lit. Instead of ice, the room was paneled in richly patterned pearwood. Mendac sat at the opposite head of the table.

“This has been the greatest time of my life,” he said.

“You must be devastated that you’re leaving tomorrow.”

He smirked. “I think you feel that way more than I do.”

Apoleia scooped up some stew and gazed at the shredded rabbit. “You’ve kept secrets from me these past few months.”

“Secrets?” he asked with surprise.

She looked up. “What were you doing in the Dev Kingdom?”

He paused. "How did you find out about that?"

"Answer the question."

Mendac leaned back in his chair. "The reason wasn't much different than why I'm here." He looked off to the side with a frown. "Haven't you ever wondered how I got to the Dark Realm?"

"I suppose I assumed you took a whirlpool."

"I didn't have time for that," he said. "They take months—years even, depending on the skill of your navigator."

"And how long did it take you?"

"Seventeen seconds."

"Impossible."

He smiled. "I took a teleplatform."

"But only the Dark Realm kingdoms have them," Apoleia said. "They require Dev Energy."

"And that's what was believed for centuries. I visited the Dev Kingdom roughly a decade ago. I was on a mission, and I failed … miserably. But I did make something of it. I saw a teleplatform for the first time in my life. I made sure to take notes and study the phenomenon. I returned years later for two reasons: to finish my mission that I had failed previously and to install my own teleplatforms that I had learned to create. And my variation was different in that it could connect the two realms."

"And how did you manage that without Dev Energy?" Apoleia asked. "You call me ignorant, but I know that Intel Energy doesn't work like that."

"I'm a supreme weaver, with an unprecedented understanding of permanence. I can make Intel Energy do a lot of things." Mendac shook his head. "We're not confined to boxes—well most people are, but I'm not."

Apoleia sighed. "That ego. And something tells me you're not telling the full truth."

The room fell quiet. Apoleia returned to her stew while Mendac stared at her intensely.

"So that's one of the reasons why I'm here," he said. "I offered your mother a lot of money in exchange for her permission to let me build a teleplatform next to the old one on the far side of the Diamond Sea. She's agreed to some limited trade—the Intel Kingdom's iron for the Still Kingdom's ever-ice."

"What do you want ever-ice for?"

"It's useful for a lot of things—cold storage for the preservation of produce or chemicals, namely."

Apoleia placed her spoon in the empty bowl. "You haven't touched your stew," she pointed out.

"I held up my end of the deal," Mendac said, ignoring her observation. "I told you my secret for being here, so that means you'll show me where—"

"Not a chance."

"That's not exactly fair."

She stood up. "Finish your food before it gets too cold for your liking. I'm turning in for the night. Chef Tria will see you out. I'll see you tomorrow when we say our goodbyes."

Mendac sat there, an empty look on his face. She could tell it was frustration, but that wasn't of her concern. He had no business knowing such information. She had heeded Titus's warnings, for she trusted him more than anyone. She walked out without another word, her heels echoing around the tall ceiling.

As she stepped into her nightgown, ready to lie down for the night, she heard the familiar giggle of her little sister. She followed the sound and found Ropinia in a study room, lying on her stomach on the floor with an open picture book in front of her.

"What are you reading," Apoleia asked.

Ropinia yelped, and then quickly covered her mouth. Apoleia laughed.

"*The Tram Ram's Treacherous Adventure across the Diamond Sea*," Ropinia replied.

"Ooh, a fun read. Though you should head to bed soon. It's getting late."

The little girl sat up with her legs crossed. "How was dinner with the stranger?"

"Uneventful."

"He's so mysterious."

"Which is precisely why we keep our distance," Apoleia said. But she went unheard, and Ropinia continued to smile as she daydreamed about the handsome stranger. With a shake of her head, Apoleia wished her sister a goodnight before heading down the hall.

She walked down the empty hall, whistling a quiet tune. She cherished late nights since they allowed her to relax the ridiculous stiff posture demanded of a princess, and her mind could shut off.

A door opened behind her. Ropinia poked her head out. The young girl hovered there for a moment, then quietly slipped out of the room on her toes.

*   *   *

Apoleia sat on a bed with her lyre on her lap. This wasn't her normal room, but she liked its relative humility. It was a place for escape—for a few extra minutes of sleep in the morning before her mother roused her, and the thick walls allowed no sound to escape in or out.

A violin rested beside the bed, a piano sat in the far corner, and a few candles were ablaze on the floor. Apoleia gazed at the bare beige walls as she plucked at the strings, following the flow of her tune.

The subtlest of noises jerked her from her trance. Her eyes fixed on the handle of the trapdoor across the room. The tiny hairs on her arms stood at attention.

The trapdoor opened, and her heart's pace increased tenfold. She crossed her arms around the lyre and squeezed it close.

"Your little sister was a big help," Mendac said.

Apoleia watched as he sat on the piano bench and stared back at her. She wanted to summon her Bewahr, but she couldn't. Her Bewahr was a man, so she was not allowed to make use of him. Many considered it a curse, that a Stillian royal first-born with a male Bewahr was bound to live a life of tragedy. She had never put much stock into such a belief.

"Do the Untenables strike fear in you?" he asked.

She took a moment to calm herself before answering. She didn't want him to hear the brittleness in her voice. "They aren't something I think of too often. Why?"

"These divine laws," Mendac said. "A couple of them make sense, such as the Untenable that prohibits taking the life of a royal first-born. It keeps a balance between the kingdoms and realms. If a first-born were to die off before having a child of their own, that link to a Branian or Bewahr would disappear for good. But there is a specific Untenable that really baffles me: 'There shall be no procreation between beings of separate realms.'"

"Get out," Apoleia commanded. Now her voice was shaking, and there was no stopping it.

Mendac tapped his fingers on his knee. "I'm glad your sister doesn't have to know the fate she sealed for you by directing me here. The guilt would likely crush her soul. Of course it didn't have to be this way. But your reluctance has rendered gentler options useless."

Apoleia squeezed the lyre tighter as her vision became drowned in tears. She stood up. "I advise you to leave. I am a royal first-born, and can dispose of you if forced."

Mendac also stood with a calm focus on his face. She waved her hand to the side as he approached her, and he shattered the shaft of ice with a surge of electricity. Her eyes widened. He didn't make the slightest gesture. How could that be?

Apoleia fought with every ounce of might she could muster up, but inevitably her energy depleted. There were holes in the wall from where she had been rammed against it. At a certain point she resorted to screaming, but the thickness of these walls—something she had come to love over the years—now betrayed her.

Finally she gave up. She was lifted off the ground and tossed into the bed, and Mendac climbed over her. The blood dripping from his face was proof that she had at least put up a fight. But it didn't matter.

Her head rolled to the side. On the floor lay her lyre—her gift from Titus—broken in half, its strings snapped and spooling loosely across the floorboards.

48
To Burn in Ice

On her second day in the Archaic Mountains, Rhyparia found a valley with vegetation and a stream. She knelt next to the slow-running water and scooped up a handful. Her eyes nearly rolled into the back of her head with satisfaction as she took a sip.

She looked both ways down the stream, curious about where this stream came from more than where it led to. According to Archaic Kingdom maps, there weren't any rivers anywhere close to these mountains, let alone leading down from them. She looked back into the water before stepping into it and allowing the weeds to tickle her feet. It was shallow, reaching only her knees, and it seemed the deepest parts were only up to her waist.

Rhyparia looked down and saw a fish dart away. She didn't have wood for fire, nor did she know how to cook, but something possessed her to go for it anyway. She stood patiently, one hand poised just above the water. A second fish swam over and she thrust her hand into the water and grabbed—no luck. She let out a groan and waited again. This time she waited for the fish to start nibbling at a weed. She spiked her hand into the water, and the fish easily darted away. She screamed in frustration, frantically slapping the river's surface.

"Quite the first impression."

Rhyparia froze, then slowly turned around. The man behind her was quite fat—not the shape of person you'd expect to see wandering the wilderness. He wore a ragged brown vest with lace that was supposed to tie it together at the front. He either chose not to bother with tying it or he was too big to even try. With his hands behind his back, he leaned forward on his toes and said, "So you are the girl I've heard about."

She eyed him a moment longer. "Who are you?"

"Ah. I believe this might answer that question." He took his hands from behind his back to reveal a tattered umbrella.

Rhyparia was excited at first, but a wave of solemnness swept over her. Did she really want it back?

The man shook his head. "Don't look at it as a burden. This is a tool that can be of great use. We shall show you that."

"Who is we?"

He slapped the umbrella in the palm of his other hand. "Follow me, and I will show you."

* * *

Bryson stood in Dunami Palace's conference room alongside Olivia. His face was a livid mess of grotesquely swollen bruises, but some of the bandages had been removed, and he could walk again.

There were eight Dev servants in the room, their eyes a deep burgundy as they recorded the conclusion of Bryson's broadcast. His eyes were wet with tears, for he had just shared the story of Apoleia Still and Mendac LeAnce with most of the Light Realm. It was time they knew the truth.

Lilu would be in Brilliance with Intel Director Jugtah for a few months, so she was absent. As King Vitio and Princess Shelly sat quietly in the back corner, Bryson concluded his speech that Agnos had helped him write:

"There is no justification or excuse for our father's deplorable actions. Olivia and I are the products of the foulest of crimes. Mendac committed his crime because he wanted to see what we would become. And for that, I'd like to apologize to Still Queen Apoleia.

"I can only put this in the plainest of words: The name Mendac LeAnce will no longer be held synonymous with the legends of the *Of Five* series. He was not a man of integrity and valor, but a violent rapist and a coward. I advise that the people across the Light Realm destroy the propaganda that extols him. As for myself, I renounce the name of Bryson LeAnce and will now only answer to Still."

Bryson glanced down at his notes and steadied his breathing. That was supposed to be the end of his speech, but he wanted to make his point clear. He looked up with wet cheeks.

"When we speak of Mendac from this point forward, we teach a lesson. Focus on his repugnant character. Science and weaving curriculum should scratch his name from existence. I don't care about his inventions and discoveries, and neither should any of you … We do not praise rapists."

He snatched his notes from the podium and walked off the stage. Scribes shouted questions from their seats about Thusia and his royal blood while he made for the exit. As he placed his hand against the door to push it open, he saw King Vitio hurrying toward him. Quickly—and without a word—Bryson bolted out of the room. He wasn't sure he could ever talk to that man again.

* * *

Bryson entered Vistas's room. "Okay, I came," he said.

"Thank you," Vistas said as he closed the door. "I'm sorry I was so persistent, but I had no choice."

Bryson said nothing.

"Take a seat, Bryson. I have something to show you."

"I really just want to head home."

"It pertains to Debo."

Bryson reluctantly sat on the sofa, and Vistas walked in front of the fireplace.

"Before Debo entered Necrosis Valley to help you, he found me hiding in the trees. He wanted to give me something for you if you ever discovered the truth about your parents. Since that has now happened, I find that I must share his memory with you." Vistas paused. "Are you willing to see it right now? See your father from Debo's eyes?"

Bryson stared at his knees. There were so many people he was infuriated with, and Debo was one of them … along with Thusia, Vitio, Poicus—everyone who likely knew this secret and held it from him. They had covered for a rapist. Thusia had sworn that Debo didn't know about the specifics—just that Mendac was not a good man and had committed the Untenable of having an intimate relationship with someone from another realm. But what was Bryson to believe at this point?

He got up from the sofa. "Not now," he mumbled, and left without another word.

*   *   *

An inferno roared in Dunami's central market while civilians of all ages massed around it. They fed books, parchments, articles of clothing—anything that bore the name or face of Mendac LeAnce—into the flames. There were scenes similar to this across the Light Realm. From massive capitals to tiny towns, Mendac's legacy was in ashes.

A mother and son approached the fire. The young boy held a leather belt adorned with dangling metal rods in his hands. He was sad, for he wasn't sure why he was doing this. When he ran out of his bedroom after school that afternoon with the belt strapped around his waist, pretending to slay demons with his mighty electrical abilities, his mother broke down in tears. When he asked her why she was sad, she had said, "You have to take that off, sweetie."

That was it, but it was enough for him. He didn't want to do anything that would make her cry. He looked up at his mom. "Go ahead," she said.

With a swing of his arm, the chime belt soared into the flames. His mother handed him a tattered leather-bound book: *The Fifth of Five: The Tale of Mendac LeAnce.* Without a second thought, he tossed it into the fire.

A thick sheet of ice spread under the Intelian crowd's feet. People gasped as the ice swathed the entirety of the market square and crept up the fronts of the surrounding buildings. It was beautiful, a reflective blue surface that sparkled in the flickering light of the fire.

A man sat on a nearby roof with his legs dangling off the edge. Hidden within the rising smoke, he wore a powder blue coat with a crystal snowflake on its back. His gaze was solemn, but his heart was appreciative. At least Titus could see that not all Intelians were of the same mold as Mendac LeAnce.

49
A Grand Stone Statue

Bryson sat in the living room of his house—or Debo's house? He wasn't exactly sure whose it was any more. He didn't even understand why he hadn't been evicted yet. Olivia was sleeping in Debo's old room, while Bryson sat with Thusia and Agnos.

"This is a nice place," Agnos said. He smiled as he looked at the painting on the wall of Bryson and Debo. "It's good to see his face again."

Bryson glanced at Thusia and got exactly what he expected: a slow shake of her head. That was her warning not to say anything he'd regret.

"What's up?" Bryson asked.

"I'll be leaving for an unknown period of time in the coming months," Agnos said. "Spy Pilot Ophala gave Himitsu a note before she was arrested. It contains information that might help me obtain the ancient I told you about. I'll be taking Tashami with me."

"Grand Director Poicus is closing down Phesaw for the rest of this school year and the entirety of the next," Bryson said. "Lilu's in Brilliance with Director Jugtah. You and Tashami will be on your own adventure.

Yama's gone for good. Toshik and Jilly will be at Brench headquarters in the Adren Kingdom. Himitsu will be in Phelos for who knows how long." Bryson sighed. "I suppose that leaves Olivia and me to find Rhyparia, track Toono, rescue Meow Meow, and deal with Dev King Storshae … and whatever else I'm missing from the list."

Agnos waited a moment before replying. "Don't just run into those mountains, Bryson. It doesn't work that way. And you'll have Vuilni to help."

"If she's ever done being interrogated by the royal heads. They're not too happy about the Power Warden's desertion."

Agnos reached into his robe pocket and pulled out the folded parchment with the mysterious letters. "I found out what this says. Sadly, I don't know what it's referencing."

"What is it?"

"It says, 'Theory of Connectivity.' I've studied a lot of theories—scientific, philosophical, and mathematic." Agnos placed the parchment on the coffee table. "And I have never heard of this."

Bryson looked at Thusia, who shrugged. "Mendac was a theorist. He had dozens of them."

Bryson rubbed his swollen face. "Why are there never any answers?"

*   *   *

After nearly a year of uncertainty for the Stillian natives, their queen had finally returned home. This was Apoleia's kingdom now. When Salia Still was murdered the previous year, Apoleia had announced her ascension as queen before departing with Toono and Olivia to the Light Realm. She told her sister, Ropinia, to act as regent until she returned.

There would be a ceremony tomorrow morning—a festival of sorts. Apoleia was to be officially crowned. This would mark a new era for the Still Kingdom, for Apoleia wasn't anything like her rigid, laconic predecessors. She was unstable and unpredictable … most called her insane. Her neck and arms were still lined with cuts. That habit hadn't stopped.

Though she didn't feel healed, there was something different about her. She had revealed her traumatic story to the public, lifting some weight off her shoulders. The city didn't respond how she thought it would. They appreciated how she was brave enough to return home and expose a part of her that she was once ashamed of. She had forgotten about the culture gap between the royals and aristocrats of the palace and the subjects in the middle class. The commoners were a lot more relaxed in their attitudes, and more equivocal about the maxims of their culture.

There was a time when Apoleia envied their free-flowing way of life. She had planned to lead the kingdom with such a mindset when she was younger. But she wasn't sure she could do that now. Mendac had left a terrible imprint on her, and only her father, Titus, and Toono had ever shown that she could put even the slightest faith in a man. And while her dad was still around, he was mute and paralyzed from the neck down. And she had sent Titus away to aid Toono in his mission.

Apoleia hurried through the halls of the glacial castle. She was hunting down her sister, who had disappeared earlier that morning. The rehearsal for tomorrow's ceremony was in an hour, and she wasn't going to go through with it without Ropinia by her side. Paranoia set in as her search brought no answers. Ropinia had been out of sorts since Apoleia's return. She'd never look her in the face, and when she'd speak, her tone was deflated and weak—the complete opposite of the Stillian woman she was raised to be.

Finally it hit her. Apoleia raced through the halls, panting as she ran. She turned one last corner and ran to the painting of the Still Mountains at the far end of a narrow hall. She yanked it open and looked through the square door.

Ropinia sat on the floor on her knees, her back to Apoleia. Her arm lay limply at her side with a blade resting in her open hand. Apoleia bolted toward her, then heaved a relieved sigh when she saw that Ropinia was unharmed.

"Don't ever do something so foolish," Apoleia whispered.

"I deserve to experience the same pain as you," Ropinia said. "But as I've come to sit here for two hours, I've learned that your bravery is unmatched. I'm scared of something as simple as bleeding."

Apoleia took the blade from her sister's hand. "This doesn't make you brave. Do you think I'm proud of my scars? I do what I do to redirect the pain elsewhere."

"It doesn't matter anyway," Ropinia mumbled. "I can't bring myself to do it."

"Good. I want you to know that I don't blame you."

"And that's stupid."

Apoleia looked at her sister for a moment before helping her up. "Let's go. I can't do this without you."

* * *

Rhyparia staggered behind the man who had met her at the stream four days ago. She was exhausted, and her body was in excruciating pain from the hike. Meanwhile, this round man—who had yet to give her a name—seemed as happy as if he were strolling through a garden. When she asked the man where they were headed, he said that she'd know it when she saw it.

They approached a cave at the bottom of a mountain. He walked straight in without hesitation. Rhyparia stopped.

His voice echoed out of the pitch black hole: "I'll leave you."

What did she have to lose? She hurried into the darkness, eager to catch up to her companion.

"Hold on to my bag," he said.

"Just be happy you can't see," he said. "And watch your step. You don't want to trip on something dead."

She wasn't sure how long they were in the tunnel, but it was definitely more than a couple hours. And the entire journey was in darkness. Finally Rhyparia saw sunlight ahead. She let go of the man's bag and sprinted forward. He said something—some kind of warning—but she didn't hear it, nor did she care. As she rushed out of the tunnel, she dug her feet into the dirt, skidding to a stop as she wheeled her arms. The path had come to an abrupt end, as it jutted out of a cliffside. For a moment she hovered over the precipice before regaining her footing and collapsing to her hands and knees.

She gulped in air as she looked down at the ground thousands of feet below her. She craned her neck upward and looked behind her. A monstrous wall of mountain soared vertically into the sky. She then brought her attention forward and gasped.

A beautiful circular valley of lush green grass and scattered homes was just barely visible behind a gap in the two mountains ahead. But it was the structure lodged directly between the two mountains—a mammoth statue of stone as big as the mountains themselves—that forced the air from her chest. Its hands grasped at the mountainsides, the muscles in its arms bulging from the effort. Its knees were buckled and shoulders squeezed its neck, as if this statue was pushing the mountains apart.

"Haven't seen anything quite like it, eh? I'm just happy you got to see it. Would've been a shame to walk all this way just to go running over the edge."

She continued with her dumbfounded stare. The man chuckled. "The villagers worship him. Basically he's a god of sorts, thought to be one of the origins of the Known History timeline."

He studied her as she continued to not say a word. He shrugged and handed her the umbrella. "Let's see what you can do. Land us safely on the ground."

Rhyparia gripped the handle as he threw his arm around her waist. She opened the umbrella, and the pair leapt off the cliff. At first they plummeted like a slab of marble in water, but then she worked a bit of weaving, and their free-fall turned into a gentle gliding descent through the sky.

"Oh, the trust I put in Pilot Ophala's words," the man said.

The comment went in one ear and out the other, as Rhyparia was still staring at the statue's face. That wasn't a god—at least not to her …

That's Meow Meow.

Delve deeper into the world of Kuki Sphaira by visiting

www.erafeen.com

Where you can find information not presented in the novels, artwork of the world and its characters, and meet the author, David F. Farris.

The *Erafeen* series:

1. The Jestivan
2. The Untenable

Printed in Great Britain
by Amazon

70395653R00255